CW01024357

A GAME OF SHADOWS

IRINA SHAPIRO

Storm
PUBLISHING

This is a work of fiction. Names, characters, business, events and incidents are the products of the author's imagination. Any resemblance to actual persons, living or dead, or actual events is purely coincidental.

Copyright © Irina Shapiro, 2013, 2024

The moral right of the author has been asserted.

Previously published in 2013 as *A Game of Shadows* by Merlin Press LLC.

All rights reserved. No part of this book may be reproduced or used in any manner without the prior written permission of the copyright owner.

To request permissions, contact the publisher at rights@stormpublishing.co

Ebook ISBN: 978-1-80508-653-6
Paperback ISBN: 978-1-80508-654-3

Cover design: Debbie Clement
Cover images: Shutterstock

Published by Storm Publishing.
For further information, visit:
www.stormpublishing.co

ALSO BY IRINA SHAPIRO

A Tate and Bell Mystery

The Highgate Cemetery Murder

Murder at Traitors' Gate

Wonderland Series

The Passage

Wonderland

Sins of Omission

The Queen's Gambit

Comes the Dawn

The Hands of Time Series

The Hands of Time

A Leap of Faith

A World Apart

Shattered Moments

The Ties that Bind

ONE

ENGLAND JULY 1624

The carriage swayed dangerously just as another bolt of lightning split the pewter sky down the middle, the electricity almost tangible in the ozone-scented air. Thunder boomed somewhere to the east, the relentless downpour continuing to soak the already oversaturated countryside. It had been raining mercilessly since they left London, making their progress painstakingly slow and trying. Now the carriage was stuck in the mud again and Valerie nearly screamed with frustration when she saw the apologetic face of the coachman through the window. The poor man was drenched, rivulets of rainwater running down his face and into his mouth as he threw her a pitying look and addressed Alec.

"I'm sorry, sir, but we can't go much further tonight. The wheels are stuck again, and the mud is knee-deep in some places. There's a village just up ahead. I'm afraid you will have to escort the ladies on foot while I try to free the coach."

"Thank you, Wilks, but I'm not leaving you here alone with night approaching. I'll help you free the coach, and we'll do our best to get to the village. I trust there's an inn of some sort we can stop at?"

Alec didn't wait for an answer and climbed out of the coach, much to the relief of the coachman, who had no chance in hell of freeing the wheels without help. The two men disappeared into the encroaching darkness as Valerie quietly dissolved into tears so as not to wake Louisa, who'd fallen asleep, lulled by the rocking of the carriage.

Stop crying, you ninny, you are made of sterner stuff, Valerie scolded herself fiercely, but the tears just wouldn't stop. Her nerves were stretched to the limit, and this was the last straw. She was tired, hungry, and frustrated beyond all reason. Nothing had gone right since last summer. Nothing. All their plans for visiting Finn and then traveling to England had to be put on hold as one crisis after another prevented them from leaving the colony. The estate had suffered greatly during the famine and Alec had to put all his energies into recovery efforts, not just of Rosewood Manor, but of the Jamestown community as a whole. Many families had lost their menfolk and needed help to survive and prepare for next winter. Alec spent much of his time at the Selby estate, helping Mrs. Selby, whose husband's death left her alone with three children under the age of eighteen. The Selbys were one of the few Catholic families in Jamestown and Alec felt it his Christian duty to help them as much as he could, since no one else would.

Valerie secretly hoped that they might finally leave after the harvest, but it proved impossible. Annabel had announced her second pregnancy during the summer, thrilled to be with child at last. She and Charles had been trying for some time and she was beginning to despair of providing a sibling for Harry. Annabel's first pregnancy had been a breeze, but the second one was completely different. Plagued with crippling morning sickness, Annabel became severely malnourished and needed to be fed every hour just to keep up her strength. She was too weak to get out of bed for the duration of the pregnancy, leaving it to Valerie and Louisa to take care of little Harry and nurse her around the clock. Valerie thought of Bridget often, wishing she could have asked for her help and advice. She felt her absence every day, never realizing until Bridget was gone how much she had taken her friendship for granted and how much she'd relied on her for companionship and support.

Much to everyone's relief, Annabel delivered a healthy baby girl in early February but was too weak to care for her for the first month, needing to get her strength back after months of illness. Valerie took over the caring of the baby, bringing Millicent to Annabel only for feedings. She worried about her sister-in-law, but kept her concerns to herself, assuring Charles at every opportunity that Annabel would soon recover. Poor Charles had aged ten years since the famine, driven to further despair by his wife's illness. Valerie knew he was more terrified of losing her than he'd ever admit. He slept on a cot in their room, afraid of unnecessarily disturbing her, but desperate to be close to her and the baby. Valerie had never expected such devotion from her self-absorbed brother-in-law, but they had all changed in the past year. The loss of Finn and the subsequent famine had brought them all to the brink, reminding them that loss was never too far away, death lurking in the shadows, ready to claim its next victim.

If it hadn't been for Frederick Taylor, they might have fared much worse. He had made it his mission to help the family get through this dark time, going out to forage several times a week and bringing back anything he thought edible. He forced the workers to eat raw onions and doled out a weekly teaspoon of strawberry or raspberry preserves to prevent the onset of scurvy. Many people in town suffered from bleeding gums and loose teeth, but no one at Rosewood Manor showed any symptoms.

Although she secretly blamed Mr. Taylor for losing Finn, Valerie was grateful to him for his tireless efforts. The funny thing was that the gray, tired old man had become a robust septuagenarian full of purpose and vigor. Marrying Cook and helping the Whitfields through the famine had given him the focus that he'd been lacking for many years and he found himself taking an interest in life again and finding joy in being part of a family.

Fred Taylor had taken a hand in Annabel's recovery as well. He had Cook add items to her diet that would help her regain her vitality, such as liver, eggs, greens, and lots of ale. Annabel normally ate sparingly, consuming mostly porridge and broth, but the extra protein and vitamins helped her get back on her feet and produce enough milk for the hungry baby. She finally began to improve by March, freeing Valerie and Alec to visit Finn for his birthday.

They'd debated telling Charles and Louisa the truth about Valerie's past and Finn's whereabouts, but finally decided that it would serve little purpose and possibly put Valerie in danger. In a time when a woman could be burned at the stake for witchery, any hint of the supernatural would arouse suspicion and give the leaders of the colony cause to investigate. Of course, no one would betray her willingly or intentionally, but it was safer to limit the secret to as few people as possible, and it was decided that Valerie and Alec would say they were traveling to North Carolina to visit Finn's grave for his birthday. Charles accepted the reason easily enough, but the only way Louisa could be persuaded to stay was with the argument that Annabel couldn't manage without her help. Louisa loved the children and took great pride in being able to care for Millicent on her own. She agreed to stay back and let Valerie and Alec make the journey.

Valerie closed her eyes, blocking out the sound of the lashing rain and the grunts of the men as they tried to push the carriage out of the mud, and pictured Finn. By the time they'd traveled back to the future, they hadn't seen him in nearly a year and a half and the boy they'd left behind was now a man. His voice was velvety and deep, and the sparse facial hair he had at sixteen was now coarse stubble by suppertime. Working on the farm had made him strong and muscular, the fabric of his shirt straining across his chest and upper arms.

Abbie had changed as well. The sweet young girl had grown into a beautiful woman, ready for marriage and motherhood. Valerie couldn't have imagined herself getting married at seventeen, but Abbie and Finn seemed more than ready, their commitment to each other absolute. They shared an obvious bond and seemed to truly understand one another. The wedding was planned for April and the preparations were in full swing by the time Valerie and Alec turned up mid-March. Mrs. Mallory was sewing Abbie a wedding dress and Martha popped by periodically with baby Joe on her hip to comment on the menu for the wedding feast and generally put in her two cents. Gil never came with her, probably overjoyed to have a few moments of peace away from his bossy wife.

The day of the wedding dawned crisp and bright, a hint of spring in the April air. The wedding service would take place at noon, followed by a party at the Mallory house. A great bonfire would be lit after dark, illuminating the yard and chasing away the chill of the spring evening. Two trestle tables had been set up, ready to be piled with countless dishes of food and pitchers of beer and ale. Valerie had squeezed Alec's hand as Mr. Mallory walked his daughter down the aisle, her golden hair hanging to her waist, adorned with a few early blooms. It wasn't the fashion for brides to wear their hair down, but Abbie had insisted, knowing how much Finn loved seeing her hair loose and shocking her parents and the minister, who thought it wanton. Valerie thought she looked beautiful, and the look on her son's face had nearly broken her heart as he took Abbie's hands in his, promising to love and cherish her forever. How achingly young and in love they looked as they were pronounced man and wife and made their way out of the church to the heartfelt congratulations of the congregation.

Valerie could remember very little of the party afterwards,

except for being whirled around the bonfire by Alec and then Mr. Mallory and the sweet sound of the violin playing a haunting melody once the guests grew tired of dancing and sat down to catch their breath and have a last drink before heading home to their beds. Jonah disappeared into the barn, possibly to meet some girl, and Sarah and Annie had fallen asleep on a bench, their arms around each other for warmth.

No one mentioned it, but the absence of Sam was felt by all. The British had just taken New York and made it their base of operations in the Colonies, forcing the Continental Army to retreat. The Committee needed people who were willing to live among the enemy in order to spy and pass back information. Sam was already in place, and their impetuous son had volunteered to join him and would be leaving shortly, with Abbie in tow. Valerie had tried to talk Finn out of going, but he was adamant, his commitment to the cause of freedom stronger than ever. He would have liked to leave Abbie at home with her parents, but she wouldn't hear of it and was already making plans for their journey north. Valerie prayed that they would be safe and not fall into enemy hands. She told Finn everything she could remember of the Revolutionary War, but it was precious little, and the basic facts she could recall would hardly keep them safe.

Once back home from their visit, they were greeted with the news that King James had declared war on Spain. Traveling to England would be a risky venture, especially once hostilities broke out and played out in the Atlantic. Valerie begged Alec to leave for England before it was too late. She hadn't seen Louisa since the night Finn had disappeared, and not a day had gone by that she didn't long for her sister. The letters came sporadically, taking months to reach them, full of news that was no longer current. Valerie read and reread the letters, cherishing every word and dreaming of a day when they would be reunited. If she had to wait much longer to see Louisa, she'd go mad with longing, not knowing how long the war would last or when they would see each other again. To her great surprise, Alec gave in to her pleas and agreed they should travel to England.

The voyage was plagued by storms, but they'd made it across safely, only to arrive in London and learn that they'd missed the Sheridans by a few weeks. Louisa and Kit had left for their country estate, Willowbrook, abandoning the city for the summer, as was the custom for wealthy Londoners who wished to avoid the outbreak of sickness that usually came with the warm weather. And now, they had been traveling for days, hampered by rain, muddy roads, and the unbearable heat that was so uncommon for England.

Valerie wiped her eyes, finally getting hold of herself. They would just have to spend the night in this village and hope that they finally reached Willowbrook tomorrow. The thought of seeing Louisa, Kit, and the children made her smile, despite her earlier bout of despair. They would be together again, and that was all that mattered. The extra day of anticipation would only make their reunion sweeter.

Valerie handed Alec her handkerchief as he got back into the carriage. The embroidered square of linen wouldn't help him, but it was the only thing she had to offer. Alec was soaked through, covered with mud up to his thighs, and scowling so fiercely that Valerie started to giggle.

"I've never realized how strange the two of you are until today," she growled, furious at being woken. "What's so funny?"

"Nothing," Alec answered, "absolutely nothing."

TWO

Valerie threw open the shutters, inhaling the fresh, and wonderfully cool, morning air. The downpour had stopped sometime during the night, taking with it the stifling heat and mugginess of the past few days. Brilliant sunshine flooded the valley, drying the soggy ground and bathing everything in a golden glow. Fluffy sheep dotted the rolling hills in the distance and the sky was a brilliant shade of blue that almost hurt the eyes with its intensity. Valerie turned from the window and pulled the coverlet off Alec, who tried to hold on to it as he burrowed deeper inside before realizing the futility of his efforts and getting up.

"We need to leave as soon as possible," Valerie said as she threw his clothes at him and poured water into a basin. "Where's your razor? You shave while I wake Louisa. You know how she loves to dilly-dally."

Valerie was already halfway out the door, disappearing into the adjoining room, where their daughter was still fast asleep. Alec smiled to himself as he found the razor and lathered his cheeks. They would have to reach Kit's estate today no matter what. Another delay and Valerie would lose her mind. He could understand her feelings; she hadn't seen her sister in nearly two years and the impatience was killing her. Crossing the Atlantic just after the king had declared war on Spain was foolhardy, but he simply couldn't say no. Poor Valerie would be devastated if they had to put off their visit yet again, so he agreed against his better judgment.

A visit to England would also take her mind off Finn's mission. Alec was worried for their son, but also proud of the brave lad Finn had grown into. Alec hoped Finn would exercise restraint and not get Abbie with child until their mission was complete. He was putting her at risk as it were, and to bring a baby into that situation would be madness. Alec sighed and wiped the remaining soap off his face. Finn was thousands of miles away and one hundred and fifty years ahead. All Alec could do was pray for his safety.

* * *

It wasn't until mid-afternoon that the towers of Willowbrook finally came into view as the carriage rattled down a wooded drive, traveling nearly a mile before finally coming within view of the house. It was grander than anything Valerie had seen in the seventeenth century. Yealm Castle was a heap of stones compared to Willowbrook, its elegant façade dotted by countless windows of leaded glass that glowed in the sunshine. The house must have been built quite recently since it didn't feature the medieval elements of a tower house, whose purpose was not only to act as a residence but as a fortress. Willowbrook was turned outward with eye-pleasing symmetry and artistry that was visible in every pilaster and roundel. Valerie looked forward to exploring the extensive grounds of the estate, recalling her love of English gardens.

"Where's your mistress?" Valerie asked the surly servant who opened the massive wooden door. She completely ignored his look of utter astonishment and asked again. "Where's my sister?"

"She's in the garden with the children," the man muttered as Valerie ran past him in the direction he'd indicated.

"Master and Mistress Whitfield," Alec informed the servant as he watched Valerie disappear through a door at the end of the hallway. "I believe we're expected."

"Yes, of course, sir. Right this way. We weren't sure when you were coming, but I will have everything prepared immediately," the servant prattled on as he led Alec and Louisa into the drawing room. Louisa looked around, her mouth opening in silent admiration.

"Dad, I think this room is larger than the entire first floor of Rosewood Manor. I had no idea Kit was so wealthy. And to think, he was mucking out stalls and chopping wood in Virginia."

"Kit's father, Lord Sheridan, distinguished himself during the battle with the Spanish Armada and was rewarded by a grateful queen, but I had no idea his estate was this palatial," Alec replied, looking around in astonishment. He hadn't expected such grandeur either.

"Do Aunt Lou and Uncle Kit visit His Majesty's Court?" asked Louisa, still gaping at the splendor around her.

"I believe they do, pet, when they're in town."

"I think I'm going to like England," Louisa stated, settling into an elegant chair and resting her arms on the armrests like a queen.

"Yes, I think you might," answered Alec, smiling at his daughter.

THREE

Valerie felt as if she'd passed through two houses before finally emerging on the other side and into the glorious July sunshine. She shielded her eyes, taking a moment to get her bearings. The formal garden stretched in front of her, neat and elegant, with its trimmed hedges and pebbled walks, but she could hear the laughter of a child coming from somewhere further away and headed in that direction. How big was Kit's estate anyway? The park stretched as far as the eye could see, and she had no doubt it all belonged to the Sheridans.

Valerie sprinted down a graveled walk past what she assumed was the maze, until she caught a flash of something white in the distance. Her breath caught in her throat as a little girl in a white frock exploded from between two hedges, giggling as she ran from her nurse. Her black curls were swept up and tied with a ribbon, but a couple of ringlets framed her flushed cheeks, bouncing as she ran shrieking toward her aunt. She stopped short, surprised by the stranger, suddenly looking for protection from the young woman who chased after her.

"Evie, don't be frightened. It's Aunt Valerie. You don't remember me, but I remember you. May I give you a kiss?"

Valerie inched closer, desperate to hug her niece and kiss that soft cheek. Oh, how she'd missed her. Evie would be two in September, but the long dress and the upswept hair made her look older than the toddlers of Valerie's time.

Evie studied Valerie with her dark eyes, unsure of whether the stranger could be trusted. "No, kiss Robbie," she said and took off in the opposite direction, clearly eager to get away. Valerie was disappointed, but there was time. She'd need to establish a relationship and build trust before Evie would accept her.

"Lady Sheridan is just over there, Mistress Whitfield," the nurse called over her shoulder as she took off at a trot after Evie. She wouldn't want to lose sight of her in a parkland as large as this. Valerie put Evie out of her mind and sprinted toward the spot indicated by the nurse. Louisa sat on a stone bench in the shade of a poplar tree, her eyes closed, and her face turned upward as she leaned back. A small boy was fast asleep in her lap, his chubby hand wrapped around Louisa's fingers. What a picture they made as they dozed, unaware of Valerie's presence. Valerie wished she could capture them on canvas, and maybe she would, if painting supplies were available.

"Lou," she whispered, "Wake up. We're here. We're finally here." Louisa's eyes flew open as her lips stretched into a huge smile.

"Oh, Valerie, I thought you'd never come. I can't believe you're really here. Where are Alec and little Louisa?"

"They're back at the house. I just couldn't wait a moment longer to see you. And is this little Robbie? Oh, Lou, he's so beautiful. He looks just like you did when you were little. Nothing of Kit in this one."

"I know," Louisa giggled. "He takes after our family in looks, and in personality too. He's so sweet, unlike Evie, who's a little monster."

Louisa brushed a stray curl from the little boy's face, her

own aglow with tenderness. Valerie couldn't help noticing that her sister looked tired and drawn, deep shadows beneath her eyes. Living in such bucolic splendor, she should be a picture of vitality and health, but something was clearly wrong.

"Lou, have you been ill?" Valerie asked, taking a seat next to Louisa. "You look exhausted."

"I'm all right. I just haven't been sleeping very well, that's all." She shifted the baby on her lap, looking away from Valerie in the process.

"Is it because you're still nursing Robbie?" She experienced a jolt of apprehension when she saw a change come over her sister's face.

"No, the milk dried up when he was barely two months old, just as it did with Evie. Robbie has a wet nurse, but he's starting to eat solid food now. He turned one last week, so I'm ready to have him weaned. He's not the one who's keeping me awake, Val. It's Kit."

"You haven't mentioned anything in your letters. Is he all right?" Louisa's last letter arrived before they'd left Virginia two months ago, but there was nothing in it that gave cause for concern. Louisa was just about to answer when the nurse appeared, holding Evie by the hand.

"Pardon the intrusion, your ladyship, but it's time for Lady Evangeline's nap. Shall I take Lord Robert inside as well?"

"Yes, thank you, Mills," Louisa answered wearily, carefully handing over the boy. "I'll just stay here for a little while."

"As you wish, your ladyship." Mills managed a curtsey despite holding a sleeping Robbie and keeping a tight rein on Evie, who was twisting and turning, eager for an opportunity to escape.

"Don't want to take a nap, Mama," she whined, but Louisa wouldn't be swayed.

"Go with Mills, darling, and later on you can meet your cousin Louisa. She's come a very long way to see you. Would you like that?" Evie considered this question for a moment, her eyes narrowing just like Kit's.

"Did she bring a present?" she asked before capitulating.

"Yes, sweetheart, more than one. Now, go with your nurse while I talk to your mommy." Valerie managed to give the little girl a kiss before she wiggled away. She clearly resented being told what to do.

"You'll have your hands full with that one," Valerie chuckled, watching her niece walk away as if she were being led to the gallows.

"I already do. She's a terror, and she's so jealous of her brother. She doesn't seem to mind me being with him so much, but God help us if Kit picks him up. She won't share her father with anyone."

"Hmm, sounds familiar," giggled Valerie. "Mom always said that you monopolized Dad and wanted to get rid of me for good. Now, tell me what's going on with Kit."

Valerie felt her heart break when she saw the look on Louisa's face. Whatever was going on was serious. Louisa opened her mouth as if to speak, then closed it again, gazing off into the distance, her hands twisting in her lap. A tear ran down Louisa's cheek, but she wiped it away almost defiantly, refusing to give in to self-pity.

"Lou, what is it?" Valerie reached out and took her sister's hand, trying to offer whatever comfort she could. It had been so long since they'd seen each other, but it felt as if they'd never been parted, instantly reestablishing their sisterly bond.

"He has a mistress, Val. There, I've said it. This is the first time I've spoken the words out loud, and it sounds even worse than I expected." Louisa leaned her head on Valerie's shoulder, tears flowing freely now.

"Lou, are you sure? That's not like Kit. He's always been so devoted to you, and you've recently had Robbie. I would think he'd be over the moon to have a son."

Valerie stroked Louisa's hair, trying to soothe her, but her mind was racing. She'd known Kit for several years, had lived with him in the same house, and had seen him in his role as husband and father. She couldn't imagine anything less likely than Kit suddenly taking a mistress.

"Yes, I'm sure. I found proof. I don't know if he'd been careless or he wanted me to find it. Maybe he hopes I'll stay here in the country when he returns to London in September. There are plenty of couples who live apart, you know. Divorce is not really an option." Louisa pulled a handkerchief out of her sleeve and wiped her eyes, her hand shaking badly. "I can't lose him, Val. I just can't."

"Tell me everything from the beginning. Maybe I can help you make sense of this." Valerie was sure that Louisa had the right grasp of the situation, but maybe she'd missed something, some vital clue to Kit's change of heart.

"It started a few months ago when King James invited Kit to sit on the Privy Council. His father was on the Council during the reign of Elizabeth, and once a seat became available, His Majesty extended the invitation to Kit. It's a huge honor, but Kit was reluctant to accept. He hates politics, but he couldn't say no. That would constitute a grave insult, so he was forced to accept." Louisa sighed dramatically.

"This means that he now has to spend a lot more time at Whitehall. Oh, Valerie, you can't imagine what that place is like. From the outside, it's beautiful and glamorous, full of people who dazzle with their beauty and wit. I felt like Cinderella at the ball the first time I was invited to court. Of course, Kit grew up among people like that, so he's not intimidated by it all, but it took me some time to learn how to conduct myself. Everyone smiles and flatters, but no one says what they mean or means what they say."

"Sounds just like Washington D.C.," Valerie quipped in an

effort to make Louisa smile. She ignored the joke and went on with her story.

"The first few weeks were fine, but then I began to sense something. Kit would come home tense and angry. I thought it was just the political maneuvering that was getting to him. It's like a pit of vipers. Your very life can be in danger if you cross the wrong people." Louisa wiped her eyes, looking to see if Valerie understood the gravity of the situation.

"You don't think Kit can handle it?" Valerie asked. She could only imagine what went on behind closed doors. In her twenty-first century life, she'd read several works that had described the clandestine dealings and underhanded maneuvering of the courtiers that frequently led to innocent victims getting caught in the web of deceit.

"I think he can handle the wheeling and dealing, but maybe it's the women he can't resist. He's became more guarded and distant as time goes on, emotionally withdrawn." Louisa sniffled, looking off into the distance. "Maybe now that we are in England, he sees me for the bumpkin that I am. I don't belong in his world."

"Lou, that's nonsense and you know it. Kit fell in love with you for who you are. If he wanted some painted courtier, he could have had one years ago. Do you still sleep together?"

"That's the strange part; he's more passionate than ever. His lovemaking is almost frenzied, as if he's trying to make up for something or is trying to eradicate his guilt."

"So, what's this proof you found? How damning is it?"

Valerie prayed that Louisa was overreacting and reading into things. Maybe Kit was under a lot of pressure, part of a government that had just declared war against Spain for reasons that seemed less than sound. Valerie didn't claim to understand the rationale, but it had something to do with the daughter of the king and her husband being defeated by the Spanish in

Flanders and the failed attempt to betroth the king's son, Charles I, to Princess Maria Anna of Spain.

"First, I found a crumpled note. It fell out of his papers when he came home from Whitehall one day."

"What did it say?" Valerie asked with a heavy heart.

"It said, 'My dearest Kit, your resistance will make it that much sweeter once you're finally mine. G.'" Louisa started to cry again as Valerie took that in.

"Any idea who 'G' is?" she asked, more to distract Louisa than because it made any difference.

"There are dozens of women at court whose names start with G. It could be anyone."

"But Lou, the note clearly indicates that he's resisting. Maybe it's just a flirtation and not a full-blown affair. Kit is an honorable man; I can't see him just jumping into bed with someone."

"That's what I tried to tell myself until I found the gift. It's an exquisite silver snuffbox, encrusted with rubies and sapphires, and engraved. It said, 'To my heart's desire. G.' I don't think this woman would be giving him such expensive gifts if they weren't lovers."

"She certainly seems very forward," Valerie noted. It wasn't common for a woman of this time to pursue a man with such singlemindedness.

"She's obviously accustomed to getting her way. She must be someone who holds a position of great power, therefore, she's likely married," Louisa replied matter-of-factly.

"So you don't think Kit wants out of the marriage?" Valerie asked, hoping there was still room to work things out.

"A divorce would cause scandal for both Kit and whoever this woman is. Likely, they'd just carry on with the relationship secretly until one of them tired of it."

"Lou, I trust your judgment, but I don't think one note and one snuffbox are enough to make a case against Kit. You have absolutely no proof that he's actually keeping a mistress. Have you confronted him?"

"I have, after I found the snuffbox. Kit swore that there's no other woman but didn't explain the inscription on the box or the note." Louisa sighed, obviously convinced that Kit was hiding something.

"Have you tried to investigate further?" Valerie asked.

"How can I? I'm stuck here in the country, away from everything and everyone. Besides, if I start poking around, I will only humiliate myself and Kit. Discretion is highly prized at court, and there's nothing more ridiculous than a jealous wife. The trouble is that I have too much time to brood. Life is so different here than it was in Virginia."

"In what way?" Valerie could see the difference in financial and social standing but wondered how it affected their daily life.

"At Rosewood Manor life was more normal somehow. Here, there are servants to see to my every need. I don't have to do anything. The nursemaid has the vapors every time I so much as walk into the nursery. Noble women do little more than give birth. Many of them pack off their children to the country to be raised by a staff of nannies, not seeing them until they are toilet trained. The ladies return to court as soon as they're able, too fearful to lose their place in society and in the affections of the king. There's no bond between parents and children. The children serve their purpose as heirs to the estates and titles, and pawns in the marriage market, the unions meant to further the interests of the family. I try to do as much as I can with the children, but time weighs heavily on my hands, especially in the country. I'm so glad you're here."

"Yes, I can see how that can be difficult, especially after having such an active life in the twenty-first century. It must be hard to have nothing to do."

Valerie could understand Louisa's difficulty. It took her a

long time to learn to accept idleness. Women of quality were expected to do very little, their days filled with endless needlepoint and walks in the garden, weather permitting. Few women cared for their children or did anything productive other than sew and manage the staff. Their lives in Virginia had been more fulfilling with a plantation to run and a family to care for. Valerie spent her days raising the children, seeing to the well-being of servants and workers, and performing various domestic chores. With a staff of servants, there wasn't much for Louisa to do but look pretty and support her husband at court when needed.

Valerie strongly suspected that there was something else Louisa wasn't saying, something that troubled her greatly. If Kit had an affair in the twenty-first century, Louisa would have options. They could go for marriage counseling, attempt a trial separation, or get divorced. Louisa would be provided for and keep custody of her children. In time, she'd move on and find someone to love, rebuilding her life step by step.

In her current position, options were few. Divorce was still rare, and a divorced woman was treated worse than a leper. Louisa would be shunned and ridiculed by society, forced into exile. Worst of all, she would have no claim to her children, since by law, they would belong to Kit. Valerie didn't believe for a second that Kit would ever be so vicious, but until a few moments ago, she'd also believed that Kit would never betray her sister. Louisa had to tread carefully if she wanted to keep her family, not making any rash decisions or unfounded accusations. If Kit denied any wrongdoing, she was better off believing him until she had concrete proof of his infidelity. Valerie was about to say so when Louisa interrupted her.

"And to make matters worse, Aunt Maud has descended on us," Louisa announced, rising to her feet.

"Aunt Maud? You've never mentioned her in your letters," Valerie observed, wondering about this new relation.

"I couldn't bring myself to. There's simply not enough paper to describe Maud. She's not even a blood relation. She's Caroline's mother's sister, but she's adopted us since Caroline passed away. She's not happy unless she has someone to torture. Kit avoids her like the plague, but he hasn't the heart to ask her to leave. She's resting now, but you'll meet her at dinner."

Louisa brushed away a stray lock of hair and retrieved her hat from the ground. "We should go inside. I can't wait to see Alec and Louisa. I've missed them so much. How is Finn?" Louisa obviously couldn't bear to talk of Kit anymore, so Valerie linked her arm through Louisa's as they walked back to the house, her mind in turmoil.

"We saw Finn and Abbie in the spring. The wedding was lovely. They're so in love, Lou. I still can't believe my baby is a husband. Where did the time go?" Valerie sighed, getting to the difficult part. "They were planning to travel to New York to spy on the British. Oh, Lou, I'm so worried about them. They are so young and naïve. I know Finn has been working for Mr. Mallory, but this is on a whole different scale. He won't be just passing messages or meeting other members; he'll be living among the enemy, and Abbie will be with him, which will make him more vulnerable. If only we had some way to communicate with them. Not knowing makes it that much worse."

"I can certainly understand that. It's like a form of death." Louisa walked slowly, every step an effort of will.

"Yes, and little Louisa keeps asking why we haven't put a marker in the cemetery for Finn, but I can't bring myself to make a grave for a child who's still living. I could tell her that it's because there's no body, but we made a marker for Bridget, so I can't use that excuse."

Valerie sighed, following Louisa into the cool shadows of the house. She'd expected this to be such a happy reunion, but now her stomach was twisting with anxiety due to Louisa's confession and her own worry for Finn. Valerie quickly rearranged her face into a mask of pleasure when she saw Kit coming toward her down the hall. Whatever happened between him and Louisa, she had no right to get involved. She would talk to Alec and see if he could suggest anything. Maybe Kit would confide in him as he used to, but then again, if he did, it would be a sign that he had no intention of working things out with his wife, since the information would surely be passed on to Louisa, and he knew it.

FOUR

Valerie studied her reflection in the mirror as the maid skillfully teased and twisted her hair into an elaborate creation. She had to admit that it looked well on her. When at home, she pinned up her hair and covered it with a mob cap, but here things were different. The house boasted an impressive staff, and a lady's maid had promptly been assigned to Valerie despite her protests. Alec was next door, getting dressed with the assistance of a manservant.

Valerie smiled as her daughter breezed into the room, wearing a lovely silk gown in a shade of dusty rose that highlighted her coloring. Her hair was piled high on her head, several ringlets left loose to artfully frame her face.

"Oh, Mama, isn't it lovely? Aunt Lou lent it to me. None of my gowns will do here, especially if I'm to be introduced at court. I have to speak to Dad about ordering some new clothes." She twirled around the room, enjoying the swishing of silk around her stockinged calves and purposely displaying the low-heeled shoes with stone-encrusted buckles.

"I think you might be right, darling, but let's not spring this on him just yet. It's our first night here, so we have plenty of time."

They both turned as Alec entered the room, dressed and ready to escort them to the dining room. Valerie hadn't expected dinner to be such a grand affair and her clothes suddenly felt dated and shabby and she wished she would have had the foresight to have a new gown made before making the trip.

The dining room was ablaze with candles, their light casting a muted glow over the polished furniture and the elegantly set table. The room was decorated in shades of cream and gold, heavy damask drapes closed against the summer night and keeping the room uncomfortably warm. Louisa and Kit were already there, looking slightly tense as they greeted their guests. This was so different from the informal dinners they used to enjoy back home. Valerie was just about to comment on the beauty of the room when an elderly woman entered the dining room, her head seemingly not attached to her body as it perched above her old-fashioned ruff. She was short and thin, with steel-gray hair and twinkling blue eyes that seemed to miss little. The air of superiority emanating from her made her appear six feet tall. She took her seat, studying Valerie and Alec with undisguised curiosity and clearly finding them lacking.

"Aunt Maud, may I present my sister Valerie, her husband Alexander Whitfield, and their daughter, Louisa. They've only just arrived this afternoon." Louisa announced, looking unusually nervous.

"So, you are the sister I've heard so much about," Aunt Maud observed with a smirk. "I certainly hope you will talk some sense into Louisa. She's had a face like a melancholy bulldog these past few weeks. Good thing she's away from court for the time being, but then, you wouldn't know anything about that, would you?" Aunt Maud looked around the table, gauging the reaction to her comment, a sly smile playing about her lips.

Valerie sensed Alec's tension, but he said nothing, taking a sip of wine instead. When Louisa said the woman was insufferable, she hadn't been exaggerating. Aunt Maud fixated her gaze on Alec, looking at him as if he weren't fit to sit at the same table with a person of quality. Louisa gasped at the rudeness, but Valerie tried to hide a smile behind her napkin. Aunt Maud was clearly trying to provoke them, her eyes dancing with merriment as she enjoyed the discord she caused. She was probably bored to tears and liked to make her own entertainment wherever she went. The trick was not to give her the satisfaction. She seemed a little deflated when no one answered back and looked around, searching for a new victim.

"And how old are you, my dear?" Aunt Maud asked, turning her attention to little Louisa. "I must say, that shade is a lot more becoming on you than it is on your aunt. She doesn't have the coloring for it."

"I'm sixteen, your ladyship," Louisa answered shyly, unsure of whether to accept the compliment or run for her life.

"Sixteen, you say? You should be married, my girl. Why, in my day you would have given your husband an heir or two by this age. When Queen Bess was on the throne, girls didn't go about picking and choosing as they do today. Their fathers arranged a marriage for them, and they obeyed, as a woman should."

Aunt Maud looked regally over the assembled company, daring someone to contradict her, but no one did, taking the wind out of her sails. Valerie thought that if Maud had been as unpleasant as a girl as she was as an adult, her father likely would have tried to marry her off at twelve to someone much older and hard of hearing.

"Aunt Maud, our guests have had a long journey, and we'd like to hear about life in Virginia," Kit interjected smoothly. "Wouldn't you like to hear about life in the New World?"

"Why would I want to hear about life in that God-forsaken

backwater? The only life worth talking about is at court. Speaking of which, is His Majesty going on Progress this summer?"

"I haven't heard to the contrary," mumbled Kit.

"It would be a great honor if His Majesty chose to visit Willowbrook, although I don't think your wife is up to entertaining such illustrious company. That's what happens when you marry beneath your station." Aunt Maud smiled at Louisa blandly, obviously revisiting an old argument. She seemed to perk up as Kit took a deep breath, finally rattled.

"Enough!" Kit roared, slamming his hand on the table. "Unless you'd like to take a tray in your room for the remainder of your stay, you will treat my guests with respect and refrain from making snide comments about my wife. Is that understood?"

Aunt Maud had the decency to look abashed, her little smile vanishing from her face as she glared at Kit with something akin to hurt.

"Perfectly. Your relations have been here for less than a day and already you're acting like a barbarian." With that, Aunt Maud swept out of the room, holding her head so high that Valerie wondered how she could see where she was going.

"Welcome to England," said Louisa, her eyes swimming with unshed tears.

FIVE

"Good God, what have we walked into?" Valerie asked as she climbed into the four-poster bed next to Alec. The housekeeper had assigned them separate bedrooms, but unlike most couples of quality, they'd always slept in the same bed, enjoying the warmth and comfort of each other's bodies.

"Things certainly seem tense," Alec observed, getting more comfortable. "Louisa looks miserable. Is everything all right between them?"

Valerie paused for a moment, unsure if she should share Louisa's concerns with Alec, but she normally told him everything and he might be able to help. Kit and Alec had shared a close bond in Virginia, so Alec might be able to talk some sense into him.

"Louisa thinks Kit's keeping a mistress. She found some evidence to support her suspicions."

"Really?" Alec asked, clearly surprised. "What sort of evidence?"

"The damning kind. There's a letter and an engraved snuffbox. Maybe you can have a talk with him," Valerie suggested, snuggling closer. "He'll listen to you. He respects you."

"Valerie, it's not my place to interfere in their marriage. I adore Louisa, and I love and respect Kit, but I have no right to intervene."

"I would want someone to intervene if you had a mistress," Valerie persisted, although she could see that Alec's mind was made up.

"Valerie, you are all the woman I'll ever need, and I have a feeling that if I even so much as glanced at another woman, it would be too late for any kind of intervention. You would kill me with your bare hands and hide my body somewhere where no one would ever find it," he said with a laugh, kissing the tip of her nose, "and that's how I like it."

Valerie couldn't say she disagreed with Alec. Confronting Kit would only cause tension between the men and ruin their stay. If Kit wanted to confide in Alec, he'd be happy to listen, but to blunder in wasn't Alec's way. Valerie had to admit that she was surprised by Louisa's handling of the situation. It wasn't like her sister to quietly sulk and pray for the best, but then this wasn't the type of life where a woman had much to gain by confronting her husband. If there really was a mistress and Kit was determined to continue the relationship, Louisa would have few options. She could either insist on living apart, in which case she might lose her children, or put a brave face on it and wait until the affair fizzled out, walking on eggshells and praying that her husband would return to her in time rather than relegate her to the ranks of unwanted wives, who were kept in the country to avoid scandal and produce more children.

Valerie couldn't imagine Kit ever treating Louisa in such a way, but then again, she'd only known him in Virginia, where he was one of the family rather than Lord Sheridan, advisor to the king. This was the role he'd been born into, not the one he'd played in Virginia.

Valerie sighed and snuggled closer to Alec despite the heat. She had doubted his faithfulness only once, but she had been the one to betray him with her lack of trust. Alec had never strayed and never would. His love for her was absolute, which was a rare and beautiful thing in any century.

SIX

Valerie looked up at the leaden sky, judging how much time she might have until the heavens opened up. They'd enjoyed several picture-perfect days, but this morning it was overcast and terribly muggy, the silk gown sticking to her flushed skin like a wetsuit. The weather wasn't ideal for walking, but in truth, Valerie just wanted a little time away from the house to think. Despite the numerous rooms, someone always seemed to find her, especially little Evie, who'd finally warmed up to her relatives and wanted to play hide-and-seek constantly, thrilled to have new friends to play with. It wasn't that Valerie didn't want to spend time with her niece or sister, but she didn't want Louisa to see the depth of her concern.

Kit was well-mannered and polite, but it wasn't hard to see that something was gnawing at him, devouring him from the inside. Valerie wasn't at all sure that Louisa's assessment was correct. He didn't seem like a man overcome with passion for a new love. Whoever this woman was, she wasn't making him happy. Valerie noticed Kit watching Louisa with unbearable longing, making her wish she could just ask him outright what was going on and put all the speculation to rest. Kit seemed happy to spend time with Alec, but hadn't mentioned anything, and Alec remained firm in his resolve not to interfere.

Louisa, on the other hand, tried to pretend that everything was well, acting normally around Kit and trying not to commit an act of violence against his aunt. Thankfully, the woman rose late, then took a nap in the afternoon, leaving them to deal with her for only a few hours a day. Louisa desperately wished she'd just leave, but it seemed the old lady was having way too much fun exactly where she was.

The latest disagreement had been about Evie wearing a corset. Aunt Maud felt that the girl was old enough to be taught good posture and bearing and needed to be trained from an early age to accept that a woman should never equate attire with comfort. Louisa was too speechless to even engage in the argument. To stuff a two-year-old into a corset would be considered child-abuse in her day, but in the seventeenth century, it was perfectly normal. After all, Evie's only value, in Aunt Maud's eyes, was how well she would eventually do on the marriage market. Her wellbeing and happiness were something that would never cross the old lady's mind. She was a mere girl, useful only in furthering the fortunes of the family. If, at some point, the king took an interest in her, Aunt Maud would no doubt recommend that Evie be sent to his bed in the hopes that the family would profit by being granted titles and estates. Being a girl of nobility in these times was a perilous business, and Valerie hoped that Kit would protect his daughter and do his best to see her happily married when the time came.

Valerie had just made it to a bench situated beneath a weeping willow when the first drops began to fall. She didn't mind. Her green retreat was waterproof and serene, just what her aching heart needed. She was so worried for Louisa, but what could she do to help other than listen and sympathize? In the twenty-first century, she might have been able to offer advice, even suggest marriage counseling, but here, there was nothing to do except to grin and bear it.

Valerie watched as heavy raindrops plopped onto the surface of the pond, making the water ripple in their wake. The surface of the pond was nearly black, reflecting the quickly darkening sky. Reeds nodded their velvety heads as the wind picked up, causing the rain to come down almost horizontally and soaking everything in its path. It would take some time for the storm to pass, but that was all right. Valerie was warm and dry in her sanctuary, if not overly happy.

She looked up in astonishment as the shaggy branches of the willow parted to admit a soggy Alec. "There you are," he said, taking a seat on the bench. "I've been looking everywhere for you."

"Why, is something wrong?" Valerie asked in alarm.

"You seemed so melancholy at breakfast; I thought you might need some cheering up," he replied, putting his arm around her and drawing her head against his shoulder.

"As long as I didn't look like a bulldog," Valerie answered sarcastically, making Alec chuckle.

"Aunt Maud is something, isn't she? I wonder if she was always so harsh or if life made her that way," he mused.

Valerie had never stopped to consider Aunt Maud's life. Was it possible that she had been a kind and caring soul at some point in her past? What would have to happen to someone to make them so horrid? She would have to ask Louisa. After all, she seemed to have no one except for her adopted nephew and his long-suffering wife. Surely, she must have had children of her own at some point, and grandchildren.

"Forget Maud for a moment, Valerie. Actually, there's something I want to discuss with you while we're away from the house. The Sheridans will be going back to town in a few weeks, and I thought this might be a good opportunity for us to escape for a little while." Alec's eyes were full of mischief, his smile conspiratorial.

"And where are we escaping to, exactly?" Valerie asked, looking up at him from her vantage point. It was always so comforting to have him nearby.

"To the future. We can see London in the twenty-first century. I have it all worked out. I thought it would be best not to tell little Louisa. She's excited to visit the palace and Kit has promised to introduce her to the king. She's asked me to have some new gowns made, so the fittings should keep her busy for a little while."

"London? But I wanted to show you New York." She had it all planned as well, and it was the next item on the list once they returned home to Virginia.

"It can't be done, sweetheart," Alec said gently.

"Of course, it can. Mr. Taylor showed me how to set a location. The new time travel device is more sophisticated and has an option to choose coordinates as well as time."

"Yes, I know; he showed it to me as well, but that's not what I meant. I know what you want to do, and it can't be done," Alec repeated, taking her hand in his and kissing her palm.

"What exactly are you referring to?"

"I'm referring to your plan to prevent the accident that killed your parents. Isn't that what you were thinking?" The look of compassion in Alec's eyes nearly made Valerie cry, but she fought back the tears, facing Alec defiantly.

"You deduced all that from one sentence?"

"I've been married to you for nearly two decades, I know how your mind works. Am I wrong?"

"No, you're not, and it can be done. I wouldn't have to show myself. Maybe you could ask them for directions or something and prevent them from crossing the street at that particular moment. It would save their lives. Oh, just think of it, Alec. They would be alive and well. I would happily return to the past knowing that they are out there, living their lives, even if they don't know that I'm still alive." Valerie had dreamed of seeing her parents again. It would be torture not to talk to them or assure them that she was well, but it would be a sacrifice she was willing to make to save them from their untimely death.

Alec shook his head sadly. "Valerie, have you mentioned this to Louisa?"

"No, but I don't see why she would object."

"Don't you? If you save your parents, Louisa will never seek out Mr. Taylor and come to the past. She will never meet and marry Kit or have Evie and Robbie. By that one act, you will negate her whole life, and not only hers. If Louisa doesn't come, neither does Mr. Taylor. Finn would never go to the future and meet Abbie, and we would likely never survive the famine, since it was Mr. Taylor who helped us prepare for the worst. You would be changing the lives of countless people, including us. Have you considered that?" Alec drew Valerie to him, holding her close. "I know you want to save them, love, but you can't. You simply can't."

Valerie buried her face in Alec's shoulder, not wanting him to see her tears. He was right, of course, but she'd never considered those things. She just wanted to help them so badly. She still missed them every day, wishing that they hadn't gone to their deaths believing her dead and buried in some unmarked grave. Her disappearance had broken their hearts, and there was nothing she could do to change any of it. She thought she was so clever by devising her plan, but as usual, Alec was the practical one. Why did he always have to be right?

"You can still show me London," Alec said softly, lifting her chin with his finger and wiping the tears away. "It would be fascinating to compare the London of today to the London of your time. What do you think?" His eyes were aglow again, full of wonder.

"Yes, of course, but we'd need a plan. It's not so easy to go to the future. You need money, identity papers, not to mention clothes. We'd look like actors from a Renaissance Faire in our finery," Valerie chuckled.

"So what do you propose?" Valerie knew exactly what he was doing. She was always happiest when planning something, so this would take her mind off her recent worries and give her something pleasant to focus on.

"Well, you have no record of being born, and if I suddenly resurface, that will flag something somewhere; I'm sure of it. We can't stay in a hotel without documents or rent a car. So, we can do day trips," Valerie announced, proud to have come up with a solution.

"Day trips?"

"Yes. We can leave in the morning and come back at night. All we need to do is bring something of value to sell, like period coins or a piece of jewelry. That would give us enough money to buy some clothes and do the touristy things we want to do in the future. As long as we pay for everything in cash, no one will be the wiser. We can ride the double-decker bus, take a taxi, and go for a spin on the London Eye. What do you think? I would love to see you in a pair of skinny jeans and a t-shirt." Valerie grinned at Alec's confused face.

"I don't think I'm ready to commit to anything called skinny jeans, but it would be fun to wear modern clothes. Do they not have breeches and shirts?"

"Ah, yes, but the breeches look somewhat different, and women wear them too. You have no idea how I miss wearing pants. And, I will make you eat sushi."

Valerie was warming up to her theme. There was so much she wanted to show him. He might be a little overwhelmed at first, but they could go a couple of times and not do everything in one day. She might even take him to the zoo. Alec had never seen any animals other than the ones common to Europe and North America. She would love to witness his reaction to seeing a tiger or an elephant, or even a shark. People of the seventeenth century still believed there were monsters lurking below the dark waters of the ocean. It would be educational for Alec to see what these monsters really looked like. Of course, his primary interest lay in all things mechanical.

"We can go to Victoria Station and take a train to the airport. We can't fly anywhere without passports, but you can watch them to your heart's content."

"I would love that," Alec answered dreamily. "What I wouldn't give to fly somewhere. It's settled then. We'll go a few days after we come back to London. Look, it's clearing up. Should we risk it and go back to the house?"

"Race you!" Valerie called out as she sprinted between the droopy branches, enjoying the gentle raindrops falling onto her flushed face.

SEVEN

The sun never came out, but the rain stopped, bringing with it a temporary coolness that was a welcome relief from the heat of the past few days. The house was strangely quiet with Evie and Aunt Maud taking their naps and the staff taking advantage of the lull to rest and have their midday meal. Valerie trudged up the stone staircase flanked by portraits of long-deceased relatives, hoping to find Louisa in the nursery. She could have sworn she'd heard Robbie squealing up there, and she wanted a few minutes with her sister.

Robbie was seated in a copper basin, his face alight with joy as he splashed away, spraying water onto an exasperated Mills. Her lips were pursed, and her face was a mask of disapproval as she tried to get close enough to Robbie to actually wash him without getting soaked. Valerie felt a pang of longing as she looked at her gleeful nephew. It wasn't so long ago that Finn had been small, splashing around in his own bath as Bridget scrubbed him to a shine.

"Please, let me," Valerie offered, coming closer and promptly getting the front of her dress soaked. "I'll give him a bath." Mills gaped at her in shock but gave a small curtsey and stepped aside.

"Leave us, Mills." Louisa walked into the room and smiled at the sight. "He loves bath time."

"Who doesn't?" chuckled Valerie, as Robbie kicked his legs and splashed water onto her face. "It wasn't that long ago that Finn and Louisa were babies and look at them now. Finn is married, and Louisa only has eyes for young men. It all went so fast, Lou. Not an hour goes by that I don't think of Finn."

"I can't imagine anything worse than losing a child. When I thought Evie might die on the crossing, I lost all will to live. Nothing seemed to matter anymore, not even Kit, or the new baby. The thought of a life without her was like a constant agony that tormented me day and night. I know Finn isn't dead, but not being able to see him or talk to him or even know if he's all right must be hell."

"Lou, did Aunt Maud have any children?"

"Yes, she did. Maud never told me about them, but Caroline did. She could barely tolerate Aunt Maud, but she felt sorry for her. The poor woman hasn't had a happy life," Louisa answered as she prepared a towel for Robbie. "She was married off at fourteen to a man more than twice her age. It was a marriage of convenience, but she fell in love with her husband, nonetheless, an unforgivable sin in those times."

"I take it her feelings weren't returned?" Valerie asked sadly.

"No. He refused to give up his mistress, and only stayed as long as it took to get her pregnant before leaving again. She gave birth to seven children—four boys and three girls. Two were stillborn, two died before the age of five, and the other three died in adulthood. I can't imagine the heartache she's endured. Her husband died by the time she was thirty-five, with his mistress by his deathbed."

"Poor woman," Valerie sighed. "Losing one child is heartbreaking enough, but to lose seven... No wonder she's so bitter."

"Yes, that's what Caroline said. She felt sorry for her. For all her venom, she's just a sad, elderly woman who's trying to cling on to the old ways out of fear. I think she would be better served if she were a little kinder to those around her, but if she lets her emotions get the better of her even once, she might just lose control and completely go to pieces. Her nastiness is just a defense mechanism against all the pain and loss she suffered as a young woman."

"How sad," Valerie sighed, seeing Maud in a whole new light. "Was there anything she could have done?"

"She could have taken a lover after her husband died, but she remained faithful to him, God knows why. She's still mourning him and the children. She doesn't even have a grandchild to call her own. Evie and Robbie are the closest she'll ever get to having grandkids, and she takes very little interest in them. They're too young to have any real value, as far as she's concerned."

Scooping Robbie out of the bath, Louisa wrapped him in a towel and carried him to his cot. He peered out of the towel, his blue eyes full of mischief. Valerie handed Louisa Robbie's gown as she toweled him dry and let him roll onto his belly, butt naked. He seemed to enjoy the moment of freedom, promptly rolling onto his back and peeing all over his mother's gown.

"You little demon," Louisa laughed, "I should have known better than to trust you." She gave Robbie a resounding kiss before putting on his clean gown and handing him to Valerie so she could go get changed.

EIGHT

MARYLAND JULY 1777

Slanted shafts of late-afternoon sun pierced the canopy of leaves above the road, striping the world in alternating ribbons of light and shade. The sun was already hovering above the horizon, painting the sky in lovely shades of fuchsia and gold. Another half hour and the first stars would start to shyly appear in the darkening sky, signaling the end of another day. Abbie loved this time of day. The sunset was a symbol of a day's promise fulfilled and a few hours of well-earned rest to look forward to before going to bed, but there would be no bed tonight. Finn would find a place to camp for the night and they would sleep next to their fire, hoping the smoking embers would keep the bugs away. Abbie didn't really mind sleeping outdoors, but after more than two weeks of travel, she was eager for a real bed and a proper bath.

She wouldn't admit it to Finn, but she was already homesick. This was her first time away from home, and she had no idea when they would be coming back. She could still see her mother's forlorn expression as she said goodbye to them. Only a few years ago, her parents had a houseful of children, but now only Sarah and Annie remained at home. Sam had been the first to leave when he joined the Continental Army, followed by Martha, and then Jonah, who joined on his seventeenth birthday in May. And now Abbie and Finn were gone as well. At least Martha was close enough to be able to visit frequently and bring baby Joe to see his grandparents. He was such a sweet, good-natured baby.

Everyone secretly thought Joe was lucky to take after his father in temperament, and not his mother. Martha was bossier than ever, especially since Gil's mother passed away a few months back. She was now the woman of the house and didn't have to defer to a mother-in-law. Martha finally had what she'd wanted all along—her own home.

"I think it's time we made camp," Finn said, looking up at the sky. "We probably have less than an hour of daylight left. Let's turn off here. I think I can hear a creek somewhere close by, so we should have water. You look tired, sweetheart. I'll set up camp, and you can have a wash if you like while I prepare supper." Finn gave her a tender look. Abbie was perfectly capable of taking care of herself and him, but it was so nice to have him cosset her this way. It made her feel special.

"We still have some bread and cheese and a few slices of cold pork. That will do for supper. How about I help you set up camp and then we can bathe together?" she asked, a seductive smile playing about her lips.

"You are a brazen woman, Mrs. Whitfield. What would the minister make of such lewd suggestions?" Finn chuckled, already envisioning Abbie's naked body, her hair damp and her skin cool from the water in the creek.

"I'm not certain, that's why I won't be making such suggestions to him, but you, Mr. Whitfield, are a different matter altogether. Unless my lewdness offends you." She giggled as Finn pulled the reins of her horse, bringing her closer and kissing her hard.

"It makes my life worth living," he whispered.

The creek turned out to be a lot deeper than expected, allowing them to completely submerge themselves in cool, refreshing water and not wash in parts as they had all week. Normally, Abbie would have kept her shift on, but they were far enough from the road and hadn't seen another person in hours, so she stripped down and walked into the water, conscious of Finn's gaze on her body. She knew the effect she had on him and relished it like a wonderful secret that only she was privy to. She leaned against him as he came up behind her, his stiff shaft against her buttocks. Finn cupped her breasts, kissing her neck and moving his hips against hers in silent intent. Abbie was about to move back to the shore, but Finn stopped her, turning her in his arms.

"Don't go," he whispered in her ear, sending shivers down her spine. The water made her feel languid and weightless, and strangely aroused. Finn lifted her up as she wrapped her legs around his waist, kissing him with abandon. She felt his fingers caress her before he slid inside her body, rocking her hips against his. Time seemed to stand still as their bodies moved in unison, creating ripples of water that swirled around them like the rings of Saturn Finn had shown her in a book on astronomy. Abbie felt like melting butter as her insides quivered with release. She laid her head on Finn's shoulder, not wanting to let go of the moment, still joined to him body and soul.

NINE

ENGLAND JULY 1624

Pouring himself a brandy, Alec settled close to the open window. A lovely breeze blew from outside, bringing with it an aroma of flowers, warm earth, and freshly cut grass. He'd missed the smells and sounds of the country while aboard the ship to England. He'd also missed having a little time alone. Being cooped up on the boat with his wife, daughter, and the crew had left him longing for a few moments of peace and staying in this house didn't help. Alec took a sip of brandy, enjoying the bouquet of flavor. This was expensive French brandy, not the merely adequate stuff he drank in Virginia.

He'd greatly enjoyed the reunion with Louisa, Kit, and the children, but now he was experiencing undercurrents he couldn't quite understand. Something wasn't right, and it wasn't just Louisa's suspicion of infidelity. Beneath the convivial façade, Kit was tense, practically thrumming with some unknown worry. He'd been like a brother to Alec in Virginia, but here things were different. Kit was back in his element: lord of the manor, confidant to the king, consummate courtier. As much as Alec longed to talk to him and draw him out, he wasn't sure it was his place to do so. If Kit wanted to talk, he'd have to make the first move. He had seemed about to say something to Alec several times over the past few days but changed his mind at the last moment and suggested some entertainment for the following day or a game of cards after dinner.

Alec was startled out of his reverie by a knock on the door. He hoped it wasn't Maud, but then she wouldn't have bothered to knock. She would have just barged in, treating him as she would a servant who happened to be in her way. Alec rarely disliked anyone to the point of hatred, but the old lady managed to offend him on every level, and he hoped they would see less of her once the Sheridans returned to London. Maud had her own residence and would hopefully find a reason to stay there for the remainder of their visit.

"May I join you?" Kit asked as he entered the room, closing the door softly behind him.

"Of course. Shall I pour you a drink?" Alec asked, already rising to his feet.

"Yes, please. A very large one." Kit sank into a chair. He looked tired and worn, his gaze overshadowed by something Alec couldn't name. Alec handed Kit a glass and sat across from him, unsure how to proceed. He had no wish to pry, but something was obviously troubling Kit a great deal.

"Kit, are you all right? I know it's none of my business, but I'll be happy to listen if you need to talk."

Kit set down his glass, burying his face in his hands. Alec heard a muffled sound, but couldn't tell if he was crying, laughing, or a little of both. "Oh, Alec, I don't know where to begin. I feel so ashamed. I can't even look you in the face."

It seemed that Kit was about to confess the affair. At least he was remorseful and ashamed, Alec thought, so maybe there was hope of him ending the relationship quietly and returning to his wife before things went too far, unless he had no wish to end it with his lover.

"Kit, you can confide in me. I won't judge you, only try to

help. Who is she?" Kit's head snapped up at Alec's question, a look of confusion on his face until he understood whom Alec was referring to.

"Alec, the she is a he. It's George Villiers, Duke of Buckingham." Kit rubbed his eyes with the palms of his hands, clearly miserable, his shoulders slumping with a resignation Alec had never seen in him before.

"Kit, I don't understand. You don't have a mistress at court?" Alec took a sip of brandy, needing a moment to compose himself. He had no idea what they were talking about and didn't want to appear foolish.

"Alec, I have no idea how any of this happened. It's laughable, really, but I'm in an impossible situation. His Majesty invited me to join the Privy Council at the suggestion of the Duke of Buckingham. As you know, my father served on the Council, but I have no good reason to be there. There are other men who could contribute much more than I ever could. I'm not a military man or an experienced statesman. I'm not sure if you know, but Buckingham is the most powerful courtier at King James's court. His Majesty trusts him implicitly, not only in matters of State, but in personal decisions as well."

"I'm not sure I follow, Kit," Alec leaned forward, his elbows on his knees. Where was this going? Was Kit simply worried about his ability to perform on the Council and feeling out of his depth? That didn't seem like him at all. He might not be an experienced politician, but he was a man of intelligence and integrity, which was more than could be said about most of James's ministers.

"Alec, Buckingham is a law onto himself. He does whatever he pleases with whomever he pleases, and he's taken a liking to me. It's no secret that he goes both ways. There's talk of him being James's lover, but to speak the words out loud is paramount to treason, despite the His Majesty's ardent proclamations of love for his *wife*, as he calls him."

"Isn't Buckingham married?" Alec asked, confused.

"Yes, but what does that matter? The king is married as well. These men perform their husbandly duties but seek pleasure outside the marriage bed. Buckingham began pursuing me shortly after I joined the Council. He's relentless, Alec. He sends letters and presents me with expensive gifts. Louisa found the snuffbox he had made for me. She thinks it's from a woman, and I simply can't bring myself to tell her the truth. I would rather she thought I was having an affair with another woman than admit that I'm being tirelessly pursued by a man." Kit finally looked up at Alec, his face a mask of misery. "Help me, Alec. I don't know what to do."

"What can you do other than reject his advances? Is he aware of your feelings?"

Kit shook his head, taking a large sip of brandy. "Yes, but you don't say no to Buckingham. He has the power to destroy me. All he has to do is present some trumped-up charge of treason to James and I could be executed, my title stripped, and my estates confiscated by the Crown. My wife and children would be left with nothing but the shame of being related to a traitor. Even my sister's sons would be affected. Their lives would be as good as over." Kit drained the brandy and held out his glass for a refill. "I'm damned if I do and I'm damned if I don't. What I wouldn't give to return to Virginia and be away from all this."

"Kit, would he really take his vengeance that far? I heard he was a reasonable man."

"Buckingham is gracious and charming, but he's like a spoiled child who'll throw a tantrum if he doesn't get his way. Only this tantrum can result in me losing my head. He's implied as much. One word to James and I would be hauled off to the Tower to await execution with no hope of a fair trial, or a trial at all, for that matter. I wouldn't be the first."

Alec exhaled loudly, his eyes sliding away from Kit's. He'd

never been confronted by such a dilemma and hoped never to be again. What advice could he possibly give? He was only too aware of what it meant to be associated with a traitor. Louisa and the children would be harassed and ridiculed, their estates seized, the noble title stripped. If it were just Kit, he'd advise him to refuse Buckingham and take his chances, but Kit would be risking the entire family if Buckingham decided on vengeance.

"Kit, I'm at a loss for words. I can't imagine myself in your situation."

"Neither can I, except I'm in it and can't do anything about it. I can't leave the country without the king's permission, but James will never grant it, not with a war coming. I'm trapped." Kit drained the second glass, his shoulders beginning to relax a little as the alcohol entered his bloodstream. "I can't sleep, I can't eat, and most of all, I can't look Louisa in the eye."

"Kit, I want you to know that no matter what happens, I would take care of your family," Alec replied, his promise sounding feeble even to himself. He could feed and clothe them, but he couldn't protect them from Buckingham's wrath nor the grief of losing a husband and father.

"Kit, I'm going to ask you an odd question. Please bear with me. Is Buckingham constant, or is he fickle and changes lovers often?" Alec asked carefully. Kit shrugged, obviously not following Alec's train of thought.

"I suppose he's fickle, although the rumors about him and James have been swirling for years. He enjoys the chase and the conquest more than the actual relationship, or so I've heard. His relationship is with his sovereign—the rest is just a game. What difference does that make?"

"It makes a difference if you submit to him. He'll eventually tire of you and you will be free."

Kit jumped up from his seat, towering over Alec, his eyes blazing with fury. "Are you seriously suggesting that I allow that man to bugger me until he grows tired of it?" he spat, his fists clenched at his sides. Kit immediately backed away, embarrassed by his reaction. Alec was not the problem.

"Yes, Kit, I am. I'd rather see you buggered than dead. You will recover in time."

"And what do I tell Louisa?" Kit asked angrily.

"Tell her that you'd indulged in a brief flirtation with some woman but assure her that it's over and will never happen again. Don't destroy your marriage over this."

Kit collapsed into the chair, hands over his face, his shoulders quaking. This time, Alec knew for certain he was crying.

TEN

Valerie climbed into bed, the sheets cool and clean against her hot skin. It was absolute heaven, as was the sight of her husband, pulling his shirt over his head and beginning to unlace his breeches. They'd barely had any opportunity for intimacy aboard the ship or on the way to Willowbrook and she was burning with desire for him. Alec's thoughts seemed to run in a similar direction as he joined her in bed.

Valerie melted into Alec's arms when he drew her to him, eager for his touch. He kissed her temple and caressed her breast, but his mind didn't seem to be on what he was doing. "Val, can I ask you something?" he said suddenly, stopping his exploration. "You mentioned before that homosexuality was widespread in the future. What do you know about it?"

Valerie looked up at Alec, her desire quickly cooling. "Are you thinking of switching sides?"

"No, but I was wondering how it works between two men." Valerie sat up, staring at Alec.

"Start talking. NOW!"

"It's nothing. Kit just happened to mention that the king

might have taken male lovers despite being married. Is that common?"

Valerie eyed Alec suspiciously. She had a feeling that Kit might have said considerably more than that, but Alec wasn't about to break his confidence, no matter how much she badgered him.

"There are men who marry in order to hide their sexual orientation but continue to take male lovers on the side. When I was a child, it was uncommon for people to admit to being gay, but as I got older, it became more acceptable. Many men are openly gay and there was even talk of making gay marriage legal," Valerie supplied, watching Alec's face.

"The Church would allow two men to marry?" Alec asked, incredulous.

"No, not the Church—the State. It would be a legal marriage though, recognized by everyone. There would be couples made up of two men or two women."

"What? Women want to marry each other as well?" Alec sat up in bed, staring at Valerie as if she were making a joke at his expense.

"Yes, women can be gay as well," Valerie explained patiently.

"Is it because they're afraid of men?" Alec needed to find an explanation that made sense, but Valerie shook her head.

"It's because they prefer women. Period. Now, why are you asking me all this?" Maybe he was in such shock he'd spill the beans, but Alec quickly recovered himself, lying back down.

"No, reason. Just curious." He still looked abashed, clearly trying to figure out how all this worked, emotionally and physically.

"How do women...?" he began, but Valerie put a finger to his lips, silencing him and nibbling on his earlobe to distract him for the numerous questions he was about to ask. Alec got the point, his hand sliding up her thigh. Valerie cried out in surprise as Alec suddenly flipped her onto her stomach, pushing her shift above her waist and grabbing her hips.

"Alec, don't you dare," she squealed as she felt his hardness against her ass. "I'll never forgive you."

"Don't squirm my dear, it won't help. Just think of it as research."

Valerie gasped as he pushed into her, silencing her protests. She wasn't sure what to expect, but aside from mild discomfort and unwelcome pressure, it didn't feel so bad. Alec began to move slowly, his thighs pushing hers further apart. She tried to relax, but her mind was still refusing to accept what he was doing to her. It just didn't feel right, and she wished he'd stop. Valerie forgot her objections when Alec's hand came around and slid between her legs, caressing her until she began to relax. His fingers probed her as he thrust slowly and deliberately, bringing her to heights of pleasure she'd forgotten she could experience.

She remained facedown when Alec rolled off her and patted her bottom affectionately, her body still quivering with the aftershocks of this novel lovemaking.

"That wasn't so bad," Alec observed. "I might be mistaken, but I think you enjoyed it."

"Don't get used to it," Valerie replied, wondering why he looked so smug, as if some important question had been answered.

ELEVEN

ENGLAND AUGUST 1624

Louisa Whitfield walked aimlessly among the perfectly manicured hedges of the formal garden, running her hand over the prickly tops. The shadows were just beginning to lengthen as the sun began its descent toward the horizon, finally giving way to a cool breeze blowing through the trees. Louisa closed her eyes and concentrated on the achingly sweet song of the lark hiding somewhere in the branches of a nearby tree, singing its heart out before another day drew to a close and silenced it for the night.

She'd looked forward to coming to England, but she wasn't enjoying herself at all. The tension between the adults was palpable, the only pleasure to be had was the time she spent with the children. She loved being with Evie, and Robbie's sturdy little arms around her neck nearly brought her to tears. They were so sweet, and completely oblivious to the undercurrents swirling all around them. Louisa had been too young to appreciate Evie when she was born, but now her response was surprisingly different. She supposed that at almost seventeen, her maternal instinct was awakening, her body reminding her that it wouldn't be long before she became a mother herself.

Of course, there'd been no offers of marriage. Her indiscretion with Tom hadn't been forgotten. Louisa pretended not to notice the sly looks or hear the snide comments she'd overheard in Jamestown after church, but deep down, she was worried. She hoped she'd marry before she turned eighteen. There wasn't much chance of her becoming an old maid, not with the shortage of women in the colony, but she had no wish to be saddled with some aging widower or rootless newcomer. She had to try her best to find a suitable husband, but no respectable family would want her for a daughter-in-law, at least not in Virginia. In England, her slate was clean, but she had yet to meet any eligible young men. Uncle Kit had promised to introduce her at court, but Louisa was nothing if not realistic. Being pretty was enough to receive an invitation to someone's bed, but not enough to elicit a proposal of marriage. Without a title or an estate in England she didn't have much to offer a prospective husband. True, their estate in Virginia was a profitable one, but for the people at court the only life worth living was in England, so a tobacco plantation, profitable though it might be, wasn't enough of an incentive to offer marriage. The only way Louisa could avoid returning to Virginia unwed was to use her wits and looks to turn the head of some unsuspecting youth and hope that his family didn't object to her too violently.

Louisa sighed and turned back toward the house. It was almost time for supper, and she wanted to take a bath. This heat was unbearable, leaving ugly wet stains beneath her armpits and making her perspire in places she didn't know could sweat. The house was a bit cooler, but not by much, and she looked forward to her soak. She'd ask the servants to fill the tub with cool rose-scented water, which would be so pleasant and refreshing. Louisa had almost reached the stairs when a commotion in the hall drew her attention. There'd been so little excitement over the past week that any distraction was welcome. Louisa held down her arms to hide the sweat stains and walked into the hall, eager to see what was happening. A young man, who bore an uncanny resemblance to Kit, was talking to the manservant, asking to see Lord Sheridan without delay. His face was flushed from the heat, his clothes and boots travel stained. He was clearly in no mood to be trifled with but stopped mid-sentence when his gaze fell on Louisa.

"I beg your pardon, madam. I didn't mean to disturb you." The young man swept her a gracious bow, his dark eyes never leaving her face and making Louisa blush. "Where are my manners? I'm Theodore Carew, Lord Sheridan's nephew. And you are?"

"Louisa Whitfield, Lord Sheridan's niece," Louisa answered coyly, subconsciously arching her back to draw the young man's attention to the creamy breasts swelling above her bodice. She tried to hide her smile when the man's gaze shifted from her face to her bosom, his breath catching in his throat.

So, this was Theo. Aunt Louisa had mentioned him only the other day. He was Lady Carew's youngest son and had been her secret, or not so secret, favorite, the son who favored her in looks and temperament. Theo's older brothers were already advantageously married, but Theo, who was around twenty, had yet to wed. Louisa lowered her eyes in mock embarrassment and smiled at Theo shyly, gazing up at him from under her thick lashes. He seemed dumbstruck, seemingly unsure of what to say to this girl who'd come out of nowhere and was looking at him with such poorly disguised interest.

"Ah, I see you two have met," Kit observed as he walked into the hall, his favorite hound at his heels. He tossed his hat to the manservant, who caught it deftly and withdrew, since the master's attention was already on his nephew. "Theo, what are you doing here? Not that it isn't a pleasure to see you."

"I bring a message from court, Uncle," Theo replied, his eyes straying to Louisa, who was still watching him.

"I hope you'll stay for a few days. Come into the library so we can talk. Do excuse us, Louisa."

Kit slapped Theo on the shoulder as they walked toward the library, leaving Louisa looking after them, a small smile playing about her lips. Suddenly, things had become more interesting, setting her mind awhirl with possibilities. She raced up the stairs to have her bath and to pick out her most becoming gown. She'd be damned if she let this opportunity pass her by.

TWELVE

STATEN ISLAND AUGUST 1777

Abbie peered at the map again, then looked around at the landmarks, if you could call them that. They were in a place called Staten Island, but it might as well have been the backwoods of Virginia. They'd passed a farm about an hour ago, but hadn't seen anything since, and there was nothing to indicate that they were on the right track.

"I think we're going the wrong way, Finn. There's nothing here," Abbie complained. She was tired, hungry, but most of all, saddle-sore. The thought of spending another couple of hours on horseback was enough to make her cry, especially since she was expecting her period and feeling crampy and achy.

"No, I think it's just up ahead. I know you're tired, but you need to hang on just a little bit longer. Sam will assume the worst if we don't show up. We're a few days late as is. Would you like to dismount and stretch your legs for a bit?" Finn asked, a look of sympathy on his face.

"No, let's just press on. Once I get off this old nag, I'm not getting back on, and that's a promise. Do we have anything to drink?" Finn passed her a bottle of cider, hoping the cool drink would refresh her. He was tired himself but didn't want to show weakness. It would only make Abbie feel worse. If they didn't find the homestead soon, they'd have to camp for the night and look for it tomorrow, but Finn hoped it wouldn't come to that. They were low on food and drink and another night of sleeping outdoors would likely push Abbie over the edge. She'd never traveled anywhere before this and the weeks of being in the saddle and sleeping rough had taken their toll. She'd need at least a day or two to rest before they took up whatever role Sam had in mind for them.

"Come on, Abs, just a little while longer." Finn squeezed her hand, willing her not to give up. Abbie nodded and dug her heels into the horse's sides, spurring it on. If she couldn't get out of the saddle, maybe she could at least feel the wind on her face.

The farm finally came into view about a half hour later. It was a desolate-looking place, but there was light in the windows and smoke coming from the chimney, which hopefully meant that someone was cooking supper. There'd be no other reason to light a fire on such a warm night. Several chickens pecked in the dirt and the lowing of cows and bleating of sheep could be heard coming from the barn as the final rays of the sun disappeared behind the horizon, bathing the homestead in a lavender glow that would quickly give way to the velvety blackness of a summer night.

A figure emerged from the house, peering into the gathering darkness as Finn and Abbie finally drew closer to the house. Abbie's heart nearly burst with joy when she recognized Sam. She couldn't see his face clearly, but the limp gave him away. It wasn't bad, but noticeable nonetheless, especially when he was tired. The bullet had penetrated his thigh right above the knee, thankfully sparing his kneecap, but preventing him from remaining in the army. Sam could no longer march for hours or run during an offensive—he was damaged goods. Their mother had hoped he might come home, but Sam wasn't ready to give up the cause. If he couldn't fight the enemy overtly, he would do so covertly, with the help of his father. Mr. Mallory was only too happy to have Sam join the Committee and put his considerable skills to good use.

Abbie slid off the horse right into the warm embrace of her brother. "Oh, Abbie, I thought you'd never get here. I was getting worried." Sam kissed Abbie on the forehead and held out a hand to Finn, who came up behind her.

"Well, maybe you should draw a better map next time. One bush looks much like the next when you are traveling through the wilds of Staten Island," Abbie retorted, already turning her attention to the house. "Who lives here?"

"A friend. Come inside and I'll introduce you. Supper is ready, as are your beds. Your assignment begins tomorrow, so you need to rest." Sam put an arm around Abbie's shoulder as he steered her toward the door. "Finn, just leave the horses. I'll see to them in a moment. Come inside and have some food. You must be famished."

"We are, actually." Finn tied the horses to a stile and followed Sam and Abbie into the house. He was touched by the relief he'd noticed on Sam's face. He must have been more worried than he let on, and now that his sister was involved it would be more difficult for him to remain detached. Finn hoped that whatever situation Sam found for them would not put Abbie in any immediate danger, but they were now in enemy territory and would have to be on their guard, always looking over their shoulder and hoping that they did nothing careless to give themselves away.

Finn wiped the last of the gravy with a heel of bread and popped it into his mouth. He would have loved to ask for thirds, but there was nothing left of the savory stew that now lay warm and comforting in his belly. Mr. Jenkins set a bowl of raspberries on the table, inviting Finn and Abbie to help themselves. Abbie took a handful and ate them one by one, savoring the burst of flavor as each berry dissolved in her mouth, filling it with juice.

"Mr. Jenkins, thank you for the meal. It was wonderful," Finn said as he pushed aside his bowl, ready to get down to business. "Sam, Abbie is exhausted, so why don't you outline our assignment before she falls asleep." He knew he and Abbie would be exposed to the British in one capacity or another, but it was up to Sam to fill in the details. He'd been working on a plan that hinged on their arrival.

"All right," Sam replied, pushing away his own bowl and pulling out a map which he unrolled on the table and pinned down at the corners with the empty bowls. "British troops are stationed here, here, and here. However, many of the officers are lodging on the isle of Manhattan. Cromwell's boarding house is located right here, on the south side of the island. It's run by a Mrs. Cromwell, the widow of Major Cromwell, who served under Cornwallis. Her reputation is above reproach as far as the British are concerned. At any given time, there are at least fifteen officers quartered at the house. Mr. Jenkins here, supplies Mrs. Cromwell with produce from his farm, as well as bacon and cheese. He's proposed that his nephew Finlay and his wife Abigail come help out at the boarding house since one of Mrs. Cromwell's maidservants is doing a lot more than cleaning the rooms." At this, Sam gave them all a meaningful look that made Abbie burst into giggles.

"Mrs. Cromwell thinks it might be best to have a married couple about the place, since the officers wouldn't trouble a married woman. I must admit that the logic of this fails me as I've troubled many a married woman myself when I was still an officer, but I digress," said Sam, grinning.

"Finn, you will see to the horses and help out with any chores that require muscle, and Abbie will clean the officers' rooms and help prepare and serve meals. Abbie, you will have a unique opportunity to read correspondence left in the rooms or see maps left lying about. We believe that the British are planning an offensive and need to know as much as possible about where they intend to strike. The information you obtain can help us win the war."

Abbie gave Sam a dubious look. "So, I have to clean chamber pots as an act of patriotism?"

"Exactly, sis."

"That could be my battle cry, "Chamber pots for Liberty!" Abbie exclaimed as she tossed another raspberry into her mouth with a saucy giggle. "I can't wait. Hopefully, Finn and I will have our own room in this military paradise?"

"Yes, you will have a room above the stables, which might not be luxurious, but will at least give you some privacy and a place to hide things if necessary." Sam rolled up the map and pushed to his feet, obviously ready for his own bed.

"Sam, how do we get the information out?" Finn asked.

"Oh, sorry, forgot about that part," Sam chuckled. "We will meet in a previously chosen location about once a week and you will pass on whatever you think is important. I, in turn, will pass it on to those who will get it to His Excellency General Washington. Now, off to bed with you two. You look dead on your feet."

THIRTEEN

ENGLAND AUGUST 1624

Louisa Whitfield looked about furtively as she slipped from the house and made her way toward the maze. The morning was lovely, cool, and fresh, with drops of dew sparkling on the grass like stars scattered by some benevolent fairy. Sounds of birdsong filled the air, making Louisa happy to be alive. She hadn't felt as hopeful as she did this morning in a very long time. Suddenly, life seemed full of promise and she wanted to do everything possible to see that promise fulfilled, and the first step to that goal was to catch Aunt Maud alone. For some reason, the old lady liked to sit on a marble bench at the center of the maze every morning after breakfast, enjoying some fresh air before the heat of the day drove her indoors. Louisa had no idea what her attachment to the maze was, but it didn't matter. It was a good place to talk privately and she needed information about Theodore Carew. Her father always said that knowledge was power, and she intended to arm herself with as much ammunition as she could get.

The message Theo brought was to inform Kit that his presence was required at some council meeting come Monday.

Monday was several days away, and thankfully, Theo had accepted Kit's invitation to stay until Sunday, when they would ride back to London together. It'd be a hard ride back, but they preferred to go on horseback rather than taking the carriage, which would take longer and possibly require an overnight stop, considerably delaying their arrival in London.

Louisa was thrilled Theo was staying. She'd discreetly observed him over supper the night before and was already strategizing. She'd always found Uncle Kit to be handsome, nursing a secret passion for him when she was a little girl. He seemed so dashing and brave, the hero of her childish dreams. Theo bore a striking resemblance to Kit, not only in looks but in personality as well. He was personable and warm, his dark eyes sparkling with humor and wit. What made Theo even more charming was his complete lack of arrogance. He seemed genuinely embarrassed when her mother had asked him about himself and even blushed when Louisa caught him looking at her across the table. His shyness was so refreshing compared to the young men she knew in Virginia, who were always boasting of their wealth and standing in the community. Theo had no need to boast; he was of noble birth and his wealth required no trumpeting. Theo's father had been as wealthy as Croesus and had provided well for his sons, tasking them with marrying well to consolidate their wealth and influence with other powerful English families. The woman Theo eventually married would want for nothing, and Louisa had every intention of being that woman.

There was no time to waste and Aunt Maud would be the best source of the information she needed, having known Theo from the cradle. Aunt Lou, who was a keen observer of human nature and as outspoken as Louisa's mother would have been her first choice, but she didn't want to ask her aunt for fear that Louisa would tell her parents, who might interfere with her plans. Aunt Maud, on the other hand, with her blunt way of putting things would surely let something important slip, something Louisa could use to her advantage in snaring her prey.

She stepped carefully, the gravel of the path hard and uneven beneath the thin soles of her slippers and the dew dampening the hem of her gown, but the misty shade of the narrow path was cool and pleasant, a strange hush permeating the maze as if it were a world unto itself, mysterious and full of old magic. Louisa slowed her pace as she neared the center of the maze, strolling as if she didn't have a care in the world and humming a wistful tune under her breath. She stepped into the square of sunlight, feigning surprise at the sight of the old lady seated regally on a bench, her face turned toward the sun, her walking stick leaning against the bench at a precarious angle.

"Aunt Maud, how nice to see you. May I join you? I was just taking a walk before it grew too hot and the maze is so pleasant in the morning, isn't it?"

Louisa didn't wait for an answer as she sat down next to Maud, her face wreathed in her most charming smile. She had to admit that although Aunt Maud managed to ruffle everyone's feathers and put a few noses out of joint, Louisa felt a sort of pity for her. How sad it must be to be old and unwanted, with no children or grandchildren to carry on your legacy. Who would really care when Maud died? Louisa supposed there would be some interest in her vast fortune, but no one would really miss the acerbic old lady or visit her lonely grave next to a husband who never loved her in life. She strongly suspected that Aunt Maud knew that as well and the truth made her more determined to torment everyone while she still could.

If only Aunt Maud were a little kinder, like Fred and Barbara Taylor, Louisa thought as she studied the old lady. Louisa only came to know Mr. Taylor after he'd decided to stay with them and marry Mrs. Dolly, but she'd learned to like the strange old man and sometimes joined him on his walks. He pointed out various plants to her, glad that someone shared his interest in nature. Louisa had always had an interest in herbs and plants, fascinated by the secrets they held. Plants had the power to heal, but some had a darker purpose and those who knew how to use them wielded power over life and death, harnessing nature's cruel beauty to serve their secret purpose. She used to follow Bridget around when she went out with her basket, collecting various items that she used in her medical arsenal. It was useful knowledge, and Louisa liked useful things. They came in handy when you least expected them to.

"Do you like the maze?" Louisa asked companionably, getting more comfortable and raising her face to the sun just like Maud.

"Yes, it reminds me of the maze at our country estate when I was a girl. My future husband followed me there one evening to inform me that my father had accepted his suit. He kissed me then and promised to make me happy." Maud stared off into the distance, her eyes clouded with memory.

"Did he?" Louisa asked.

"Did he what?" asked the old lady, startled out of her reverie.

"Make you happy."

"No child, he made my life a misery for over twenty years before he finally died with his mistress by his bedside, but at that moment in the maze, I was the happiest girl in Christendom." Maud sighed and turned her attention to Louisa. "And what are you doing here?"

"I like to walk in the maze. I got lost a few times, but now I know the way. Did you know that Theodore will be staying for a few days?" Louisa asked innocently. "He'll be traveling back to London with Uncle Kit on Sunday after church."

"Hmm, that's welcome news. He's a good boy, Theo. He was always Caroline's favorite, you know. She spoiled him, if you ask me, mothered him too much since his father died when he was only a child. A boy like him needs a firm hand to beat the nonsense out of him; that's what I would have done." Aunt Maud slapped her hand against the bench for emphasis, obviously still reliving an old argument with her niece.

"What nonsense, Aunt Maud? He seems very serious to me." Louisa turned her face to Maud, her mouth parted with curiosity.

"He was always soft-hearted that one. Didn't have the driving ambition of his brothers. They will go far, just you wait and see. They've already made advantageous marriages and gained the favor of His Majesty. Theo, on the other hand, will find some damsel in distress and fall head over heels in love. He always needed someone to rescue, often dragging stray dogs and injured birds home to his mother. She should have tossed them out, but she helped him take care of them, encouraging his weakness. He fancied himself the patron saint of broken things," Maud said acidly.

"For a smart woman, Caroline was a fool when it came to her youngest. I suppose she couldn't resist his need for her. Robin and Walter gravitated toward their father, but Theo only wanted his mother, sniveling like a girl. He was her only comfort after his father died, until she took that young lover. Now, that was a scandal in the making, but she wouldn't hear a word against her new love. Sure enough, he deserted her as soon as she became ill. She'd outlived her usefulness. I hear he married a girl just barely out of the nursery. Must be a nice change after a woman nearly twenty years his senior." Maud sniggered, still annoyed with the niece who'd been dead for nearly two years. Forgiveness did not come easily to her.

"Now, make yourself useful and help me to my feet. Time I went back inside. It's getting unbearably hot out here. You may walk me back," she announced imperiously, taking Louisa's arm.

"Of course, Aunt Maud. It would be my pleasure." Louisa

offered her arm to the old lady, smiling serenely. She didn't mind walking Maud back. After all, she had just told her exactly what she wanted to know, making her task that much easier. Louisa glanced away as Maud's piercing glance skewered her face. Had she known all along what Louisa was after?

FOURTEEN

NEW YORK AUGUST 1777

Abbie refolded the letter and sat wearily on the neatly made bed of Captain Gordon. It was barely mid-morning, but already the room was hot and stuffy, sunlight streaming through the window with relentless intensity. The heat made Abbie feel faint, but it wasn't the reason for her flushed cheeks. What she felt was shame. All her life she'd thought of the British as the enemy, but she'd never actually had any dealings with them except for that horrible moment in the woods when Finn saved her from a brutal attack. To her, all British soldiers were alike: cruel, belligerent, and intent on taking away everything and everyone she held dear.

Now that she'd come into contact with actual people, hating them wasn't as easy. Some of the older officers were more rigid and high-handed, but the younger ones just seemed lonely and homesick, eager for any human connections they could make. They were courteous and polite to Abbie and Libby, who managed to retain her position after Millie was dismissed in disgrace two weeks ago. Abbie wondered whom Millie had actually been caught with, but Mrs. Cromwell made no mention of the girl and Libby refused to gossip, terrified of losing the job that helped her take care of her elderly mother. It didn't really matter. Millie's dalliances led to Abbie getting her job, and in the grand scheme of things that was all that mattered. Abbie was now ideally placed to spy on the British officers, a task that suddenly made her more ashamed than proud.

Abbie and Finn had been at the boarding house for over two weeks now, and although they had come across some useful tidbits which they'd passed on to Sam, most of the information Abbie uncovered in her snooping was very personal. She now knew that Captain Gordon's wife had given birth to a boy, their first, and Lieutenant Llewellyn's mother had sent him woolen underwear and a tonic for his bowels, and Major Weland's younger brother had recently been shot during a skirmish in Canada. What she didn't know was what the British were planning to do next. It seemed that any important information was kept very well-guarded. Abbie tried to listen in as she served meals to the officers, hoping they might discuss some vital details of the upcoming invasion, but the conversations were banal, restricted to gossip, news of home, and veiled remarks about visits to Madame Mabel's establishment, which Abbie took to be a house of ill-repute.

Abbie put the letter back into Captain Gordon's writing desk and picked up her bucket and broom. Thankfully, this was the last room and she could have a short break before starting in on the laundry. Mrs. Cromwell offered laundry as a part of her service at the boarding house, ensuring that Abbie had a never-ending supply of unmentionables and shirts to wash. At least she got to go outside to hang up the wet garments, giving her a few moments of fresh air and a possible peek of Finn, who was busy chopping wood, carrying pails of water, and bringing hay and oats for the horses of the officers.

Stowing the bucket and broom in a cupboard off the scullery, Abbie looked around. Mrs. Cromwell didn't seem to be about; she must have gone to the market for supplies. She liked to choose everything personally, not trusting Abbie or Libby to get the best price for the best goods. Libby was already elbow-deep in laundry, so Abbie snuck out the back door to the garden. All she needed was a few minutes. She walked toward the back and sat down in the shade of an ancient maple tree, grateful to be out of the blazing sun, and facing away from the boarding house toward the burned-out husk of Trinity Church rising over the roofline of the neighboring houses. It had been less than a year since the fire of 1776 and many houses and businesses west of Broadway Street were just piles of burned beams and soot-covered bricks. The city was slowly rebuilding, but evidence of the disaster was still obvious.

As Abbie looked at the ruined church, she couldn't help but wonder if the fire had been an act of arson, its sole purpose to do as much damage as possible rather than handing the city to the occupiers undamaged. The fire had started at the Fighting Cocks Tavern near Whitehall Slip, so it could have just as easily been an act of carelessness by some drunken patron. Abbie supposed no one would ever really know the truth. She wished the fire had done more damage, making it impossible for the British to stay, but although about a fifth of Manhattan had been destroyed, New York still became a British stronghold after the withdrawal of Washington's troops.

FIFTEEN

For the first week, Abbie felt awkward around the British, but eventually the novelty began to wear off. She had to act natural around the lodgers and being as nervous as a cat in a room full of rocking chairs wouldn't help the cause. The only time she felt at ease was when she and Finn took their afternoon off. She'd never been to a city larger than Williamsburg, and New York was teeming with people and life. Mrs. Cromwell gave them every other Thursday afternoon off and two hours to attend church on Sundays. It wasn't enough time, but it was a welcome break from the boarding house.

On their first afternoon off, Abbie and Finn walked around the city, taking in the sights and sounds of the metropolis. They'd gone to East Side Wharf to see the ships at anchor, but left quickly, suddenly overwhelmed by the might of the British Navy. The great ships towered above their heads, a sea of masts piercing the summer sky and reminding them that victory would not come easily or swiftly.

The Revolution relied on men to fight for the cause voluntarily, but Britain still pressganged able-bodied men into service, swelling their ranks considerably and providing the Navy with unlimited manpower. The men might not care about defeating Americans, but they had no choice but to fight for their country, else they be persecuted for treason or desertion. In either case, the penalty was death, so their only hope of returning home lay in winning the conflict with the colonists.

Abbie and Finn passed Fulton Market where the vendors brought fish caught only that morning in the East River. The smell of fish kept them from stopping to take a closer look and they continued to walk until they reached Battery Park, where Finn took Abbie to a coffeehouse. It was still several hours till supper and they were tired and hungry from walking for so long. Abbie tried a currant scone with clotted cream and found it to her liking. She'd have to learn the recipe and show her mother how to bake scones when she came home. The girls would love the crumbly pastry with its tangy burst of currants.

Thinking of Annie and Sarah made Abbie homesick, so she tried to focus on the sights and sounds of the city, pretending that she and Finn were just travelers in a new land, rather than spies working against the people who barely noticed their presence. It was better that way. To the soldiers who lodged with Mrs. Cromwell, they were just servants, there to see to the smooth running of the boarding house. The less attention they paid them, the better.

After their coffee break, Finn and Abbie took a walk in the park, grateful for the shade the trees provided. A crowd had gathered around a makeshift stage where a show of some sort was in progress. Most of the audience was made up of soldiers, but there were a few civilians in the crowd, some of them with small children perched on their shoulders to get a better view of the stage.

"Let's go see," Finn suggested, pulling Abbie along and maneuvering her through the crowd. Two puppets were going at each other, eliciting uproarious laughter from the spectators. One was dressed in the colorful outfit of a court jester, his beaky nose the most prominent feature on his malicious face. The bells on his hat jingled violently every time he swung his stick at the female puppet, causing everyone to laugh. He had an unnaturally high-pitched voice, making it nearly impossible to make out what he was saying, but his antics were comically deranged. He was berating the woman, trying to get in as many blows with his stick as he could while the female managed to dance out of his reach every time.

The female puppet was round, with a bosom that came up to her pointy chin and a voluminous cap that quivered every time she ducked the jester's stick and screamed abuse at him to the delight of the crowd. It was so silly, Abbie couldn't help but laugh. Eventually, the woman managed to get the stick from the jester and beat him over the head until he retreated behind the painted screen, bringing the show to a close. The crowd reluctantly dispersed, leaving the puppet master to put away his set and dolls and move on before the park grew dark.

"What was that?" she asked Finn as they finally walked away.

"I think it's called a Punch and Judy Show. It's popular in England, so they perform it here for the soldiers. Did you like it?"

"It's silly," Abbie replied, shrugging. She preferred something a tad wittier than two puppets pummeling each other.

"I think that's the idea. It's meant to cater to a large crowd where people don't really get too involved in what the puppets are saying. I bet Annie and Sarah would like it."

"Yes, they'd love it. I miss them so much, Finn. It must be hard for them with everyone suddenly gone. I hope Jonah is all right. How soon do you think he'll get leave?" Abbie knew her parents were terribly worried and would love to see Jonah, if only for a couple of days. He'd been so eager to go, he barely took the time to say goodbye.

"I don't know, maybe you should ask Sam. I hope we hear from him soon. I'm a little worried that he didn't turn up for our meeting this week."

Finn instantly regretted his words, seeing the anxious look on Abbie's face. He'd waited for Sam in the designated spot for over an hour, but Sam never showed, forcing Finn to return to the boarding house before he was missed by the ever-watchful Mrs. Cromwell. He couldn't afford to draw attention to himself by disappearing for too long, even in the evening.

"I'm sure he's just fine, Abs. We'll hear from him soon. Now, where would you like to go next?" Finn asked in an effort to distract Abbie from worrying.

"I think I'd like to go back to the loft if you don't mind. I'm awfully tired today." Abbie slid her arm through Finn's, leaning her head on his shoulder. It would be absolute heaven to get out of these clothes and lie down for a little while before the evening meal.

"Abbie, where in God's name are you? If you think I'm going to do all this laundry by myself, you are gravely mistaken." Libby was standing in the doorway, her arms on her ample hips, her face tight with indignation. She was a good sort, really. Abbie couldn't blame her for being annoyed. There was enough work for both of them and they needed to pull their weight to get through the day.

"I'm coming. Sorry, Libby. Just felt a bit faint." Abbie rose laboriously to her feet, reluctant to come back inside. She took a few last breaths of the briny air coming off the river before following Libby into the steamy laundry room, heat coming off the cauldron of laundry in suffocating waves.

"You do look a bit peaky. Have a cool drink while the Dragon Lady is not here. There's an open barrel of beer in the cellar. She'll never notice a cupful or two missing. I just had one." Libby gave her a mischievous smile as she disappeared into the laundry room. "Don't worry, the laundry will keep till you come back."

Abbie wiped her forehead with the sleeve of her dress. It was clammy and her upper lip was covered in perspiration. Libby was right. A cool drink would set her to rights.

SIXTEEN

Abbie viciously tore off her cap, her shaking fingers already undoing the buttons of her dress. "God, I can't take this heat. Help me with these buttons, Finn."

Finn obediently went to help, trying to sneak in a kiss when Abbie lifted her hair away from her neck. She jerked her head away, irritated and upset.

"Sweetheart, it's not so bad in here. The breeze off the river is nice tonight. Here, take off your dress and lie down. That will help you cool down."

He'd opened the little window as soon as he came up, letting the heat of the afternoon dissolve in the briny air blowing off the river. Abbie seemed unusually flushed when she finally came up with a pail of stew, some bread, and a bottle of beer. Normally, they ate in the dining room, but some nights they preferred to eat in the loft, enjoying a little alone time after a day of never-ending chores. Finn wouldn't have minded eating at the main house, since there was a good chance of getting seconds and an extra cup of beer, but Abbie said she couldn't stand being at the boarding house a second longer than she needed to be. Finn quickly agreed to have supper in the loft, not wishing to upset Abbie further.

Abbie barely touched her food, drinking her beer in one gulp and slamming the cup onto the scarred wooden table that also served as a nightstand and holder for the pitcher and ewer. Finn didn't think it was just the heat that was making Abbie so angry. True, it was hot, but not any hotter than it was in Virginia at this time of year, and Abbie hardly ever complained there. She was worried about Sam. It was safer for her not to know where Sam was staying or who his contacts were, but it also made her feel isolated and vulnerable. Finn was used to the ways of the Committee, knowing that the lack of information was meant to protect him and the others, but Abbie was still new and felt as if she were purposely being kept in the dark.

Abbie lay down in her shift, using a pamphlet to fan herself. "Aren't you coming to bed?"

Finn busied himself with tidying the small room in an effort to avoid Abbie's intense gaze. "Actually, I have to go out for a while." There, he'd said it, and now he could brave the storm that was about to rage through their little room.

"And where are you going at this time of night?" Abbie sat up in bed, her eyes boring into him.

"I received a message from Sam this afternoon. He wants to meet with me."

"Why didn't you say so?" she asked happily. "I'll come too. Maybe he has news of home." Abbie was already reaching for her stockings when Finn finally turned around to face her.

"Sweetheart, you can't come," he said quietly. Damn Sam for putting him in this position.

"Why ever not? I'd like to see my brother." Finn gently took the stockings from her hand and replaced them on the chair by their bed. It was probably wiser to stay back as he told her the news, but he felt awful for upsetting her when she was already out of sorts.

"I'm meeting Sam at Mabel's brothel." There, it was out. Abbie's mouth opened in shock, no sound coming out for a few moments until the shrieking began.

"You can't be serious! Why, in the name of all that's holy, would Sam want to meet in a brothel? What's the meaning of this?" Finn quickly clamped a hand over Abbie's mouth before the officers at the boarding house heard her. She struggled for a brief moment before realizing her mistake and hanging her head in shame. Finn slowly removed his hand, studying her for signs of further outrage before replying.

"I don't know, but I'm sure he has a good reason. Why don't you stay here and get some rest, and I'll be back as soon as I can? I'll tell you everything that happened, I promise." Finn was already backing out of the loft in the hope that Abbie would calm down once he left. Now that she knew Sam was alive and well, maybe she'd be able to rest and calm her frayed nerves.

In truth, Finn was just as puzzled as Abbie. Sam certainly didn't live a monastic existence, but why a brothel? That wasn't like him. Finn jammed his hat onto his head and stepped out into the sultry night. Sam was one of the most patriotic and clever people he'd ever met, aside from Mr. Mallory, so whatever he was up to must have a purpose. In this situation, they had to trust each other implicitly since even the slightest mistake could lead to their capture. Sam would never knowingly do anything to endanger Abbie and Finn, so his reasons for meeting in a whorehouse had to be sound. Besides, Finn was more than a little curious. He'd heard of the existence of such establishments but had never been to one. Abbie was the only girl he'd been with and that was how he wanted it to be for the rest of his life. Some men still visited brothels despite being married, but Finn felt no such desire. Both his father and Mr. Mallory were faithful husbands, who treated their wives with the utmost respect, and Finn intended to be the best husband he could be.

Finn chuckled when he thought of Sam. His brother-in-law certainly never missed an opportunity for a roll in the hay. To him, sex had nothing to do with emotional love and was to be enjoyed as long as both participants were willing. Sam loved women, so the notion of settling down with just one was probably one step up from a prison sentence. Would Sam ever find a girl clever enough to tame him? Finn hoped he'd be around to see the woman who finally took Sam in hand.

Jonah, on the other hand, would probably fall in love with the first girl who showed him any affection, following in his father's footsteps and settling down at an early age. Finn said a silent prayer for Jonah's well-being every night. He missed him more than he could have imagined, often carrying on a silent conversation with him as he worked. Sam and Jonah were the closest thing Finn had to brothers and he prayed that they would survive this war that was to last for another four years. A lot could happen in four years.

SEVENTEEN

Finn walked down the street, checking out his surroundings. He wasn't sure what he'd been expecting, but it was a nice street with two-story houses on each side, some of them with shops on the first floor. All the shops were shuttered for the night, but there was a tavern at the end of the street, snippets of song and loud conversation disturbing the silence every time someone opened the door. Otherwise, all was quiet. Finn stopped outside the address Sam had given him. The building didn't look like much and was built of wooden planks and punctuated by small windows with black-painted shutters. All the shutters were firmly closed, most likely to keep whatever was happening inside from being seen from the outside. Finn knocked on the door, his stomach twisting. What if Sam expected him to participate in whatever was going on? He just couldn't do that, not only because of Abbie, but because that went beyond the call of duty.

A middle-aged man opened the door, studying Finn for a few moments as if he could learn all he needed to know just by staring at him. He was bald and stocky, with a nose that looked as if it had been broken more than once. Several of his teeth were missing, leaving dark gaps that made him look even more threatening. He was clearly no stranger to violence and would gladly pummel anyone who displeased Madame Mabel.

"In with you," he grunted as he held the door open wider, allowing Finn to walk past. The dark, narrow hallway led to a well-proportioned room, decorated in crimson and gold. There was a pleasant aroma of something flowery and sweet, reminding Finn of being in a garden on a spring afternoon. A large mirror hung on every wall, reflecting the light from the candles and giving the room an aura of intimacy. Several British soldiers were dispersed throughout the parlor, enjoying the charms of the girls, who were surprisingly attractive and healthy-looking. The men didn't seem in any rush to take them upstairs but were enjoying their drinks and flirting with the unoccupied girls, prolonging the pleasure and soaking up Madame Mabel's hospitality before getting what they came for and retreating back to their lonely barracks.

Finn spotted Sam, who was seated in a large armchair in the corner, a buxom redhead on his lap. Finn couldn't help but stare. The woman was beautiful, with mischievous blue eyes and luminous skin that looked pale against her rouged lips. Her large breasts swelled above the low-cut bodice, barely covering her nipples and occupying all Sam's attention. The woman arched her back, bringing her breasts closer to Sam's face and running her finger seductively over his lower lip. Sam appeared to be in heaven as he planted a sensuous kiss on the creamy flesh before turning to Finn.

"Ah, here's the friend I told you about," Sam said, gesturing to Finn to come closer. "When I promised you an unforgettable evening, I meant it. John, may I present Diana—the Goddess of the Hunt." Sam smiled at Finn, willing him to cooperate. He'd mentioned that use of real names wasn't wise, so for tonight they were Patrick and John.

"It's a pleasure to meet you," Finn stammered, trying not to stare at the woman's tits.

"Oh, the pleasure is all mine, I'm sure." Her voice was throaty and seductive, her eyes taking Finn's measure and pausing meaningfully when they reached his manhood.

"Any friend of Patrick's is a friend of mine." Diana slid off Sam's lap and wrapped her arms around Finn, whispering into his ear. "Don't worry. Your virtue is safe with me, Johnny."

"Shall we go upstairs then?" Sam asked, rising to his feet. "Don't worry, John, she's all paid for." Sam slid his arm around Diana's waist, maneuvering her toward the stairs, slightly unsteady on his feet. "Lead the way, princess."

Diana beckoned them to follow as she started up the stairs, calling a bawdy greeting to the man by the door. He responded with a huge grin, suddenly much less intimidating.

"What are you doing?" Finn hissed as Sam fell a few steps behind Diana. "Abbie is livid, not to mention worried for your safety."

"Just play along, John, and trust me. I wouldn't steer you wrong. She's worth the money; I promise you," he said a little louder for the benefit of the thug manning the door.

Diana led them to a room at the back of the house. The hallway was lit with only two candles mounted in sconces, shadows dancing on the dark upholstery of the walls. Finn heard moaning and giggling as he passed a room on his right, and muffled screams of pain from the left. What the hell was Sam playing at?

The room was decorated in shades of cream and green, surprisingly clean and pretty. Most of the space was taken up by a large bed, hung with gauzy bed hangings that parted in the center opposite a large mirror strategically situated across from the bed. Diana lay down on the bed, smiling invitingly.

"Get on the bed, John," Sam ordered as he lay down next to the woman. He was still dressed, so that was promising. Finn did as he was told, lying down without touching the girl and hoping that was as far as it was likely to go. Sam began to bounce lightly, making the bed creak as Diana moaned theatrically, winking at Finn and trying to suppress a giggle. She sounded as if she were in absolute ecstasy, the sounds coming from her low and exciting.

"Easiest money I ever made," she whispered as she slid her hand up Finn's thigh, amused by his reaction.

"Now listen," Sam whispered, "the reason I had you come here is to meet Diana and know where Mabel's is. Diana is one of us, and she's doing what we're doing, only in a slightly different capacity. I need to lay low for a few weeks, so Diana will be your contact. Come here only if you have some important information or you're in trouble. She will be able to help. Otherwise, wait for me to contact you. Now go. I'll follow you shortly. Diana and I have some business to wrap up."

"Are you actually going to stay with her?" Finn asked, amazed. Sam looked as if he had every intention of getting his money's worth.

"That's classified information, brother. Now away with you and remember what I told you."

Finn heard Diana's giggle as he bolted from the room, impressed and horrified in equal parts. He stopped for a moment, adjusting his clothes and taking a breath to calm himself. He had to look like a man who had just enjoyed a threesome. Suddenly, he couldn't wait to get home to Abbie and for the first time since meeting him, Finn felt sorry for Sam. There was no one waiting for him at home. No one who loved him.

EIGHTEEN

ENGLAND AUGUST 1624

Louisa twirled in front of the cheval glass, admiring her image. Aunt Lou had given her a few gowns and they were finer than anything she'd ever owned before, made of silk and brocade, with lavish embroidery and bodices worked in seed pearls and gold thread, the sleeves adorned with the finest lace. Just running her fingers over the rich fabric made her shiver with pleasure, reminding her how much she longed for a life of luxury. At home, she had one pretty gown, but the rest were made of homespun, suitable for everyday chores that she was expected to perform to help Minnie.

The gown she had chosen today was a primrose yellow, with an underskirt of cream satin and matching lace at the bodice and cuffs. The color accentuated the auburn highlights in Louisa's hair and her amber eyes, making them appear almost tawny, like a panther she'd once seen on the plantation. She was about to pinch her cheeks to give them some color but decided against it. She looked flushed enough, and overly rosy cheeks weren't in fashion. Women painted their faces to make them look like fine porcelain and hide blemishes and the ravages of time, but Louisa didn't need to apply layers of rice powder. Her skin glowed from the inside, nurtured by fresh air and a lifetime of good nutrition. Anyway, it was time to stop admiring herself and put her plan into action.

She found Theo in the parlor talking to Uncle Kit, a glass of brandy in his hand. He looked happy and relaxed, the breeze from the window ruffling his unbound hair as he gestured with his hand to emphasize his point. She heard the Duke of Buckingham mentioned, which seemed to upset Uncle Kit. They were so intent on their conversation they didn't even hear Louisa enter until she was halfway across the room. Both men sprang to their feet, Theo stopping in midsentence and blushing furiously at the sight of her.

"I'm so sorry. I didn't mean to interrupt, but I thought I heard Mama in here. I was hoping she would join me for a walk in the garden. I'm so tired of walking alone, but it's such a lovely day and a shame to stay indoors." Louisa ignored Kit's knowing smile as he turned to Theo.

"Why don't you take a walk with Louisa, Theo? We can talk more later."

Louisa threw Kit a grateful look before turning to Theo. "Oh, that would be wonderful. We haven't really had a chance to talk, have we? I wager you can show me parts of this estate I haven't seen yet." She smiled prettily as Theo buttoned his doublet in an attempt to make himself more presentable.

"It would be an honor to walk with you, Mistress Whitfield."

"Please, call me Louisa, and may I call you Theo?" The young man nodded happily, already following Louisa from the room and down the hall toward the door to the formal garden.

It was in shadow at this time of day, so Louisa didn't have to worry about unattractive perspiration marring her beauty as she charmed her prey. She slid her arm through Theo's as they walked down the graveled path that was lined with stone urns and boxy hedges. Thankfully, there was no one about, so she had Theo's undivided attention. Louisa purposely chose the formal garden to avoid the children, who would cling to her and want to play a game of hide-and-go-seek if they saw her. Evie was especially fond of the game, always wanting to be the one to hide, but the nurse never took them to the formal garden, leaving it for the adults.

"So, you grew up in Virginia?" Theo began shyly. "I've always longed to visit the New World. It must be so exciting. I'm afraid I've never been further than Kent."

"I think you are the one whose life is exciting," Louisa replied, looking up at Theo through her eyelashes. "Jamestown is so primitive compared to London. I believe your aunt called it a backwater. Not many would disagree with her."

"She enjoys shocking people with her observations. It's the only way she can get them to pay attention to her, at least, that's what my mother used to say. She always asked me to be kind to her."

"Oh, I don't mind Aunt Maud. She's amusing if you don't take her too seriously. It must be nice to have such a large family. Do you see your brothers often?" Louisa gazed up at Theo. He was almost as tall as Kit, with the same black hair and eyes, but he lacked the swagger of her uncle. Kit exuded confidence and decisiveness, whereas Theo seemed shy and reticent, eager to please. Louisa strongly suspected that Theo preferred to observe rather than to be observed.

"I live with my older brother Robin and his wife, but they're in the country for the summer. Walter was married a few months ago. I haven't seen him since the wedding. He's enjoying time with his new bride. I miss him," Theo added quietly. "It's strange when people begin a new chapter in their lives and leave one behind."

"I miss my brother as well. He was my best friend," Louisa whispered dramatically.

"I'm sorry, Louisa. I didn't mean to be callous. I heard what happened to your brother at the hands of the savages. It must have been awful for all of you. The stories of the Indians seem so exciting and romantic, but the reality is quite ugly, isn't it? You must still be grieving."

Louisa stopped walking and turned to face Theo, her eyes full of unshed tears. "It's as if I lost a part of myself when Finn died. I've been terribly lonely without him. My parents were so torn apart by grief that they couldn't even bring themselves to put a marker for him in the cemetery. There was no body, you see, so they couldn't bury him. At least baby Alex has a grave that I can visit." She glanced away, wiping a phantom tear.

"I can only imagine your despair," Theo said, subconsciously drawing her a little closer. "If there's anything at all I can do to cheer you up, please say the word. I'm entirely at your disposal."

Louisa glanced away from Theo as if to hide her emotion. He was so sweet. She could see the compassion in his eyes and her heart melted. There was something in his expression that reminded her of Finn. She wasn't lying when she told Theo about missing Finn. She genuinely grieved for him every single day, and the loss was not something she would easily get over. True, she told Theo about Finn in an attempt to gain his sympathy, but there was a part of her heart that broke the day she learned of Finn's death. Maybe Theo could help. He wasn't just a coveted prize to be won; he was someone she could grow to love, and hopefully he could love her in return. He liked to care for damaged things, so maybe he could care for her and make her whole again.

"I've been terribly lonely since coming to England. My parents are preoccupied, and there's no one here close to my age. I enjoy playing with the children, but I long for more age-appropriate company. Any time you could spare would earn my undying gratitude. My brother used to take me for picnics by the lake on fine days. Do you think that's something I might be able to persuade you to do? It would mean so much to me." Louisa looked up at Theo, smiling beguilingly.

"It would be my pleasure. Would this afternoon be too soon? I could ask Cook to pack us a basket of food, and I know just the place. My brothers and I used to play there when we came to visit grandfather. That was before he died and left the estate to Uncle Kit. I can barely remember him now. My mother is buried next to him. She died in this house, you know." Theo suddenly looked upset, obviously grappling with the sad memory of his mother's final days. Louisa placed her hand on his arm in a show of sympathy.

"I'm sorry, Louisa. I didn't mean to get all maudlin. It's just that this house holds sad memories for me. I hope you can forgive me."

"There's nothing to forgive. I suggest we make new memories, ones that will make you smile when you recall the summer you met the girl from Virginia. Anyway, this afternoon would be perfect," Louisa said, standing on her tiptoes and planting a kiss on Theo's cheek. "You've made me so happy."

NINETEEN

NEW YORK AUGUST 1777

The loft finally cooled down, a gentle wind blowing from the open window directly onto the bed. Feeble starlight barely lit up the sky, black as pitch on this moonless night. All was quiet around them, the only sound being the chirping of a cricket and the scurrying of rats somewhere in the rafters. Abbie hated rats, but there was no escaping them this close to the water. She sighed contentedly and snuggled closer to Finn, pressing her butt against his thighs. She never bothered to put her shift back on after Finn's frenzied lovemaking and lay naked in his arms, languid and satisfied.

"Finn, did Sam really stay with that woman?" Abbie asked quietly.

"I don't know. I expect she had some important information to pass to him," he improvised, hoping Abbie would drop the subject.

"Thank you for that, but you don't need to lie to me. Sam was always one for the girls, even at a young age. Funny how different he is from Pa and Jonah," she mused, sounding sleepy.

"How is he different?" asked Finn, although he already knew.

"My mother was the first girl Pa courted, did you know that? He said she was always the one for him. And Jonah breaks out in hives every time a girl so much as looks at him." Abbie giggled and turned onto her back, her eyes on Finn's. "Pa caught Sam with a girl when he was just thirteen. She was a neighbor's daughter, two years his senior."

"What did your father do?" He couldn't help wondering what his own father would have done had he caught him with a girl.

"Oh, he took a strap to him. Said Sam had no business being with a woman until he was in a position to marry and support the child he might have gotten on her. Sam took the beating without a peep, although he had trouble sitting for about a week." Abbie smiled at Finn in the darkness, obviously remembering Sam's discomfort.

"Did he stop?"

"No, I suspect he just got better at not being caught."

"What happened to the girl?" Finn asked. "On their way back from the British fort, Sam had mentioned a girl he'd loved when he was very young. Maybe she had been the one.

"You don't want to know." Abbie's shoulders started to shake as she dissolved into giggles, snorting with mirth.

"Oh, now you have to tell me. Please, Abbie." Finn started tickling her to get it out of her, enjoying her squirming against him.

"Oh, all right. Just stop tickling me." She took a moment to compose herself, no doubt to draw out the suspense.

"Well?"

"She married the minister," she announced.

"What? Mistress Greene is the girl Sam had been with? Does the minister know?" Finn had to admit that he was shocked. Mistress Greene was about as right and proper as they came, so the thought of her frolicking in the barn with Sam was a little hard to countenance.

"I highly doubt it, but Pa never was able to look her in the eye, considering how much of her he had seen when he found them. I'm worried about Sam, Finn," Abbie said, her laughter fading away. "He almost died because of that girl at the tavern, and now there's this Diana. I hope he knows what he's doing."

"So do I, sweetheart, so do I." Abbie had vocalized his own concerns, reminding him of how close Sam had come to being executed two years ago. Finn hoped he'd learned his lesson.

"Get some sleep, Abbie. We have a long day ahead of us tomorrow." He kissed her tenderly, brushing away a stray curl. "I love you."

"I love you too. Goodnight, Finn, and God help you if I ever find you in a brothel," she added before closing her eyes.

TWENTY

ENGLAND AUGUST 1624

Louisa carefully removed the food from the basket, laying it out on the cloth. There was some bread, cheese, cold chicken, and a bunch of grapes. Theo had already taken out the bottle of ale and was pouring it into pewter cups. The spot he'd chosen was perfect, far enough from the house to give them privacy, but still sufficiently exposed to prevent any malicious talk. They were seated on the grassy bank of the pond, shaded by the interlaced branches of the trees above their head, shafts of sunlight creating patterns on their faces as it pierced the canopy of rustling leaves overhead. Birdsong and the incessant buzzing of insects filled the air, reminding them that the pond was teeming with life.

Theo took a sip of his ale and reclined on the grass, his face shadowed by the leaves overhead. Louisa took in his long legs and allowed her gaze to travel up his body toward his face before finally meeting his gaze.

"Why don't you remove your doublet?" Louisa asked innocently. "You must be stifling under all that velvet."

"I am, actually. Would you mind terribly?" He was already

unbuttoning the heavy garment and breathing a sigh of relief as he pulled it off, remaining in a linen shirt and breeches.

"Why should I mind? I hate being hot. Is it always this warm in July?" She reclined close to Theo, making sure the hem of her gown rose just above her ankle, offering Theo a glimpse of her leg. "I can hardly wait to peel off my gown once I get back to my room. It's so liberating to get undressed." Louisa gave Theo a moment to enjoy the image she'd just planted in his mind before looking at him expectantly.

"Not usually. This summer is the hottest one I can recall. Summers in England are usually quite pleasant, especially if you have a country home. Whitehall is nearly empty at this time of year with everyone going to the country for fear of the plague."

"How frightening," Louisa breathed, putting her hand on Theo's chest as if by accident. She could feel the beating of his heart beneath her palm, steady and strong. His skin felt warm through the fabric of his shirt, and she inhaled his scent, so pleasantly masculine. He was watching her, his mouth slightly open and his eyes full of desire, but it was too soon for anything more. He'd taken the bait and now Louisa had to reel him in slowly, so as not to scare him away, as she had Tom. Louisa pulled her hand away.

"Would you like something to eat? I'm famished." She popped a grape in her mouth, enjoying his gaze on her mouth. She made sure to part her lips slowly before wrapping them around another round grape, her eyes never leaving Theo's face. Oh yes, he'd taken the bait.

"Ah, yes, thank you. That would be nice," Theo stammered, sitting up. Louisa smiled into his eyes, reaching for a pewter plate and piling it with goodies. She was fairly sure he was ravenous, but not necessarily for the food. Her plan seemed to be working.

* * *

"You should send him away." Aunt Maud had come down from her nap earlier than expected and was already holding court in her favorite chair by the unlit hearth.

"Why? I like having him here. He's a fine boy." Kit retorted, his voice low. Maud had ambushed him, since he'd never willingly spend time alone with her.

"Because, if you are not careful, my boy, those two will be wedded and bedded by the end of the month. Didn't you see them sneaking off together? It's a disaster waiting to happen." This statement was followed by a thud. Maud used her cane as much for punctuation as for walking.

"Theo is one of the most honorable men I know, Aunt Maud, and they weren't sneaking. Theo asked Alec for his permission to take Louisa for a picnic and Alec granted it. There's no disaster brewing, I assure you. Besides, I'd have no objections if they formed an attachment. Louisa is a lovely girl, beautiful and intelligent. She would be an asset to any man," Kit replied defensively. He didn't appreciate being scolded by Maud. Thank God she wasn't privy to what happened with Thomas Gaines two years ago. That would really give her something to sink her teeth into, and with good reason. Louisa knew exactly what she was about, and she was sure to get her way. Maud just picked up on it quicker than the rest of them.

"You are even more of a fool than I thought, Christopher. He is a nobleman with a brilliant future ahead of him. She's a commoner with nothing to recommend her but a pretty face and a charming manner. She would harm his chances of advancement. He needs to marry well to solidify his position." This was followed by another thud of the cane.

"Aunt Maud, you are sorely trying my patience. Now, if you will excuse me." Kit left the parlor and headed outside, but not before he saw Louisa duck into the adjoining room. He sighed heavily. Louisa might have fooled Alec, but she hadn't fooled Maud, who was a sly old fox. Maud had a point, as usual, and although Kit had outwardly dismissed her concerns, he resolved to keep an eye on the situation.

TWENTY-ONE

Another flash of lightning split the sky, thunder rattling the stone walls of the manor as a brisk wind blew through the open windows, making the damask curtains billow like the sails of a ship. Torrents of water poured from the sky, mercifully relieving some of the heat of the previous few days. Louisa was tired of this crazy English weather. It was either blazing sun or torrential downpours. For a brief moment, she missed Virginia, but then berated herself for being silly. She watched in irritation as the candle guttered, a thin whiff of smoke curling to the ceiling. Louisa climbed into bed and drew her legs up, hugging them and resting her chin on her knees. She knew perfectly well that it wasn't the weather or the candle that had caused her such frustration—it was Theo. He would be leaving with Kit tomorrow after church, so her time was up.

True to his word, Theo had spent most of his time with her, taking her riding, to see a Norman church in the village, and even taking her out in a rowboat on the tranquil pond. He was charming, sweet, and smitten, but he hadn't so much as taken her hand other than the time he helped her in and out of the boat. Once he left for London, God only knew when she'd see him again, and her opportunity would have passed.

Louisa took a deep breath, enjoying the smell of rain and wet earth. As much as she loved her parents, she had no intention of returning to Virginia with them. This was her one chance, and she wouldn't let it pass her by. Having had a glimpse of London and the splendor of Kit's country estate, she had no desire to return to the primitive conditions of America. This is where life was, and this is where she meant to stay. She was sure she had Theo wrapped around her finger, but the silly pup was too noble for his own good.

Louisa stilled, a plan forming in her mind. Could she really do that? If she miscalculated, the consequences could be dire, but she was sure of Theo's feelings for her. All he needed was a nudge in the right direction. Even Aunt Maud kept cautioning everyone about the budding relationship. She saw it too. Louisa slowly got out of bed and went to stand in front of the cheval glass. She looked pretty and virginal in her white nightdress, her hair spilling down her back in dark silky spirals. Would he really resist? She walked over to the walnut cabinet where she kept her things and took out a vial of rose oil. It had been a present from Bridget, but she'd had little opportunity to use it, until now. Louisa dabbed on two tiny drops, so as not to overdo it, and returned the vial to its place.

The corridor was quiet and dark, everyone most likely asleep. It had to be close to midnight, so even all the servants were in their beds, resting after a day of hard work. Louisa crept down the hall, careful not to make a noise. If she were caught, she'd just say she was thirsty and was going to the kitchen for a cup of water. She turned the corner and approached Theo's door on silent feet. Her heart was drumming so hard she thought the beat must echo through the whole house, waking everyone, but no one stirred. Louisa stopped in front of the door. It still wasn't too late to turn around and flee, but she forced herself to try the handle. It turned easily, the door opening silently on well-oiled hinges.

Theo was sitting up in bed, reading by candlelight. He wasn't wearing a nightshirt and his dark hair was tousled and falling into his face as he absentmindedly brushed it away. He was so absorbed in his book, he didn't even notice her standing there.

"Theo," she whispered, closing the door behind her and inching further into the room.

"Good God, Louisa, what are you doing here?" He nearly bolted out of bed but remembered his nakedness and remained where he was. "You shouldn't be here."

"I'm sorry. I'll go. I was just frightened by the storm. I shouldn't have come." Louisa turned around slowly, as if to leave. If he didn't stop her, she'd just go back to her room and die of mortification.

"Wait. I'm sorry. I was just shocked to see you." He seemed genuinely confused, unsure of what to do. Louisa watched the emotions playing over his face, his desire for her to stay battling with what he knew to be the right course of action. She needed to press him before the rational part of his brain took over.

"Theo, I lied. I didn't come here because of the storm. I just wanted to see you alone one last time before you left. I wanted a kiss, just one kiss to remember you by." Louisa lowered her gaze to the floor, trying to look innocent and beguiling.

"Louisa, what are you talking about? We'll see each other all the time once you come to London. I'll call at the house, and with your father's permission show you something of London. We can go see a play or go sailing on the Thames. I wouldn't just disappear. You know how I feel about you."

"How *do* you feel about me?" she asked shyly, raising her eyes to his in a silent plea for his love.

"I adore you. You're all I can think about, but I was afraid of being too forward and frightening you off. These last few days have been some of the happiest I've ever known."

He looked so earnest that Louisa allowed herself to relax. She'd made the right choice coming here. All Theo needed was something to force his hand. Louisa glided over to the bed, her gaze never leaving his face and climbed in, straddling him. She bent over him, her hair cascading to shield their faces from the world and kissed him softly. Theo froze momentarily, but then his arms came around her, flipping her onto her back as his face loomed above hers.

"Louisa, please," he whispered, stroking her cheek with his thumb. "If you don't go now, I can't be responsible for my actions. I've tried so hard to keep my distance, and now you're here and I can't find the strength to ask you to leave."

"Please don't ask me to leave," she murmured, wrapping her arms around his neck. "I want to stay with you."

Her words broke his resolve and he finally kissed her with all the passion he'd been trying to hold back. His kiss was all she hoped it would be: passionate, intoxicating, and full of promise. She hardly noticed when Theo pulled her nightdress over her head, his hands and lips exploring every inch of her body. Thunder crashed outside, masking her moans of pleasure. So this is what it was like. She must be awfully wicked to want it so badly, but she could barely contain herself. Louisa wasn't sure what exactly she yearned for, but she knew it was something only he could give her at that moment. She gasped as she felt him inside her, not painful exactly, but strange and unfamiliar. He began to move slowly, watching her face in the candlelight. Louisa closed her eyes, moaning as discomfort was replaced by something else entirely.

"Oh, Theo," she breathed as he kissed her again, never stopping the rhythmic movement of his hips against hers until she forgot everything but him and the feelings coursing through her.

"Will you speak to my father tomorrow?" Louisa asked as

Theo held her close, his body warm against hers, still joined together in the aftermath of their lovemaking.

"I'd like to, but I think it's too soon. I must see to some things before asking your father for your hand. I need to show him that I'm able to take care of you, financially and emotionally. I need a few weeks. Can you wait that long?" he asked tenderly, kissing her temple. "I won't let you down. You have my word."

"I'll wait, but don't take too long. I can't wait to proclaim my joy to everyone. Oh, Theo, I've never been so happy. It's as if you saved me," she added for good measure.

"I think you're the one who saved me. Now, I think you should return to your room before someone notices you're gone. It's not long till dawn and you can't be seen leaving my room. I don't want to do anything to mar this moment or ruin our future together."

Louisa gave Theo one last kiss and slid out of bed reluctantly, giving him a warm smile. "I love you, Theo," she said before slipping out into the darkened hallway. Louisa tiptoed to her room, the grin never leaving her face. She'd made the right choice, and now her future was assured.

TWENTY-TWO

Theo galloped after Kit, the countryside a blur of verdant green all around him as they passed fields and villages on their way to London. Sunday was the best day to travel since most people were at home after church, enjoying a few hours of well-earned rest and time with the family. Theo had been sorry to leave Willowbrook, especially after what happened last night, but he had no choice. He'd had only a moment to bid Louisa a brief farewell, promising to write as soon as he spoke to Robin. Robin was at Beachwood with his family, enjoying annual domestic bliss that he was most likely dying to escape. Robin was happiest when at court, scheming and plotting to further his interests and those of the family. He was a true Carew, as his mother always pointed out with pride.

Clumps of mud flew from the hooves of Kit's horse, forcing Theo to keep his distance for fear of getting splattered from head to toe. The road was still muddy from last night's storm, making galloping unwise, but Kit seemed unusually restless, driving the horses hard and making no plans to stop for a rest. Theo was glad he wasn't expected to carry on a conversation; he wouldn't have been able to. Last night was still fresh in his mind, a combination of wonder and disbelief mixing with joy and hope. He'd never expected Louisa to come to his room last night, and he should have been a gentleman and asked her to leave, but he simply couldn't find the will to send her away. She was so beautiful in her white nightdress with her hair cascading down her back, her pouty mouth slightly open as she gazed at him with longing. He'd never seen her with her hair down and the feel of it between his fingers had been like the finest silk from the Orient, sensual and arousing.

Spending time with Louisa these past few days had been an exquisite torture. She was like no one he'd ever met before. There were plenty of beautiful young girls, who paraded in front of him at Whitehall Palace in a tireless attempt to catch his eye, but no one had touched him as Louisa had. She was a complete paradox. At first, he thought her vulnerable and fragile, a girl who needed to be healed and mended, but her grief often gave way to a charming playfulness that beguiled and intoxicated him with its lack of artifice. She was seemingly unaware of her power over him, drawing him in with her innocence and complete trust and tormenting him with desire. Theo was ashamed of his wicked thoughts, but they kept coming back unbidden as he continued to spend time with her, his attraction growing and demanding to be acted upon.

Of course, Aunt Maud only made things more difficult, reminding him of his duty to the family. He had to marry well, like Robin and Walter, but he wasn't like his brothers. Robin had kept a mistress at court before he married Beth and never ended the relationship, continuing to see Celia Kilbourne on a regular basis, even after she'd delivered a son last autumn. Theo strongly suspected the child was Robin's, since Celia's husband seemed too old and feeble to have fathered the infant. Lord Kilbourne took great pride in the child, nonetheless, thanking God for finally granting him a son and heir in his old age.

Walter was likely tumbling every female servant under the

age of forty right under his wife's nose and enjoying every minute of it. He never stayed faithful to one mistress as Robin had; he liked variety and excitement. The possibility of being caught was as much of a draw as the women he pursued, their faces indistinguishable in the shadows of a dark corner.

They'd both married where their interests lay, the unions nothing more than a contract between consenting parties. Theo wanted a real partnership, a marriage of body and soul that would fill his heart with the love he'd been craving. He'd glimpsed that kind of happiness between Uncle Kit and Aunt Louisa and he'd seen it again between Alec and Valerie Whitfield, making him believe that it was possible with the right person. Louisa Whitfield had all the qualities he dreamed of in a wife and he intended to keep his promise to her as soon as he faced down his brother.

Robin was the head of the family and a marriage had to be sanctioned by him. If the potential bride didn't meet with Robin's approval, Theo could either forfeit his sizable inheritance or give up the woman of his choice. Theo hoped Robin wouldn't decide to exercise his brotherly control at this moment, since he hardly ever involved himself in Theo's affairs, but a marriage was serious business and Robin just might have some reservations, especially if Maud had already written to him in her never-ending quest to meddle in other people's lives.

At least Theo didn't have to appeal to Walter. Walter would refuse immediately, laughing at Theo's childish infatuation and calling him a spineless turd, as he had when they were children. Walter only did things that benefited him in the long run and would never even consider something as utterly ridiculous as marrying for love. If Theo wanted love, he could find that outside the marriage. Better yet, he could have as many women as he wanted and feel no obligation to them or their bastards.

Theo followed as Kit finally slowed down and headed

toward an inn located on the outskirts of a village they'd just passed. They would change horses, have some food, and stretch their legs before continuing their journey. It would be a good opportunity to talk to Uncle Kit privately and hopefully gain his approval, which would go a long way to swaying Robin and clearing Theo's way to marrying Louisa.

TWENTY-THREE

The house seemed strangely silent once Kit and Theo left for London, leaving Valerie feeling listless. Little Louisa floated from room to room like a ghost, alternating between secret smiles and sudden tears, and Lou was preoccupied with the children and her own worries. Despite Kit's assurances that he wasn't in love with another woman and cherished her more than ever, Lou wasn't convinced. She wanted to believe Kit, but her woman's intuition refused to be fooled, nagging at her day and night. Valerie didn't blame her. Alec swore Kit wasn't having an affair, but refused to elaborate, which left Valerie to surmise that there was much more to the story.

Valerie was eager to return to London. This beautiful house was starting to feel like a tomb, reminding her of a saying about a gilded cage. She looked forward to exploring London with Alec and enjoying all it had to offer. It had been nearly two decades since she'd seen a proper play or visited an actual book shop. What a pleasure it would be to ride in Kit's fine carriage and take in the sights and sounds of the city. One could walk the length of Jamestown in ten minutes, not that there was any reason to go there, especially once Charles and Annabel had settled at Rosewood Manor.

Valerie hoped spending time in London would distract her from constantly worrying about Finn and Abbie. She often found herself frowning, desperately trying to remember obscure facts about the Revolutionary War, anything that might ease her mind. Of course, nothing she could remember could keep Finn and Abbie out of danger. They were living among the enemy, putting themselves at risk each and every day. Valerie had actually remembered something just the other day and ran from the room in tears, needing a few moments to compose herself.

It was strange how tidbits of information suddenly shifted into place after decades of being buried in one's subconscious. In this instance, Valerie remembered learning about Nathan Hale, an idealistic young man who was captured and hanged when caught spying for the Revolution. Valerie suddenly recalled walking past a statue of Hale in City Hall Park when she was still a student. She'd even stopped to read the inscription, feeling sorry for the young man who became a hero long after his death.

Valerie sighed, wishing that particular memory had stayed buried. How many other spies had been discovered and executed before the war finally ended? Valerie wiped away a tear, berating herself for being a worrywart. Finn was smart, and she'd told him everything she could think of to prepare him for his task. The British were nothing if not honorable. They would not hang a person without evidence and as long as Finn and Abbie trusted no one but Sam they'd be safe. Nathan Hale had betrayed himself to someone who pretended to be a patriot, but Finn would never make such a foolish mistake.

"How about a boat ride on the pond?" Alec asked, interrupting her melancholy thoughts. "It's a lovely day out and I want you all to myself." Valerie followed him out the door, still sulking. There were things she wanted to discuss with Alec, but she wasn't sure if she was ready to voice her concerns. Valerie slid her arm through Alec's as they walked toward the pond, each lost in their own thoughts.

"You don't need to keep it from me, you know," Alec said suddenly. "I have eyes."

"What are you referring to?" Valerie asked carefully, although she already knew.

"I'm referring to our heartsick daughter. She's been wandering about listlessly ever since Theo left yesterday. I'd feel sorry for her if I didn't want this romance to fizzle out so desperately."

Alec tried to sound lighthearted, but Valerie could hear the pain beneath the words. Louisa had always been the apple of his eye and the idea of losing her was more than he could bear. Alec had been secretly relieved that Thomas Gaines had chosen to run away rather than stay and marry their daughter. He wasn't ready to part with her just yet, no matter how desirable the potential suitor.

"I think she loves him, Alec, and Theo seems equally smitten. Did it never occur to you that she might meet someone in England?" Valerie had worried about this, but had never really brought it up to Alec, afraid he might not want to make the trip.

"It did, but I didn't expect it to happen so quickly. They hardly know each other. Surely it can't be love." He pushed the rowboat into the water and handed her in before getting in and taking up the oars.

"Alec, how long did it take you to fall in love with me?" Valerie asked, smiling at him.

"I fell in love with you the minute you walked into the room," Alec replied, a guilty smile on his face.

"The minute I walked into the room you thought I was a madwoman wandering about the countryside in her undergarments," Valerie suggested helpfully.

"All right, I fell in love with you a few minutes after that.

You looked so scared; all I wanted to do was keep you safe from harm. I should have locked you in the tower and never let my brother lay eyes on you, but it's too late for recriminations. You are mine, and that's all that matters." Alec rowed toward the middle of the pond, seemingly lost in thought.

"Will we really lose her, Valerie? First, we lost the baby, then Finn, and now we are going to lose Louisa. Is there no end to how much loss one person should be expected to bear?" he asked, his eyes full of misery.

"Aunt Maud lost seven children. I suppose we should be grateful that at least two of ours are still alive. I will resign myself to losing them as long as they are well and happy. That will keep me going in my darkest moments. Of course, we can stay in England to be close to her if she marries Theo. Charles is happy running the plantation and Finn is no longer there, so there's nothing forcing us to return. Don't you want to visit Yealm Castle?" Valerie asked carefully. Alec hadn't mentioned returning to his home once since they left Virginia.

"I have no desire to go there, not even to visit Finlay's grave. It holds nothing but painful memories. Charles stopped there when he was in England. I instructed him to sell the estate. It doesn't belong to us anymore."

"Why didn't you tell me?" Valerie always wondered what Alec planned to do with the estate. He hardly mentioned the place, especially since Louisa had come to them and described the derelict state of the place.

"I didn't want to rake up the past. You endured such suffering there. I was glad to move on and start a new life. We've been happy in Virginia, haven't we?" he asked, finally looking at Valerie.

"Yes, we have," she replied, smiling into his eyes.

TWENTY-FOUR

The chamber of the Privy Council was as hot as the deepest level of Hell, the windows firmly shut against the August sun and the heavy velvet drapes open to allow the merciless rays to stream into the room, making it even hotter. The men seated around the table were all red in the face, looking desperate to leave and go somewhere where they could rip off their wigs and strip off their heavy doublets. His Majesty wasn't there, but Buckingham spearheaded the meeting, addressing issues that could easily have waited until the members of the council returned to town in September. What had been the great urgency?

Kit shifted in his seat, eager to escape. There was no point returning to Willowbrook, so he would just go back to his London house and wait until the family returned the following week. A few days alone might be beneficial in his current state of mind. He'd taken Alec's advice to heart and supposed it made sense in an abstract type of way, but to actually go through with it would be a lot more difficult than making the decision to do so.

Kit looked up when he felt Buckingham's gaze on his face. Several members of the Council were debating something he hadn't been paying attention to as Buckingham leaned back in his chair, watching Kit much like a cat that watches the unfortunate bird it's about to devour. Kit tried to look away, but Buckingham gave him a half-smile, his dark eyes hooded with desire. Kit felt a trickle of sweat run down his back more from anxiety than heat. How long would these buffoons keep talking? He'd go take a walk by the river as soon as he could decently get out of here; maybe it would be a little cooler there and he could go over his options one more time. *Who are you trying to fool?* he asked himself as he pretended to concentrate on the document before him. *You have no options. May as well get on with it and pray that it burns out quickly.*

Buckingham suddenly stirred, abruptly calling an end to the meeting. He looked remarkably cool compared to the others but blamed the heat on their inability to come to a decision and suggested they await the invaluable input of His Majesty before making a final recommendation. Buckingham gathered his papers and prepared to leave the room, glancing up just as Kit was about to depart.

"Lord Sheridan, a word if you please." His voice was low and seductive as he gazed at Kit from beneath his dark lashes. "Would you care to join me for a drink in my rooms to discuss the issue at hand further?"

Kit threw a longing look at the door before turning back to face his tormentor. There was nothing he wanted less, but it may as well be now. There was no point in putting off the inevitable any longer. Villiers was getting impatient; that much was obvious.

"That would be most welcome, Your Grace," Kit replied, giving Buckingham a slight bow. "Shall I see you there in a few minutes?"

"Yes. I'll be expecting you, so don't disappoint me." Buckingham collected his papers and strolled past Kit, lightly brushing his thigh as he walked past. Kit was grateful the room was now empty as he sank back into his chair, his legs refusing to hold him up.

TWENTY-FIVE

Kit's stomach clenched with anxiety as he neared Buckingham's rooms. In theory, Alec was right, but now that Kit was actually here, what he was about to do was unthinkable. Kit tried not to allow the unbidden images spring into his mind as he rapped on the door. Buckingham had the grandest apartments at Whitehall, aside from the king, and the most private. No one would know he'd been here, but that didn't matter—he'd know. Kit felt a wave of nausea when he heard quickly approaching footsteps on the other side of the door. A bland-faced servant held the door open, ushering Kit in as if he came to visit his master every day.

"Come through here, if you please, Lord Sheridan. Hammond, we have Council business to attend to. Make sure we are not disturbed," Buckingham instructed the servant before pouring Kit a cup of wine. He was informally dressed in breeches and a white shirt, his stockinged feet in simple buckled shoes. Kit had never seen George Villiers without his wig and had to admit that the man looked a lot less intimidating without all those black curls cascading down his back. His hair was cut short, as dark and curly as Kit's own, with a few tell-tale gray strands silvering the sides. Villiers smiled seductively, his gaze warm and inviting.

"Don't be so nervous, my pet; I won't bite. I know you don't normally do this sort of thing, so I promise to be very gentle with you. Come, let us have a drink. What shall we drink to? How about new experiences and forbidden pleasures?"

"Yes, Your Grace," Kit answered quietly. He thought he might be sick.

"Please, Christopher, let's us not stand on ceremony. It's George. Come now. Let me hear you say it."

"George," Kit repeated obediently, swallowing down another wave of nausea. He wanted to run for the door and never come back, but that wasn't an option. Still, this was better than mounting the steps to the scaffold and facing one's imminent death, although not by much.

Villiers took a dainty sip of wine and set down his cup, coming closer to Kit and pulling him to his feet. The kiss was strange, prickly where the man's beard touched Kit's face, and warm, his lips surprisingly soft. Villiers drew Kit closer, kissing him as he would a woman.

"You're shaking, Christopher. Is it so distasteful?" The smile was knowing and full of mischief. Villiers had probably done this a time or two before. Kit shook his head, unable to find his voice.

"Just close your eyes and let me show you how wonderful this could be."

Kit obeyed, closing his eyes, his hand on the ornate desk for support. He squeezed his eyes harder as Buckingham's fingers deftly unlaced his breeches and pushed them down over his thighs.

Oh, God, help me get through this, Kit prayed, his knees buckling. He gasped as Buckingham's mouth closed around his cock, sucking slowly and deliberately. The sensation wasn't all that different from when his wife did it, except for the tickling of the beard. *It's Louisa. I'll just pretend it's Louisa,* Kit thought as the sucking became more insistent, the tongue teasing and arousing him despite his fiercest protests. His breathing quickened as waves of pleasure surged through him, taking him utterly by surprise.

Kit couldn't help but open his eyes. Villiers was on his knees in front of him, his laughing eyes watching as he continued with his task. Kit turned away and caught sight of them in the gilded mirror hanging above a cabinet inlaid with mother-of-pearl flowers and vines. Buckingham must have deliberately chosen the spot, hoping Kit would peek. Kit watched in mute fascination, unable to look away as the second most powerful man in Christendom shamelessly pleasured him. He grabbed onto the desk as his seed spilled into Villiers's hot mouth.

"Oh, dear God," Kit whispered, unsure what he meant.

"That wasn't so bad, was it, pet?" George's smile was full of triumph as he wiped his mouth with a lacy handkerchief, his gaze never leaving Kit's face. "You'll grow to like it. Others have."

"Are there many at court who enjoy this kind of thing?" Kit asked, suddenly wondering about men of his acquaintance. Who else had Buckingham taken as a lover?

"More than you think, but it's a game best played under the cover of shadows, which makes it even more delicious. See you soon, pet."

George planted a soft kiss on Kit's lips, then turned and walked into an adjoining room, leaving Kit stunned and shaken.

TWENTY-SIX

Theo opened his eyes to find the room bathed in brilliant light. He hadn't bothered to close the shutters last night and judging by the position of the sun it was close to noon. He squeezed his eyes shut against the merciless light, his head banging like a drum, bursts of light exploding against his eyelids in a rainbow of color, that sort of display possible only after a night of heavy drinking. He got to bed very late last night, having stopped at Kit's house for a late supper once they'd finally arrived in London. Cook, who'd been sound asleep when they got in and had to be dragged out of bed, was only able to provide some cold meat, cheese, and bread on such short notice, but that had suited them just fine as they took their plates into the parlor rather than sitting down in the formal dining room and facing each other across the long table. Kit wasn't a stickler for formality, and Theo loved that about him. There was enough of that at court.

Kit seemed unusually restless and reluctant to be alone, so Theo stayed late into the night, drinking and playing dice until he could barely see straight. The dice swam before his eyes, refusing to stay in one place long enough for him to calculate the points before Kit took his turn and making it impossible to keep score. Eventually, they gave up, since neither of them was able to make heads or tails of the game, having drunk enough to down a horse or two.

Theo had no reason to rush home since he was the only one in residence until the rest of the family returned from Kent, but it was time to go. Kit invited him to stay before stumbling off to bed, but Theo declined. His initial plan had been to collect some clean clothes and head to Beachwood in the morning, but the unbearable aching in his head quickly made him change his mind. Hours in the saddle on such a bright day would no doubt finish him off, and in the end, accomplish very little. He would make it to Beachwood just in time for the family to leave for London, everyone distracted by packing and closing up the house. Robin normally didn't involve himself in that type of activity, but Beth tended to complicate things, turning every little task into a mammoth undertaking and whipping the servants into a state of nervous frenzy. It would be best to talk to Robin once he got home.

Theo willed himself to get out of bed and close the shutters, blocking out the merciless light before stumbling back and falling face down onto the pillow. Just a few more hours of sleep and he would feel somewhat human again. Damn Kit for letting him drink so much. He smiled as he briefly thought of Louisa before falling into a dreamless sleep.

The room was dark and stifling by the time Theo finally woke. He was thirsty and hungry. His mouth felt like dry wool and his shirt was stuck to his body, glued by sweat. At least the headache had abated, and he could think straight once again. Theo was considering a bath when he heard a woman's voice outside his door. He didn't need to look out into the corridor to know who the voice belonged to—it was Celia, giggling as Robin planted a few more kisses on her powdered cheek. She was perfectly coiffed and exquisitely painted, ready to return home to her husband. So, Robin was back and in good spirits if Celia's happy laughter could be believed. She was a consummate actress, always playing whatever part Robin wanted her to. It was no wonder she'd been his lover for years. She knew him better than he knew himself.

Theo had just stripped off his damp shirt when Robin walked in without knocking. He was unshaved, tousled, and unmistakably happy.

"Theo, I'm glad you're back. How's Kit and family?" Robin collapsed into a chair, watching Theo as he pulled off his filthy shirt. "Hard night?"

"I rode back with Uncle Kit and stayed for a few hours. I'm afraid we drank too much," Theo replied in embarrassment. He didn't like Robin seeing him this way, but Robin just nodded, unconcerned. Who didn't get blind drunk once in a while?

"I arrived back yesterday as well; told Beth I had urgent business." Robin scratched his stubbly jaw, scowling as he thought of his wife, who had no idea that the only urgent business he had was to bed his mistress.

"That bad?" Theo asked.

"She's with child again. I suppose I should be happy, but you know how she gets—unbearable. I just have to glance at her the wrong way and she's in tears for hours, accusing me of God knows what." He shrugged as if his wife's tears were of no consequence. "I needed to spend some time with Celia. She always gives me what I need."

"Actually, Robin, there's something I'd like to discuss with you," Theo began, but Robin was already halfway out the door.

"And I will gladly listen to you over supper. I'm famished. Get dressed and come down. You look in need of a drink, but perhaps you should bathe first. I can smell you from here."

TWENTY-SEVEN

When Theo came down, Robin was already seated at the table, which was laden with enough food to feed ten people. *No eating in the parlor for him*, Theo thought as he took his place and reached for a piece of pheasant. He'd let Robin eat before telling him about Louisa. Robin was always happier when well fed with a few cups of wine in him.

"Have you seen Walter?" Robin asked, filling his plate with food.

"No."

"I wager he's playing the happy bridegroom," Robin chuckled, taking a sip of wine and smiling benignly. "Wonder how long that will last before he gives some maid a full belly? What did you want to talk to me about?" Robin took a bite of steak pie and chewed slowly, his eyes on Theo. "Are you going to tell me, or do I have to guess? Is it a woman?"

Theo nodded, suddenly tongue-tied. Why was he so nervous? Robin seemed in fine spirits and he'd never denied his younger brother anything. All he had to do was present his case.

"Robin, I wish to marry," Theo began as Robin's face split into an unexpected grin.

"That's wonderful news, Theo. I actually have someone in mind for you. She's young, comely, and her family is well-connected. They have a vast estate up north, close to the Scottish border. If that comes to you through marriage, we will own nearly a quarter of this country."

"Robin, I have someone in mind already," Theo interrupted. "It's Uncle Kit's niece, Louisa Whitfield. She's beautiful, sweet, and clever. I think you'd really like her."

Robin leaned back in his chair, studying Theo for a moment, his eyes narrowed in thought. "So, you've finally fallen in love. Have you had her yet?"

"Robin, I want to marry her," Theo repeated, his stomach twisting with apprehension. This wasn't going quite as planned.

"I heard you, brother." Robin seemed to think for a moment, his pie forgotten. He opened his mouth to speak, but then closed it again, taking a gulp of wine to buy time. Theo pushed away his plate, the food no longer appealing. He hadn't expected Robin to be so apprehensive.

"Theo, you know I hate to deny you," Robin began.

"Then don't," Theo pleaded. "I love her, Robin."

"The girl might be beautiful and charming, but she has no title or fortune. A plantation in Virginia, no matter how profitable, is not nearly as valuable as an estate here in England. Property is power, Theo; you know that."

"Robin, we have more than enough property. Her father is not titled, but wealthy, so she's not without fortune," Theo replied, knowing that he'd lost the argument already.

"Brother, the lack of fortune is not my only concern—she's a Catholic, for God's sake. We are a Protestant family and have been for generations. I won't have a Papist in the family." Robin shook his head as if contemplating the horror of having a Catholic sister-in-law. He wasn't particularly fond of Louisa Sheridan, and now Theo understood why. The subject of her religion never came up, but Robin always kept his distance, preferring to deal with Kit at Whitehall rather than at home.

"Robin, we have a Catholic king, whose son will no doubt marry a Catholic princess. Would it really be so dire if I married a Catholic woman?" Theo knew that wouldn't help his cause, but he couldn't help using every last bit of logic to convince Robin. "Uncle Kit married a Catholic, and it hasn't hindered him. He's on the Privy Council and seems to have the backing of Buckingham."

Robin shook his head, clearly upset. Theo knew this wasn't easy for him, but he took his duty to the family very seriously and would oppose Theo to the last if he truly believed himself to be right.

"Theo, Aunt Louisa is a fine woman, but she's not a devout Papist and has agreed to raise the children in the Protestant faith, which is what really matters. In either case, Uncle Kit has always been somewhat unconventional in his choices. I will not permit such division within the family. It leads to nothing but trouble." Robin looked away, unable to face his miserable brother.

"I'm truly sorry, but I must decline your request. I'd tell you to use her to your heart's content, but she's Uncle Kit's niece, so it's probably best if you don't see her again. I know you're not in the right frame of mind just now, but when you are, I'd like to talk to you about Lady Mary Winslow. Her father is eager to see our two families united."

Theo's chair scraped the stone floor as he pushed away from the table, walking out of the dining room without another word. His hands were shaking, his heart pounding as he realized the impact of Robin's decision. Louisa was now lost to him forever unless he turned his back on his title and inheritance. Would she even want him if he were penniless?

Theo stepped out into the muggy evening, unsure where he was going. The streets were dark, illuminated only by patches of light spilling from windows onto the muck-strewn sidewalk. Few people were out, keeping to the middle of the road for fear of being set upon in the shadows and robbed, or worse. The occasional carriage rattled by, but otherwise, all was quiet. Theo walked toward the Thames, hoping it was cooler by the water. The smell of seaweed and rotting fish accosted his senses, but he hardly noticed; he was too wrapped up in his misery.

Orbs of yellow light bobbed above the black surface of the water as packet boats crossed the river, ferrying people across even at this time of night, the boatmen calling out to each other from time to time. Theo sat on a barrel and watched as the river lazily flowed past him, oblivious to his troubles. He'd given Louisa his word of honor, and he would keep it. He just needed to think of something he could use to change Robin's mind, but for the life of him, he couldn't come up with a damn thing. One thing he knew for certain—he wasn't going to lose her.

TWENTY-EIGHT

Alec poured himself a glass of brandy but set it aside for the moment. The amber liquid glowed in the late afternoon sun pouring in through the leaded windows, casting golden shafts of light onto the polished walnut table conveniently situated between the two high-backed chairs. Alec loved this room. Yealm Castle had had a passable library, but the library at Kit's London residence far surpassed it. He walked along the nearest shelf of books, running his finger along the spines of the well-read volumes. How he'd missed reading for pleasure. There were some books in Virginia, but not nearly enough, and most of them were religious texts rather than the "frivolous musings of degenerates," as the minister had put it in one of his sermons.

Alec pulled out *Richard III* by William Shakespeare and smiled. It had been one of his favorites when he was a young man. He'd been enthralled by Richard's Machiavellian tactics during his rise to power, horrified and impressed that someone would go to such lengths to gain the throne. Alec settled into a chair, grateful to have the library to himself. He briefly wondered what the women were up to before opening the book to the first page and reaching for his drink. He'd see them soon enough.

Alec was so engrossed in the play that he didn't notice her at first. The servant approached him shyly, clearing her throat to get his attention as she hovered by the door, unsure whether she should come further into the room. Alec reluctantly put the volume down, turning his attention to the maid. "Was there something you wanted?"

"Ah, I'm sorry to disturb you, sir, but there's a young woman asking to see you. What should I tell her?"

"A young woman?" Alec asked, confused. "Did she give a name?"

"No, sir. She only said that she must speak with you urgently and will wait as long as it takes for you to receive her." The maid gave him an inquisitive stare before hastily looking away. Alec had no idea why some unknown young woman would want to see him, but he'd find out soon enough.

"I'll receive her in here. Thank you," he added as the girl slipped out of the library. Alec threw a longing look at the book before setting it down on the table. He'd pick up where he left off later. Whatever this woman wanted couldn't possibly take too long. He turned at the sound of the door opening behind him, distracting him from his thoughts.

At first, she just stood there in the shadows until Alec beckoned her to come forward. He could sense her apprehension, so he sat down, hoping to put her at ease by not towering over her. She was just a slip of a girl, thin and pale with almond-shaped green eyes that stood out in her childish face. She seemed vaguely familiar, but Alec couldn't place her. Anyhow, he hadn't been in England in eighteen years, so he couldn't possibly know her.

"You wanted to see me," he prompted. "Would you like to sit down?"

The girl remained standing by the door as if she would flee

at any moment and studied him with those eyes. She seemed to make up her mind and advanced further into the room, pulling off the hood of her cloak to reveal chestnut hair that was piled high on her head with several strands escaping the pins to frame her face. Alec noted that it was too warm outside to be wearing a cloak, but it seemed she wore it more for protection than for warmth. He gestured to a chair, but the girl mutely shook her head, stopping a few feet away from him.

"Would you like a drink?" Alec asked. He had no idea what to make of this strange young woman, who was studying him with an intensity he couldn't quite understand.

"No, thank you, sir," she replied shyly, taking a few steps closer to him. "I'm just so overcome. It's taken me so long to find you." The girl had a trace of a French accent, English clearly not her first language.

"Why were you looking for me, if I might ask?"

"My name is Genevieve, and I believe you're my uncle, sir."

The poor girl looked so nervous as she uttered the words that Alec thought she might faint. He absentmindedly gestured for her to sit down again and this time she took a seat, perching on the edge of the chair as if to sit down comfortably might somehow derail her cause. Now that she was closer to the light, he could see her face more clearly. He placed her somewhere in her late teens, although it was hard to tell. Finlay had been dead for nearly nineteen years, so conceivably, she could be his daughter. Charles had visited England before his marriage to Annabel, but this girl was too old to be his daughter.

"Are you Finlay's daughter? Who is your mother, child?" Alec thought Finn would have told him if he had an illegitimate child, but then again, he might never have even known of her existence. God knows, Finlay had been no saint. He had his pick of women before he married Valerie, and one of them could have given birth to this girl. Alec saw a momentary look of confusion on Genevieve's face as she raised her eyes to his, holding his gaze for a moment before answering.

"I'm not Finlay's daughter. My mother was Rose—your sister."

Alec was glad that he was sitting down because he felt as if someone had bashed him over the head with a blunt object. He hadn't seen Rose in over twenty years, not since she ran off to join a convent right after the death of their parents. Could this girl truly be her daughter?

"Forgive me if I seem surprised, but my sister left home to become a nun. Had she married? Who is your father?" Alec didn't want to interrogate the girl, but despite the obvious resemblance, he had a hard time accepting her claim. Rose feared marriage, and the idea of submitting to a man left her repulsed and terrified. She wanted to dedicate her life to God, so what happened to change her mind?

"I don't know who my father was, sir. I was born at the Convent des Ursulines in Loudun, France. My mother died a few days after my birth. The nuns raised me and gave me an education, but I knew nothing of my family until I was ready to leave the convent."

Alec gripped the armrest as if his life depended on it. He'd accepted that he'd never see Rose again, but to hear of her death still left him gutted. He wanted to believe that she was alive and well, living in some convent and enjoying a life of peaceful contemplation and order, and all this time she'd been dead.

"Did she die of childbed fever?" Alec asked miserably. Rose had been frightened of childbirth since she was a young girl and had seen their mother in labor with Charles. She'd sworn she'd never have children if it meant going through such agony. Was her dying in childbirth some cruel cosmic joke?

"No, sir, she drowned herself." Genevieve looked away for a moment, her eyes filling with tears. Clearly, she still mourned the mother she'd never known.

"She drowned herself?" Alec exclaimed.

"Yes. They found her body downstream from the convent. She took her own life. Do you mind terribly if we don't discuss her death? I find it very distressing." Genevieve angrily brushed away a tear, as if she were ashamed of her weakness, and turned back to Alec.

"I didn't want to join the order, so Mother Superior helped me secure a position as a nursemaid with an English family. I wanted to come to England to find my mother's family, but by the time I got here, everyone had gone."

Genevieve suddenly sprang to her feet, as if she had overstayed her welcome. "I'm sorry to have bothered you. I only wanted you to know that I exist, that's all. I will go now." She made for the door, but Alec grabbed her arm before she had a chance to run.

"Wait, please. I'm sorry if I seem less than overjoyed, but you've taken me completely by surprise. I'd like to talk more with you and get to know you. I've always regretted the way things turned out and wished I could find Rose, if only to tell her that I understood and didn't blame her for leaving. Had she discussed her decision with me, I would have helped her get to France and had seen her settled. She never even told us which convent she was going to."

Alec lifted Genevieve's chin with his finger and looked into her eyes. "You look so like her when she was a girl. I can't believe I didn't see it right away." Genevieve turned her face away, her eyes full of grief.

"I'd like to get to know you too, Uncle," she whispered. "I've felt alone for so long. It would be wonderful to have someone I can call family." Genevieve kissed Alec on the cheek and ran from the room before he had a chance to stop her.

"I'll come back tomorrow," she called out before disappearing through the door.

TWENTY-NINE

Theo finished his apple and threw the core over his shoulder, his eyes never leaving the house across the road. He'd been at his vantage point for nearly three hours but had yet to see any activity. Servants came and went through the rear exit, and a wagon had pulled up earlier, delivering something to the kitchens, but the carriage hadn't been brought around yet. He was hot and hungry, but he didn't dare leave. If his information was correct, then today was the day Lord Kilbourne had a meeting with his solicitor, leaving Celia alone for several hours.

The old man rarely went out, so this was an opportunity not to be missed if Theo wanted to speak with her privately. Celia had spent most of her time at the palace when she had been a lady-in-waiting to Queen Anne, but Her Majesty had dismissed Celia when she found out she was with child, giving her leave to return home for the remainder of her confinement. Theo wondered if Celia would return to her post now that the queen was back at the palace after the Royal Progress. He was sure Celia longed to be at court, where she was free of her husband and able to meet Robin discreetly in the myriad rooms available at the palace for the use of secret lovers.

Theo stepped from foot to foot, hoping something would happen soon. A few minutes later, the carriage finally appeared, ready to take Lord Kilbourne to his meeting. The old man gingerly walked down the steps, his cane tapping on the stone as he laboriously descended assisted by a strapping young servant. He climbed into the carriage with great difficulty, looking like a man who'd just accomplished a mammoth task. Theo could see his profile as he settled in for the ride, his waxy skin glowing white in the dim interior of his equipage. Lord Kilbourne was in his early sixties, but appeared much older, possibly due to illness. The carriage finally began to move, blending into the midday congestion within moments.

Theo waited a few moments before approaching the door and banging the brass knocker. Celia wouldn't be pleased to see him, but he had to try; she was his only hope. He was led through a cavernous foyer, the soaring ceiling and flagstone floor reminiscent of a church, and into a receiving room. The house was eerily quiet. There must be an army of servants going about their tasks, but it felt as if the house was completely empty, devoid of any occupants. Dust motes twirled in the light flowing through the windows, settling on the heavy wooden furniture and tapestries decorating the walls. They looked old, the colors faded and the faces of the people almost indistinguishable. Theo suddenly felt a pang of pity for Celia. What must it be like to live in this tomb with a man who was as good as dead?

"I'm afraid you've missed my husband by mere moments," Celia said as she swept into the room, escorted by the same servant Theo had seen earlier. "Is there anything I can assist you with, your lordship?" She gave Theo a hard look, demanding he play along. Any connection between Celia and the Carews had to be underplayed, even in front of a servant, who was likely to report Theo's visit to his master.

"I'm terribly sorry to hear that, Lady Kilbourne, but perhaps you might be able to help me. It's a matter of some delicacy," Theo replied, glancing at the servant.

"I see. Leave us, Grady." Celia waited until the door closed behind the man, putting her finger to her lips, her eyes large in her face. "He listens at the door," she whispered. "Perhaps we should take a stroll around the garden, my lord. It's such a pleasant day outside," she suggested in a louder voice, no doubt for the benefit of the servant, who was clearly her husband's man.

"Yes, that would be most agreeable," Theo replied, playing along. He didn't care what they did as long as he got to speak to Celia. Theo followed her out into the neatly manicured garden behind the house. It seemed as quiet and lonely as the rest of the residence, the only sound coming from several bees that buzzed from one flower to another, intent upon their task and oblivious to the vexed woman and anxious man who dared to violate their domain.

"What are you doing here?" Celia hissed as soon as they were out of earshot of the house. She looked genuinely scared, her face pale and drawn without its usual paint. Theo had been so eager to resolve his own situation that he never stopped to think of the danger he was putting Celia in.

"Celia, I'm sorry to descend on you this way, but I was hoping you might be able to help me," he said, feeling contrite.

"Help you with what?"

"Robin has forbidden me to marry Louisa Whitfield and I thought you might be able to talk to him for me. You are the only person he'll listen to, the only one who can sway him." Theo gave Celia a pleading look. "Please, Celia."

Celia sank onto a marble bench, her dainty hands folded in her lap as she looked up at Theo. She absentmindedly played with a ruby ring that appeared way too large for her small hands. "What are his reasons for forbidding the marriage?" she asked, her voice flat.

"Lack of title, fortune, and desirable religion."

"Ho!" Celia cried, smiling for the first time. "What can I possibly say to him in the face of that?"

"I don't know, but he listens to you. It's not fair, Celia."

Theo didn't mean to sound like a petulant child, but he'd thought of nothing else since his interview with Robin and longed for sympathy from someone who understood the cruelty of not being able to marry one's lover. Celia's head snapped up, her eyes flashing in her pale face.

"Oh, it's fairness you want, is it?" she cried. "And what makes you think you are entitled to fairness when the rest of us aren't?

"What do you mean?" Theo asked, confused by her reaction.

"Is it fair to be married off to a man nearly forty years your senior when you are sixteen? Well, is it?" she demanded, her eyes never leaving his face. "Is it fair to have no say in your own life? Is it fair to attend on an old and sour queen day and night when all you want to do is run away and be with the man you love instead of being tormented by thoughts of him with his wife? I'm sorry, Theo, but Robin's love is the only thing that makes my life worth living, so I won't do anything to jeopardize my relationship with him. You must figure this one out for yourself."

Celia rose to her feet, her ire spent. "Did you know that I'm Kilbourne's third wife?" she suddenly asked. "He sent the other two to their graves with his abuse for failing to give him a child when it's he who's the problem. The old goat is so proud, he can't even fathom the notion that Will is not his and boasts to anyone who'll listen of his prowess. Well, sometimes we have to let people believe what they want to believe and deceive them in order to snatch a little bit of happiness for ourselves. That's the way of the world, Theo, and that's the only advice I can give you."

Theo sighed as he followed her back to the house. "Is there nothing I can do?" he asked, miserably. He hadn't expected Celia to be so belligerent, but he supposed he could see her point of view. He never stopped to think what her life must be like with a man old enough to be her grandfather, who kept her on a tight leash and had the servants spy on her. She was lucky he had acknowledged her son as his own rather than getting rid of him immediately after the birth and putting out a rumor that the baby had died. No wonder Celia was so afraid. She had a lot to lose and little control over her situation. Celia turned around, looking up at Theo with narrowed eyes.

"Check your father's will," she said cryptically before walking Theo to the door.

"It's been a rare pleasure to see you, Lord Carew. I will pass on your regards to my dear husband," she said with a coy smile as the servant appeared behind her shoulder. "He'll be so very sorry he missed your visit. Do come again soon," she added as Theo bowed and took his leave. What did she mean about the will?

THIRTY

Valerie opened the window and inhaled the fragrant air of the summer night. Their bedroom faced the back of the house, thankfully sparing them odors of raw sewage, manure, and human waste that wafted from a nearby alley. The heady smell of the rose garden filled the room, chasing away the stale air of the evening and cooling the room by a few degrees. Valerie could understand the servants' reluctance to open the windows for fear of letting in disease, but the rooms were like ovens by midafternoon, making one break into a sheen of perspiration as soon as one crossed the threshold. How wonderful it would be to have air-conditioning, or even just a good old ceiling fan, but alas, those inventions were hundreds of years away, and at this point, indoor plumbing would be at the top of her list.

Valerie propped up the pillows and got into bed, knowing full well that she wouldn't be going to sleep anytime soon. Alec had tossed his doublet across a nearby chair but was still dressed and wearing out the floorboards with his pacing.

"Alec, I'm getting tired just watching you. Why don't you come to bed?" Valerie patted the space next to her invitingly, but he shook his head stubbornly without skipping a beat.

Valerie had seen him this way before and knew he wouldn't be able to sleep until he exhausted himself. She could feel the tension coming off Alec all through supper, but he didn't tell her of Genevieve's visit until they came up to their bedroom, not wanting to share the news with the rest of the household until he could make sense of it himself.

"Alec, do you believe she's really Rose's daughter?" Valerie asked carefully. They needed to talk this through, but she had to tread carefully, not knowing what Alec's feelings were yet. It seemed he didn't know himself.

"She seemed sincere enough, and then there's the resemblance," he answered absentmindedly. "You should have seen her eyes."

"You thought she was Finn's, didn't you?"

"Yes, I did. I wouldn't have been nearly as shocked. Don't you see, Valerie, none of this makes any sense. My sister was a devout Catholic who wanted to spend her life in the service of God. The idea of her having a child out of wedlock and then taking her own life is absurd. If Genevieve is truly hers, then who is the father? Does he even know that he has a daughter? If I had a child out there, I'd want to know." Alec stopped pacing and faced Valerie across the room, his gaze clouded with confusion.

"I can't say I'd be thrilled to find out you have a child, but I see your point. Do you think she never told him?" Valerie had never known Rose, so it was difficult to guess what she would or wouldn't have done when she found herself pregnant.

"I can't imagine Rose willingly lying with someone, especially if they weren't legally wed. She caught Finn kissing a maid once and subjected him to such a scolding that for a mad moment he actually considered giving up women and taking the priesthood," Alec recalled with a smile. "Rose would never consent to premarital relations." Alec stopped in front of the window and gazed into the darkness of the night, not really seeing anything beyond his own thoughts.

"Of course, there's always another explanation," Alec continued as he resumed his pacing. "Perhaps Genevieve's father had seduced Rose, or even raped her, and then left her to her fate, which would explain why she wasn't married and still hiding behind the walls of a convent. Maybe it was the only place she felt safe." Alec grew tired of pacing and sank into a chair, facing Valerie across the room. "But that still doesn't explain why she would drown herself. Suicide is a mortal sin. No matter how desperate she felt, I can't imagine Rose would resort to taking her own life."

"Alec, I can understand your frustration, but I think you'll have to resign yourself to never knowing what really happened. You can accept Genevieve as your niece and take comfort in the fact that you are doing something for your sister and her child. I can't see what more you can do."

Valerie felt a pang of apprehension when she saw the look on Alec's face. She knew what he was going to say before he even opened his mouth.

"That's just not good enough, Valerie. I'm going to France."

"To do what?" Valerie exclaimed.

"To find out what happened to Rose. I owe her that much."

"And how do you plan to do that? It was over twenty years ago. Are you suggesting using the time travel device to go back?" Valerie asked, wondering how Alec meant to proceed.

"No, I don't think so. I have no idea how it would work if I went back within my own lifetime. Would there be two of me, one in France and one in England? Besides, Rose left before you ever came to us, so how would that change what happened in the future? I don't want to risk changing history. I will just go to France and try to determine what happened."

"You mean, *we* will go to France," supplied Valerie, giving Alec a hard stare and daring him to disagree with her.

"All right, we will go to France. I think the only logical place to start is the convent, don't you? They must know something." Alec's decision seemed to calm him down a little as he began to undress for bed. He always felt better once he had a plan.

"What about Louisa?"

"I see no reason to involve Louisa in this. She can stay here with Lou and Kit and I will ask them to extend their hospitality to Genevieve. She will be my ward and will not need to work any longer. Besides, she can be a good companion for Louisa. What do you think, Val?" Alec climbed into bed, pulling Valerie closer to him, obviously feeling more at peace.

"We don't know anything about her, but I suppose we'll have to find out. Let's see how she feels about your plan."

THIRTY-ONE

If Valerie felt any doubts about Genevieve's claim, they were dispelled as soon as she saw the girl the following afternoon. She'd never met Rose, for Alec's sister was long gone by the time Valerie showed up at Yealm Castle, but this girl could have easily been the daughter of Finlay or Charles. The resemblance was uncanny. She had something of Alec as well, but it wasn't as pronounced. Valerie could see why Alec was so shaken by her appearance. She had to admit that the girl was lovely. Besides being beautiful, she possessed the kind of charm and humility one didn't often see, especially in daughters of the nobility. Valerie liked her self-effacing manner and hoped that maybe their daughter could learn something from her.

Over the past two years, Louisa had become increasingly willful and contrary. Valerie supposed it was normal at her age, but she worried for her girl. If Louisa wanted something, she went after it with single-minded determination that left no room for doubt or caution; she just plunged in. At home at Rosewood, there weren't too many dangerous situations she could get into, especially since Alec kept a tight rein on her after the fiasco with Tom, but here in England, God only knew what she could get up to. She was already making plans to be introduced at court and secretly plotting a future as Lady Carew. Theo was unquestionably in love with her, but as that old English proverb warned, "There's many a slip twixt the cup and the lip."

Theo had come by the day before and taken Louisa for a drive around London, but he hadn't spoken to Alec about the future, and excused himself shortly after bringing Louisa back, claiming he had a previous engagement. Louisa looked a bit crestfallen after he left but was soon her old self again, alternating between moments of happiness and long stretches of moodiness.

Valerie had serious reservations about leaving Louisa in London, but to take her to France would only complicate matters. Lou promised that she'd enlist the help of Aunt Maud in guarding Louisa. If anyone knew the ways of the court, it was the old lady, and she would keep Louisa in line with her unflinching honesty.

Valerie turned her attention back to Alec and Genevieve, putting thoughts of Louisa aside for the moment. Genevieve was telling Alec about her childhood at the convent.

"Did you mind growing up at the convent?" Valerie asked, sitting down across from Genevieve and inviting her to take some grapes, which she accepted shyly.

"Mind? No, I didn't mind in the least. If the nuns hadn't taken me in, I would have most likely died of disease or neglect. The nuns were very kind to me and saw to my well-being and education. Most of them had known my mother, so I was able to extract bits of information that helped me to paint a portrait of her in my mind. I tried to picture her face every night before falling asleep, praying that she'd keep watch over me from Heaven. Mother Superior said that my mother's suicide cast her soul in Hell, but I never believed it. She was a kind and gentle soul according to the sisters, so whatever had driven her to take her own life would surely be forgiven by a just and loving God."

"I'm glad you don't think ill of your mother. She *was* a kind and gentle soul, almost childlike sometimes. All she ever wanted was to devote her life to God. I'd like to think He forgave her as well."

Alec reached out and took Genevieve's hand. She nearly yanked it away, but stopped herself in time, smiling up at Alec. Valerie didn't suppose she was used to being touched. The nuns would not have shown her any physical affection, especially once she got older. Alec seemed to notice the girl's discomfort and let go of her hand, reaching for a bunch of grapes instead to give her a moment to compose herself.

"Genevieve, I intend to go to France to find out what happened to my sister. Is there anything you can tell me that might help me discover the truth?"

Genevieve's gaze flew to Alec's face in alarm. "What do you mean, Uncle Alec? What truth do you hope to discover?" She seemed suddenly nervous, her fingers pleating the fabric of her skirt.

"I need to find out why my sister took her own life and I'd like to discover who your father is. Wouldn't you like that?" Alec asked gently, obviously realizing that his quest might not be welcome news to his niece.

"When I was little, I used to dream that my father would come to the convent and take me away to be a part of a family. I imagined that I might have brothers and sisters who would welcome me and love me, but Sister Marie-Jeanne said that it was a silly dream that would never come true and I should just forget it. In time, I did. No one ever came, so I stopped thinking of my father. He didn't want me, so I convinced myself that I didn't want him either." Genevieve looked toward the window, her expression wistful. Her dream was obviously not forgotten and the pain of being deserted by both parents still haunted her.

She turned back to Alec, her face full of resolve. "I would like to know why my mother killed herself, but if you happen to find out who my father is, please don't tell me. At this point in my life, it would only cause me pain. I'm so excited to have found you all; surely, that's more than anyone can ask for."

"We are very excited to have found you as well," Valerie piped in. She could see that Alec was shaken by Genevieve's speech. She supposed he expected her to jump at the chance to find out the truth, without taking into account what her life might have been like as a child or the disappointments she'd faced. "Would you like to meet Louisa? She's your cousin, and she's anxious to get to know you."

That was overstating it a bit, but Valerie wanted Genevieve to feel welcome. Louisa was less than thrilled to learn of her cousin's existence and hoped she wouldn't interfere with her plans to take the court by storm. "She's probably as quiet as a church mouse," she'd exclaimed, making a moue of distaste.

Alec had said sternly, "Louisa, you will welcome your cousin, and you will be kind and gracious. Is that understood?" He generally made a Herculean effort to ignore his daughter's moods and outbursts, but he wouldn't be defied in this. Genevieve had never known her family and he would do everything in his power to make her feel welcome and cherished.

"I'd like to meet Louisa very much, and I look forward to meeting Uncle Charles and Aunt Annabel. Do you think that might be possible at some point in the future?" Genevieve asked, her hands gripping the sides of the chair. *Poor girl,* thought Valerie. *She's scared we'll leave her behind.*

"Charles and Annabel will be thrilled to meet you, as will their children. You will have a home with us for as long as you want it," said Alec. He'd noticed her anxiety as well and wanted to assure her she wouldn't be left on her own again.

"Thank you so much Uncle Alec and Aunt Valerie. I never

dreamed I'd get such a warm welcome." Genevieve's eyes were full of joy as she smiled at them, overcome by gratitude.

THIRTY-TWO

Genevieve watched the carriage until it disappeared from view, then entered the house and raced up the stairs. She tried to be as quiet as possible, hoping not to run in into Master or Mistress Walker or any of their three children. Normally, she would have been happy to spend time with them as they had been the next best thing to a family of her own, but tonight she needed to be alone. Her tiny room was stuffy and dark, but Genevieve never noticed. She closed the door behind her and leaned against it, slowly sliding down to the floor in a heap of skirts. She wasn't sure when the tears came, but they flowed down her cheeks unchecked as she stared at the tiny square of twilit sky visible through the window above her bed.

Genevieve's mind feverishly reviewed every detail of the past few hours, still unable to believe that she'd actually not only been invited to dine with the family but to come live with them as a ward of Alexander Whitfield—Uncle Alec. A fresh flood of tears overtook her, sobs tearing from her chest. She fished out a handkerchief and wiped her face before blowing her nose. This was just a moment of weakness. She had to stop crying before someone heard her and came up to find out what was wrong. She should be crying tears of joy, but the torrent that took her so completely by surprise was a mixture of the emotions that had been building inside her since she was old enough to understand her position.

Genevieve had observed her cousin Louisa across the table, amazed by the arrogant assurance of the girl. She'd grown up in a family where she never had to question her place or the affection everyone felt for her. Genevieve couldn't help noticing Uncle Alec's indulgent smile and Aunt Valerie's pursed lips as Louisa blurted out something she shouldn't have and giggled prettily to hide her embarrassment. How blessed Louisa was to have been born into a real family, a family that loved her. She couldn't possibly imagine what it was like to grow up in the frigid silence of the convent, surrounded by people who proclaimed their undying devotion to a loving God but couldn't spare an ounce of affection for a lonely little girl who had no place in the world. Not a day had gone by that someone hadn't reminded Genevieve of her illegitimacy or her mother's sin. She'd prayed and prayed that someday her father would come and take her away from the cold, judgmental looks of the sisters, but he never did.

"No one is coming for you, ma petite," Sister Marie-Jeanne said, giving Genevieve a stern look. "Your papa has better things to do."

The words had cut like a knife, and she'd never mentioned her father again. If he came, it would be a wonderful surprise, the best day of her life, but if he didn't, she'd just have to learn to live with her disappointment.

No one ever came. The only man to visit the convent was Father Marc, who later became a bishop and then a cardinal. He was always kind to her and asked after her health and studies, but he was aloof and wouldn't answer any questions about her mother when asked. He petted her on the head kindly, making a sign of the cross over her and instructing her to be obedient and grateful. After all, the nuns had been extremely kind to take in a bastard and not only clothe and feed her but give her an education that would someday help her earn a living and make her way in the world.

As time went by, Genevieve formulated a new plan. She would try to find her mother's family, but no one at the convent would give her any information. She'd even tried to speak to Mother Superior, to ask for the name of her mother's people, but the woman wouldn't tell her a thing beyond that Sister Rose had come from England. Mother Superior knew nothing of her family. Genevieve accepted the answer but refused to give up. Her mother hadn't hatched out of an egg. Somewhere out there, there were people who belonged to her and maybe, just maybe, she could belong to them.

It had been Sister Clothilde who finally took pity on her. She was an old woman, who'd spent the better part of fifty years at the convent. She was one of the few people to be truly kind to Genevieve, believing that the sins of the parents should not be visited upon the children. One day, she asked Genevieve to help her pick some medicinal herbs, taking her for a walk along the riverbank. It had been a glorious summer day a week after Genevieve's sixteenth birthday. Sister Clothilde stopped periodically, poking a stick through the grass in search of some particular plant. Finally, she stopped, needing to rest. Genevieve sat down next to the old woman, enjoying the warm sun on her face and the sound of insects drawn to the slow waters of the river, its surface sparkling in the midday sun.

"Genevieve, I'm the oldest sister at the convent and I think I'm not long for this world," the nun began.

"Don't say that, Sister Clothilde," Genevieve wailed pitifully. "I don't want to lose you. You're my only friend."

"I don't want to lose you either, child, but I've had a long life and whenever the Good Lord chooses to take me, I will be happy to go to Him. However, there's something that's been on my mind."

"What's that?" Genevieve asked, her curiosity piqued.

"Your mother. She was a good girl, pious and kind, and you are just like her in that respect. Would you like to be a nun, Genevieve?" Sister Clothilde asked, shielding her eyes from the sun as she looked at the girl.

"No, Sister. I would like to find a position and leave the convent. I haven't been happy here." Genevieve had never complained to anyone, but she couldn't stop the words from spilling out.

"Just as I thought," replied Sister Clothilde, nodding to herself. "Genevieve, I've done something I wasn't supposed to do. I've asked Monsieur Barras to deliver a note for me, and I received a reply yesterday." She handed Genevieve a piece of paper folded into a tiny square. "Destroy it after you've read it."

"May I look at it now?" Genevieve asked, confused. The old nun nodded, turning away to rummage in her basket.

Genevieve unfolded the note with shaking hands, nearly dropping it to the ground. There were just two lines and no signature, but Genevieve knew exactly what the words meant.

"Alexander and Finlay Whitfield, Yealm Castle, village of Newton Ferrers, Devon, England."

Genevieve stared at the words for a long time, unable to believe that after all this time she finally had a name, an actual name. "Genevieve Whitfield of Yealm Castle," she mouthed experimentally. She knew she had a long way to go until she could say that out loud, but at least now there was something concrete, something solid. She had no idea who Alexander and Finlay were, but she would find them and pray that they didn't turn her away without hearing her out. Now she had a quest.

"Oh, thank you, Sister. Who is this from?"

"It's from someone who knew your mother well. That's all you need to know," the Sister replied with a kind smile.

"You don't know what this means to me."

"I know exactly what this means to you, child. Now, destroy the note, tell no one, and make your plans accordingly. You'll be leaving the convent next year. If you try, you might find a position with an English family, which would make your search easier. May God be with you, Genevieve. I will pray that you find what you are looking for." With that, she gave Genevieve her hand, needing assistance to stand. "Time we got back to the convent or we will be missed."

* * *

The tears finally dried up, leaving Genevieve tired and sore from sitting on the floor for so long. The room had grown completely dark, and it was time to wash and get ready for bed. Tomorrow was another day, a day where anything was possible, a day she never thought she'd see.

"I found him, Sister Clothilde," she whispered into the darkness. "I've found him, and he's so much more than I ever expected."

Genevieve smiled to herself, the years of fruitless searching and disappointment forgotten. Finlay Whitfield might have died years ago, but his brother was still alive, and he promised to take care of her and make her a part of his family. Genevieve sighed happily as she climbed into bed after saying her prayers and making the sign of the cross.

"Good night, Mama," she said before closing her eyes.

THIRTY-THREE

Valerie sat across from Louisa, taking a deep breath of the evening air. It wasn't the custom of seventeenth-century Londoners to sit outside on a pleasant evening for fear of catching disease, but Valerie could think of nothing more enjoyable. Most people wore herb-filled pomanders around their necks, hoping the herbs would keep sickness at bay. The pomanders helped mask the terrible smell coming off people who thought bathing was bad for their health, but they had no power to ward off infection. Louisa, who was notorious for disliking cats, kept several cats in the London house, since they were the only viable shield against the rats and mice that carried disease. The cats weren't allowed upstairs, especially near the children, but kept to the kitchens and storerooms where they could hunt to their hearts' content.

The stars were just becoming visible in the evening sky, a hint of autumn already detectable in the air fragrant with the tang of the Thames and the smell of earth and flowers. Alec joined them a few moments later, having seen Genevieve home in the carriage. He had convinced her to stay for supper, and she'd shyly accepted. She wasn't in the habit of dining with the family in her position as nursemaid and felt visibly awkward until Louisa began to chatter away, putting her more at ease. To everyone's astonishment, Genevieve and Louisa got on well, since at twenty-three, Genevieve wasn't very worldly due to her monastic upbringing.

"So, how did you leave things with Genevieve?" Valerie asked when Alec sat down next to her.

"She's agreed to give up her position and allow me to assume the role of guardian. She will move in here by the end of the week, with Kit's consent. I wish I had more time to get to know her, but time is of the essence. I'd like to leave as soon as possible."

Alec took Valerie's hand, holding it in his own. He realized she was disappointed about their canceled trip to the future, but this was too important to put off until spring.

"Where exactly are you going?" Louisa asked, surprised. They hadn't broken the news yet, not before they had a viable plan. Valerie knew Louisa would be upset. They'd only just been reunited a few weeks ago and now she would be leaving again, possibly for several months.

"We are going to France to visit the Convent of Loudun where Genevieve grew up. I want to find out what happened to Rose that drove her to suicide."

Alec didn't really want to talk about it, but they had to tell Louisa and Kit sooner or later. Kit had just joined them outside, squeezing in next to Louisa on the wrought iron bench and putting his arm around her shoulders. Things seemed better between them, so maybe Kit had been able to resolve his situation at court.

"Wait! Did you say the Convent of Loudun?" Louisa exclaimed, staring at Alec as if he had just done a headstand.

"Yes, I did. Why do you ask?"

"Valerie, don't you remember?" Louisa exclaimed again, gazing at Valerie expectantly.

"Lou, I have no idea what you are talking about." She really didn't. The name sounded vaguely familiar, but she couldn't recall where she'd heard it before.

"Don't you remember how Billie dragged us to that horrible opera, *The Devils of Loudun* at the Met?" Louisa was staring at Valerie, willing her to remember.

"Oh my God, of course. I hated it. Is it the same Loudun?"

"Of course, how many can there be? What year did that happen in?" Louisa jumped off the bench and was pacing now, trying to remember.

"What are you two talking about? What's an opera?" Kit asked, bemused.

"An opera is a play where everyone sings," Louisa replied, still pacing.

"So, it's a comedy?"

"No, it's usually a tragedy," supplied Valerie, enjoying the men's confusion.

Kit looked at Alec, rolling his eyes in exasperation. "I think they're making a joke at our expense, Alec. Can you imagine everyone singing, and it not being funny?"

"Actually, this opera was based on real events that took place at the convent," Valerie said, trying to recall the plot.

"Wait," chimed in Alec, "what devils? What happened there?"

"Valerie, do you remember?" Louisa asked as she paced in front of them, hands on hips. "What I wouldn't give to Google it."

"Maybe you could sing it instead," Kit piped in. "It'd be more amusing."

"I don't remember the details, but it had something to do with a large number of Ursuline nuns being possessed by the Devil. They had convulsions and spoke in tongues," Valerie supplied.

Alec and Kit stared at her as if she were the one speaking in tongues. They'd probably never even heard of such things. After all, they'd never been exposed to modern media, so the concept of demonic possession would be foreign to them unless it was mentioned in the Bible.

"When did this happen?" Alec asked, doubt written across his face.

"Sometime in the seventeenth century, but I can't recall the year. I don't think it's happened yet. I actually looked it up after the performance and it mentioned an earlier case in 1611 in a different town, but Loudun happened later," Louisa recalled.

"So what happened to the nuns?" Kit was bursting with curiosity, probably thinking that this could only happen to Catholics. Protestants didn't indulge in such theatrics.

"They were exorcized by a priest, who later went mad. That's all I can remember." Louisa sat back down as if exhausted by her trip down memory lane.

"Exorcized? And you are saying this happened at the convent where my sister died, and Genevieve grew up?" Alec was incredulous. "I must admit, I find this a little difficult to believe. I've never heard of such a thing. And they turned it into a play?"

"Where everyone sang," added Kit helpfully, trying not to laugh.

"I'm telling you what I know. You don't have to believe me," replied Louisa defensively.

"I'm sorry, Louisa. I wasn't questioning your word. It's just somewhat surprising. I hope you're right, and it hasn't happened yet. I would hate to think that Rose might have been a part of it. You would think a convent would be a place of refuge, not a den of evil."

Alec shook his head, obviously trying to rid himself of the images Louisa had planted in his mind. "I must admit that I'm dreading this journey, but I feel compelled to undertake it. I think I'm going to retire now. Goodnight."

Valerie followed Alec into the house. She could understand his feelings. All these years he'd comforted himself with the thought that his sister was safe behind the walls of a sanctuary, not realizing that she was not only gone, but had clearly been driven to self-murder. Valerie was glad Genevieve agreed to accept Alec's offer. Making her happy would be a balm to his troubled soul.

THIRTY-FOUR

The sound of cutlery on plates and the clinking of glasses could be heard coming from the dining room, the smell of roasted meat wafting through the house and made Theo's mouth water. He ignored his rumbling stomach and crept past the closed doors of the dining room to the staircase leading to the bedrooms. Robin kept his room locked when he wasn't at home, but tonight he and Beth were entertaining guests, so technically Robin was in. The corridor was quiet and dark, the servants serving supper.

Theo looked around to make sure no one was coming before trying the door. Thankfully, it wasn't locked, so he slipped inside, closing the door quietly behind him. Robin's bedroom was much like his own: masculine, uncluttered, and spacious. He hated any kind of ornament or artifice, preferring to keep only items necessary for his everyday life. Beth's bedroom next door was a woman's paradise filled with ornamental boxes, perfumes, and tapestries, but Robin's was as stark as that of a Spartan warrior.

Theo didn't bother to light a candle, relying on moonlight to find what he came for. Robin kept all the important papers in an

Oriental box he received years ago as a gift from some foreign merchant. Its black-lacquered lid was decorated with a whimsical mother-of-pearl design, a pearly pink stone used to represent the blossoms of a cherry tree. The box was very pretty, and Beth had asked Robin to give it to her several times, but he refused. He had some kind of strange attachment to it. Robin kept the box hidden in a specially built alcove behind a painting of their father, which was the only decoration in the room. Lord Carew Senior stared sternly from the canvas, willing his sons to do his bidding even in death, his light eyes so different from Theo's and Robin's. Only Walter had taken after their father, his light-brown hair and shrewd blue eyes just like the ones in the painting.

Theo moved the frame to reveal the alcove and pulled out the box. He was glad it wasn't locked. He would have hated to force the lock and upset Robin. All he wanted was to look at their father's last will and testament to see if there was anything to Celia's comment. Robin never need know he'd even been there. Theo told him that he was dining with a friend, so no one would be expecting to see him for a few hours yet.

Riffling through the papers, Theo finally came to the rolled-up document bearing a broken seal. He unrolled the scroll and brought it closer to the window, quickly reading through the details of their father's final instructions. He'd been very young when Lord Carew died, so whatever he knew of the document, he knew from Robin. His mother never mentioned a thing, leaving all business matters to her eldest son and spending her time in pursuit of pleasure, which had been denied her during her marriage. Robin and Walter hadn't approved, but Theo didn't mind, pleased to see his mother smiling and happy after years of tight-lipped misery.

Theo scanned the numerous paragraphs looking for his own name. He saw it several times in relation to property, but there was nothing about marriage until the very last paragraph. Theo read it twice to make sure he got it right before rolling up the document and replacing it in the box. Maybe Celia hadn't been referring to Theo when she talked of deception, but Robin. Seemed his brother had some explaining to do.

Theo slipped out of the room and headed to the kitchen. It would be a while yet till Robin returned to his room for the night and he might as well face him on a full stomach.

THIRTY-FIVE

It was several long hours before Theo heard Robin on the stairs, his voice loud as he bid Beth goodnight. He'd obviously had too much to drink and was eager for his bed, grateful not to have to visit his wife's bedroom in order to perform his husbandly duties. Robin never turned to Beth to satisfy his lust, and now that she was with child, he was free from her for a while. Despite being a straying husband, he was surprisingly devoted to Celia and felt as if he were being unfaithful to her when with his wife. Beth's soft voice replied to Robin before she retired to her own room, equally happy not to have to deal with her husband. Theo hoped to God that he'd never have to endure such a marriage, but that would be his fate if Robin got his way.

He waited a few minutes before leaving his sanctuary and going to face his brother. Theo had always loved and respected Robin, but tonight he was angry and full of resentment. Robin had taken advantage of his trust and wanted to manipulate him to serve his own ends. Well, he was in for a shock.

Robin turned around in surprise, his hand on his flies. He was a little unsteady on his feet as he plopped down on the bed, kicking off his shoes. It would probably have been better to wait until Robin was stone sober, but Theo was too upset to put off the confrontation any longer.

"I thought you were out," Robin said, finally managing to get his breeches off and throwing them to the floor before pulling his shirt over his head. "I'm off to bed, if you don't mind." Naked, Robin crawled into bed and pulled a sheet over his middle in an attempt at modesty.

"I'd like to talk you," Theo said quietly as he pulled a chair closer to the bed. He wanted to see his brother's face while he talked to him to gauge his reaction.

"Can't it wait? I'm tired. You should have been there tonight. We dined with Lord and Lady Winslow, and the subject of your marriage to their daughter came up more than once. They are very eager to see you two wed before the year's out."

"I'm afraid that's not possible, because the only person I will be marrying before the year is out is Louisa Whitfield." Theo watched Robin's astonished face as he absorbed the announcement.

"Theo, we've already had this discussion and as far as I can tell, nothing has changed. I forbid you to marry that Papist. Now, go to your own room and let me get some sleep." Robin scratched his stubbled cheek, making a rasping sound with his fingers as he watched Theo in the fruitless hope that he'd leave.

"Oh, but something has changed, at least for me, and it will for you if you keep on denying me. First, if I marry her without your consent, it will result in embarrassment for you, which is never desirable when you are concerned with your political future. Second, it wouldn't look good to have a penniless brother married to a Papist, and third, and most importantly, you lied to me, Robin." Theo watched Robin's face as he took in what he said.

"What are you talking about? Are you saying that you will marry her without my consent and forfeit everything?"

"No, I'm saying that I will marry her without your consent and forfeit nothing. It seems you forgot to tell me that your guardianship ends on my twenty-first birthday, which is only two months away. So, either you can give me your consent and we can do this amicably or you can withhold it and try to disinherit me. Father's solicitor has a copy of the will, which will prove that you have no say in my affairs as of November 2nd. Which shall it be, Robin?"

Robin sat up in bed, suddenly looking tired and sober. He'd obviously never expected this turn of events and he stared at Theo, his mouth open in shock. "How did you know about the will?" he asked, his eyes cold.

"It doesn't matter. What matters is that you lied to me and tried to manipulate me in order to serve your own ends. I've always trusted you, Robin, and you betrayed me." Theo didn't mean to sound as hurt as he did, but Robin's lie cut deeper than he allowed himself to admit.

Robin rubbed the bridge of his nose, his eyes closed as if it hurt to look at Theo. He finally looked up, his gaze clear and unflinching.

"Theo, I would never have said no to you had you picked someone even remotely suitable; you know that. I love you, and I want to see you happy, but this union is a mistake and you will live to regret it. You hardly know the girl. Can you honestly tell me that she loves you and isn't only after your wealth and position? She has much to gain and little to lose."

Theo stood, not bothering to allow Robin to finish. He didn't want to hear an argument against Louisa. He had the upper hand now, and he'd use it. Even if the document hadn't stipulated that Theo was a free man at twenty-one, Robin dreaded scandal more than he'd ever admit. He never imagined that Theo would go against him, but if Theo still chose to marry Louisa and accept the consequences, it wouldn't look good for the family and the only way to avoid embarrassment would be to put a good face on the marriage. Robin was now with his back against the wall, and he would support the marriage, if only not to lose face at court.

"Goodnight, Robin," Theo said as he walked out the door. He'd won this round, but his heart was sore, aching with the knowledge that his relationship with Robin would never be the same. He would have to look out for his own interests from now on.

THIRTY-SIX

NEW YORK SEPTEMBER 1777

Abbie wiped the perspiration off her face as she made her way down the corridor. The day was quite pleasant, but she felt unusually warm and weak, her legs refusing to cooperate as she swept the hallway before cleaning Major Weland's room. He was one of the last to leave this morning, having had an upset stomach the night before. Two more officers were also still about, but they were downstairs breakfasting, so Abbie was able to quickly clean their rooms and move on. She couldn't wait to finish her chores and have a quick lie-down before the midday meal. She'd see Finn then. Mrs. Cromwell had sent him on an errand to buy fresh hay for the stables and collect several bags of oats for the horses, generously provided by the quartermaster of the regiment the lodgers belonged to. She had become adept at cutting corners and using her rank as the widow of a major to get some perks through the officers quartered at her establishment.

Abbie was glad to see Major Weland finally leave his room, returning his greeting as he made his way downstairs, his boots thudding on the wooden steps. He was one of Abbie's least favorite lodgers, always uptight and guarded unlike some of the younger men. They were only too happy to exchange a few words with her, their playful manner a reprieve from the likes of the major. Abbie picked up her bucket and mop and entered the major's room. She opened the window and was just about to make the bed when a sudden wave of vertigo forced her to sit down. She'd had several bouts of dizziness these past two weeks and it was time to face the obvious.

Abbie forced herself to get up and walk to the major's desk where he kept a calendar. She counted carefully and slowly, knowing the answer would change her life, although she knew it already. She was nearly three weeks late and that could mean only one thing. She suspected she was pregnant for a week now but was reluctant to tell Finn. He would insist they return home immediately, aborting their mission, their contribution not valuable enough to risk their baby. She'd been able to pass on some useful tidbits to the Revolutionaries, but nothing that would change the course of the war, so she was entirely dispensable.

Abbie decided to take a look at the major's papers since she was already sitting at the desk. There was letter from his wife, who seemed even more tightly wound than the major, and a rolled-up document of some sort. Abbie spread the document on the desk, studying what appeared to be a map. Now this was interesting. It was a detailed map of Pennsylvania with certain points circled and starred. Abbie shuffled through some of the other papers. If she was reading the map correctly, then the British were planning to move some of their companies toward Philadelphia in an effort to capture the capital. There were markings in blue of where units of Washington's army were stationed near a place called Brandywine. This had to be important, but there's no way she could remember all these details. She needed to write the information down and pass it on to Sam. It might be vital intelligence.

Abbie looked around for a sheet of paper and pulled out a quill. She'd clean the quill, so the Major would never know she'd used it. Abbie began to copy the document to the best of her ability, making sure to place the troops accurately on the map. Even the slightest mistake could provide misleading information. She was so caught up in her task, she didn't immediately turn when the door opened behind her.

"I'm coming, Libby. I'm almost done in here." Libby made it a habit to come in search of Abbie if she took too long about her task. She fancied herself in charge, which was just fine. She'd still be there long after Abbie and Finn departed. Abbie wasn't too concerned about Libby finding her at the major's desk. She was just as nosy, although her purpose was different. She was fascinated by the personal lives of the officers and liked to read their private correspondence. She'd recently confided to Abbie that she was nursing a secret love for Corporal Tennant, who was one of the few unattached men lodged at Mrs. Cromwell's establishment. Libby checked his letters from home feverishly, hoping there was nothing from a young lady who might be a possible fiancée.

Abbie looked up in surprise as her wrist was seized roughly by a male hand. Major Weland stood over her, his nostrils flaring, his face beet-red with fury as he glared at Abbie's drawing.

"How dare you?" he hissed at Abbie, tearing the quill out of her hand and whipping the sheet of paper off the desk. "You are spying for the rebels." Major Weland yanked Abbie to her feet, his fingers wrapping painfully about her wrist just as Libby's eager face appeared in the doorway.

"All right, Major Weland?" she asked, nearly bursting with curiosity.

"No, not all right. Kindly summon the two officers from the dining room this minute, as well as Mrs. Cromwell."

"Sir, I wasn't spying," Abbie stammered, her heart beating wildly against her ribs. How could she have been so careless as to assume that it had been Libby coming into the room? Although it probably wouldn't have made any difference. The writing desk was clearly visible from the doorway, so any attempt to hide her map would have been noted by the major, who would have seized it anyway. Why couldn't he have come in when she was still looking at the calendar? God, what would he do with her?

"Save it for the court, Mistress Whitfield, for a court you will face. Have no doubt of that."

The major folded Abbie's drawing and stuffed it into his breast pocket, safely out of Abbie's reach. She opened her mouth to protest, but there wasn't much she could say. The major had caught her red-handed. Abbie felt another wave of dizziness wash over her as she slumped against the rigid form of Major Weland, who took her by the arms and roughly sat her down in the chair he'd yanked her from only a few moments ago.

"Don't bother swooning. It won't work," the major hissed at her as the two remaining officers came in followed by a red-faced Mrs. Cromwell. Libby brought up the rear, her eyes round as saucers as she watched from the corridor, her mouth open in shock.

"I've apprehended Mistress Whitfield going through confidential papers and making copies to pass on to her cohorts," Major Weland informed the two officers. "I'm going to take her to the residence of General Campbell. I believe I have enough evidence for a tribunal. Captain Gordon, Captain Mara, you are to remain here and take the husband into custody as soon as he returns. Bring him to me at General Campbell's house. He will be put on trial alongside his wife. I can't imagine that a mere woman would spy on her own initiative. You are to do nothing that might alert Master Whitfield and give him a chance to flee. Is that understood? Mrs. Cromwell, please keep the maidservant out of sight. She's just dimwitted enough to give the game away. Captain Gordon, saddle my horse."

Mrs. Cromwell threw Abbie a look of pure poison before

following the captains out of the room. Abbie heard her berating Libby as their steps receded. Major Weland closed the door behind them and turned to face Abbie.

"How long have you been spying for the rebels, Mistress Whitfield?" He looked as if he wanted to hit her but was too much of a gentleman to strike a woman, even if she were the enemy.

"I'm not a spy, Major Weland; I'm just a nosy girl. I didn't mean any harm," answered Abbie, sounding feeble even to her own ears. If he fell for that one, he wasn't fit to bear his rank.

"I will ask you again. How long have you been spying for the rebels? Where do you meet your contacts?" The major towered above her in an effort to intimidate, but there was no need. Abbie was trembling with fear, her hands shaking in her lap.

"I'm not a spy, Major. I was merely bored and rifled through some papers. I have no contacts."

The room swam before her eyes as she slid off the chair and onto the cool wooden floor. Abbie closed her eyes, willing the room to stop spinning, but it didn't work. She felt as if she were being sucked into a black hole. Abbie would have happily stayed where she was, but the major hauled her up by the arms, sitting her back in the chair, his face mere inches away from hers.

"Your feminine antics won't work with me," he barked, giving her a good shake. He was about to continue interrogating her when Captain Gordon appeared in the doorway. "Your horse is outside, Major, and there's still no sign of the husband."

"Don't let him get away," the major barked as he led Abbie outside. She was surprised when he asked Captain Gordon to give her a leg-up, then mounted behind her. It felt awfully intimate to feel his hard body behind her as he dug his heels into the horse's flanks, leaving the boarding house behind.

Please don't get caught, Finn, Abbie prayed as the major

cantered down the street, his thighs rigid against her own. *Please get away*. General Campbell's residence was only a few streets eastward, just off 5th Avenue. He occupied a sizeable house, the first floor serving as headquarters. The house boasted several outbuildings discreetly situated behind the main residence. A few soldiers were in the yard, unloading stores and stowing them in one of the outbuildings. Major Weland helped Abbie dismount and marched her through the gates past two astonished sentries. It wasn't often that a woman was anything other than a skivvy, and those went through the back door.

"Can I help you, Major Weland?" A young officer greeted them at the door, eyeing Abbie with undisguised curiosity and noting Major Weland's grip on her arm.

"I'm here to see the general."

"Right this way, sir." The officer led them down a corridor toward what must be the general's private office. He was seated behind a massive desk, writing something as he scratched his unwigged head absentmindedly. The iron-gray curls stood on end as he composed his missive, oblivious to the commotion outside.

"General, Major Weland is here to see you on urgent business, sir," the officer announced before showing them into the office.

General Campbell looked up in surprise, jamming his wig on his head almost as an afterthought before inviting Major Weland to sit down. Abbie thought a general of the British Army would look more menacing, but General Campbell looked anything but. His round blue eyes peered out from a florid face, jowls spilling over the collar of the uniform which gave every impression of strangling him, his wig slightly off-center, making him look comical. Abbie would have laughed had she not been so terrified. This ridiculous man had the power to send her to the gallows, and there was nothing comical about that.

"Thank you. I'll stand, General. I've arrested this young woman for spying. I caught her in the act of copying maps of the Philadelphia campaign to pass on to the rebels. I left two men at the boardinghouse to arrest her husband, since I've no doubt he's behind this enterprise."

Major Weland was rigid as ever, his chest puffed out with righteous indignation as he delivered his speech. Abbie stood quietly, unsure whether she should face the general or look down. Staring him down could be construed as either courage or insult, just as looking down could be seen as proof of guilt. She looked up, meeting the man's bemused gaze.

"I see," said General Campbell as if he didn't see at all. He leaned back in his chair, studying Abbie. "Is it true? Were you spying?" His voice was soft and friendly, almost sympathetic, giving Abbie a tiny bit of hope.

"No, sir. I was just curious, that's all. It's a very dull job cleaning rooms, so I occasionally snoop to make things more interesting. I have no ties to the rebels, sir." The general looked at Abbie with something akin to pity.

"I might have been inclined to believe you had you not been caught copying the documents. Boredom only goes so far. You obviously had a greater purpose to your snooping. Do you deny it?" General Campbell asked.

"I do, sir."

"I expect you would." Sighing, the general shook his head in dismay. "You're a patriotic lot, I'll give you that. As distasteful as I find it, I must order you to be executed by hanging. That's the penalty for spying. Do you have anything to add?"

"Do I not get a trial?" Abbie asked, desperate for another chance to state her case.

"I'm afraid this was your trial, young lady. You've been caught in the act of copying vital documents. The major has concrete proof, written in your own hand." The general stabbed his finger into the map to support his argument. "There's nothing more to be said. If there's something you'd like to add, you may do so now, otherwise it's the gallows for you."

He looked up at Abbie, as if expecting her to suddenly produce some proof that this was all a lie and she hadn't been caught copying the map, but Abbie had nothing more to say in her defense. She felt as if a great chasm opened up beneath her, ready to swallow her in a sea of blackness. Bright spots appeared before her eyes as all sound faded, leaving a strange buzzing in her ears. She felt weightless as she crumpled to the floor.

THIRTY-SEVEN

The room was upholstered in pale-blue silk, well-proportioned and elegant, with high ceilings that gave the impression of air and space. Sunlight spilled through the tall windows, casting squares of light onto the carpet covering the wooden floor, and a carriage clock ticked loudly on a marble mantel. The silk of the sofa felt cool against Abbie's cheek as she came to, enjoying a few blissful moments before her mind turned to the fearful sentence. She was to hang. The room spun again, but she managed to hang on just as smelling salts were shoved under her nose. A beautifully dressed woman sat down on the sofa next to Abbie, putting a cool compress on her head.

"I'm Camille Campbell, the general's wife. Are you all right, my dear?" She looked as if she were about to cry as she smoothed back a strand of Abbie's hair. "You poor girl. I can't imagine what you must be feeling right now. I tried to intervene on your behalf, but the general won't be swayed. I'm so sorry. Is there anything I can do?"

Abbie was about to say that she needed to get a message to her husband when she realized that Finn had either been arrested or managed to avoid capture. "My husband..." she whispered.

"Your husband got away. I hope that brings you comfort, although I'm sure he got you into this, didn't he? A lovely girl like yourself wouldn't be spying for any other reason than to please a man."

Camille Campbell looked like the type of woman whose entire existence was dedicated to pleasing a man, so Abbie kept her counsel. She had been about to tell her that she wasn't some feebleminded female who could be induced to spy simply to please her husband, but what was the point? The woman was only trying to be kind in a situation where she didn't need to be. Abbie shook her head in misery, tears running down her face.

"I'm pregnant," she whispered. "They will kill my baby." She hadn't meant to tell anyone, but the woman's sympathy made her feel sorry for herself and the child who would never be born, thanks to her foolishness.

"How far along are you dear?" Camille wiped a tear from her lovely face, her eyes full of compassion.

"About two months."

"That's a shame. If you were further along, they might commute your sentence until the babe was born, but not at two months. I'm afraid it won't sway them. I will talk to my husband though. Maybe there's something I can do." Mrs. Campbell rose from the sofa, her gaze still on Abbie.

"Why are you helping me?" Abbie asked, confused. This woman was the wife of a British general, yet she was carrying on as if spying for the Revolution was just a minor offense, like breaking a vase or forgetting to change the linens. Did she not understand what Abbie was accused of?

"You are just a slip of a girl, no older than my own daughter. Women do crazy things for the men they love, but I don't think they should hang for it, especially if they're with child. You are hardly a danger to the monarchy."

With that, Camille Campbell floated out the door, leaving Abbie to face the harsh reality of her sentence. A maid offered her a cup of water, but Abbie's hands shook so badly she couldn't hold it without spilling the water all over her bodice. The cup fell to the floor as Abbie doubled over, her face distorted by the silent cry that tore from her, tears streaming down her face. She would die soon, and in a very brutal way. Abbie gulped mouthfuls of air as if the rope was already around her neck, choking the breath out of her body, then tore off her tucker, feeling as if she were suffocating and desperate to breathe. Good God, was she really to die at eighteen with a new life just beginning to grow in her womb?

Abbie didn't even notice when Camille Campbell came back into the room, followed by two soldiers. "I'm so sorry, dear. I tried." She looked away as the soldiers picked up Abbie under the arms and dragged her toward the door.

"Where are you taking me?" Abbie cried, terrified the sentence would be carried out immediately.

"You will be held in a cell until tomorrow morning when you will be taken to the place of execution," one of the soldiers replied. Abbie could see the compassion in his face, while the other shoved her roughly out the front door and into yard.

"She's a spy, Diggory. Save your compassion for someone who deserves it."

The man spit on the ground in front of her before marching her around the side of the house and toward a structure at the back. He used the butt of his musket to push Abbie inside before locking the door, the metal padlock clanking against the wooden door like clumps of dirt hitting a coffin. The room was small and dim, with a bench along one side and a bucket in the corner. Abbie sank onto the bench, her hands folded in her lap. There was nothing left to do but pray.

THIRTY-EIGHT

Finn watched in dismay as Major Weland trotted away from the house, Abbie seated before him, looking terrified. Her back was rigid in an effort not to lean against the major, her gaze bewildered. Finn was on his way back to the house when he noticed Captain Gordon leading the major's horse from the stables, glancing around nervously as if he expected to be ambushed. It was unusual for Captain Gordon to saddle the horse himself, and even more so to look so worried, so Finn stopped to watch. If only he could talk to Libby, but she was nowhere to be seen. Maybe she was hanging out the wash. Finn left the sacks of oats behind a bush and doubled back. He'd approach the house from the back and see if he could catch Libby at her work. It took him a few minutes to get to his vantage point, but it felt like an hour, his mind teeming with unanswered questions. Where had the major taken Abbie and why? What was happening?

Libby wasn't in the garden. She was likely still laundering since she was on her own today and the daily laundry took several hours to complete, even with Abbie's help. Going inside was risky, but Finn had to try. He needed to know what happened and Libby was the only person in a position to tell him. If Abbie had been arrested, it would be only logical to assume that Finn would be next, so he had to be extra careful not to get caught. Whatever happened, he was Abbie's only hope, and if he were caught, there'd be no one to get word to Sam. Finn vaulted over the low fence and made his way quietly to the open door. Mrs. Cromwell went marketing at this time, so Libby should be alone, but under the circumstances, he couldn't be sure. Major Weland might have left men to guard the premises, making sure Finn didn't get away.

The laundry room was in the cellar and smelled of soap, ammonia, and hot steam, the heat enveloping him as soon as he crossed the threshold. Libby was standing by the steaming copper tub, red in the face as she pulled garments out with a long wooden stick. She would put them through the mangle to squeeze out the water before finally taking them outside to hang in the fresh air. Libby's hands were red as a lobster from the hot water, her forehead beaded with drops of sweat from the effort it took to get the clothes out. The wet garments were heavy and hot, making it awkward to lift them without getting boiling water all over yourself. Normally, Libby sang while she worked, but today she was silent, her lips compressed into a thin line. She nearly jumped out of her skin when Finn whispered her name, spinning around and splashing Finn with scalding water.

"Get yourself away from here quick as you can. The major caught Abbie in his room copying some map. He arrested her for spying and bid Captains Gordon and Mara to arrest you as soon as you came back. Now go. Abbie wouldn't want you to be taken. The Dragon Lady is on the lookout for you as well."

"Thanks, Libby. Where'd they take her?"

"General Campbell's. She looked so scared," Libby said, her eyes filling with tears. "Get her back, Finn."

"I will. Don't tell Mrs. Cromwell you've seen me."

"As if I would." Libby looked indignant that he would even suggest such a thing. "Go with God, Finn."

Finn felt as if his heart might explode. It was so much worse than he could have imagined. If the major took her to the general's house, he meant to see Abbie persecuted. If she couldn't talk her way out of it, the sentence was death. *Oh, Dear God, Abbie, what were you doing?* What would have made the major arrest Abbie? They'd agreed that she would just look at the papers and put them away if she heard anyone coming. Even if they caught her snooping, they'd have no reason to believe she was actually spying and not just being nosy.

Finn was just about to step out into the yard when he saw Captain Gordon. He stood with his back to the house, surveying the fence and the alley behind it. Finn stepped behind a cabinet, hoping the man would go back in, but Captain Gordon seemed in no hurry to leave. The captains must have decided to split up, with one guarding the front and the other guarding the rear of the building. The captain was armed, his musket in his hands and surely loaded. He wouldn't hesitate to use it, so Finn's only chance was the element of surprise.

Captain Gordon kept gazing out over the fence, never suspecting that Finn was right behind him, which was to his advantage. Finn quietly stepped from his hiding place and looked around for something he could use as a weapon. Most tools were kept in the stables, but there had to be something he could use. His eyes lit on a shovel propped up against the wall. He'd used it when Mrs. Cromwell asked him to dig a new privy and fill in the old one. He could still remember the stench that clung to his clothes and burned his nose until tears ran down his cheeks.

Reaching for the shovel, Finn weighed it in his hands. It would do. He didn't want to kill the man, just knock him out so he could make his escape. Finn sighed, wishing there was another way. Captain Gordon was only a year or two older than Finn, with a young wife and a newborn baby back in England. He was a nice fellow, always ready with a smile, courteous, and polite. He often chatted to Finn while Finn saddled his horse, telling him amusing anecdotes about the regiment and his commanding officer, who sounded like a real horse's ass. Under different circumstances, they might have been great friends, but this war set them on opposite sides, pitting them against each other against their will.

Finn wrapped his hands around the handle, holding it at the ready as he stepped into the yard. The captain was still looking the other way, his left hand shielding his eyes from the sun as his right gripped the musket. Finn stepped behind the captain just as the man started to turn around. Finn hadn't wanted to hit him in the face, but he had no choice. Captain Gordon had seen him, his mouth opening in shock as he raised his musket, ready to fire. Finn swung the shovel and brought it across the man's temple. Captain Gordon went down like a sack of potatoes, crumpling to the ground in a heap of red tunic and white trousers, his wig stained with blood. Finn didn't stay long enough to see if he'd killed the man. He dropped the shovel next to the captain and made for the fence, jumping over and running down the alley before Captain Mara could come after him. He prayed Captain Gordon wasn't dead, just unconscious, and Captain Mara would find him in time to get help.

Finn needed to put as much distance as possible between himself and the boarding house. There was only one place to go, so he raced in the direction of the brothel, having no idea what to do once he got there. All he knew was that he had to get to Sam.

THIRTY-NINE

The brothel didn't look any different during the day than it had at night. All the windows were shuttered, even though it was nearly noon. Finn's banging went unanswered for a painfully long time. He was just about to try the back door when the thug who manned the door finally opened it a crack, looking at Finn as if he were daft.

"What'ye want here? Can't ye see we're closed? Come back after dark." He was about to slam the door shut, but Finn pushed his way in, taking the sleepy man by surprise.

"I need to see Diana right now. It's urgent."

"Or what? Yer cock will explode?" The man laughed at his own wit, sounding like a creaky door.

"Now," Finn hissed, giving the man a look that implied that a lot more than his cock would explode if he didn't call Diana. The man wasn't intimidated by Finn, just annoyed to be disturbed so early in the day. He'd probably been sleeping when Finn's banging woke him up. His clothes looked grubby and rumpled, and his face was covered with a day-old growth of beard, making him look even more disheveled. He squinted at Finn, taking his measure.

"All right, all right. Wait here."

The man lumbered away, leaving Finn in the darkened hallway. He could smell the aroma of coffee coming from somewhere down the hall and the smell of frying bacon and fresh bread. The girls were probably sitting down to breakfast having just woken up after a night of earning their keep. Normally, the smell of bacon would have made Finn hungry, even if he'd just eaten, but it made him sick to his stomach, bile rising in his throat and threatening to choke him. He tried not to think of what Abbie must be going through at that very moment and concentrate on coming up with a plan. He was Abbie's only hope, especially if Sam had left New York as he'd implied he might.

"John, what are you doing here?" Diana came floating down the stairs, her wrap barely covering her bare breasts and long legs. She pulled the wrap tighter around herself, covering her nakedness and pushing her long, red hair out of her eyes. "I was asleep when Bill woke me. He said it was urgent. Now what could be so urgent before noon?" she asked with a forced giggle, her eyes worried as she studied Finn's anxious face.

"I need to talk to Sa— Patrick. It's an emergency. Where is he?"

Diana gave him a once-over, suddenly looking very awake. "It's your wife, isn't it?"

"Yes," Finn whispered. "Now, where is he?"

"I don't know, and that's the honest truth. I only know he left Manhattan for a while because of some scuffle he got into with a British officer."

Diana took Finn by the arm and dragged him upstairs to her room. He followed obediently, since this would be the last place anyone would come looking for him. If Sam couldn't be located, he'd need to rescue Abbie on his own.

"Listen," Diana whispered, "I need to run out for a little

while. I know of someone who might know where Patrick is, but you need to stay here and wait for me. I'll tell Mabel that I have a personal errand to run and lock you in here, so no one comes in. Just try to sleep or something. You need to be very quiet, since this room is directly above the kitchens. Do you understand?"

Finn nodded, sitting down on the bed as Diana got dressed. She pulled off her wrapper, standing completely naked with her back to Finn. He could see her reflection in the mirror, her full breasts and flat stomach clearly visible. He wondered if she'd done that on purpose. She was probably so used to men seeing her unclothed she hardly noticed anymore. Diana quickly pulled on a chemise, stockings, and stays before stepping into a skirt and tying it at the back, then putting on the bodice. She hastily pinned up her hair, then jammed a straw bonnet decorated with silk flowers onto her head. She almost looked like a lady as she put a finger to her lips and disappeared through the door, the key turning smoothly as she locked Finn in.

Finn reclined on the bed, breathing deeply in an effort not to panic. He had no time to waste, but he desperately needed help. If Diana didn't come back within a half hour, he'd climb out the window. And do what? he asked himself. He had no idea. If he went to the general's house, he would be arrested immediately, so that was out of the question. Going back to the boarding house to get his hatchet was paramount to suicide, but he needed a weapon. He supposed he could get Diana to pilfer a knife from the kitchen but that wouldn't be very useful against a loaded musket. Besides, what chance did he have against several well-armed British soldiers? He needed a cunning plan, one that would give him an advantage and an element of surprise. That was the only way he would have any chance in hell of saving Abbie.

Finn sat bolt upright as an idea suddenly popped into his

head. Yes, it just might work, but it would take more than one man. He prayed Diana would be able to locate Sam, since he was the only person Finn would trust to help him, and who'd be just crazy enough to pull it off. Finn suddenly felt very alone and isolated, reminding him of his first few days in the eighteenth century. If only Mr. Mallory or even Jonah were nearby to turn to for help. If Diana couldn't find Sam, he'd be completely on his own and Abbie would most likely be doomed.

Finn thought of his father and what he must have felt when he discovered his brother was in the Tower. He must have entertained thoughts of a rescue until he realized there was nothing he could do other than try to spare his brother a horrible death. What if he couldn't save Abbie? What if he had to watch her die, gasping as the last bit of air left her body, her thrashing stilling as she slowly suffocated? He'd never gone to a hanging, but he'd seen the crowds dispersing, ready for a cool drink after the spectacle.

Finn curled into a ball, trying to hold in his fear and misery. A sob escaped his lips, forging the way for another and another. Finn covered his face with his hands, desperate to stifle the sobs that were coming fast now, tears flowing down his cheeks. It was all his fault. He'd been a reckless fool and now Abbie would pay the price. She hadn't bled in August, but he barely noticed, intent on seeing them settled at the boarding house without arousing suspicion.

Abbie was normally a strong girl, accustomed to hard work, but she was feeling faint by the end of the day, eager to rip off her confining clothes and lie down, fanning herself with anything that was to hand. She was irritable and unusually emotional, which he attributed to her fear at being behind enemy lines. He now realized she hadn't bled since they left Virginia. How could he have been so blind? She was pregnant, and he'd ignored all the signs, putting her in danger. He should have made the decision to leave a fortnight ago, but he was too intent on his mission, paying no attention to his wife, who would now die because of his carelessness.

Finn forced himself to calm down. He needed to think clearly. Getting hysterical wouldn't save Abbie. He had to focus on his plan and work out all the details before presenting it to Sam. It had to work. It simply had to. Even if Diana didn't find Sam, he'd have to try it on his own. He would be at a disadvantage, but at least he'd have a better chance than just charging in with a weapon and hoping for the best.

There was no clock in the room, but the minutes seemed to crawl by at glacial speed as the sun reached its zenith in the cloudless sky. He was getting restless, needing to do something, anything, but he had to wait a little bit longer. If Diana hadn't been able to locate Sam, she would have come back right away, Finn reasoned in a desperate attempt to justify her long absence. Oh, what was taking her so long?

He nearly jumped out of his skin when the key finally turned in the lock, the door slowly opening to admit a flushed Diana. She breathed out a sigh of relief when she saw Finn on the bed, tossing her reticule onto a dressing table and taking off her hat before sitting down on the bed next to him and pulling a piece of paper out of her bodice.

"Sorry it took so long. It seems Patrick returned a few days ago, but no one knew exactly where to find him, except Maury Baker, who refused to tell me for fear that I would give Patrick away. Or maybe he just wanted to see how badly I wanted the information. I had to use everything I had to get him to trust me."

Finn unfolded the paper, looking down at an address. "What do you mean you had to use everything you had?" he asked, realizing what Diana just said.

"Never you mind," she replied, suddenly businesslike. "One

more won't make a difference, will it? Now, go find Patrick so it would have been worth it. Tell the woman at the house that Master Baker sent you, or she won't let you in. Patrick should be there. If he isn't, ask Mistress Morse to get a message to him. She'll know how to reach him. Now go."

Diana unlatched the door, looking left and right before allowing Finn to leave. He slipped out the door without looking back, needing to get away as quickly as possible. Finn wished he could have given her something for her trouble, but everything he had was back at the boarding house, not that a few coins would make up for Diana having to sell herself for information. He couldn't imagine what it must be like to use your body as a bargaining tool. Even as a man he would have a hard time lying with someone as part of a business arrangement. He supposed she was used to it, but he still felt sorry for her.

What had happened to her to drive her into a life of prostitution? She seemed like such a lovely girl, pretty and smart. Had there been no other way for her to survive? He'd seen the look on her face when she admitted to having lain with the man to get news of Sam and wished he could have spared her that sacrifice. As she'd said herself, one more man wouldn't make any difference, but he hated to think that she'd done it for him. He supposed some women preferred to toil long hours for little pay keeping their honor intact, while others chose the life of easy money, their virtue of little consequence. Diana didn't seem like the type of girl who'd be happy taking out chamber pots and polishing the silver. She was too saucy for that, too spirited. Finn hoped the choice had been hers and that she'd never regretted it.

He looked down at the paper, hoping the information was accurate. The address was on the Lower East Side, so it would take at least a half hour to get to his destination. Finn pulled his tricorn lower to cover his face and kept to the side streets, trying to lose himself in the midday crowds. There were so many men who looked just like him that he eventually began to relax, darting between the carts and delivery wagons to save time.

The address was near Old Slip Wharf, located on a side street that smelled of fish, tar, and refuse. The wooden houses looked as if they were slightly drunk, leaning against each other for support. Finn knocked on the door of number seventeen, holding his breath without even realizing it. What would he do if Sam had gone? He was relieved to hear someone coming. The woman who opened the door was a surprise. He wasn't sure what he'd expected of Mistress Morse, but it wasn't the young, pretty girl who looked at him from beneath sooty lashes with an expression of amusement. She couldn't be more than seventeen. Mrs. Morse folded her hands over her huge belly, eying Finn as if he were about to do something very entertaining.

"I'm looking for Patrick. It's urgent. Master Baker sent me," he added hastily.

"I see. Come in then. It was a surprise to see Patrick again, I'll tell you. I haven't seen him in nearly nine months. I'll just go get him."

She showed Finn into a parlor and made her way laboriously up the stairs. She'd said nine months. Could her baby be Sam's? Finn put the thought out of his head. Whatever Sam did in his private life was his own affair and nothing to do with the business at hand. Finn paced the small room, too anxious to sit down. He heard muffled voices coming from upstairs and then a thud as Sam's feet hit the floor. He came flying down the stairs, wearing breeches, but no stockings or shoes. Sam's dark hair was tousled, his jaw stubbled. His shirt hung out of his breeches, open at the chest, his face white with shock.

"What's wrong?" he demanded, tucking his in shirt and running a hand through his hair. "Sorry, I was asleep. Late night dicing with some British soldiers. I did pick up a tidbit or two," he added as an afterthought, his eyes taking in Finn's troubled face.

"Abbie's been arrested for spying. I don't know exactly what happened, but she's been taken to General Campbell's house. There's a warrant for my arrest as well." Finn coughed slightly to hide the tremor in his voice, not wanting Sam to think him weak and frightened.

Sam ran a hand over his jaw, lost in thought. "What do they have on her?"

"I don't know, but it must be something concrete. Libby said she was caught copying some map." Finn wanted to act now, this moment, but Sam seemed to be moving in slow motion, his mind still not fully awake.

"Sam, we need to get her out," he yelled.

"Shh, I'm Patrick here. I know we need to get her out, but we need to think this through. Campbell has a reputation for fairness, but he's very by the book. If he truly believes Abbie was spying, he will order her execution. We don't have much time, and we need a plan." Sam began pacing the room just as Mistress Morse looked in, probably wondering what the commotion was all about.

"Would your guest like some refreshment, Patrick? I can organize some bread, cheese, and ale. I was about to have some myself." Sam waved her away, his mind on rescuing Abbie. Mistress Morse took in Sam's bewildered appearance and retreated. "Let me know if you change your mind," she called over her shoulder.

"Thank you, Deborah, we will," Sam replied, turning back to Finn.

"Sam, I already have a plan, and I think it's a good one. Now listen to me. If Abbie's been sentenced to hang, they won't carry out the sentence at the general's house. They will transport her somewhere, most likely to City Hall Park. That's where they hanged Nathan Hale for treason last year, and probably a few people since. That's where the prisoner camp for American Revolutionaries is and they would want to make an example of her. Our only chance to get to her is between the general's house and the place of execution. If we fail, she dies. Can we stay here till nightfall?"

"Yes, I'm sure Deborah won't mind. What happens after nightfall?"

"You'll see."

FORTY

LONDON SEPTEMBER 1624

Louisa yelped as a hand fan slammed against her back, hurting more than something so flimsy should. "Keep your back straight and smile, girl," Aunt Maud commanded, stepping aside and allowing them to continue. Kit scowled, but didn't say anything, knowing it to be pointless. The sooner they got it right, the sooner he could escape the clutches of his relentless aunt. He would have sent her on her way long ago if it hadn't been for the promise he made to Caro before she died. Caro said that Aunt Maud was like a loaf of bread—crusty on the outside but soft and warm on the inside. He was still waiting to see the warm side.

"Those parents of yours have a lot to answer for, neglecting your education this way. There's nothing more important for a young lady than knowing how to conduct herself in public and being able to dance without looking like a milkmaid at a barn dance. Keep your shoulders back or you'll look like a hunchback."

Louisa bit back a retort as Uncle Kit skillfully took her by the waist and lifted her into the air, making a graceful turn before setting her back down. She could have asked Theo to partner her in this lesson, but she didn't wish to humiliate herself. She only knew the dances popular in Virginia, not that there had been much dancing going on. Such frivolity was frowned upon by the religious leaders of the colony and her parents never took the time to teach her the modern dances since they didn't know them themselves. There had been a few parties at Rosewood Manor with lots of food and music but when her mother and Aunt Louisa danced, they did it with joy and abandon, not this rigid formality that made her feel as if she had a stick up her backside. Another smack of the fan brought her out of her reverie as she missed a step and fell into Uncle Kit's arms.

"I'm hopeless," she complained, looking up at a laughing Kit.

"Let your partner lead you and try not to let your tension show. Just follow and smile."

"What are you telling her?" Aunt Maud interrupted. "If she looks relaxed and smiles too much, she will appear to have lax morals, like most women of your generation," she scolded, tapping her fan against her voluminous skirt.

"Then she'll fit right in. Now, if you will excuse me Aunt Maud, I'm expected at Whitehall. I think your pupil is ready for her grand entrance."

"Hmm, that's doubtful, but we don't have much time. Will you be presenting her to at court tonight?" she asked.

"Yes. His Majesty has permitted me to invite Louisa to court. I will return for you and your aunt before six. Please be ready." Kit was already halfway out the door, eager to escape the forced dance lesson.

"I will, Uncle Kit," Louisa called after him, giddy with anticipation. Theo wouldn't be there tonight, having gone to visit Walter on some urgent business, but Louisa was still excited to go. Being introduced at court was beyond the wildest dreams of a girl who grew up on a tobacco plantation in

Virginia. Her breath caught in her throat as she imagined standing in front of the king, but then she reminded herself that Uncle Kit and Aunt Louisa would be with her, and all she had to do was follow their lead. She would be all right. She was no country bumpkin, no matter what that awful woman said. If only she wouldn't accompany them tonight.

Louisa finally escaped, running to her room before she could encounter anyone, especially Genevieve, who floated through the house like a ghost, unsure what to do with herself since Louisa's parents had left for France. Louisa wanted to rest so she could look her best when she was presented tonight, wearing the beautiful new gown that had been ordered especially for this occasion. She wished Theo could see her in it, but then he preferred her without her gowns, she thought, giggling. He'd been shy with her the first few times, but their relationship had progressed over the past few weeks, going from a budding romance to full-blown passion. Theo had taken her for a drive through London as soon as she came back to town. Making love in the carriage had been uncomfortable and risky, and they couldn't go to Kit's or Robin's house for fear of getting caught.

Louisa had to admit that the thought of being discovered was somewhat exciting, but she didn't want to ruin her chances of a respectable marriage. Theo was devoted to her, but things could still go wrong, and she didn't want Uncle Kit to know that she'd been spreading her legs for a man she wasn't married to. Louisa talked Theo into renting a room at a lodging house where they could be alone. All she had to do was make sure her face was sufficiently covered so that no one would recognize her and tattle on her to Lord Sheridan. No one cared if a young man kept a mistress, but Louisa's reputation needed to be preserved.

Louisa stretched out on her bed and smiled as she remembered lying in Theo's arms the day before. He was passionate but gentle, worshipping her body as if she were a goddess and he her faithful servant. Louisa's body tingled with the memory of Theo inside her, bringing her to heights of pleasure she'd only dreamed of before she discarded her maidenhood the night of the storm. She hoped Theo come back soon; she was aching for him to make love to her again. If only they were married.

Theo had finally spoken to her father before her parents left for France, asking for her hand in marriage. Louisa thought his brother Robin had some objection to their union, but Theo assured her that Robin supported the marriage, as would Walter, once he told him the news. Louisa longed to tell the world of her betrothal, but her father had been reluctant to make the news public. He said that he was in favor of the marriage but wanted Louisa and Theo to take the time until her parents returned from France to get to know each other better and allow their feelings to grow.

Of course, her naive father had no way of knowing that she was already lying with her intended, not willing to wait for her wedding night like a whimpering little virgin. Thinking of her father made her feel guilty, so she pushed the thought away, knowing how angry he'd be if he learned of her disgrace. He was such a dear that she couldn't bring herself to disappoint him, or her mother. They'd been so fragile since losing Finn that she wanted nothing more than to see them rejoice in her good fortune. So, she and Theo would wait. Her parents would hopefully be back before the first snow and then they would be married, her future as Lady Carew finally assured.

FORTY-ONE

"Close your mouth and stop gawking," Aunt Maud hissed from somewhere behind her as Louisa passed through several well-appointed rooms on the way to the king's reception chamber. She had been in a state of nervous excitement ever since the carriage drew up to Whitehall Palace and uniformed guards admitted them, their weapons held at the ready should anything untoward occur. Louisa tried not to stare as she followed her aunt and uncle through the palace, taking in the breathtaking splendor of her surroundings. She'd never seen such finery before—or such excess.

The palace was ablaze with candlelight, the flames reflected in gilded mirrors, suits of armor, and frames of the paintings covering the walls. Heavy brocade curtains hung at every window, the fabric worked in whimsical patterns of gold and silver thread. Countless candelabras made of silver stood on every surface, filling the rooms with brilliant light. Louisa glimpsed the supper table as they passed the dining room, the table as long as their entire house in Virginia, set with gold-plated dishes and ornate goblets for every guest.

Louisa straightened her shoulders and held her head high as

they finally reached the reception hall. Dozens of magnificently dressed men and women milled around, talking and laughing as they waited for His Majesty King James, to make his entrance. The women strutted like peacocks, their gowns made of silk and satin, the colors glowing and shifting in the light of the candles. Their jewels were breathtaking. Louisa hoped that once she married Theo, she would have such finery and not be forced to wear Aunt Lou's castoffs. She'd lent Louisa a necklace and earbobs made of rubies and gold, but they were embarrassingly dainty compared to what some of the ladies were wearing.

Louisa noted the powdered faces and rouged cheeks of the ladies and wished she'd had the foresight to do the same, but Aunt Lou hadn't painted her face, so she probably wouldn't have allowed her to do it anyway. Some ladies looked ravishing with their cherry-red lips and rosy cheeks, but some, especially the older women, just looked like painted corpses, their faces unnaturally white against the bright hue of the rouge. Aunt Maud was one of those, her waxy features coated in white powder and her cheeks as pink as those of a young maid in love. She kept a watchful eye on Louisa as she circulated the room, chatting with old acquaintances and exchanging bits of gossip and flattery.

Most men wore dark, curly wigs, their tresses hanging down their back like dead poodles. Louisa remembered Finn making fun of the style and felt a piercing sadness at the thought of her brother. How she wished he could be with her tonight to gossip and laugh with after they got home. Instead, he lay rotting in some unmarked grave, his young life cut short by savages. Had he even known what it was like to be with a woman before he died? Finn had been fond of Minnie, but Louisa didn't think their relationship ever went further than friendship. Finn would never have pushed Minnie into something she didn't want to do. He was honorable, like their father, a man of his word. Louisa sighed, forcing herself to put Finn out of her mind. He was gone forever and now her parents were in France, so far away from her at a time when she needed them by her side.

She was safe with Uncle Kit and Aunt Lou, but she felt strangely alone and insecure, thrust into a world she didn't fully understand. She watched as her aunt and uncle exchanged greetings and comments with other couples, circulating around the room in the endless dance of the courtier. Her aunt was smiling and nodding as some woman told her something behind a fan, giggling prettily. Aunt Lou laughed along, but Louisa knew her well enough to see the tension in her shoulders and the faraway look in her eyes. She'd rather be anywhere but here, away from all this forced gaiety and speculation.

Uncle Kit bowed to a handsome man who was dressed in a gorgeous suit of burgundy velvet, a large diamond glittering on his left hand. The man moved closer to Kit, taking him by the arm and whispering in his ear. His eyes never left Kit's, watching for a reaction. Uncle Kit took an involuntary step back before forcing a smile and saying something to the man that made him smile. Would this be her life once she married Theo? The thought was exciting, yet off-putting at the same time. Uncle Kit said life at court was tedious and full of peril. *What did he mean?* Louisa wondered as she continued her silent study. No one looked particularly dangerous or bored. She saw several men talking quietly in a far corner, and a woman to her right looking at another woman's husband with a suggestive smile that left her intentions quite plain.

A sudden ripple went through the crowd as everyone took their places, forced looks of rapture suddenly lighting their faces. The doors at the end of the room opened just as the royal couple were announced. His Majesty walked in with his wife on his arm, taking his seat on the dais and surveying the room. Louisa looked down like everyone else but couldn't help examining the man from beneath her lashes. He was middle-aged, with a dark curly wig like all the other men, and a tired, thin face that looked awfully pale against the dark curls. His dark eyes swept over the room, taking everything in.

James's eyes gleamed for a moment as they settled on the man in burgundy, but a look of boredom quickly settled on his unattractive face as he continued to gaze at the assembled courtiers. Louisa paid rapt attention as various people came up to greet the king at his bidding and curtsied until they nearly fell over. Soon it was their turn and she walked up to the dais woodenly, sinking into a well-practiced curtsey before the king made some comment of welcome and waved his hand summoning the next victim.

"Was it as exciting as you had hoped?" Aunt Louisa asked, smiling at her niece. She looked weary of the whole thing, probably longing to be at home with her children.

"Not really," Louisa replied truthfully. "He's just a regular man." They had adjourned to another room for the dancing, which was about to begin.

"Don't let him hear you say that," whispered Uncle Kit as he held his hand out to his wife. "Shall we?"

"If we must," Aunt Lou answered and allowed herself to be led to the dancefloor.

Louisa looked around for Aunt Maud. As long as she stayed on the other side of the room, this evening would be bearable. If only someone would invite her to dance. Couples were already performing the elaborate steps of a Baroque dance Aunt Maud had taught her last week. They all appeared to be in time as if they'd been practicing for years, but then again, they probably had. According to Kit, things didn't change much at court unless it was some new fashion, which everyone was determined to follow with feverish devotion.

Louisa wished Theo could be there. His warm smile and admiring gaze made her forget all her fears and misgivings, and she felt like a flower opening up to the sun in his company. Too bad his brother had summoned him to his estate. Theo would be back in a few days and Louisa couldn't wait to feel his arms around her and his lips on hers, full of promise and passion.

"You look even more beautiful than I remember," a voice whispered in her ear, raising gooseflesh on her arms. She whirled around, unsure she'd heard correctly, but there he was, right behind her, his eyes full of mischief. Two years had done much to change him. The golden boy she'd pined after had grown into a man who looked confident and at ease in this setting. He'd put on a little weight, no longer the thin young man she'd said goodbye to but a powerful man, dressed in a suit of dark blue velvet, his unwigged honey-blond hair framing his face and falling into his eyes. His blue eyes sparkled with merriment, enjoying her look of shocked surprise.

"Tom, how wonderful to see you. Uncle Kit hadn't mentioned you were at court."

"I don't suppose he would. We rarely see each other, and he moves in different circles," Tom said with a sly smile, his meaning unclear to Louisa. "Will you dance with me, Louisa?" he asked, holding out his hand to her and guiding her to the floor before she even agreed. He was a skilled dancer and Louisa followed his lead easily enough, trying to remember all of Aunt Maud's endless commands. She smiled prettily, held her head up, kept her shoulders back, and most of all, tried not to show Tom that she was quaking in his arms, her knees buckling at his touch and her heart pounding as it had on that afternoon behind the hedge. Had he forgotten it?

He could be married, Louisa suddenly thought, nearly missing a step. A man of his age and position would likely have found a suitable bride by now, but then again, Annabel would have mentioned it had Tom married. Or would she? She'd been so ill before they sailed for England that her brother's betrothal or marriage would not have been uppermost in her mind.

Tom put his hands on Louisa's waist, lifting her and executing a turn before setting her down and taking her hand again. His eyes never left hers as he led her around the floor, making her feel like warm honey pouring out of a jug. Louisa looked around as the dance finally ended, suddenly recalling that she was in a room full of people, two of whom were looking daggers at her.

"Tom, I must return to my aunt and uncle," she said, trying not to look at Aunt Lou's frowning face and Uncle Kit's narrowed eyes.

"I must see you again," Tom whispered in her ear. "Shall I come to you?"

Louisa lowered her eyes to the floor, giving him an imperceptible nod as he squeezed her hand before letting her go. Louisa's heart pounded in her chest as she rejoined her aunt and uncle, smiling innocently.

"How did I do, Uncle Kit? I think Aunt Maud would be proud," she prattled on, trying to distract Kit from whatever he was thinking. He nodded curtly, clearly still upset.

"Louisa, you are to stay away from Thomas Gaines, is that clear? I've given your father my word that I will keep you safe and I intend to keep it. Gaines is not to be trusted." Uncle Kit glared at Tom, who led an older woman around the floor, a satisfied smirk on his handsome face.

"Oh, Uncle Kit, it was just a dance, nothing more. He was most charming."

Louisa looked to her aunt for help, but Aunt Lou looked equally displeased, her lips pursed in a way that made her look very unattractive. Louisa sighed and looked away. What did they think she was going to do? Tom had done enough damage to her reputation in Virginia; she wasn't about to repeat the same mistake. After all, she had Theo now, and he was everything she could hope for. She wouldn't do anything to jeopardize their future together.

"Please don't worry. I've learned my lesson," she said

quietly, looking from Kit to her aunt. "I will be on my very best behavior."

Kit nodded, accepting her promise. He still looked skeptical, but allowed the subject to drop, giving Aunt Lou his arm to escort her into supper. Louisa trailed behind, her eyes scanning the room for Tom. She didn't see him until everyone was seated, but their eyes met across the table, locking in a gaze of understanding like two co-conspirators. This game was far from over.

FORTY-TWO

The note from Tom arrived the following day, asking Louisa to meet him in the garden. She wasn't sure how he planned on getting into the garden, but it didn't matter. He wanted to see her, and she wouldn't pass up the chance. She was thrumming with curiosity and excitement. What would he say to her? Surely, there was no harm in hearing him out. She wouldn't allow him any liberties though, just enjoy the game. Theo was still away, and she was bored and restless, eager for something to occupy her mind. Her father had instructed her to spend time with Genevieve, but the girl bored her to tears with her modesty and pious ways. Spending a few stolen moments with Tom would be a welcome reprieve from that silly goose who only wanted to sew or read.

Too bad she couldn't talk to Genevieve. It would have been nice to have a confidante, but Genevieve would be shocked and dismayed if she ever found out what Louisa was really up to. She had to keep her own counsel if she wanted to keep control of the situation. Genevieve just might be silly enough to tell her aunt and uncle in her misguided devotion to her newfound family. Better to keep things to herself.

Louisa instructed the maid to help her with the rose-colored gown, knowing it brought out her dark hair and golden eyes. She turned in front of the glass, examining her image. She didn't think of herself as vain, but she knew she looked fetching, especially with her cheeks glowing pink with anticipation. Tom would see her and realize what he'd lost. She hoped he would be really sorry.

Making sure the corridor was empty, Louisa slipped out of her room and skipped down the stairs. She felt unusually happy, on the verge of an adventure as she stepped outside into the garden. It wasn't large but well-tended, with lovely autumn flowers blooming in their beds and tall hedges lining the walk. Would Tom be hiding behind one of them as he had at Charlie's house?

Louisa felt the kind of thrill she hadn't felt since she tiptoed to Theo's room last month. Should she let Tom see that she was happy to see him, or should she be cold and unattainable, reminding him of what he'd done to her? In truth, it hadn't really been his fault. She'd been a willing participant in their trysts, but it was easier to blame him since she was the one who'd suffered the consequences and Tom got to escape to England and start a new life. He looked happy and comfortable in his new surroundings, whereas Louisa had been forced to endure snide comments and a lack of social opportunities thanks to Charles's indiscreet handling of the situation.

Tom was sitting on a bench at the end of the paved walkway, conveniently hidden from view by the hedges lining the path. His hair shone in the light of the sun, his smile warm and inviting as he patted the space next to him, inviting her to sit down. Louisa lowered herself onto the bench, leaving enough room between her and Tom to keep things proper.

"You look lovely, Louisa, even more beautiful than you did last night." Tom's eyes were drinking her in, his admiration obvious.

"Surely not as beautiful as some of the ladies at court," she remarked coyly, fishing for a compliment.

"The women at court would sell their last piece of finery to look as lovely as you. Your youth and beauty just accentuate their tired old faces, painted like trollops in an effort to disguise the cruel march of time they'd give anything to stop." Tom took her hand as he gazed into Louisa's upturned face.

"I've been such a fool, Louisa. I ran away to England, thinking I would find adventure and excitement, when all along the things I wanted had been right in front of me." Tom was caressing Louisa's hand gently, his thumb stroking her palm in a circular motion that made her feel slightly weak.

"You must have met many beautiful women," she replied breathlessly, wanting him to deny it.

"I have, but I never realized how common their beauty was until I saw you again. There wasn't a woman last night who didn't envy you. The king himself couldn't take his eyes off you."

The king had barely glanced at her, but Louisa wasn't about to point that out. If Tom thought she was so captivating, she wasn't about to tell him otherwise. He hadn't wanted her enough before, but maybe things could be different now. He'd changed and so had she. She was no longer a naïve little girl. She was a woman on the verge of a betrothal to a lord, and she wouldn't let him deceive her again. All she really wanted was to see the regret on his face and the longing in his eyes. That would be enough for now.

"You are very kind, Tom, and it's been such a pleasure to see you again, but I must go back before I'm missed." Louisa withdrew her hand, gazing at Tom from beneath her thick lashes. His face fell in obvious disappointment, but he wasn't ready to give up.

"Louisa, say you'll meet me again. Maybe I can take you for a drive or on a pleasure cruise on the Thames. I wager you've never been on a barge equipped with every comfort, with players to entertain us and servants to see to our every need."

"That sounds very pleasant, Tom, but my aunt and uncle would never allow me to go on my own. Shall I invite them along?" she asked playfully, enjoying Tom's discomfiture.

"Perhaps you could bring along a maid or a female relative?" he asked hopefully.

"Well, there's always Aunt Maud. I trust you two have met?" Louisa nearly burst out laughing at the look on Tom's face. He'd rather drown himself in the river than go on a cruise with Aunt Maud, but then again, so would she.

"I think Aunt Maud would ruin the mood, my sweet, don't you? Maybe a young female relative? How about your cousin, Genevieve?" Tom took her hand again, gazing into her eyes.

"How do you know about her?" Louisa asked, suddenly jealous. What if he decided to woo Genevieve instead?

"Word gets around, but it's not her I long to see; it's you. Will you come?" His eyes were full of longing as he looked at her, her hands warm in his.

"I don't think Lord Carew would approve of me meeting with you. We are about to announce our betrothal, or did you already know that too?" she asked with a coy smile. "You seem to know everything."

"All I know is that you are not married yet," replied Tom, pulling a startled Louisa into his arms and giving her a hard kiss before letting her go and disappearing behind a hedge. Louisa raised her hand to her mouth, touching her tender lips. She should be offended and upset, but instead she felt a sense of loss at the thought of not seeing Tom again. What would be the harm in meeting him one more time? She just had to keep her head, that's all.

FORTY-THREE

Kit had almost convinced himself that Buckingham had changed his mind and was willing to forget the entire episode when the summons came, inviting him to the duke's apartments for a light luncheon. Kit stared at the note as if it would burst into flames just from the intensity of his distaste, but the paper remained intact, the scribbled lines just words that when strung together had the power to destroy a man's soul. Kit sighed, bracing himself for the worst. He doubted he would get off as easily as the first time. Buckingham liked to play games, and the next move would be more strategic than the first. Kit couldn't help remembering how it felt to have George on his knees, worshipping him in a way he'd never expected. The thought of returning the favor nearly made Kit sick, but he stuffed the note into his pocket and put on a brave face. He'd survived the last encounter and he would survive this one, as long as his family was safe from the far-reaching specter of Buckingham's power.

Kit knocked on the door expecting to be admitted by a servant, but Villiers opened the door himself, smiling benignly at a bemused Kit. He was dressed much as before, informally and comfortably. A table was set for two, several covered dishes already in the center, waiting to be sampled. Villiers gestured for Kit to enter before locking the door behind him.

"I'm so glad you've decided to accept my invitation. I wasn't sure how eager you'd be to come after our last meeting, but I was hopeful." Villiers poured a cup of wine and handed it to Kit before pouring one for himself.

"Do you mean to imply that I had a choice, Your Grace?" Kit asked, watching the man.

"There's always a choice, my pet, but one must be prepared to deal with the consequences of one's decision, mustn't one?" Buckingham took a sip of wine, putting the cup back on the table and taking the untouched wine from Kit's hand.

"My man left us a cold luncheon. I think I prefer to wait, don't you?" Villiers was watching Kit as a cat watches a mouse just before it bites its head off. He was probably enjoying this little dance as much as he would enjoy what followed.

"As you wish, Your Grace," Kit replied, bracing himself for what was to come.

"Please, Christopher, I've asked you to call me George. Your Grace is so formal and inappropriate under the circumstances, unless you enjoy the act of submission to someone in a position of power. We can explore that if you like." He smiled, the humor never reaching his eyes. "Shall we?"

Villiers took Kit by the hand, leading him into the adjacent room. The bedroom was decorated much like a woman's boudoir. The bed was hung with gauzy bed curtains, their pretty pattern worked in gold thread and pastel colors. The furniture was gaudy and ornate, not the usual masculine design favored by men for their private chambers. A marble statue of a nude Roman stood in a place of prominence on a round table next to the bed. Kit couldn't help but stare, for the man in the statue had the posture of a warrior: shoulders back, head held high, and legs spread to give him better balance, his erect manhood long and thick and worked in exquisite detail. Villiers put his hand on Kit's shoulder, "Beautiful, isn't he? I like to look at him before falling asleep."

Kit looked away, unable to meet Buckingham's gaze. He didn't protest as George removed his coat and shirt, his lips fastening around Kit's nipple like a hungry babe's. The feeling was not unpleasant as long as Kit closed his eyes and tried to forget that it was a grown man suckling him and not his wife. The breeches and stockings came next, leaving him naked and vulnerable. He kept his eyes closed as Villiers continued to kiss him, his gentle hands stroking his chest and cupping his buttocks. Kit wanted nothing more than to punch the man until he was a bloody mess begging for mercy, but that was out of the question. Attacking Buckingham was like signing his own death warrant, so he willed himself to relax and remain calm.

Buckingham pushed him onto the bed, ordering him to lie on his stomach. Kit was grateful for the pillow that he could bury his face in. At least he didn't have to look the man in the eye. Buckingham pushed Kit's legs apart with his knee, cupping his bollocks as tenderly as any woman, and caressing them for a few moments as he whispered obscene things about what he was about to do in Kit's ear. Suddenly, the hand was withdrawn as Buckingham got off the bed.

"I want you to look at me, Christopher," he ordered, gently turning Kit's head to the side. He stood next to the bed, making sure Kit could see him, his head cocked to the side as he watched Kit's reaction. The man was in good shape from riding and playing games, his stomach taut and his legs and arms well-muscled. George commanded Kit to watch as he stroked himself, his lips stretched into a satisfied half-smile at Kit's discomfort.

"Are you ready for me, pet?" Buckingham whispered as he slid his finger inside Kit, lubricating him with rose-scented oil. Kit gritted his teeth, his mind screaming in protest, but he couldn't leave. Buckingham would never forgive the insult. If only he could get on the first ship back to Virginia but leaving court without express permission from the king carried its own risk, not to mention what would happen once Louisa was back in the colony. He was trapped.

Kit balled his hands into fists as Buckingham got behind him, his thighs brushing against Kit's. He gasped with pain as Buckingham penetrated him, moving slowly and rhythmically, and whispering words of love. He was glad it hurt. He wanted to feel pain for it took his mind off the terrible humiliation and feeling of helplessness. *Let it hurt like hell,* he thought. *Let it be agony, for then I can at least pretend that I'm being tortured for the sake of my family.*

The pain began to recede, replaced by a feeling of fullness and pressure. Villiers was moving faster, moaning with pleasure as he neared his climax. *Just a little longer,* Kit thought, desperate for it to be over. He felt a revolting wetness as Buckingham spilled himself inside Kit, pulling out with a sigh of contentment.

"You'll grow to like it. I enjoy lying with my wife from time to time, but there's nothing like the tightness of a man's arse. I'll let you try it next time. I prefer to be the dominant one, but I will do it for you. I want you to have the full experience. Would you like that, pet?"

Kit nodded into the pillow, not trusting himself to speak. What was he supposed to do now, make polite small talk with a man who'd just violated him in the most disgusting way possible?

"Shall we have some lunch? I'm famished." Villiers wiped himself and pulled on his breeches, not bothering with a shirt. He was watching Kit, that little smile still playing about his mouth. How Kit wished he could wipe it off with a few well-placed blows, but he hid his thoughts as he pulled on his own clothes, his hands shaking badly.

"George, would it be all right if I left? I'm afraid I can't eat just now." He prayed to be released, if only for a short time so that he could regain his composure, if not self-respect.

"You may go," George said, kissing him softly on the lips. "I know you are shaken, but say you'll come back. Please do." Kit nodded again. If he had a choice, he'd come back in order to plunge his sword in Buckingham's chest, twisting it until his tormentor was dead, but all he could do was make his escape, hoping he wouldn't see anyone on his way out.

Kit couldn't remember walking through the halls or exiting into the street, but the sound of the city finally brought him to his senses. Wagons rumbled by, the sound of wheels and neighing of horses loud in his ears. Vendors were calling out their wares as they sold anything from oranges to bunches of flowers and hot sausages. Kit leaned against the wall of a building, gulping air like a man who was suffocating. The street stunk of manure and rotting fruit, but he didn't care. It was preferable to the smell of rose oil, following him about like a miasma. He was out of that room and away from Buckingham, but he wasn't free.

Recalling the sensation of having George inside him, Kit was violently sick, his forehead covered in a cold sweat, his knees buckling under as the magnitude of what just happened to him finally crashed over him like a tidal wave that destroys everything in its path. If Louisa found out he'd never be able to face her again or muster the courage to be a proper husband to her. For the first time in his life, he wished death on another human being—a sudden, violent death.

FORTY-FOUR

The room was lost in darkness, only the distant light of a crescent moon silvering the peaceful faces of the children. Their even breathing soothed Louisa's heart as she sat between Evie's bed and Robbie's cot, reluctant to leave. They'd been asleep for some time now, their demand for another story willingly granted as Louisa recounted some of the stories of her childhood, eliminating anything that might be an anachronism, not that they'd know. Most of the fairy tales from Louisa's time hadn't even been written yet, since Hans Christian Andersen and the Grimm brothers wouldn't be born for approximately another two hundred years.

A church clock struck the hour, startling Louisa out of her reverie. She knew she should go down and join Kit in their bedroom, but she just couldn't bring herself to go just yet. He'd sworn there was no other woman, and Alec and Valerie seemed to believe him, but in her heart, Louisa knew something was terribly wrong. Kit was the same kind and loving man he'd always been, but despite the façade of calm and good humor he hadn't been himself for months. Louisa finally admitted to herself that she didn't think he was keeping a mistress. No love affair could account for the haunted look in Kit's eyes or the tension radiating from him whenever Louisa was near. It had to be something else, something serious, but she had no idea how to find out the truth. Kit smiled and reassured her that everything was well and there was no need to worry. Louisa wasn't so sure.

She found him in the library earlier, a glass of port in hand, his eyes closed, his face as pale as a marble statue. He hadn't heard her come in or he would have rearranged his features to mask the look of agony on his face. Louisa walked quietly into the room, putting her hand on Kit's shoulder. She hadn't meant to startle him, but he grabbed her wrist, nearly breaking it as he exploded out of the chair, a look of pure hatred and revulsion in his eyes. It was only when Louisa cried out in pain that he regained awareness, begging her forgiveness and pulling her into a hug that nearly crushed her ribs.

Kit's heart hammered against her breasts, his breath coming fast and hard as he tried to calm down, but no amount of questions would force him to tell her why he was so agitated. He just kissed her and held her, swearing that he would love her and protect her until the end of his days, and she might have believed him had the whiff of rose oil not overwhelmed her senses.

Louisa forced herself to get up and walk out of the peaceful sanctuary of her children's bedroom. It was time to go down and face her enigmatic husband. She suspected that he'd want to make love to her tonight and knew it would be frenzied and all-consuming, but the thought didn't arouse her as it might have done before. It just scared her further.

FORTY-FIVE

Valerie took a last bite of duck and pushed her plate away, thoroughly satisfied. The duck had been prepared with some kind of blackcurrant sauce and served with roasted potatoes, their skins browned to a crisp, the potato inside soft and flavorful. She hadn't had food this good since leaving the future. One thing hadn't changed—the French still knew how to cook. They'd been in France for a week now, but still hadn't reached their destination. The closest port to Loudun would have been St. Nazaire, but Alec couldn't find a ship heading that way on such short notice. Instead, they had to sail to Calais and then continue over land. Had Alec gone alone, he would have hired a horse from the nearest livery, but with Valerie in tow, they needed a carriage, which thankfully came with a coachman. The man was only too willing to take them where they needed to go, provided he got well paid for his trouble. Loudun was nowhere near Calais.

Despite the grim nature of their errand, Valerie was enjoying the trip. She'd never been to France in her twenty-first century life, so this was a first, and after years of living in Virginia a breath of fresh air. She spent most of her time gazing out the window, enjoying the distinctly different flavor of the country. She was charmed by the beautiful chateaux that perched on hillsides, overlooking their verdant fiefdoms. Acres of vines heavy with clusters of grapes gave way to fields ripe with wheat and barley. Peasants dotted the countryside, working in the fields. One field they passed had already been harvested, golden haystacks standing like runes beneath the cloudless blue sky. It reminded Valerie of Monet's *Haystacks* and she told Alec about it.

"Someone painted hay? How eccentric," he remarked, gazing out at the bucolic paradise. Valerie wished he could enjoy their trip more, but he was preoccupied with his thoughts and what they'd find at the convent. Secretly, Valerie didn't think they'd discover anything, but she kept that opinion to herself. Even if they came away from this with absolutely no new information regarding Rose's life and death Alec would still get some form of closure, which is what this whole thing was about anyway. She doubted that after more than twenty years anyone would even remember anything relevant. They might know the basic facts, but that would most likely be it.

"We should reach Loudun by midday tomorrow. Thank God the weather held, or it might have taken longer. I must admit that now we're almost there, I feel a little apprehensive." Alec looked at Valerie, needing her understanding.

"It's absolutely normal that you would. You are afraid to find nothing, but you are even more afraid to find something. Isn't that right?" she asked, wishing she could comfort him.

Alec nodded, glad to see she understood his reservations. "I'm not sure what I hope to find. I suppose I just want to be able to lay her to rest in my mind."

Valerie took his hand, offering silent support. She hadn't brought it up with Alec, but it was likely that Rose wasn't buried in a cemetery. Suicides were buried at crossroads and not in hallowed ground. As a Catholic, Alec knew that, but he had probably chosen not to dwell on it until he had to, since it would cause him great pain.

Drawing Alec's hand to her mouth, she kissed it tenderly. She hoped that whatever they found tomorrow wouldn't break his heart. At least he would have Genevieve to return to. Alec asked her if she'd like to accompany them, but she opted to stay in London and keep Louisa company. Valerie was worried about leaving Louisa behind, but with her imminent engagement to Theo, Alec thought it best. He hoped they'd use the time to get to know each other better before rushing to the altar. Theo seemed like a sensible young man, but Louisa had turned his head and was now in a position to manipulate him and toy with his feelings.

Valerie hoped Louisa wouldn't do anything to jeopardize their relationship. She hated the thought of leaving their daughter in England, but the rational part of her brain had to admit that it was the best place for her. Louisa's prospects in Virginia were limited and she was too hungry for life and fulfillment to enjoy spending the rest of her days in a small and puritan community such as Jamestown. Louisa would make the perfect courtier, enjoying the intrigue and politics as an actor enjoys stepping on stage and taking on the role of someone else.

Valerie sighed. Strange how different two children in the same family could be. Finn and Louisa shared a certain physical resemblance, but they were like night and day in their temperament. Despite being Finlay's son, Finn was more like Alec than Valerie could have imagined but Louisa was like neither of her parents. She was vain and selfish, always ready to sacrifice someone else's feelings for her own benefit. She would trample anyone who stood in her path and not look back. Valerie never shared these thoughts with Alec for fear of hurting him, but she was secretly disappointed in the daughter they'd raised. She prayed that Louisa wouldn't hurt Theo. Despite being older and more sophisticated, Theo was the innocent one.

FORTY-SIX

Valerie wasn't sure what she'd been expecting, but Loudun was no different from the towns they'd passed on their way from Calais. The narrow winding streets were flanked by buildings made of gray stone, fighting for space closer to the center of town. Loudon Castle could be seen in the distance, perched on a hill above the town like a stern overlord watching over his domain, and a Gothic church occupied a place of prominence in the square, its spire the tallest point of the town, reminding its citizens that God was above all. If Valerie hadn't known what year they were in, she might have thought she was in medieval France, since nothing had changed in centuries other than fashions. The common people lived much like they had in the Middle Ages, subservient to the nobility and to God.

They happened to arrive in Loudon on market day, so the streets closer to the town square were congested with traffic, wagons and people making the streets almost impassable.

"Why don't we get out and walk?" Valerie suggested. "We can meet Andre by the inn." Alec nodded, his mood growing grimmer by the minute.

Despite Alec's stormy mood, Valerie enjoyed seeing the

market. The square was choked with stalls boasting everything from fresh produce to bolts of fabric and trinkets made of silver, pewter, and bronze. Vendors called out their wares, trying to lure the customers with false promises and witty slogans. It was the modern form of advertising, and it seemed to work very well. Young girls drooled over colorful ribbons, while matrons argued over the price of fish and asked to sample the cheeses proudly displayed on a wooden counter. The smell of freshly baked bread and rolls filled the square, making Valerie's mouth water.

She pulled Alec over to a stall selling pastries, the display a feast for the senses, especially for someone who hadn't eaten in a while. Alec pulled out a coin, handing it to the vendor. "Whatever the lady wants," he said, smiling at Valerie's consternation as she tried to decide between a fruit tart with custard cream and a cream puff sprinkled with powdered sugar. Valerie finally settled on the tart and turned to Alec. "Don't you want anything?"

"No. I don't have much of an appetite just now, but you go ahead. It looks wonderful." He took her by the elbow, maneuvering her through the crowd until they emerged on the other side of the square and across from the inn. Their coach was already there, the horses being watered and fed while Andre enjoyed a tankard of ale in the taproom.

"I took the liberty of sending the trunk up to your room," he announced. "Would you care to rest, or will we be going to the convent soon?" The poor man looked tired, having been driving them for days with stops only for the night.

"Why don't you rest, Andre, and we'll walk to the convent when we're ready," suggested Alec. "It's not far and we could use the exercise after spending so many days in the carriage."

Andre seemed happy with this suggestion, ready to spend some quality time drinking and dicing with some locals seated at a table in the corner who invited him to come and join them in their game.

Alec exchanged a few words with the innkeeper, then led Valerie to their room. It was just like all the other rooms they'd stayed in: small, clean, and very French. Valerie stretched out on the bed, trying to ease the pain in her back from so many hours of sitting. It felt nice to lie down, if only for a few minutes. Alec was anxious to get going, and she was eager to get the interview over with. She wished she had better knowledge of French, but she only knew some basic phrases, which were enough to get her a meal and find the way to the privy. Alec, however, was fluent, which was a boon since few people spoke English.

Valerie reluctantly got up and went to wash her hands and face. She wished she could remain at the inn and rest for a while, since she wouldn't understand a word of what was said anyway, but Alec needed her support, so she felt she should go with him. He was pacing the room like a caged tiger, his arms folded defensively, his lips pressed into a thin line. Valerie genuinely liked Genevieve and wanted to help her, but it would have been better for all involved if she'd never shown up on their doorstep. Alec's quest could bring him nothing but pain, no matter what he found out, and he'd had enough to deal with in the past few years. He rarely spoke of Finn, but Valerie knew how deeply he missed him and longed to have his son back, especially since they'd finally come to appreciate each other as a father and son should. Alec had hoped that Finn would inherit the plantation and the ships, but ever since Finn left Alec had lost interest in running the estate, gladly passing the reins to Charles. If Louisa remained in England, it would be Charlie's Harry, not Finn, who'd inherit the estate when the time came.

"Ready?" Alec asked, eager to get going. Valerie dried her hands and adjusted her hat before following Alec out the door. They may as well get this over with.

FORTY-SEVEN

NEW YORK SEPTEMBER 1777

Abbie woke with a start, feeling disoriented and confused. She looked around the cell, suddenly remembering that this was her last night on earth. She'd fought valiantly, trying to stay awake, but she must have fallen asleep, overwhelmed by stress and fatigue. Abbie walked to the little window and peered outside. A giant moon hung above the rooftops, casting a silvery glow on everything in sight. It was round and bright, surrounded by a halo of light that almost eclipsed the meager light of the countless stars twinkling in the cloudless sky. A fresh breeze stirred the trees, bringing with it the smell of the river. Abbie inhaled deeply, her legs shaking as she tried to walk around the cell. The sun would come up in a few hours and she would be taken down for execution to the gallows at City Hall Park. They would carry out the sentence next to the camp for American prisoners, considering it a fitting place for her to die.

Abbie wrapped her arms around herself and gazed up at the heavens, begging God for mercy. If she were to die, she hoped to at least do it with some dignity and not like a sniveling little girl. She thought she could manage that until she thought of the baby and Finn, and then the tears came again. She'd known the risks when she volunteered to come with Finn to New York, but deep down, she'd never understood that she might die. It all seemed so theoretical. What possible danger would she be in working in a boarding house? She'd been so naive, and oh so careless. She wiped the tears, putting a hand on her belly.

"I'm so sorry," she whispered. "I would have loved to know you, as would your father. At least he'll never know of your existence, which will spare him pain. We'll die together, you and I, together in life and death."

Abbie sank back onto the bench, her legs no longer able to hold her up. She could see a strip of gray just beginning to appear over the horizon. The dawn was near, and so was her end. She looked at the plate in the corner. General Campbell had offered her a last meal, but she couldn't eat it. Her throat closed up at the sight of the meat and potato, making her sick. The chunk of meat lay cold and fatty next to the shriveled-up potato, their smell filling the cell. Abbie didn't want the food, but the ale wouldn't come amiss. Maybe it would dull her senses a little, if only for a short while.

She didn't resist when two soldiers came to get her. It was fully light now, the beautiful moon of last night just a memory —her last one. They walked through the gates and handed her into a cart that would take her on her last journey. Abbie looked around, trying to focus on buildings and taverns they passed, unable to accept what was about to happen. She moved her hands, trying to ease the pain of the rope cutting into her wrists. The hemp was chafing her skin, making it bleed in some places. It would take days to heal. Suddenly, Abbie realized that it didn't matter. Her wrists would never have time to heal since she'd be dead soon, the hemp of a different rope choking her until she suffocated.

She lowered her head, too proud to allow the soldiers to see her tears. She'd give anything to get a last glimpse of Finn or say goodbye to her parents. Would Finn know what happened to her? Would she at least have a proper grave or be thrown into a pit with the other prisoners, who'd died of neglect and disease? Abbie wiped her eyes with the sleeve of her dress. She'd never have done that before, but the cleanliness of her dress no longer made any difference. She pulled up her legs and laid her head on her knees, closing her eyes against the brilliant sunshine of the September morning.

The cart continued its progress down the street, the two soldiers making casual conversation to pass the time. One was driving the cart, the other was seated across from Abbie, his musket across his thighs. He barely glanced at her as he recounted a story about a brawl in a tavern a few nights ago to the great amusement of the driver. It seemed that someone they both disliked got the stuffing beaten out of him and they rejoiced in their enemy's comeuppance. The soldiers were sniggering and making plans to visit the tavern next time they had leave. Abbie wished she could put her hands over her ears to tune them out, but her hands were bound, and she was forced to listen to their laughter. At least they weren't laughing at her; she couldn't have borne that, or their pity. It was best that they completely ignored her and treated her as if she were already dead. She supposed to them she was.

Abbie hardly noticed when two officers drew up alongside the cart, cantering on either side. The street was almost deserted at that time of the morning, but it wasn't uncommon to see British soldiers. New York was teeming with them. The officers called out a greeting to the soldiers, asking them where they were headed.

"Just over to City Hall Park," the driver replied in a friendly voice. "Delivering a spy to the gallows. Poor girl will die all alone. Seems her husband ran out on her, leaving her to her fate, the scoundrel."

The officers glanced over at Abbie, their tricorns pulled low over the faces, shielding them from the sun. She never bothered to look up, indifferent to their scorn. Abbie stared straight ahead, suddenly wishing to have it all over with. In an hour she'd no longer care. She'd be dead and all the suffering would be behind her. She only hoped it would be quick. She suddenly remembered someone saying that the easiest way was to have the neck instantly broken, otherwise, it could take as long as an hour to actually die. Abbie began to shake, her teeth rattling in her head at the thought of the agonizing death awaiting her.

The cart turned a corner, entering a shadowy side-street flanked by shops that had yet to open for business. It would be another hour or so before the street began to fill with traffic and the shops opened their doors, eager to welcome the maids and housewives about their daily marketing. Most folk were just getting out of bed, having breakfast and preparing for the long day ahead. The patrol continued alongside, seemingly escorting the cart to City Hall Park for lack of anything better to do.

"Maybe he didn't," one of the officers suddenly said quietly.

"Didn't what?" the driver asked, looking up at the man curiously.

"Maybe he didn't run out on her," the officer replied. Something in Abbie's mind snapped at the sound of the soldier's voice. He sounded so like Finn that tears began to flow again, her vision blurring to the point where she couldn't see anything at all. Her head snapped up as the officer suddenly jumped onto the bench of the cart, startling the driver and the horses. The horses reared, taking off at a gallop, the cart rocking from side to side. The driver tried to rein in the horses, managing to slow them down to a trot.

"What the hell are you doing?" he yelled at the officer, turning to face him, his mouth opening in shock when he saw the glint of the dagger in the officer's hand. He barely made a sound as it slid between his ribs, piercing the heart with fatal precision, his body sliding off the bench and into the dirt road like a sack of oats.

The soldier who sat with Abbie in the cart was already on his feet, musket drawn, frozen with indecision. Killing an officer was an offense punishable by death, and he had no idea what was happening. That split moment of uncertainty cost him his advantage as the second officer leapt into the cart, knocking him down. The two struggled, knocking Abbie right out of the wagon. She flew into road, landing painfully on her bound hands. The fall knocked the wind out of her, leaving her dazed, her ears ringing. Abbie's mouth and nose were full of dirt, making her cough and gasp for air as she rolled over onto her back, trying to sit up and get her bearings.

She looked around in panic, not understanding what was happening. Why were British soldiers fighting British soldiers, and what did they want with her? The cart rocked from side to side as the soldiers wrestled, evenly matched in size and strength. The horses stomped their feet, their nostrils flaring as they sensed danger. The other two horses had wandered off, grazing peacefully halfway down the street. Abbie's vision was still blurred, but she froze in terror as the officer who stabbed the driver jumped off the bench, heading toward her, knife in hand. Was he going to kill her too? She tried to scoot away from him as he got closer but her bound hands and tangle of skirts prevented her from moving more than a foot or so. He got on his knees next to her, taking her by the shoulders, but she struggled against him, screaming in fear.

"Abbie, are you all right?" Finn was shaking her by the shoulders, his face inches away from hers. "Abbie, it's me." She stared at him, still in shock, unable to comprehend what just happened while Finn sawed through the rope binding her wrists.

"Abbie, look at me." Finn took her face in his hands, forcing her to focus on his face. It took her a few moments to comprehend that he was really there and not a figment of her imagination. He pulled her close, holding her tight as she sobbed into his chest, her arms around his neck like a vice, afraid to let go.

The scuffle in the wagon seemed to be over. The guard had put up a good fight, but Sam finally managed to knock him out, using the butt of his own musket. The man lay sprawled in the bed of the wagon, his face bloody and his body limp, but still alive. Sam turned away, distracted by Abbie's screams and needing to see that she was all right.

Abbie had never been so happy to see Sam in her whole life. She tried to smile at him to reassure him that she was fine when she noticed movement behind him. The soldier had come to and was reaching for the musket Sam had carelessly left in the cart.

"Sam, behind you!" Abbie yelled. Sam spun around, but it was too late. The soldier got hold of the musket, his hands shaking with effort. Abbie watched in horror as he drove the bayonet into Sam's stomach. Sam fell to his knees, blood soaking his red tunic, his mouth open in shock as his hand went to the wound. He stared at the blood on his hands as if unable to comprehend that the blood was his own and he'd really been wounded. The soldier was still in the cart, musket pointed at Finn and Abbie as he tried to rise to his feet. Finn shoved Abbie out of the way just as the guard fired, thankfully missing them both. Finn ran toward the wagon before he had the chance to prime and load again. He wrenched the gun out of the soldier's hands, turning it on him and driving the bayonet into his chest. The man fell over the side of the wagon and hit the ground with a thud, already dead.

"Finn, help me," Sam moaned. He was on the ground next to the wagon, his hands clutching his belly. "Finn, please."

"Abbie, help me," Finn called out. "We need to get Sam in the wagon." Abbie grabbed Sam's legs while Finn grabbed him beneath the arms, lifting him into the wagon. He shrugged off his tunic and folded it beneath Sam's head then tore off both his sleeves, wadding them up and stuffing them into Sam's tunic to staunch the blood. Sam looked ashen, his eyes shut, his chest rising and falling as he gasped for breath.

"Abbie, keep pressure on his wound. We need to go, and quickly." Finn removed the driver's coat, putting it on as he took the reins, turning the cart toward Eastern Wharf and away from City Hall Park. Abbie felt as if someone suddenly poured a bucket of ice water over her head. This wasn't some dream. This was real, and Sam could die. All thoughts of her execution were forgotten as she held the wadded cloth against the wound, begging Sam to hold on.

"Finn, where are we going?" she cried, terrified.

"There's a boat waiting for us at the wharf. We'll cross to Staten Island and then go back to Jenkins farm. We need to get away from here as quickly as possible."

Finn jumped onto the bench and grabbed the reins, driving the cart down the street at breakneck speed. Several people had seen them and might raise the alarm before they had a chance to get away. Abbie noticed a curious female face in a second-floor window, the woman's hand pressed to her mouth as she took in the carnage, but she didn't care. All she cared about was getting Sam to safety. The streets were filling with traffic, making it more difficult for Finn to maneuver and forcing him to slow down. Several people stared after them, curious to see what the hurry was. Abbie breathed a sigh of relief when she finally saw the water sparkling in the sunlight. They were almost there. Just a little further.

The boat was waiting for them, a grizzled old man at the oars. He reluctantly got out and helped Finn carry Sam into the waiting boat, laying him on the bottom where he wouldn't be seen. Finn got in after Abbie, eager to leave Manhattan and the manhunt that would soon be under way.

The boat was old and weathered, hardly large enough for the four of them. Sam lay on the bottom, frighteningly still as

Abbie tried to talk to him, but he wasn't responding. His face was clammy to the touch, his lips devoid of color. The old man began to row, humming a tuneless melody as if there was nothing remotely strange about transporting a wounded man and a woman sentenced to hang. He was surprisingly strong for a man his age, his muscles bunching under his dirty shirt as he rowed steadily across the Narrows. Finn sat erect, trying to look like an officer crossing to Staten Island with his lady. The less attention they attracted the better. There weren't many boats on the water, but all it'd take was one person to notice that something wasn't quite right.

"You have my coin?" the man asked suspiciously. "Mistress Morse said you'd pay me well. Should keep me in drink for at least a week."

He grinned at the thought of spending his well-earned money at the tavern, oblivious to the bleeding young man at his feet. Finn silently handed over a few coins, his attention on Sam. Abbie tore off the hem of her chemise, wetting it and using it to wipe Sam's face. It was the color of whey, but he opened his eyes, looking up at Abbie with a slight smile.

"You just hang on, you hear me? We'll get you back to the farm and take care of you. Don't you even think of dying on me after you just saved me." Abbie wiped his face again, planting a kiss on his forehead. "Don't die on me, Sam. Please."

Finn drew her to him as she began to shake. The shock was beginning to wear off, reality setting in. They were still in danger and would continue to be until they reached Jenkins's farm. It was imperative that they dock in some remote place and then make their way on foot to the farm.

"Dock at South Beach," Sam croaked. "We should be able to walk to Dongan Hill from there. Finn, do you remember where the farm is?"

"I'll find it. Don't you worry. Just rest. How do you feel?"

"Cold," Sam whispered, his eyes closing. Finn put his arm

around Abbie as she looked at him in panic. Sam's gaze was glazed, unfocused. He seemed to be bleeding a little less, probably because he was lying down.

"We're nearly there. He'll make it, Abbie. You'll see."

Abbie leaned against Finn, closing her eyes. Her arms and legs felt like lead, and her head was pounding, the light hurting her eyes, but she couldn't afford to let herself fall apart. She'd rest later, once Sam was safely at the farm. She couldn't believe how much the situation had changed in one hour and the irony of it all.

"I thought I'd never see you again. I thought I'd die alone, and now it's Sam that's dying. Oh, Finn, how did it all go so wrong?"

Finn held her close, not knowing what to say. They'd taken a great risk, and this was the price they had to pay for saving Abbie's life.

Sam moaned as they helped him out of the boat, setting him on his feet. "Godspeed," the old man called out as he rowed away, a big grin on his face. He'd earned his money and was eager to spend it. He didn't care what happened to them now.

"Can he be trusted not to betray us?" Abbie asked.

"Yes," Sam mouthed as he nearly collapsed onto the sand. "He'll go to the gallows too if he betrays us. Finn, you have to leave me. Help me to a sheltered spot and go on. Take Abbie to the farm and come back for me with the wagon. I can't walk on my own and I don't want to hold you back. They'll be looking for her once they realize she's gone and two soldiers are dead. Keep her safe, Finn." Sam's eyes were rolling into the back of his head, his lips turning bluish.

"I'm not leaving him, Finn. I'm not," Abbie said fiercely.

"Listen to me," Finn ordered. "If you get caught, Sam's sacrifice would have been for nothing. The best thing we can do is go back to the farm and get the wagon. Mr. Jenkins and I will come back for Sam. We'll hide him over there for now. All we can do is pray that he lasts few more hours. Now help me make him comfortable."

Finn dragged Sam to a secluded spot, laying him down in the shade. He hoped he'd bleed less if lying down. He poured some water into Sam's mouth, putting the bottle within his reach should he want a drink.

"Sam, I'll be back for you very soon. Just hold on, all right? Don't give up, no matter what." Abbie looked away as Finn held Sam's head to his chest, kissing the top of his head. "You hold on."

"Just go already," Sam whispered. "I'll be here, waiting." Abbie kissed Sam, smoothing away a lock of dark hair from his clammy forehead.

"I love you." She turned away to hide her tears from her brother. "Let's go." Finn followed at a brisk pace, knowing better than to talk. She was in hell, and all he could do was return for Sam as soon as he could.

FORTY-EIGHT

FRANCE SEPTEMBER 1624

Alec felt a chill as soon as he passed through the doors of the convent. It wasn't just the cold reception he and Valerie received at the gate, but also the bone-chilling cold of a building made entirely of stone, with windows no wider than arrow slits, allowing in very little light and warmth. The sunshine of early September did not penetrate the gloom of the monastery, giving the impression of being in a tomb. The silence was so complete that it almost hurt his ears as he followed an elderly nun to the office of Mother Superior.

The nun initially refused to admit them, saying that their order was almost entirely cut off from the outside world and did not permit visitors, but he wouldn't be turned away so easily. After several minutes of arguing, the nun finally agreed to consult Mother Superior, and returned for them with a look of severe disapproval on her weathered face, her lips pursed to the point of being almost invisible. She glided down the stone hallway as if her feet didn't touch the ground, frowning at the sound of Alec's boots echoing through the dim halls.

They passed the chapel, where countless candles burned at the feet of Christ, casting eerie shadows on his face and making it appear almost lifelike. The chapel smelled of wax and wood polish, but there were no signs of life, not even nuns at prayer. What had it been like to grow up in a place like this? No wonder Genevieve was so timid and shy. Most likely, she'd never known the sound of joy or laughter, or the comfort of a loving touch.

Their guide brought them to an arched doorway at the end of the corridor and knocked lightly before turning on her heel and leaving without a word.

"Ready?" Valerie asked. She looked as if she'd rather be anywhere but there, and suddenly Alec felt the same way. Why had he come? What was he hoping to find? Whatever information lay on the other side of the door wouldn't really change anything. Nothing Mother Superior could tell him would change the fact that his sister was dead by her own hand and that her daughter was the product of an encounter that most likely led to her suicide. All he could do now was offer Genevieve the love and protection she'd lacked since the day she was born, and in that small way hope to make up for the actions of her parents. But it was too late to turn back. Alec gave Valerie a rueful smile before turning the brass handle of the door.

"Ready."

Mother Superior sat behind a carved desk, her hands steepled in front of her as if in prayer, a shaft of light illuminating her stern face. With a narrow face, serious eyes, and lips that were so colorless they blended into her pale skin, she had to be somewhere in her mid-fifties. Unlike the other sisters, who worked in the garden and tended the animals, she probably spent most of her time on administrative tasks, rarely setting foot outdoors. There was no sign of welcome as she gestured toward two high-backed chairs facing the desk.

"How can I help you?" she asked, clearly displeased by their presence.

"Reverend Mother, a few weeks ago a young woman named Genevieve came to find me in London, claiming to be the daughter of my sister, Rose Whitfield, and informing me of her death. I must admit that I was shocked to learn that my sister gave birth to an illegitimate child and then took her own life. I am here to find out what happened to Rose."

It hadn't been Alec's intention to be so blunt, but Mother Superior's frosty reception left him in little doubt that putting things in a more diplomatic way would do nothing to help their cause. She didn't look inclined to give them any more time than was strictly necessary before showing them the door.

Mother Superior took a moment to answer, studying them as if they were specimens she'd never come across. She never moved, her hands still in front of her like a shield. Alec hoped that a woman who spent her life tending to the well-being of nuns would have a little more compassion, but the woman's eyes were cold, her back rigid as she faced him and Valerie across the desk.

"Mr. Whitfield, I'm afraid I can't offer you more information than you already possess. I never knew Sister Rose. I came here from another convent after my predecessor died. I knew of her, of course, because of Genevieve. It was an unfortunate chapter in our history, if you'll pardon me saying so, but we have managed to move on." She didn't look as if she much cared if Alec pardoned her, but she was being coolly polite.

"There must be something you can add," Alec persisted. "Surely there are still sisters here who remember Rose and can tell me something of her final days."

"Mr. Whitfield, we are a closed order, so the sisters will not speak with you, nor will I permit them to. Besides, I highly doubt they remember something that happened so long ago to someone who was with us for only a short time. I will, however, give you the facts."

Mother Superior rose from her desk going to a dusty bookshelf full of identical leather-bound volumes. She ran her finger along the spines until she found what she was searching for and pulled out the volume, carrying it back to her desk and leafing through it very slowly.

"Here's what I can confirm. Rose Whitfield came to us in the autumn of the year of our Lord, 1600. She was a novice for a year before taking her vows the following autumn. In July of 1602 she gave birth to a female child in her cell. Three days later, she died by drowning herself in the river. Most likely she couldn't live with the disgrace she brought on herself and this house of God." Mother Superior closed the book with a finality that suggested she wasn't going to tell them anything else.

"Who is Genevieve's father?"

"I don't know. No one ever came forth to claim the child. I'm sorry, but I must ask you to leave now. I have duties to attend to." She rose once again, walking to the door and holding it open for them. The interview was over.

"Where is my sister buried?" Alec asked as he stopped in front of the woman, towering over her. He hadn't thought it possible to feel such animosity toward a person who dedicated herself to the service of God, but he wanted nothing more than to grab her and shake her until he could see the person beneath the cold exterior she presented to the world and maybe catch a glimpse of compassion for his poor sister and her orphaned child.

"As I'm sure you are aware, suicides are not buried in consecrated ground. Sister Rose is buried at a crossroads about two miles outside Loudun. Good day to you both. I trust you can find your way out." Mother Superior swept past them, disappearing down the hallway, her black habit billowing behind her like the sails of a ship.

"What did she say?" Valerie whispered as they left the walked out. "I only caught a few words."

"She didn't reveal anything we didn't already know," Alec

replied, taking Valerie by the arm as they walked toward the village. He was oblivious to the beauty of the day as he went over every detail of the interview.

Valerie squeezed his arm in an effort to get his attention. "Alec, I can hear you thinking from here. What's on your mind? Are you very disappointed with what she said?"

"I can't honestly say that I expected her to tell me anything more, but I was surprised by the hostility of the woman. I don't believe she told us the whole truth," he said, walking faster in his agitation. "Did you see how desperate she was to get rid of us? She knows more than she admitted to, and she's terrified that we'll find out the truth, which obviously still has the power to hurt someone."

"Do you really think so? How do we find out?" Valerie was almost running to keep up with Alec, his boots raising a cloud of dust as he strode down the dirt lane, oblivious to everything around him.

"The only thing we can do is talk to some locals, starting with the innkeeper and his wife. A nun giving birth to a bastard and drowning herself in the river is not something people forget in a hurry. It would have been a great scandal in a place like this. Someone must know something. Small towns thrive on gossip, and there's always someone who's eager to talk, especially when there's money to be made. I will offer a reward to anyone who can give me any information, then wait for them to come to me." Alec slowed down a little, taking Valerie's arm as she stumbled over a stone, nearly losing her balance.

"Are you sure you want to stir all this up again? It was over twenty years ago. Maybe it's wiser to let it rest." Valerie looked up at him, imploring him to move on. Nothing he could learn from the locals would bring him any comfort, if anything, it would raise more questions that he wouldn't be able to find answers to. Rose was dead, and nothing anyone could say would change that.

"Val, you are probably right, but I will never be able to rest if I don't at least try to find out the truth. Someone fathered that child, someone here in Loudun. Rose became pregnant after being at the convent for a year, so that greatly narrows down the number of men she might have been exposed to, rather than if she had already been pregnant by the time she arrived, so someone must know something."

"You're right, but Mother Superior said no one laid claim to the child. If the father had been a local man, surely, he knew the child was his. Most likely, he either had no way of caring for it or was a married man who didn't want his indiscretions to ruin his life. If he's managed to keep his secret this long, what makes you think he would allow it to come to light now? He must have had some way of protecting his secret."

"He could also have been someone who forced himself on a nun and didn't see fit to take responsibility for his actions. His cowardice resulted in the death of my sister and the less than happy life of his daughter," Alec replied stubbornly. "I must see this through."

FORTY-NINE

STATEN ISLAND SEPTEMBER 1777

Abbie pulled the pot from the fire, leaving it on the hook by the hearth to keep the stew warm. She'd made supper, washed her shift and stockings, swept the floor, washed last night's supper dishes, and saw to the animals. She needed to keep busy to stop herself dwelling on the fact that if it hadn't been for Finn and Sam, she would have been dead hours ago, her life cut short by the hangman's rope, her body tossed into some stinking hole full of rotting corpses. And now it was Sam who could be dead, and all because of her. She couldn't stop seeing his pale face and glazed eyes as they left him behind at South Beach, bleeding and helpless.

Abbie glanced out the window again, but Mr. Jenkins and Finn still weren't back. She stepped outside to check if her things had dried and gazed up at the sun, shielding her eyes from the still-bright rays. It was around 5 p.m., but there was no sign of the men. What was taking so long? They'd gotten to the farm around noon, Finn and Mr. Jenkins setting off as soon as Finn changed out of his uniform into plain clothes and made sure she was all right. She wasn't really, but her priority was getting Sam. He was all that mattered at that moment, and she wouldn't delay Finn by a second, knowing that it could make the difference between life and death. She had to believe that Sam's wound wasn't fatal and that she'd be able to nurse him back to health. The bayonet could have punctured some vital organ, but Abbie pushed the thought away, unable to accept the possibility. If only they would come back.

It had taken Finn and Abbie nearly two hours to walk to the farm, so by cart it should have taken less than half the time. They should have gotten to Sam by one and been back by two; no later than half past. Abbie sat on a wooden bench, leaning against the wall of the farmhouse. She was exhausted physically and mentally but couldn't allow herself to rest. She had to stay alert and ready for when they brought Sam back. She'd prepared some rags to use as bandages and even found some silk thread and needles in case Sam needed to be sewn up. She'd never done anything like that before, but she would if she had to. Mr. Jenkins didn't have much in the way of medical supplies, but there was whiskey and even a small vial of laudanum. The vial was more than half-full, enough to keep Sam sedated if necessary.

Abbie wondered what happened to Mrs. Jenkins. Her things were all over the house, her clothes in the wooden chest by the bed and a silver-backed hairbrush on the dresser in front of the small mirror mounted on the wall. A tortoiseshell comb was next to the brush, both items likely prized possessions of a woman who wasn't accustomed to luxury. Jim Jenkins hadn't mentioned his wife, and Abbie hadn't asked, not wishing to pry. He was likely a widower, who didn't have the heart to get rid of his wife's things, needing to hold on to that last bit of her just a little longer before letting her go and settling into a lonely, barren existence.

The shadows slowly began to lengthen, the air cooling

slightly as the treetops swayed soothingly above her head. Abbie could hear the animals moving restlessly in the barn and the chickens clucking about in their enclosure, but there was no sound of a wagon approaching. She took her things off the line and went back into the house to put them on. She'd washed as best she could and was nearly naked beneath her dress, unwilling to borrow something belonging to Mrs. Jenkins for fear that her husband might object.

Abbie put on the clean shift, stockings, and stays, pulled on the bodice and skirts, and brushed her hair before pinning it up and donning her cap. She felt marginally better now that she was wearing clean things, but her anxiety was increasing by the minute. It had to be around six now. What was keeping them? She bolted from the room when she heard the rumble of approaching wheels, exploding from the house just in time to see the wagon coming down the road. Thank God, she thought, running to meet it. Abbie slowed down when she saw Finn's face, unable to take another step forward. The idea of Sam being dead pierced her like a dagger straight through the heart. They must have waited for him to die before loading his body into the cart, not wanting to fill his last moments with more agony than was strictly necessary. Mr. Jenkins slowed down next to Abbie, but she was afraid to look at the bed of the wagon. She couldn't bear to see Sam dead. Tears streamed down her face as she stepped closer, forcing herself to look. It was empty, a layer of straw undisturbed and unsoiled.

"Where's Sam?" she asked, turning to Finn, her heart pounding. She tried to read Finn's face, but she couldn't comprehend what she was seeing there. He seemed nervous and afraid, but most of all apologetic.

"I don't know. He wasn't where we left him. We searched for hours, going several miles in every direction. We found no trace of him, save the blood on the grass where we laid him this morning." Finn jumped off the bench, taking Abbie into his arms. "I'm sorry, Abbie—he's gone."

"I don't understand," Abbie muttered. "Gone where?"

"Sweetheart, Sam was in no condition to go anywhere on his own. He didn't leave—someone took him."

"Oh, God," Abbie moaned as she slumped against Finn. "Why would anyone take him? Do you think they meant to help him? How will we ever find him now?"

Finn shook his head, having no answers. He'd asked himself the same questions over and over as he searched the area, desperate for any clue to Sam's whereabouts. The shady copse where they'd left Sam had been deserted, not near a road or a village. It was unlikely that someone would have come across him by accident. They'd left him well hidden. Even if someone did find him, what would be the purpose of taking Sam unless they hoped to help him? Or maybe they wanted to rob him and leave him for dead somewhere. Sam didn't have much on him, but he did have a few coins, a musket, and the brass buttons of the uniform that could be worth something. But why would someone need to take him to rob him? He was badly injured; they could just take what they wanted and leave him to his fate.

"Abbie, Jim and I will go out again first thing tomorrow morning and look for Sam. In the meantime, you need to get some rest. You look done in. Have you eaten?"

Abbie just shook her head. She tried eating some of the stew she'd made, but it stuck in her throat, tasting like ashes.

"You need to take care of yourself. Come, let me take you inside." Finn put his arm around Abbie, guiding her toward the door. "Something smells really good."

He was ravenously hungry, having had nothing to eat since last night. Deborah Morse had given him supper and a bed for the night, but Finn hadn't slept. He and Sam slipped out close to midnight, ready to put their plan into action and be in place just in time for Diana to do her bit.

Finn was exhausted, but he couldn't allow himself to rest until he knew Abbie was all right, at least physically. She needed to eat and get some rest after the terrible ordeal she'd been through. She was near collapse, her face white as a sheet and her eyes full of pain and fear. She'd come precariously close to a violent death and now her brother was missing, injured and helpless somewhere out there, at the mercy of whoever took him. Finn sighed, not wanting to think of what Sam might be going through at that very moment. Perhaps he was already dead.

After washing his hands and face, Finn sat down at the table, the events of the day crashing over him now that he had a moment to think. Jim Jenkins sat down heavily across from him, his eyes full of sorrow as he looked at Abbie, who busied herself with serving the stew and pouring ale into pewter mugs. She didn't look at either Finn or Mr. Jenkins as she set the bowls on the table, biting her lip in an effort not to cry.

"I'm so sorry, Abbie. We'll do everything we can to find Sam." Mr. Jenkins squeezed her hand as she set a bowl of stew in front of him, her hand shaking with stress and fatigue. A tear slid down Abbie's cheek and she angrily wiped it away, refusing to give in to her worst fears.

"I know you will, Jim," she replied, sitting down in front of her own bowl and staring at the contents. She was hungry, but she couldn't eat a bite, her throat closing at the mere thought of food. She dumped the stew back into the pot and left the room, curling into a fetal position on her cot.

"Where are you, Sam?" she whispered into the silence, praying that he was alive somewhere. Abbie turned to the wall, pulling the thin blanket over her head and wrapping her arms around her knees. She didn't stir as Finn lay down next to her, folding his arms around her and burying his face in her hair. He didn't say anything, just held her as she cried for Sam, her shoulders quaking with silent sobs.

"Abbie," Finn whispered, "you are alive, and we don't know that Sam is dead. Maybe some Good Samaritan helped him. Please, don't torment yourself so. I can't bear to see you like this."

"Finn," Abbie said suddenly, turning to face him. "I wouldn't have died alone today."

"Of course not; I wouldn't have let you die." He pulled her close, holding her as if she would vanish.

"That's not what I meant. Our baby would have died with me." Finn held her as tears ran down her face, soaking his shirt. "My stupidity and carelessness would have been responsible for killing our baby, and now Sam is somewhere out there, hurt and alone, because of me."

"Nothing will happen to you or our baby; I promise. I will take care of you both, now and forever."

"You don't seem surprised," Abbie said, looking up at him, her nose red from crying. "How did you know?"

"Oh, Abbie. I've been such a fool, such a blind, idiotic fool. You looked so tired and pale. You were starving half the time and sick the other half, and your flow is late. I should have realized it sooner, but I was preoccupied with getting the information out, not paying attention to you as I should have done. When I found out they'd taken you, I nearly lost my mind. I should have taken you away from here weeks ago, but I foolishly thought we were safe."

"How on earth did you get those uniforms anyway?" Abbie asked, recalling her dramatic rescue. Things happened so quickly, she hadn't had time to wonder how Finn and Sam had been able to pass for British soldiers without anyone noticing.

"Oh, that was Diana's doing," Finn said, smiling at the memory. "Seems she has a few regulars who come like clockwork. She invited two of them up to her room, for a... well, never mind, but they were only too happy to oblige. They took their time about it too, I can tell you that. Diana made sure they were soused by the time they finally came back down, and she told them their commanding officer was in the parlor, being entertained my Madame Mabel. She helpfully offered to lead them out the back way to avoid any embarrassment. They were so drunk they never even bothered to question how Diana might know who their commanding officer was. She led them into the alley where Sam and I were waiting. Don't worry, Abbie," said Finn, watching her anxious face, "We didn't kill them, just knocked them out. I think the only thing really hurt was their pride when they came to and found themselves stripped of uniforms and weapons."

"Diana is very patriotic, isn't she?" remarked Abbie with a smug grin. "Not many people would take on two men just to help a fellow rebel."

"Something tells me she enjoyed it," replied Finn, still watching Abbie intently. "And speaking of patriotic, what was it you found, Abbie?"

"I found a map for an invasion of Philadelphia. I was copying it when Major Weland caught me. It seems he forgot something and came back to retrieve it. He caught me red-handed, Finn."

"An invasion of Philadelphia? Do you remember anything you saw?"

"I remember some things. If I could have a map of Pennsylvania, I could recall where the troops were meant to be and where the Continental Army is encamped. Do you think we can still get the information out?"

"I'll ask Jim for a map. I think it's imperative that we let the Committee know, even if the information is not one hundred percent accurate. At least they will know what to expect, and they can find out the rest on their own. Do you have any idea when it's meant to happen?" Finn asked. British troops had been moving toward Pennsylvania for the past several weeks, so it must be very soon.

Abbie shook her head. "I don't know when. I only saw where the troops were stationed and where Washington's forces are expected to be. I'll look at the map just as soon as I have a little rest." Abbie's eyes were already closing, but Finn pulled her up, brushing a stray curl out of her face.

"It's got to be now, love. Jim can get the information out tonight. Come, let's see what you can remember."

Finn led Abbie into the other room and sat her down at the table. She desperately needed rest, but there was no time to lose; the British were on the move and anything they could tell the Committee might make a huge difference. Jim pulled out a map and rolled it out in front of Abbie, who stared at it, her eyes barely focusing.

"Abbie, I know you are exhausted, but you must concentrate. What did you see?" Finn put a quill in Abbie's hand, sitting down next to her. "Come now."

Abbie rubbed her eyes, trying to remember what she had seen. It seemed like years ago that she'd sat at Major Weland's desk, copying the map, but it had only been yesterday morning. She closed her eyes in an effort to envision the map and began drawing, marking the places on the map where British forces were amassing.

Jim Jenkins was already putting on his hat and coat, ready to leave with the map. Abbie didn't know where he was taking it or if it would get there in time, but she continued to draw, details coming back to her now that she was concentrating.

"That's all I can remember," she said apologetically as she handed the map back to Jim Jenkins.

"Don't you worry, Abbie. It's priceless information, and I will get it into the hands of the Committee tonight. You just get some rest. You've earned it."

Mr. Jenkins tipped his hat and disappeared into the night. Abbie tried to stand up, but her head was spinning, her legs refusing to hold her up. Finn swept her up and carried her to the bed, gently laying her down and covering her with a blanket.

"Go to sleep, love. I'll clear up and wait for Jim to return." He kissed her forehead, but Abbie was already asleep, unable to hold on any longer.

FIFTY

Finn finished tidying up the kitchen, but although he was physically exhausted, he couldn't go to sleep. The events of the day kept replaying in his mind, leaving him hunched with tension, his mind on fire. He stepped outside, sitting down on the bench and leaning back against the wall of the farmhouse. The moon was obstructed by clouds, their fluffy shapes lit up from behind and casting an eerie glow onto the world around him. The croaking of frogs and chirping of crickets filled the night with sound, making him feel slightly less alone. Finn wished he could go to bed and slip into oblivion like Abbie, but thoughts kept racing around and around in his head, keeping him awake.

Visions of Sam, lying helpless and bleeding, kept popping up in front of his eyes, making him ball his hands into fists with frustration. They shouldn't have left him, but what choice did they have? Abbie had been on the verge of collapse after her ordeal and he needed to get her to safety. Dragging an injured and bleeding Sam would have taken hours and left a trail of blood for the British to follow had they come looking for them on Staten Island. Finn loved Sam like a brother, but Abbie was his first priority, especially in her condition. He'd made a difficult choice and now the blame lay with him. Where was Sam, and was he still alive? Finn jumped to his feet, walking to the stile and leaning against it in frustration. Was there anything he could have done differently? Probably not, but it didn't make the situation any easier to bear.

And then there was Abbie. She was doing her best to keep her emotions under control, but eventually the shock would wear off and the events of the past forty-eight hours would come crashing over her. She'd come very close to dying today and her life might have been saved at the expense of Sam's. That realization was sure to wreak havoc in her mind, causing her to blame herself for something she had no control over and had no power to prevent.

Finn looked up at the overcast sky, wishing he could see the stars. Looking at the familiar constellations always helped him find balance and remember that he was just a speck in a vast Universe, his existence nothing but a fleeting moment in time, part of a greater whole that made up life on earth. He felt a pang of sadness as he thought of his parents. He missed them so much, especially at moments like this when he felt like a helpless child. What he wouldn't give to talk to his father and tell him everything, wishing he would absolve him of blame and reassure him he'd done the right thing.

Finn walked back sat down again, exhaustion rolling over him and leaving him shaking with fatigue. He had been so lucky to get Abbie back, but what if he hadn't? What if he had been unable to rescue her and prevent her execution? The thought of losing her made him shake even harder, a chasm opening up somewhere inside his guts, making him feel hollow and fragile. After all, his father had lost his young wife and newborn baby, and his mother had lost his natural father shortly after they were married. Finn suddenly understood those events in a whole new way, the magnitude of his parents' losses leaving him gutted. How had they coped with the death of people they loved? Both his parents had managed to move forward and rebuild their lives together, but what had they gone through before coming out on the other side of such devastating pain? Was it possible to ever be whole again after such tragedy?

Finn forced himself to his feet and stumbled inside, crawling into bed next to Abbie and holding her against him as if she'd vanish if he didn't hold on hard enough. He mouthed words of a prayer, thanking God for allowing Abbie and their child to live, and begging him to spare Sam. Finn was still praying when he fell into a dreamless sleep, his mind and body depleted, both physically and emotionally.

FIFTY-ONE

ENGLAND SEPTEMBER 1624

Louisa Whitfield sank into a chair, grateful to be alone. She felt lightheaded and queasy, more so after breaking her fast. Normally, she was hungry in the mornings, but lately, all she wanted was something to drink. The ale soured her stomach, so she asked the maid for a glass of milk; a request which was greeted with a look of shock. Milk was for small children, not young ladies. The milk and bread seemed to settle her stomach for the moment, but she still felt odd. Louisa closed her eyes enjoying the silence. Maybe she would go out into the garden. It was lovely outside, the heat of August having been replaced by the crisp freshness of September.

"'Isa, help me." Louisa's eyes flew open as Evie ran into the room, lugging Louisa's work basket and something white that got caught under her feet making her lose her balance. Louisa caught Evie just as she was about to fall, taking the work basket from her hands and settling her on the settee.

"What are you doing, pet? Where's your nurse?" Louisa asked, noting the guilty look on Evie's face.

"She's with Robbie. I ran away," she added proudly. "I

brought my nightdress." She held out the white fabric to Louisa, expecting her to take it.

"Whatever for?"

"I want flowers, Isa," the girl said, pushing the work basket toward Louisa.

"Ah, I see. You want me to embroider some flowers on your nightdress? What color would you like?" Evie had been enthralled with the pattern Louisa had embroidered on her own nightdress, one of flowers and vines around the bodice and hem. She hated sewing, but embroidery was something else entirely. To take a plain piece of cloth and turn it into something beautiful gave her a feeling of accomplishment and pleasure, not to mention peace.

"I want bluebells and primroses," Evie informed her. She'd obviously had time to think this through.

"All right, what about vines? Would you like those?" Louisa tried to fight a wave of nausea as she looked at her eager cousin.

"What's a vine?" Evie asked, confused. "I want some leaves."

"There you are, you little monster," Aunt Lou exclaimed as she burst into the room. "Mills is looking everywhere for you." Evie gave her mother an imperious look that nearly made Louisa laugh. "I want flowers," she announced as if that explained everything.

"I see. Well, if Louisa is willing to do it, then you shall have flowers, but you are not, and I repeat, not to run away from Mills ever again." Evie nodded, as if she couldn't understand what all the fuss was about. She'd only gone downstairs by herself, not outside. Evie turned to Louisa, waiting for her to reply.

"I'll do it, and I promise to make the flowers extra pretty for my favorite cousin." Louisa opened the basket looking for blue thread. Evie swung her legs back and forth as she peered into the basket, wanting to choose a color herself.

"That one," she exclaimed as she spotted something she liked. Louisa pulled out the skein of thread and a needle and rose to her feet. She'd need a little extra light to thread the needle since the eye was so small. Louisa walked to the window, the lightheadedness returning as soon as she stood. The room seemed to shift around her, everything dissolving as she slid to the floor, needle still in hand.

"Louisa. Louisa," her aunt called out. "Can you hear me?"

Louisa opened her eyes to see her aunt's anxious face above her own. Her limbs felt strangely heavy as if they were weighed down with something, but the dizziness had passed, and she felt better. Evie was on her knees next to her, peering into Louisa's face, her dark eyes glistening with tears. The poor child was scared, so Louisa sat up and wrapped her arms around the little girl, needing Evie's comfort as much as the child obviously needed hers. Evie wrapped her arms around Louisa's neck, her wet cheek against Louisa's, her little body trembling.

"I'm all right. I don't know what happened." She patted the floor, feeling for the needle she'd just dropped. She wouldn't want Evie to hurt herself.

"Ah, there it is," Louisa exclaimed, picking up the needle and getting up off the floor. She still had flowers to embroider.

"I'm going to summon the physician. Doctor Wells treats some of the ladies at court and has even seen Her Royal Highness when her own physician was ill. Come, let's get you to bed." Aunt Lou took the needle and stuck it into a pin cushion before taking Louisa by the arm and maneuvering her toward the door.

"Aunt Lou, I'm much better, really. I don't want to go back to bed." Louisa tried to protest, but it was pointless. Her aunt would brook no argument. She guided her past Mills, who was just coming down the stairs with Robbie, her expression one of relief that Evie had been found.

"Mills, please see to Evie. Would you like to play in the

garden, darling?" Aunt Lou asked just as Evie was about to protest that she hadn't gotten her flowers yet. She nodded reluctantly, tears filling her eyes again.

"Evie, I promise to embroider the flowers as soon as I can. You'll have your nightdress by the end of the week," Louisa called out as her aunt marched her up the stairs.

Doctor Wells was younger and more handsome than Louisa could have imagined. She expected some old man, smelling of leeches and potions, but the man who walked into her room was likely in his early thirties, with a pleasant smile and warm gray eyes that made her feel slightly more at ease. She was secretly glad Aunt Lou had summoned him. She hadn't been feeling well for about two weeks now and was beginning to worry. Her monthly flow had come on time, so at least that wasn't a concern.

Aunt Lou took a seat by the window, refusing to leave while the doctor examined her. It was reassuring to have her aunt in the room. She didn't like being prodded by a stranger, no matter how pleasant and handsome he happened to be. The doctor started with her head, looking at her eyes, throat and ears, and feeling her forehead for any signs of a fever. He seemed satisfied because he moved down to her chest. Dr. Wells used a wooden tube to listen to her heart and lungs before palpating her stomach gently with his hands, a look of concern on his face.

"Lady Sheridan, do I have your permission to examine your niece further?" he asked, giving her aunt a meaningful look.

"Is that really necessary, Doctor?"

"I'm afraid so. I need to be certain." Aunt Louisa nodded miserably, turning away to look out the window while the doctor continued his examination. He pushed Louisa's shift over her thighs, making sure that she was still decently covered.

"Now, don't be frightened, Louisa. This might hurt a little, but it will be quick. I promise." The doctor's voice was soft and calming, helping Louisa to relax. She didn't like the idea of being so exposed, but he was a physician after all, and she didn't have anything he hadn't seen before. She forced herself to relax, tensing a little as the doctor pushed her legs apart, sliding his fingers inside her and feeling around. She had no idea doctors did such things.

"Try to relax, Louisa," the doctor said kindly as he continued his exploration. He pressed on her stomach in several places before removing his hand and turning to her aunt.

"She's with child, Lady Sheridan."

"Are you sure?" her aunt choked out. "How far along?"

"I can't be sure at such an early stage."

"But I had my flow not two weeks ago," protested Louisa. "You must be mistaken, Doctor." It had been such a relief. Getting with child before the wedding had not been part of her plan.

"Some women do get their menses during the early stages of pregnancy. I've seen it happen. I have no doubt that you are expecting, young lady." Louisa turned away toward the wall, unable to face the doctor or her aunt. What would her parents say? And Uncle Kit? With her parents gone, he would be the one to decide on a course of action. Louisa wiped away the tears as her aunt walked the doctor out and then returned, sitting on the side of the bed.

"I will speak to Kit and we will make arrangements to have you married as soon as possible. I'm sure Theo will not object. He's besotted with you. It will be all right, Louisa. I only wish your parents were here. This is the second time something's happened on my watch," she said miserably. She took Louisa's hand. "Louisa, look at me."

"I can't," Louisa mumbled. Her aunt had no idea how miserable and scared she was.

"It will be all right. I promise. It's not an ideal situation, but Theo loves you, and no one has to know." Aunt Louisa stroked her hair, trying to soothe and comfort her, which made Louisa feel even worse. Her aunt was so loving and trusting. She had no idea how wicked she'd been, and now she was being punished for her sins.

"You don't understand, Aunt Lou. It's not as simple as you think," Louisa sobbed, burying her face in her aunt's shoulder. "I don't know if the baby is Theo's."

Louisa felt her aunt stiffen as she absorbed the words. She took Louisa by the shoulders and held her away from herself, their faces only inches apart. All sympathy was gone from her aunt's eyes, replaced by shock and disgust.

"Who else have you been with, girl?"

"Thomas Gaines," Louisa whispered as her aunt let go of her shoulders and walked out of the room, slamming the door behind her.

FIFTY-TWO

Louisa curled into a ball, bringing her knees up against her flat stomach. She shouldn't have blurted out the truth to Aunt Louisa, but the doctor caught her off-guard with the news. She had been so sure that she wasn't with child. Of course, it had always been a possibility. She had been with Theo several times since leaving Willowbrook, and then there was Tom. She never meant for it to happen, had never meant for things to go that far, but she knew they would before she even entered Tom's lodgings in Blackfriars, her face covered by her hood should anyone recognize her.

She'd lied to everyone, but most of all to herself. She'd wanted Tom all along and known that she'd never be satisfied until she had his love—only it wasn't love he was offering. He'd changed since she'd known him in Virginia, going from a spoiled, selfish boy to a hard, cunning man who saw right through her. The irony was that Tom understood her better than she understood herself, seeing through the façade of a refined young lady to the dark parts of herself that she refused to acknowledge, even in private.

Louisa thought Tom would romance her and make promises

of love, but he never bothered with all that once she agreed to come to his lodgings. He pushed her up against the wall as soon as she walked in, kissing her hard and sliding his hand between her legs, stroking her until she was shaking with desire, desperate to be his, but Tom wasn't quite ready to give her what she'd come for. This was a game and it would be played by his rules, not hers. She'd nearly ruined his life the last time they played, and he hadn't forgotten that.

"Take that dress off unless you want me to rip it off you," Tom ordered, removing his own clothes, his eyes never leaving hers. Louisa undressed slowly, leaving only her stockings. They were a pale-blue silk tied with bows mid-thigh and they brought attention to her slim, shapely legs, the bows drawing the eye to the dark triangle between her thighs. She wanted him to look at her and hunger for her, but Tom was past that. He was ravenous. He threw her on the bed like a rag doll, teasing her until she was begging him to take her, her body quivering with need, but he wasn't ready.

"Tell me you want me, Louisa," he breathed in her ear. "Tell me I can do anything I want. His hands explored her mercilessly, followed by his lips. He didn't bother to be gentle, his fingers rough inside her, his lips fastening around her nipples until she nearly screamed with frustration.

"I want you, Tom. I always have," she moaned, arching her hips against him in the hope that he would finally make love to her.

"Tell me you are here to finish what you started," he commanded, biting her lip until she tasted blood. She didn't care. She was on fire. She tried to touch him, but he pinned down her wrists, his knee forcing her thighs apart.

"Finish what you started," she pleaded as Tom finally rammed into her, making her cry out. He pounded her with savage force, pain turning into exquisite pleasure as her body surrendered to his, totally giving up control. The sensations that coursed through her forced all thoughts from her mind, her whole being focused on the point of their joining, wanting to pull back, yet arching her back to get closer to him as he continued his onslaught, merciless and demanding. Something inside her let go, her body convulsing in a climax that shook her to the core, leaving her breathless and spent as Tom finally rolled off her, a mocking smile on his handsome face.

"Did I satisfy, your ladyship?" he asked, using her future title to belittle her.

Louisa pulled a sheet over her nakedness, her body still thrumming from the force of his attack. She squeezed her legs in an effort to contain the ache and hold on to some of the feelings that he'd roused in her. She never felt this way with Theo. It had been pleasurable and romantic, but it was like comparing a summer shower to a tempest that rages for hours and leaves a trail of devastation and destruction.

She wanted to rage at Tom and pummel him with her fists for using her so roughly and making her feel little more than a whore, but at the same time, she wanted to thank him for making her feel alive, and complete. She wished he'd say something kind to her, tell her how beautiful she was, or how he'd hungered for her for so long, but Tom just lay there, watching her with that infuriating smile as if he could read the thoughts racing through her mind.

"I must go," she said, slipping out of bed and reaching for her clothes with shaking hands. "And I won't be back."

Tom laughed. He was sprawled on the bed, his legs spread, his hands behind his back. He looked obscenely beautiful as he taunted her with his lack of modesty.

"Oh, you'll be back, maybe not tomorrow or the next day, but you'll be back. You see, Louisa, your little lord will never be enough for you. You are not the kind of woman who welcomes her husband into her bed once a week and sighs with happiness when he leaves. You want someone who will tear you apart, love you and hurt you, and leave you crying and begging for more. That's the only time you feel truly alive." Tom was still sniggering as she let herself out, her legs buckling as she ran down the street.

She swore she wouldn't go back, but she had, again and again. She fell asleep dreaming of Tom and woke up wanting him like a starved person wants food. He'd been right; she enjoyed him hurting her. It aroused her and made her want him more. He didn't stop her when she slapped him or clawed at him as he took her hard, making her cry out with pleasure and pain. They were one and the same, and only he could make them irresistible.

And now everything would change. She was pregnant and would have to marry as soon as possible to save her reputation. Louisa closed her eyes, trying to picture herself married to Tom, but all she saw were visions of violent sex that left her shaken and fulfilled. Was there any part of Tom that wanted her for more than her body? Did he care for her even a little? He never spoke of love or a future beyond the little room in Blackfriars, and she'd never asked, but now everything was different.

FIFTY-THREE

Louisa's hand flew to her cheek as the sting of the slap shocked her out of her complacency. She'd been in denial since the doctor's pronouncement, but she had to face reality, and that time was now. Uncle Kit's furious face floated above her own as tears began to flow, her cheek hot and throbbing.

"Don't you cry!" he roared. "Don't you dare cry!"

"What will you have me do then?" she whimpered, afraid he'd hit her again. But the fight had gone out of Kit, leaving him looking ashamed and defeated as he took a step back from Louisa's cowering form in an effort to control himself.

"I would have *you* tell me what I'm meant to do with you. I defended you to Charles the first time you disgraced yourself with Gaines, but this time you've gone too far. Am I supposed to lie to my nephew and tell him the child is his so that he could marry you and spare you the humiliation, or am I supposed to confront Gaines, not that it would do much good, since he's betrothed already?" Kit drew a deep breath, obviously trying to control his rage, but it was lost on Louisa. She stared at him in shock as his words finally penetrated her shroud of desperation.

"He's betrothed?" she whispered.

"Of course. Were you too busy lifting your skirts to inquire?" Kit yelled. "He's to marry the daughter of his employer at Michaelmas, or haven't you heard?"

"Kit, don't be cruel," Aunt Louisa said quietly, laying a hand on Kit's arm. "She's miserable enough."

"Not as miserable as she'll be when she's round as a melon and has no ring on her finger from either man. What am I to do, Lou? What would Alec want me to do?" he asked, turning to his wife for guidance.

"He'd want you to handle this with discretion and tact." Aunt Louisa replied, giving Kit a pleading look. "Do this for Alec and Valerie."

"Do what? How can I force Theo's hand when I don't know that this child is his? And why should I encourage him to marry a woman who has no moral standards or self-respect? Thank God Aunt Maud isn't here, or she'd crucify all of us, and with good reason this time."

"How did you even manage to see him alone?" Kit asked suddenly, changing tack. "And where did you see him?" He'd kept a close eye on Louisa, never allowing her to leave the house unchaperoned unless she was with his nephew. He'd been so vigilant, and yet she still managed to deceive him and spend time with Gaines without his knowledge. The girl was obviously much cleverer than he'd given her credit for, and an accomplished liar. When Charles accused Louisa of plotting to trap Gaines, Kit thought he'd been exaggerating and that it was Louisa's innocence and trust that landed her in a precarious situation, but now he wasn't so sure.

Maybe Charles had the right of it. After all, he'd known Louisa since birth and Kit had only known her since coming to Virginia with his wife, but he had to admit that he'd had his suspicions about her all along. Kit had seen enough of life to know that people were capable of changing and adjusting to their circumstances, but there were certain core traits that remained unchanged, regardless of time and position. If a person lacked basic decency and honor in their youth, those characteristics were not about to appear in later years, regardless of the life that person made for themselves.

Louisa had always been sweet and charming, but underneath the façade, Kit saw a selfish, self-serving girl, who had no compunction about sacrificing someone else's happiness to suit her own needs. Alec was blind to his daughter's failings, but Valerie was well-aware of Louisa's faults. No wonder she'd been eager to announce the engagement to Theo. Having Louisa safely married was probably the best course of action under the circumstances, and now time was of the essence. Kit turned back to Louisa, his eyes boring into her as she withheld her answer.

"How did you manage to see him alone?" he repeated, not backing down. He would have his answer if she wanted his help. He deserved to know the truth.

"I saw him when I went out with Genevieve. I forced her to lie for me," Louisa stammered, seeing renewed anger in Kit's eyes.

"How could you have forced her to lie for you? Was she a willing accomplice in this?" He looked incredulous, knowing that Genevieve would never have willingly lied to them, her position in their household so uncertain.

"No, Uncle Kit. It's not her fault. I took advantage of her fear," Louisa mumbled, looking at her feet to avoid Kit's furious gaze. Her fingers were intertwined in front of her, her knuckles white with tension as she took a step back in fear.

"How?" her aunt asked, shocked.

"I told her that if she didn't help me, I would tell my father that she was unkind to me and he would ask her to leave."

This time the slap came from her aunt, who looked furious. "You little bitch! How could you do that to her after everything she's been through? No wonder she lied for you. When did you become such a cold-hearted, calculating person? I'm ashamed to call you my niece," Aunt Louisa said.

Her voice was quiet, but the words hurt worse than the slap. Louisa genuinely loved her aunt and uncle and to see their anger and disappointment was almost the worst part of her predicament. And then her parents would find out once they got back. Her mother would be livid, but her father would be heartbroken. He always took her side and gave her unconditional love, but now he would despise her for the disgrace she brought on herself, and in turn, him.

"Please, help me, Uncle Kit," she pleaded. "I'll do anything you say. Please don't tell my parents. I know you can help."

"Louisa, I will speak to my nephew against my better judgment, but only because I love your parents and don't want to see them humiliated. You don't deserve Theo's love or protection, but I will speak to him, nevertheless. However, if you EVER do anything to hurt him again, I will personally see to it that you live to regret it. Do I make myself clear?"

Louisa nodded, tears rolling down her face. She'd never seen Uncle Kit so angry. He was always so kind to her and full of good humor, but at that moment, he looked as if he hated her and wanted nothing to do with her ever again. Louisa turned to her aunt, but she turned away, not wishing to meet her eyes.

"Go to your room and stay there. I can't bear the sight of you right now," Aunt Louisa said, turning to the window. Louisa ran out of the room, wishing she were dead.

FIFTY-FOUR

FRANCE SEPTEMBER 1624

Valerie checked the room one last time for any forgotten belongings before closing the lid of the trunk. Alec had gone downstairs to pay their bill as Andre came up to fetch the luggage to be loaded onto the back of the carriage. Valerie was secretly happy to leave the place. They'd been in Loudun for a week, and it was a week too long as far as she was concerned. None of their inquiries produced any results, despite the handsome reward Alec offered to anyone who came forward. Everyone remembered the scandal that rocked their town twenty-three years ago, but no one knew anything more than what they'd already been told, or if they did, they weren't willing to share the information, even for money. Sister Rose had never left the confines of the convent, so no one in town could even say what she looked like, much less if she'd ever been seen with someone. People did know Genevieve and asked after her, sending her warm regards and kind wishes. Alec was sorely disappointed, but after so many years, the trail had grown cold. There were no clues left to find.

There was one last thing they had to do before leaving, and that was to visit Rose's grave. Alec kept putting it off, knowing it would break his heart to see the sad final resting place of his sister. For a devout Catholic, there was no worse fate than being buried like a dog at a crossroads, the soul forever banned from the gates of Heaven and condemned to Hell for eternity. Valerie wasn't sure if Alec believed that Rose was really in Hell, and she didn't want to ask. He was heartbroken enough, believing that he'd failed her in death as well as in life. Rose had chosen her own path the day she decided to flee Yealm Castle, but as a man of the seventeenth century, Alec saw it as his duty to protect his sister and take responsibility for her, regarding her actions to be a result of his failure to help her rather than Rose's desire to get away from a marriage she didn't want. The only marriage Rose had been interested in had been as a bride of Christ, so whatever happened to her once she reached France had likely not been of her choosing. Alec knew that and blamed himself, despite the fact that there was nothing he could have done to prevent Rose's sad fate. The sooner they left Loudun the sooner he could begin to come to terms with Rose's death and hopefully, in time, learn to accept that the fault did not lie with him.

Valerie took one last look at Loudun as the carriage rattled down the cobblestone street toward the outskirts of town. Somehow it didn't seem quaint or charming anymore, just sad and full of secrets. Alec must have felt the same because he closed his eyes, not wanting to see the last of the town or the convent that was on their left as they passed, its gray walls cold and forbidding in the light of the overcast morning. They would visit the grave and then begin their journey to Calais.

Alec opened his eyes reluctantly when the coach came to a stop at the crossroads. A lonely cross, weathered by time and elements rose out of the ground, the crude inscription nearly worn away. The wood was bleached by the sun and split in places, making it look as if it had been standing at that lonely spot for centuries rather than decades. Tall grass choked the lower part of the cross, the grave itself unkempt and neglected after two decades. No one would have bothered to take care of Rose's final resting place, her existence as irrelevant as the lonely marker covered by a layer of dust.

Valerie silently followed Alec out of the carriage as he took off his hat and stood in front of the grave, tense and dry-eyed. He reached out and touched the wood of the cross, running his finger over the name. "I'm sorry, Rose," he said quietly. "I wish I'd listened to you and tried to understand. Maybe things would have turned out differently for us both. Rest in peace, knowing that I will take care of your daughter as if she were my own."

He looked as if he wanted to say something more, but suddenly turned toward the carriage, wiping his eyes with the back of his hand. Valerie was sure that the memory of Rose's grave would haunt him for the rest of his days, taunting him with his failure to do anything more for her.

"Monsieur." A man was walking briskly through a field, waving his hand in greeting. He broke into a run as Alec got into the carriage, ready to leave.

"Wait, monsieur," he called out as he finally reached the carriage, holding up his hand as he tried to catch his breath.

"Who's that?" Valerie asked as she studied the man through the window of the carriage. They had met many of the inhabitants of the town, but she was sure they hadn't seen this man before. He was dark-eyed and lean, his skin bronzed by frequent exposure to the sun, his moustache and trim beard hiding the lower half of a face that was younger than she originally thought.

"I don't know. Maybe he's mistaken us for someone." Alec seemed distracted, eager to get away from the place.

"Monsieur Whitfield, please wait. I'd like to speak to you." The man took off his hat, holding it in his hands and shifting his weight from foot to foot in agitation.

"I'd better see what he wants," Alec sighed, getting out of

the carriage and leaving the door open so Valerie could hear what transpired.

"My name is Maurice Barras. I heard that you've been making inquiries about Sister Rose, but I didn't want to come to you in town for fear of drawing attention to our meeting. You might think that no one remembers anything of that time, but you are quite wrong. Everyone does, but they are too afraid to speak up, even in the face of a large reward. There's something I'd like to tell you, and I think this is the right place to do that."

Alec stilled, watching Maurice Barras with weariness. He'd given up on learning what happened to Rose, and this man was suddenly offering information at the eleventh hour. Was he simply hoping to claim the reward before it was too late, knowing that Alec would have no choice but to pay up regardless of the authenticity of the information? He'd have no way to verify that what the man was telling him was the truth, but at this point, money was the last thing on Alec's mind. He was eager to hear what the man had to say, his eyes lighting with hope at the prospect of learning something, anything, of what happened to his sister.

"Please, go on, Monsieur Barras," Alec invited, uncrossing his arms and talking off his hat in a gesture of friendliness. The man glanced toward the cross for a long moment before finally facing Alec, a look of determination on his face.

"My grandfather worked at the convent many years ago. He wasn't permitted inside, but he tended the grounds and made minor repairs to the outbuildings. He was an old man, so the sisters felt safe with him. I helped my parents on the farm during the year, but in the summer, I used to sneak onto the convent grounds to help my grandfather. He was getting on in years and things were getting too much for him, although he wouldn't readily admit it. I met your sister. She was a kind lady and said I reminded her of her little brother, Charles."

Maurice Barras paused, looking out over the empty road as if he could see Rose clearly in his mind.

"Thank you, Monsieur Barras. It was kind of you to tell me that," Alec said, turning to leave.

"Wait, I haven't quite finished. You see, I was the one who found your sister's body. I'd gone swimming in the river and there she was, floating in the water. I wasn't sure if she was dead, so I pulled her to the bank and ran for my grandfather. He tried to revive her. I was only ten at the time, but I remember it as if it were yesterday. She was so pale and still, just lying there on the grass in a white gown. Her habit had been left further upstream, folded neatly with the cross on top."

Maurice Barras paused again, a look of sorrow on his face. It must have been traumatic for a ten-year-old child to find a corpse floating in the river, but he had obviously been a quick-thinking lad and pulled Rose out in the hope that she might still be saved.

"You see, Monsieur Whitfield, Sister Rose didn't have any water in her lungs and there were terrible bruises around her neck and wrists. My grandfather pointed them out to me. He left me to watch over the body while he went to fetch Mother Superior. He showed her the bruises, telling her that they were inconsistent with drowning, but she wouldn't listen. She told him that Sister Rose couldn't live with her shame and had chosen to end her life rather than to spend another day in the hell she'd created for herself. They took her away then, and Mother Superior had chastised my grandfather for allowing me to come to the convent, threatening to fire him from his job. He didn't earn much, but it was enough to allow him to live modestly and independently, so he kept his suspicions to himself and let the matter drop."

Alec regarded Maurice Barras silently for a few moments, digesting what he'd just heard. "So, your grandfather believed Sister Rose had been murdered?"

"He said that he thought she was dead before she went into the water. Her throat was nearly purple with the bruising, but Mother Superior said that she might have tried to hang herself first. It didn't look as if the bruises had come from a rope. They were wide, as if made by large hands."

"I see," Alec said. "Thank you for telling me." He took some coins out of the leather pouch at his waist, handing them to Maurice Barras, but the man shook his head, holding up his hands as if trying to ward off evil.

"I don't want the reward, Monsieur Whitfield. I told you this because I felt it was my duty to your sister and to my grandfather. I promised him that if ever the chance presented itself, I would tell the truth of what I saw that afternoon. I only wanted to right a wrong, not profit from it."

Alec nodded in understanding, putting the coins away, his eyes clouded with confusion. "That's very decent of you, Mousier Barras. I must admit that I have no inkling of what to do with this information. Knowing that my sister didn't take her own life would ease my soul, but the possibility that a murder had gone uninvestigated and unpunished disturbs me even more."

Alec ran a hand through his hair in his agitation, completely taken aback by the possibility that Rose might have died at someone else's hand. They had been on their way out of town, but what were they to do now? Could they leave knowing that Rose might have been murdered? Alec suddenly looked up, remembering something the man had said earlier.

"You said that people were afraid to talk to me. Who are they afraid of?" Clearly, someone still cared to keep the truth from coming out, and Maurice Barras knew who that might be.

Maurice Barras didn't answer the question directly, just cocked his head to the side, studying Alec before coming to a decision.

"There's someone I think you should talk to, Monsieur

Whitfield. Her name is Berenice Jarnot. She lives on a farm ten miles south of Loudon and likely knows nothing of your inquiries, or she would have come forward. She was one of the sisters at the convent but left the order shortly after your sister's death. My grandfather said that she was the one who delivered the baby that night, and that she didn't leave the convent of her own free will."

"Thank you, Monsieur Barras. I'm very grateful. May I tell Madame Jarnot that you sent us?" Alec asked, watching the man's face.

"Yes. She knows me well and will make you welcome. I hope she can help you. Good day."

Maurice Barras shook Alec's hand and walked away in the direction he'd come from, never turning back. Alec stood looking after him, conflicting emotions playing over his face. Had the man readily accepted the reward, Alec might have had doubts about the veracity of the information, but Barras had nothing to gain and something to lose by confessing what he knew. The question was, just how much could he lose if someone found out that he'd spoken to them? Who would kill a nun, and why? And why would they still want to protect their secret after two decades?

"Shall we go see Madame Jarnot?" Valerie asked, startling Alec out of his reverie. "Do you think she might be able to shed some light on any of this?"

"I hope so, although if she knew something, she would have spoken out at the time, don't you think?" he asked, getting back into the coach.

"Maybe someone wanted to keep her quiet," Valerie replied, pondering the situation. "If someone had really killed Rose and tried to make it look like suicide, they might go to great lengths to keep it from coming out, and Madame Jarnot might have been too afraid to speak out."

"Yes, I suppose that's possible. There's only one way to find out."

FIFTY-FIVE

The Jarnot farmhouse sat on a slight hill surrounded by lush pasture and newly reaped fields, golden haystacks filling the air with their lovely smell. Several cows chewed their cud, completely disinterested in scandals of long ago, while chickens pecked in the dirt of the front yard under the vigilant eye of a fat orange cat that meowed with displeasure as a plump middle-aged woman smacked its behind in order to get him off the bench and make room for her laundry basket. She shielded her eyes from the sun, watching the carriage rolling toward her home. The road wasn't well-traveled, so visitors were probably rare.

Alec had been quiet since they left the gravesite, lost in thought, his fingers drumming a steady tattoo against the side of the carriage in agitation, his body taut as a spring. Barras's account cast a whole new light on what might have happened to Rose, and if Madame Jarnot had nothing to tell them, would leave things even more convoluted. Valerie almost wished they'd never spoken to Mousier Barras and had left as planned, but now the situation had changed, and Lord only knew what new revelations would come to light. Alec finally stopped his drumming and turned to Valerie, a look of understanding on his face.

"I have to do this," he said stubbornly. "I know you don't want me to, but I must. This woman might have nothing of importance to tell us, but I can't leave without speaking to her. Even if all she can do is tell me about Rose's mindset during those days, I might be able to piece together something of what she'd been going through. Bear with me, Valerie." He squeezed her hand, rearranging his face into a warm smile as the carriage pulled up in front of the house.

The woman called out a friendly greeting, asking if they needed directions as they stepped from the carriage. Valerie had expected some dried-up old nun, but this woman had a broad, open face with round blue eyes that sparkled with good humor and deep dimples that appeared when she smiled. Her dark hair was liberally streaked with gray, but her face was unlined, her skin as supple as that of a young girl. She had that rare quality that made people feel instantly drawn to her, and considering the nature of their errand, that was a great start.

"Madame Jarnot, I wonder if we might have a word with you," Alec began, not wanting to just blurt out the purpose for their visit. "Maurice Barras thought you might be able to help."

"Why, of course, Monsieur. Do come in. I don't have much to offer you as I wasn't expecting guests, but I have some fresh bread just out of the oven and some goat's cheese and pâté. Please make yourselves comfortable."

The farmhouse was a low structure made of gray stone with small, muslin-curtained windows overlooking the yard. It consisted of one large room with a hearth, table and benches on one side, and a large bed shielded by a curtain on the other. Several tools hung neatly on nails to the left of the hearth, and a pine cupboard held an assortment of cups and plates painted in gay colors. It was swept clean, a jug of wildflowers in the middle of the scrubbed table adding a little cheer to the dimness of the cottage. Madame Jarnot put out a plate of thickly cut bread, butter, cheese, and pâté on the table, as well as a bowl of apples. The table looked like a still-life hanging on the wall of some museum. Valerie was taken aback by the woman's hospitality. She hadn't even asked them what they wanted but was willing to share whatever she had with them, making them feel very welcome.

"Is beer all right?" she asked, putting out three cups and a pitcher covered with a cloth.

"Now then, how can I help you? Do try the pâté. It's rather good," she added with a proud smile. No doubt she made everything herself from ingredients produced on the farm.

Valerie spread a piece of bread with pâté and took a bite, chewing slowly. It was very good, better than anything she'd tasted so far. She wished she could participate in the conversation, but Madame Jarnot spoke no English, making it impossible for Valerie to follow. Alec would give her an account of what had been said once they left the farmhouse instead of translating sentence by sentence. It wasn't wise to interrupt a person in the middle of their narrative; it gave them time to regret sharing too much.

"Madame Jarnot, I believe you knew my sister, Rose Whitfield," Alec began, watching the woman's face as he said the name. She paled visibly, her hand stilling in the act of peeling an apple.

"Mon Dieu, you've come at last," she said. "I always thought you would, but I must confess, I was expecting you somewhat sooner. Rose spoke so lovingly of you. She said you were the best of men." Berenice Jarnot put down the knife and the apple, wiping a tear from her cheek. "She didn't deserve what happened to her."

"The convent never saw fit to inform us of Rose's death or Genevieve's existence, and I was secure in the knowledge that my sister was safe and at peace in a house of God," Alec said by way of explanation. It obviously never occurred to Madame Jarnot that Rose's family knew nothing of her death or her child, casting a new light on events that were already murky at best.

"Will you tell me what happened?" Alec asked gently. Berenice nodded, emotions passing over her kind face like clouds racing across a summer sky. She was obviously thinking of how to phrase it best in an effort to spare Alec the pain of hearing the details of Rose's death. She finally began speaking, her voice low and laced with sadness.

"You see, Rose and I came to the convent at about the same time. We were novices together. Particular friendships are not encouraged in that type of life, but it's hard not to become fond of people, especially when you are both young and more than a little scared. Rose said that she'd longed to become a nun since she was a little girl, but I had my reservations. It had been my mother's dying wish that I join the order. Her life had been hard, and she thought I would be spared some of the harsher realities of life as a nun."

Madame Jarnot looked away for a moment, her eyes full of tears. It must have been a painful time in her life, having to leave home soon after the death of her mother, thrust into a life she hadn't chosen for herself. She didn't seem like the type of woman who would ever willingly renounce the world; she was too much a part of it. She finally turned back, continuing her story.

"Back in those days, there were more nuns than there are now, so Rose and I had to share a cell, which we secretly liked. We whispered long into the night, talking of our families and our devotion to God. I'd never been away from my family before I came to the convent and I felt lonely and cut off, frustrated by the fact that this feeling of isolation would likely stay with me for the rest of my life. Rose was lonely too, and still grieving. She felt some guilt about the way she'd left you all, especially young Charles. How is he?" Berenice asked suddenly.

"He's very well. He lives in Virginia with his wife and children. He loved Rose very much and was devastated when she left," Alec replied, leaning forward in his eagerness to hear the rest of the story.

Berenice took a sip of beer and went on with her story. "Rose met Father Marc in Calais. She'd made her way to France, but once she'd arrived, she wasn't sure where to go or how to get there on her own. He happened to be staying at the inn where she took a room and told her of our convent. Rose took that as a sign from God that that's where he wanted her to go. She said Father Marc was the kindest, most devout man she'd ever met, and they had some wonderful conversations on the way to Loudun. It was a great relief to her to have a trustworthy traveling companion that took her under his wing."

"Did you know him?" Alec asked, instantly suspicious of the priest.

"Oh, yes. Father Marc was our parish priest for years and came regularly to perform Mass and hear our confessions. He was always very kind and understanding—and too charming and handsome for a man of his calling." Madame Jarnot giggled prettily, revealing a glimpse of the young girl she must have been when she joined the order.

"Was Rose ever alone with him?" Alec asked, his voice tight with suspicion.

"Yes, during confession and when they walked in the gardens from time to time. He took time out to talk to all of us, especially the novices, since he was preparing us to take our vows. I had been alone with him as well, more than once."

"Did my sister still wish to take her vows?" Alec asked.

"Oh yes. She was eager to take her vows and devote her life to God. She asked to speak to Father Marc on several occasions, and he came to see her. She always seemed uplifted after his visits, almost ethereal. I must admit that I envied her unwavering faith. She seemed so sure of what she wanted, whereas I would have been much happier had I been allowed to marry my Jean, which I would have done, had mother not insisted that I go to the convent."

"Did you know Rose was pregnant, Madame Jarnot?" Alec asked Berenice looked away in embarrassment before answering.

"I noticed that she didn't seem to get her menses, but I didn't dare ask. Sisters weren't encouraged to speak of physical matters, only spiritual, and we never undressed in front of each other, even though we shared a cell. I thought she might be ill, especially since her appetite was much diminished, and she was paler than usual. It never occurred to me that she might be with child. It's not something that comes to mind when dealing with a woman who took a vow of celibacy. I only found out when her pains began. She tried to keep very quiet and begged me not to call anyone. She kept saying that he would come, and everything would be all right." Berenice took another sip of beer, her face flushed with the memory of that night.

"I couldn't be sure if she was referring to the baby's father or God. She had become even more devout in the months leading up to the birth, often speaking as if God was right there with her, privy to her every thought. She kept saying that she would make him proud and give him a son just like Mary. I delivered the baby. I'd seen plenty of babies being born, so thankfully I knew what to do. She was so small; I thought she might have been premature. Rose cried when she saw the baby and asked to hold her right away, although she kept referring to the baby as him. She whispered to her and kissed her head. She didn't look like a woman burning with shame, but she didn't seem fully aware of the fact that she'd just given birth to a baby girl. She seemed almost vacant; her spirit a million miles away."

"What happened then?" Alec asked.

"The child began to cry, and Sister Marie-Jeanne came to check on us. Then all hell broke loose. Mother Superior ordered me to take the baby and leave the cell. She questioned Rose for a long time. She must have gotten what she wanted because she called for old Monsieur Barras. She needed him to deliver a message."

"Who did she send a message to?" Alec asked. Valerie could see the tension coursing through him, his desperate need to know what happened. She couldn't understand most of what Madame Jarnot was saying, but she knew that her account was as close to the truth as Alec was likely to get, and that this new information had the power to change everything.

"I don't know. Monsieur Barras had gone to his daughter's house that night, so Mother Superior went out herself, which was highly unusual. Three days later Rose was dead." Berenice was crying softly now, her round face desperately sad. "She didn't drown herself; I'm as sure of that now as I was then."

"Is that why they asked you to leave?" Alec asked.

She nodded, wiping her eyes with her apron. "I helped prepare the body for burial and saw the marks on her neck and wrists. She didn't do that to herself. Someone had killed her. I asked to speak to Mother Superior, but she tried to dismiss me, feeding me the usual platitudes about the will of God. I said that I would go to Father Marc with my suspicions. That's when she flew into a rage, ordering me to leave immediately since I clearly did not understand the meaning of obedience and humility. She said that I wasn't suited to the life of a nun and that no one would believe me anyhow; she'd make sure of that. She said Rose brought shame on herself and the order and deserved to die a horrible death."

"You married your young man?" Alec asked, watching Berenice Jarnot intently.

"I did, and I must say that despite the terrible circumstances that led to my dismissal it was the best thing for me. Jean and I have had a wonderful life and raised three children. I was never cut out for the barren life of a nun."

"And what of Genevieve?"

"Father Marc approached a young couple who'd recently had a child of their own and asked them to care for the baby. He must have offered them an allowance of some sort for the support of the child. Monsieur and Madame Collot raised Genevieve until she was three years old, and from what I heard, had offered to adopt her, but Father Marc had other ideas. He wanted her to be raised at the convent, where she would get a good education. If she'd stayed with the Collots, she would have likely grown up to be an illiterate farm girl, although she would have grown up with kindness and love, which is in short supply at the convent."

"Madame Jarnot, do you think Father Marc is Genevieve's father?" Alec asked, his voice shaking.

Madame Jarnot shrugged her shoulders in a typically Gallic gesture. "To be perfectly honest, Monsieur Whitfield, I don't know. Rose never named Father Marc as the father, and believe me, I asked, as I'm sure Mother Superior did. Father Marc had the opportunity, but I had been alone with him on several occasions and there was never a hint of inappropriate behavior, but then again, maybe he simply didn't find me appealing." She shrugged again, looking from Valerie to Alec.

"There isn't a person in Loudun who doesn't suspect that Father Marc is Genevieve's father, but they would never speak the truth for fear of Le Mayor's wrath. Did you know that he is Father's Marc's father? He's a hard man, and to cross him can be hazardous to one's health, both physical and financial, but I've kept this secret for over twenty years, and I'd be damned if I didn't tell what I know now. You see, Rose wasn't the only one. There was Martine as well."

"Was she also a nun?"

"No, Martine was the daughter of the cobbler. She was a

beautiful young girl who spent a lot of time in church, confessing her sins, although I can't imagine what sins a pious fourteen-year-old might have other than nursing a secret love for the handsome priest. She died in childbirth before her fifteenth birthday, the child with her. Everyone believed the child to be Father Marc's." Berenice took another sip of beer, obviously distressed by the memory of that time and the injustice of young girls dying in shame while the priest escaped unscathed, protected by his powerful father and the Church.

"What happened to Father Marc after Rose died?" Alec asked.

"Father Marc left shortly after. He's a cardinal in Paris now, but he comes to Loudon all the time. He still visits the convent and he always took a particular interest in Genevieve."

"Thank you, Madame Jarnot. You've been truly helpful. I'm glad that things worked out well for you." Alec took a slice of bread, spreading it with a thick layer of pâté. He seemed suddenly hungry after days of hardly eating anything.

"I've made a good life for myself here, for that I am grateful. It gladdens my heart to see that Genevieve finally found her family and has someone to look after her interests and welfare. She was such a lonely child. I would have gladly adopted her myself had Father Marc allowed it, but I suppose I'd be the last person on Earth he'd want as a guardian for Genevieve. I know too much."

Berenice moved the plate of cheese toward Alec, glad to see him eating. She seemed like the kind of woman who got pleasure from feeding others, equating food with love. Alec gratefully took a piece of cheese, chewing thoughtfully as he considered the next step. This was a bitter-sweet victory, finding answers that only led to more questions and renewed feelings of guilt and pain, but at least he now had something to go on.

Madame Jarnot placed her palms squarely on the table,

leaning in and rising from the bench reluctantly, ready to return to her chores. She'd told them all she could and the relief of having shared her suspicions after all these years was obvious in her face.

"Thank you again, Madame Jarnot," Alec said, shaking her hand as she walked them to the waiting carriage.

"What will you do now, Monsieur?" she asked, brushing a stray lock out of her face as the wind picked up, moving the trees above their head with a sudden force.

"The only thing I can do—find Father Marc and make him pay for his sins." Alec handed Valerie into the carriage, giving Berenice Jarnot a final wave as the carriage rolled away, swaying in the gathering wind.

FIFTY-SIX

STATEN ISLAND SEPTEMBER 1777

The room was bathed in the soft light of an autumn afternoon, surprisingly cool and airy as both windows were open to allow for ventilation. Several cots were set against the walls, spaced with geometrical precision and neatly made. They were all unoccupied, except for the one closest to the window. The man on the far side lay silently, his form unmoving, his arms folded over his stomach as if laid out for burial, the even rise and fall of his chest the only sign of life.

Sounds of vigorous activity, clanging of metal, and voices of men could be heard from the yard below, but the hush inside the room was almost church-like. Sam looked around, wondering where he was. Judging by the nasal British voices that shouted commands in the yard below this could only be one place, the worst possible place he could have ended up. Sam tried to rise, but the sharp pain in his belly was like a hot poker that was being twisted this way and that to inflict the most damage. He lay back, breathing heavily and sweating despite the freshness of the air. He gingerly touched the wound. It had been cleaned and dressed, but Sam had no recollection of it. Someone had removed his clothes and dressed him in a nightshirt which reached almost to his knees and smelled pleasantly of soap and fresh air.

Sam licked his lips, desperate for a sip of water. His mouth was so dry he could barely swallow. He reached for a cup on the low table beside his bed, drinking gratefully once he actually managed to get it without causing himself undue pain. How did he get here? Sam lay still, allowing his heartbeat to return to normal. Even the act of reaching for the cup had left him drained and shaky. Sam closed his eyes, his face tense with concentration. He could remember everything that happened up to the time Finn helped him out of the boat, but after that, he drew a blank. He hoped Finn got Abbie safely to the farm but had no way of knowing that they hadn't been ambushed as they made their way across Staten Island. The place was crawling with British soldiers, who must have come across him on one of their patrols. The uniform had been the only thing that stood between Sam and a sure death, but it had also landed him among the enemy, making an attempt at escape difficult, especially in his weakened condition.

Sam tried to outline his options, but his mind refused to cooperate, getting fuzzier by the moment, his limbs growing heavy. He must have fallen asleep because the next time he opened his eyes it was already getting darker, the last glimmer of daylight leached from the sky and a single candle burning on the table beside his cot. A short man with bushy whiskers was standing over him, his hand on Sam's head, his face full of concern.

"How are you feeling?" the man asked, smiling down at Sam. "I'm glad to see you awake."

"I'm better, thank you," Sam answered carefully. "Where am I exactly?" He already knew, but he wanted to hear it, nonetheless.

"Oh, you're at Fort Flagstaff. A patrol came across you in the woods by the beach and brought you here. I'm Doctor

Freeman. I don't suppose you remember much of what happened?"

"No," Sam mumbled. The less said the better.

"They found you just in time. I daresay you would have died had you been left out there for much longer. You were bleeding quite heavily. You seem to have gotten lucky twice," he said, beaming at Sam, his eyes large behind his round spectacles.

"In what way, Doctor?"

"Your wound is painful, but not fatal," replied the doctor, taking Sam's pulse.

"I'm very relieved to hear that." Maybe he could make his escape tomorrow, or even tonight, although the gates of the fort were likely locked for the night, making it difficult to get out undetected.

"What I mean to say is that if the bayonet entered your abdomen a little to the left, it would have perforated your intestine, which would have resulted in eventual death. As it is, it didn't damage any vital organs. You should be on your feet in a few days. I'm sorry, but I didn't get your name." The doctor smiled at Sam benignly, obviously happy for his patient's good fortune.

"It's Corporal Patrick Johnson, sir." How long would it take them to learn that Corporal P. Johnson didn't exist? Sam wondered, calculating his chances.

"A pleasure to meet you, Corporal Johnson." Doctor Freeman let go of Sam's wrist and pulled back the coverlet and nightshirt to examine the wound. He seemed satisfied and replaced the blanket, patting it into place absent-mindedly.

"I can give you a few drops of laudanum to help you sleep if you are in great pain, but it's up to you. I think you've had quite more than enough already. You were in terrible pain when the patrol brought you in, so I took the liberty of giving you some laudanum before cleaning and dressing your wound to spare you unnecessary pain."

"Thank you, Doctor Freeman," Sam began, but the doctor waved his hand dismissively.

"Think nothing of it, my boy. That's what I'm here for. Your improved health is thanks enough." The doctor became distracted as a young woman walked into the room, carrying something on a tray. She was slight and graceful, with warm, brown eyes, much like Doctor Freeman's. The doctor's face lit up as she came closer, a look of deep affection on his homely face.

"And who is this Angel of Mercy?" Sam asked, smiling up at her. She looked away shyly, her cheeks turning a lovely shade of pink, visible even in the feeble light of the candle.

"That's my daughter, Susanna. She insists on helping me take care of the patients. What did you bring, my dear?"

"I heard you talking to our patient and thought he must be hungry. I brought some porridge and milk." She set the tray down on the table, making Sam's mouth water. He hated porridge, but couldn't remember the last time he'd eaten, and would have been equally excited about anything she had to offer that would fill his empty belly.

"Very thoughtful of you, my dear, very thoughtful, indeed. I was just about to suggest some food myself. I think Mr. Johnson might require help eating though. Would you be so kind?" Doctor Freeman looked at his daughter with undisguised pride as she sat on the side of the bed, reaching for the bowl and spoon.

"I'll check on you in a little while, Corporal," the doctor said before walking over to the far side of the room to check on his other patient.

Susanna held out a spoonful of porridge to Sam, who obediently opened his mouth, enjoying the taste of the warm mush. She'd put some butter and honey into it, just as his mother did, making it slightly more palatable. Her blush faded, but she still looked self-conscious, her eyes barely meeting his as he studied her openly.

"How long have I been here?" Sam asked, accepting another mouthful.

"Nearly three days now. You were unconscious when the patrol first brought you in, but you became delirious later, calling for Abbie over and over. Is she your wife?" Susanna asked shyly. Sam suddenly realized that she was older than he initially thought. He assumed she was Abbie's age, but on closer inspection, she had to be around twenty-five. He let his gaze slide to her left hand, but there was no wedding ring on her finger.

"Abbie is my si...—fiancée," Sam replied, looking away from Susanna. He didn't want to lie to her, but he was now trapped at a British fort, the only way out being as a deserter of an army he never joined. He would need help, and if Susanna believed that he was trying to get to the woman he loved, she might be more willing to assist him.

"Is she in England?" Susanna asked, giving Sam a drink of milk before continuing to feed him the porridge. He noticed that despite her warm smile, her eyes were awfully sad, making him wonder what her life was like at a British fort, helping her father. Had she come willingly, or had she not been offered a choice, being an unmarried woman?

"No, she's here. As a matter of fact, I was taking her to her aunt in Richmond Town when we were set upon by the rebels. I tried to fight them off, but I was vastly outnumbered. I have no idea where she is, or if she's safe," Sam whispered. "I need to find her." He felt like an awful cad, seeing the distress in her eyes, but at the moment, she was his only hope of escape. He prayed she was gullible enough to believe his story but couldn't think of anything else that would explain his presence on Staten Island and his wound.

"Oh, how awful. I do hope she's all right. You are not in any condition to leave yet, but once you are better, I'm sure your commanding officer will give you leave to go look for her. You must love her very much." Susanna replaced the bowl and cup on the tray, reluctantly rising to her feet. Sam would have liked more time to cultivate Susanna's friendship, but he didn't have that luxury. He had to get out of the fort, and he had to do it very soon. He reached out and took Susanna by the hand, forcing her to look at him.

"I do love her. Susanna, you have to help me. I can't wait until I recover and get leave. I must go tomorrow. Abbie could be out there, frightened and alone. They might have taken her and done her an injury." Sam could see a look of indecision on Susanna's face. She would help him with just the right amount of persuasion.

"You can't just walk out of here, Corporal. That would be tantamount to desertion, and you know what the penalty for that is. You must report to a ranking officer here at the fort and ask for help. He can send a messenger to your garrison and get a letter from your commander." Susanna gently extracted her hand, picking up the tray and holding it against her chest in an effort to put some distance between them.

"Susanna, please. I can't wait. What would you think if your intended left you alone and unprotected? Surely, a woman of your compassion and sensitivity can understand my predicament." Sam gave her a pleading look. He hoped he was wearing her down.

"I suppose I can see your point. You don't think she got to her aunt's house?"

"You see, even if she did, I still have to get to her," Sam improvised. He glanced away, trying to look embarrassed. "She just found out she's with child, so I must marry her right away before her family finds out. I must do the right thing, don't you see?" He looked up at her, begging her to understand. She seemed disappointed for a moment, as if shocked by the fact that he might have gotten a woman he wasn't yet married to with child, but then her mind turned to his escape.

"All right, Corporal, I will help you leave here if you promise to come back as soon as you've found and married your Abbie. Do we have a deal?" She looked so earnest that Sam loathed himself for lying to her, but he had no choice. He had to get out of this fort before anyone realized he was an imposter. If an officer marched in here asking questions, he was finished. His only choice was to escape before anyone had a chance to question him. If found out, he'd hang.

"How can we do it?" Sam asked eagerly.

"There are some local farmers that make deliveries to the fort. They bring meat and produce several times a week. There are a lot of men here, and they need to be fed. I don't normally interact with the locals, but I know one man. He brought his son here two weeks ago. The boy fell out of a tree and needed to be stitched up. I helped my father do it. He wanted to pay, but my father wouldn't hear of it. He was happy to help. I think he wouldn't refuse me if I asked him for a favor. He should be here tomorrow morning. You would need some civilian clothes, and I would need to distract my father long enough to allow you to walk out of here. I'll speak to Mr. Miller tomorrow and let you know. In the meantime, get your rest. I will pray for you and your intended tonight," she said as if that would take care of everything.

Mistress Freeman awkwardly touched his shoulder, obviously moved by compassion for him, making Sam feel even worse. He'd been known to tell a lie or two to get out of a scrape, but this woman didn't deserve to be taken advantage of. Sam sighed and tried to go to sleep. Recriminations would have to wait till later. Right now, his only goal was to get the hell out of the enemy fort.

FIFTY-SEVEN

Sam woke sometime in the middle of the night, at least he thought it was the middle of the night. He was terribly hot, but the heat was coming from somewhere inside, consuming him like a raging inferno. *That's what it must feel like to be burned alive,* he thought before throwing off the blanket and gulping lungfuls of air in an effort to cool down. Sam felt his side, yanking his hand away. Even the slightest touch sent waves of excruciating pain throughout his entire torso, setting his guts aflame. He wished he could call out, but his mouth felt like cotton wool. He felt better when he fell asleep after talking to Susanna. She was going to help him escape, and now he'd gone and ruined everything.

Sam tried to shift position, but even the slightest movement resulted in unbearable pain, causing him to cry out. The man in the other bed looked up, concern on his face. "Are you all right, mate?" he asked.

"Can you call Doctor Freeman, please?" croaked Sam. "Something is wrong."

"Of course, just hold on." The man got out of bed laboriously, grunting with effort. Sam barely noticed that his right leg ended just below the knee, the bandage covered with pus and dried blood as he used a wooden crutch to limp to the door.

Sam looked up to see his mother coming toward him, a reassuring smile on her face. She was saying something, but he couldn't quite make it out. It didn't matter, she was there, and everything would be all right, just as it had been when he was a little boy and was ill. She always nursed him back to health. She hadn't been able to save Luke though, his mind protested as he remembered his brother. Abbie had been heartbroken after Luke died, taking to her bed and refusing to eat for days. Where was Abbie? Sam looked around, almost expecting to see Abbie appear out of thin air, but she never materialized. His mother seemed to vanish as well, leaving him alone and in pain. Sam's brain felt terribly muddled and the room swam before his eyes, making him dizzy and forcing him to squeeze his eyes shut. Where was everyone?

He wasn't sure how much time had passed. It might have been five minutes or five hours, but Doctor Freeman appeared at last, still wearing his nightshirt, which was tucked into his trousers. His hair was standing on end, but his face was alert and full of concern. Susanna was right behind him, a long braid snaking down her shoulder from beneath her cap, her shoulders covered with a shawl. She held a candle as her father moved aside the blanket and pulled up Sam's shirt. Another time he might have been embarrassed to be naked in front of a woman he barely knew, but the delirium chased all shame away.

"Bear with me, Corporal. I'll just take off the dressing and see what's going on." He peeled off the dressing very gently, finally exposing the wound. Sam heard Susanna's intake of breath, but kept his eyes shut, having finally gotten a handle on the dizziness.

"It's festered," the doctor said quietly. "Quite badly. I don't know what caused it. I cleaned it most carefully before stitching it up." Sam's eyes flew open, the meaning of the words sinking into his fevered brain. Doctor Freeman scratched his head, his eyes huge behind the glasses.

"Will I die, Doctor?" Sam asked. He preferred to know the truth.

"Not if I can help it, son, but you won't be rejoining your regiment for some time to come. Susanna, we must operate immediately. Any delay will cause the putrefaction to spread. Please get me all the necessary instruments and ask two soldiers to come in here. I'll need to move Corporal Johnson to an operating table where I can work with greater ease."

Sam could see the other patient peering over Susanna's shoulder, his face full of curiosity. "That looks awful," he said before Susanna shooed him back to his own bed. After that, everything was a blur. Two uniformed men came in and lifted Sam off the cot, placing him on a wooden table in a different room. Susanna was laying out instruments while Doctor Freeman consulted a medical text. That didn't seem like a very good omen. The sun was just beginning to rise, filling the room with a rosy glow that moved across the walls, casting a pink pall over them and chasing away the shadows of the night. Waves of heat rolled over Sam as he tried unsuccessfully to push aside the sheet with which he was covered, which Susanna kept adjusting.

"Daylight will be most helpful," Doctor Freeman said, glancing toward the window. "Much better than working by candlelight, I say."

"What are you going to do, Doctor?" Sam stammered, although he wasn't sure he really wanted to know. The doctor stopped what he was doing and looked over at Sam, coming to stand where Sam could easily see him.

"I'm going to reopen the wound and clean it out once again. I might have to shave away some of the infected flesh until I'm satisfied that all the putrefaction has been removed. I will then clean it with wine and pour boiling turpentine into the wound before applying a salve and dressing it once again. I'm sorry, Patrick. It won't be pleasant, but it must be done. If I'm successful, it will save your life."

"And if you're not?"

"If I'm not, then the infection will spread and eventually enter your bloodstream, resulting in death. I will do everything in my power to make sure that doesn't happen." Doctor Freeman took Sam's hand, squeezing it gently. "I need you to be brave for me."

Sam tried to answer, but he had a lump in his throat the size of a brick. He just nodded, returning the pressure of the doctor's hand. "Do what you must," he whispered, barely able to get the words out. He closed his eyes when he saw Doctor Freeman pick up a small knife that was about to be used on his tender flesh.

"Susanna, give him some laudanum, then I need you to stand on the other side and sponge off the blood and pus. You there," he turned to one of the soldiers still hovering in the doorway. Hold this metal container over the candle until it boils. There's no sense lighting a fire just to boil a bit of turpentine. Let me know when it's ready."

"Yes, sir," the soldier replied, holding the little pot over the candle very carefully and throwing looks of pity at Sam, who was still shivering with fever.

Sam sucked in his breath as Doctor Freeman touched his abdomen, ready to begin the procedure. He knew it would hurt, but the pain that tore through him was like nothing he'd ever experienced. It was white hot and all encompassing, but most of all relentless despite the laudanum. Sam tried to hold on, but then a merciful blackness enveloped him, and he welcomed it with open arms, unable to take the pain any longer.

He slipped in and out of consciousness, waking up to an agony beyond anything he'd ever known. The doctor was scraping away inside his stomach, intent on his task. Sam tried to hold still, but his legs shook of their own accord, his back arching from the unbearable pain. Susanna wiped his forehead as she continued to sponge out the wound, the putrid smell of pus filling the small room. Sam passed out again, grateful for the respite. Mercifully, he stayed unconscious for the grand finale. Doctor Freeman poured the boiling turpentine into the wound, then proceeded to stitch it up before applying a smelly salve of some sort and dressing the area once again.

Sam felt the touch of a cool hand on his forehead as he began to surface from the dark hole he'd been sucked into during the surgery. He was still in pain, but it was nothing compared to the agony he'd felt earlier. His legs were no longer jerking, and the inferno that had taken over his belly seemed to have cooled a bit. Susanna sat on the side of the bed, holding a cup of water to his parched lips. It was dark outside once again and he had no idea whether it was evening or early morning.

"How do you feel, Patrick?" she asked, cupping his cheek in an unexpectedly intimate gesture. Her eyes were full of sorrow as she looked at him lying there, making Sam feel sorry for himself. Maybe he wasn't really feeling better and the surgery hadn't worked.

"Am I dying?" he asked. He was suddenly scared, not wanting to die among strangers and under a false name. No one would know what happened to him or visit his grave. Sam sighed, bracing himself for the answer.

"We won't let you die. Father thinks he got everything out this time, and the turpentine and wine should do the rest. You are still much fevered, but not like you were earlier. Father thinks it must be working. Do you want something to eat?"

Sam just shook his head. The thought of food nauseated him. "I just want to sleep, if that's all right." Susanna nodded, touching his cheek again.

"Sleep then. I'll sit with you until you fall asleep, then lie down on one of the empty cots so that I can be close to you should you need me."

She smiled down at him, his large hand in her small one, tethering him to the world. Sam closed his eyes and allowed himself to drift away, secure in the knowledge that an angel was watching over him as he slept.

FIFTY-EIGHT

The milky light of dawn was just creeping across the floor and walls of the room as Sam woke. He wasn't sure what woke him because everything was quiet, both inside and out. Even the yard below was silent, the soldiers still in their beds, getting a few more minutes of sleep before their wake-up call. The room was pleasantly cool, the air fresh and clean, despite the closed window. Doctor Freeman gave orders to air out the room twice a day, but the windows were firmly shut after that to prevent infection and the possibility of catching a chill. Sam didn't think it was possible to catch a chill on a glorious September day, but what did he know?

Doctor Freeman had checked on him during the night, shuffling in with his glasses jammed onto his face at a strange angle and his nightshirt swishing against his legs. He seemed satisfied with Sam's progress as he checked for temperature before examining the wound. He nodded in satisfaction, then quietly retreated to his own room at the end of the hall, but not before pulling the blanket over Susanna and tucking it around her shoulders.

Sam slowly turned his head, half expecting Susanna to be

gone, her cot empty and neatly made, but she was still there, sleeping soundly. Her breathing was even and shallow, her face luminous in the morning light. Her cap had come off during the night, her hair fanned out on the pillow as she slept. It was a few shades darker than Abbie's, a honey-blonde that caught the rays of the rising sun and shone like a halo around her head. Susanna's mouth was slightly open, her full lips rosy against her pale skin. Sam tried to look away but couldn't. She was so lovely just lying there, completely unaware of his scrutiny. The blanket her father so carefully tucked around her had slipped off, exposing the curve of her breast against her nightdress. Sam suddenly wished he could go over to her and adjust the blanket to keep out the chill of the morning, but even the merest motion left him sweating and pressing his hand against the wound in a fruitless effort to hold in the pain.

Sam lay back against the pillows panting and tried not to stare at Susanna's sleeping form, but his eyes kept sliding to her face, his lips stretching into a silly smile. Susanna was nothing like the women Sam normally found attractive. He liked them buxom and saucy, the kind of women who weren't shamed by their desire or need for a man. They were honest and refreshing compared to the demure damsels he was normally exposed to, whose only goal was to catch a husband and breed like cattle.

Susanna was slight and graceful, her somber-colored, high-necked gowns doing little to disguise her natural beauty. She wasn't the kind of woman who needed to display her bosom or make suggestive comments to get attention. She exuded a quiet dignity as she moved about the empty ward, helping her father and doing her best to make her patients feel cared for. Under different circumstances, Sam might have found her to be cold or repressed, but he noticed sadness in her eyes and a look of longing as she gazed out the window, most likely wishing to return home to England rather than molder in a fort in the middle of a war she probably cared nothing about.

She seemed heartbreakingly earnest and dedicated, and her concern for him touched Sam deeply, for no girl had ever really cared about his wellbeing. She seemed drawn to him, whether because he needed her help or because she genuinely liked him, but he had to stay aloof for fear of causing her pain. He felt terrible enough lying to her the way he had, knowing that she believed every word and prayed for him to be reunited with his nonexistent betrothed.

And suddenly Sam wished he did have a betrothed. He'd had his share of romance, but no girl had ever really touched his heart. He secretly envied Finn when he saw him with Abbie. It wasn't just physical love. Theirs was a union of souls as well, and Sam prayed that he would be blessed enough to experience something similar before he died. It was ironic that the girl who wormed her way into his soul was the daughter of an enemy surgeon, someone he could never have. Maybe in another life they could have had something special, but for now, he had to keep his distance while still taking advantage of her kindness. Sam sighed and turned to his side, suddenly feeling lonelier than he ever had in his life.

FIFTY-NINE

ENGLAND SEPTEMBER 1624

Louisa carefully opened the door and peeked into the empty corridor. It was just past noon and the best time to slip out unnoticed. The servants were in the kitchen having their midday meal, Aunt Lou was in the nursery putting the children down for a nap, Uncle Kit was predictably out, and Genevieve was in her room doing God knows what, probably thumbing through the Bible. Louisa tiptoed down the empty hallway and out the door, breathing a sigh of relief as she trotted down the street, melting into the midday crowd. By the time they discovered her gone, it would be too late. She would have accomplished what she set out to do. The plan was two-fold, and the first part had gone off without incident.

Convincing Uncle Kit to allow her to go to church to pray for forgiveness had been easy enough, although he was slightly taken aback by her desire to attend All-Hollows-by-the-Tower church rather than the one they normally attended for Sunday services, but Louisa had her reasons. Genevieve had been surprised as well, especially when ordered to accompany her, but she didn't protest and did as she was told, the silly little mouse. Louisa thanked her lucky stars that she hadn't grown up in a convent. The poor girl seemed to have virtually no free will. She was so used to being told what to do that she simply complied, never questioning the order.

Louisa found she felt sorry for the girl, but compassion would have to wait. She had more important things to do. She only hoped that Genevieve hadn't figured out the real purpose of their visit to the church and wouldn't feel morally obligated to report it to her aunt and uncle. Louisa thought she'd been discreet, but Genevieve was more observant than people gave her credit for and her knowledge of herbs and medicines certainly didn't help in this case. Louisa pulled on her hood and proceeded to Tom's lodgings on foot.

She'd never been out on her own and felt a thrill of excitement at the unexpected feeling of freedom. She could just keep going and no one would know where she'd gone. But where would she go alone and pregnant with no money of her own? Foolish idea, really. Louisa looked around to see if anyone noticed her, but the street was full of people going about their business. Handsome carriages fought for space as cumbersome wagons loaded with produce and barrels of fish made their way down the narrow road. People walked carefully, keeping close to the buildings, careful not to slip on rotting cabbage leaves and apples, periodically glancing upward in case some overzealous maid decided to empty a chamber pot onto their head. One could never be too careful, especially in Blackfriars.

Louisa walked past the Blackfriars Theater, quickly glancing at the handwritten notice to check what play was to be performed this week. How she'd love to attend the theater, but Uncle Kit had kept her under lock and key for the past week, allowing her an hour a day in the garden to get some fresh air and exercise. Even Theo had been turned away, told by Uncle Kit that she was unwell and needed to stay abed for a few days. Louisa had never felt so frustrated and alone. At least her parents were still away, which was a blessing in disguise. By the time they returned from France, everything would have blown over, giving them no reason to be displeased with her. Everything would be resolved today.

A pleasant breeze blew off the river, making Louisa's use of a cloak more acceptable. She didn't want anyone to see her face or know that she had visited Tom's lodgings. She'd been there several times while poor Genevieve walked along the riverbank, watching the packet boats crisscrossing the Thames and the elaborate barges of the wealthy gliding down the sparkling waters on fine days, music drifting to the shore as they were entertained by players and mummers. Genevieve was strangely drawn to the river, refusing to go anywhere else while she waited for Louisa. Louisa had even offered her money for a ticket to a play, but the silly girl wouldn't take it. Maybe it had something to do with her mother's body being found floating in the river, but that was just morbid.

Louisa's thoughts turned to Tom and her impending visit to his rooms. He wasn't expecting her, but hopefully he'd be at home. This might be her only chance to see him alone and put her plan into action. Funny how she'd meant to teach Tom a lesson and show him what he gave up by not marrying her, but instead the joke was on her. She'd learned a valuable lesson about playing with fire and getting burned. Tom would get away unscathed, but her life would be forever tainted by doubt and fear.

What would Theo do if he ever found out about her betrayal? Aunt Lou and Uncle Kit would never breathe a word, but what about Tom? He would be able to hold the secret over her head for the rest of her life, and once her child was born, things would get even worse. Thomas Gaines was many things, but stupid wasn't one of them. He made his dislike of Theo very clear, so what if he implied to Theo that the child wasn't his or better yet, decided to blackmail Louisa into paying him for his silence? Tom showed off the finest suits of clothes and trinkets when he came to court but judging by the location and state of his rooms, he was short of funds. Having an extra income from a secret source would not only line his pockets but bring him a perverse sense of satisfaction while Louisa's life could be ruined forever. He'd proudly told her how he blackmailed one of his employer's associates, having been privy to information that could ruin the man. No, that would never do. She couldn't give him that kind of power over her.

Louisa patted her pocket before knocking on the door. The little pouch was still there, her ticket to freedom, but did she dare use it? Thinking thoughts of revenge was one thing but carrying it out something completely different. She never intended for things to go this far, but Tom had been so charming and persistent at the start, sending her letters full of pretty verses and lovely promises, berating himself for the fool he'd been for not appreciating her when he had the chance. Louisa had wanted nothing more than to heal her wounded pride, but instead she allowed him to use and humiliate her and turn her into a willing participant in his little game. Tom had played her so skillfully, she never even realized he was using her. He wanted to fuck her into submission, to bring her to her knees and show her that she was no better than a whore at heart, ashamed, but hungry for anything he could give her.

Louisa sighed as she stood in front of the door, her trembling hand raised to the iron knocker, a last opportunity to change her mind and flee. Her head knew the truth about Tom, but her heart still needed convincing, and that was ultimately the purpose of the visit. Tom's response would decide everything, sealing his fate and hers.

Tom opened the door himself, surprised to find Louisa on his doorstep in the middle of the afternoon, a self-satisfied smirk playing about his lips as he invited her in. Louisa made sure to cross to the other side of the room before he could kiss her or slide his hand between her legs, awakening the surge of desire that would no doubt land her in his bed, the purpose of her visit forgotten. She wouldn't let it happen. This time she would be in control, and she would bring him to his knees.

"What are you doing here?" Tom asked carefully, watching her with narrowed eyes. Normally, she went straight to him, but this time she was keeping her distance, alerting him to the shift in power. Tom smiled a predatory smile. Whatever she had planned, he was ready to play.

"I had to see you, Tom. Lord Sheridan has forbidden me to leave the house, but I slipped out and must return before I'm missed," she said guiltily, looking at Tom from under her lashes.

"What have you done to deserve such treatment from your uncle? He's normally an understanding man." Tom sat down, inviting Louisa to sit next to him, but she remained standing. She needed to see his face.

"I'm with child, Tom. It's yours." Louisa held her breath as she blurted out her news, hoping against hope that Tom would surprise her and offer words of love and comfort, but Tom leaned back, cocking his head to the side, as if watching an amusing play. He gave Louisa a lazy smile, studying her for a few agonizing moments before finally answering. "Sweetheart, I greatly enjoyed our trysts, but you could have done the same with any number of men. Your bastard is your problem."

Louisa felt as if she had been kicked in the stomach by a horse, the cold look in Tom's eyes cutting her to the bone.

"You said you loved me, Tom." She didn't mean to let him see her distress, but her voice shook, and her eyes filled with tears, betraying her hurt.

"All men say that to women they hope to seduce, but it's not always true."

He continued to watch her with an expression of wry amusement as if trying to guess what she really wanted from him. "Were you hoping I'd declare my undying love for you and offer marriage? I'm afraid you have a bit of a problem, my little dove," he said, smiling cruelly. He was mocking her, his blue eyes twinkling with sarcasm as he studied her pale face. "My, my, what will little Louisa do?"

"Actually, I don't have a problem," Louisa replied haughtily. "I'm to be married to Lord Carew." She held her head high, willing herself not to cry anymore. She had the answer she'd come for.

"Ah, I see Lord Sheridan didn't waste any time. He's a clever man, no wonder Buckingham is so enamored of him, in more ways than one." He smirked as if he knew something she didn't.

"What do you mean by that?"

"Don't worry your pretty little head about it. It's nothing to concern you, but what might be of concern is your sweet lord finding out about what you're really like. Does he make love to you tenderly or does he think you are still a virgin and is looking forward to deflowering you on your wedding night? What a surprise it will be when he realizes you've a full belly already."

Tom laughed, his face contorted by malice. "Oh, how I will enjoy watching you squirm, sweeting, especially when you'll do anything I ask to keep your dirty little secret. Now, let me see, would I like to keep fucking you, or would I like you to pay me for my silence?" He furrowed his brow as if in deep thought, then smiled viciously. "I think I might enjoy both, now that I think of it. We will discuss the details of our arrangement another day. Now, I must get back to Whitehall; Lord Seton will be expecting me. It was kind of you to call." Tom got up from the settee, obviously ready to show Louisa the door.

"Wait, Tom. Will you at least have a glass of wine with me to celebrate my upcoming marriage?" Louisa asked with a sweet smile, shocking him into silence. "I would really like that. You've made your position clear and I will do whatever you ask." If Tom seemed taken aback by the change in her mood, he made no comment, just shrugged.

"All right, but then you have to go. I'll get the wine." He turned toward the door, but Louisa held up her hand.

"Let me. I know where you keep the wine. I won't be a moment. Here, sit down." She gave him a winning smile before disappearing into the dingy room beyond. The wine was exactly where she expected it to be and she emptied the contents of her pouch into it, swirling the wine before picking up two pewter cups and bringing them back to the small parlor. Tom was watching her as she poured the wine, handing him a cup.

"May you be happy in your marriage, Louisa," Tom said, dripping sarcasm as he raised his glass and drained it in one gulp. He made a face as he peered into the cup. "The wine tastes bitter."

"Yes, it does, but what do you expect from this cheap swill? Uncle Kit keeps a good cellar, so I'm accustomed to fine wine," Louisa said, putting on her cloak. "Well, goodbye Tom. We won't be seeing each other again."

"Oh, I'm sure our paths will cross sooner than you think," Tom replied, wiping his mouth with the back of his hand. "Are you leaving London once you're married?"

"Oh, I'm not going anywhere," Louisa replied cryptically, "you are."

"What do you mean?" Tom stared at her as if she'd gone mad. "Is your uncle coming after me?" He seemed suddenly nervous, but Louisa gave him a warm smile.

"No, Tom. I try to fight my own battles whenever possible; it's more efficient that way, not to mention discreet. But I won't let you hurt me ever again."

Tom was about to say something when his hands started to shake, his pupils dilating in the dim light of the room. He grabbed his stomach as if trying to hold in his guts, but the pain only increased, forcing him to double over, moaning.

"What have you done?" he croaked as his body began to convulse.

"I added ground yew seeds to the wine. Did you know that many English graveyards have yew trees? There's a particularly impressive one in All-Hollows-by-the Tower cemetery. They seem to represent death or some such nonsense. My nurse told me that. She was very knowledgeable about such things, but then you don't really care about that, do you? You don't care about anything other than your own ambition and lust."

Tom tried to say something, but his eyes were bugging out of his head, his body shaking uncontrollably. It wouldn't be long now. Yew killed quickly if properly administered. Louisa felt a pang of guilt as she watched Tom's agony, but there was no turning back now. She hadn't really wanted to use the seeds, but Tom's cruelty forced her hand. All she'd really longed for was to hear that he loved her and would never forgive himself for letting her marry another man. Instead, he had been vicious and menacing, his heart untouched by the child growing inside her womb.

Tom slowly slid to the floor, a look of astonishment on his frozen features. He was just as beautiful in death as he had been in life, but there was no time to dwell on that. The church bells were ringing, and it was time to go back home before anyone noticed her gone. Louisa rinsed out the cups with water from a pitcher and poured the wine out the back window. No one would know how Thomas Gaines died, least of all his intended.

Louisa took one last look at Tom's face, his blue eyes so beautiful now that all malice was gone from his expression. He looked so young as he sat on the floor, his back propped up by the settle and his arms still crossed over his belly. She was in love with the boy she knew in Virginia, but this Tom was callous and cruel, eager for whatever power he could grasp, even if it meant stooping to blackmail. She supposed he always had a mean streak, but life at court had brought it out into the open, the constant backstabbing and maneuvering of the courtiers all the encouragement Tom needed to embark on a life of social climbing at any cost. He had implied that he knew something about Uncle Kit, smirking as he mentioned him in the same breath as the Duke of Buckingham, but now he'd never get to use the information against him. Whatever he knew would go to the grave with him, just like Louisa's own indiscretion. Tom couldn't hurt anyone anymore.

Louisa closed the curtains, plunging the room into semi-darkness. She wasn't sure why she did that, but it seemed appropriate somehow. She took one last look around before letting herself out of the house and hurrying down the street, her mind surprisingly blank. She expected to feel remorse, fear, agony of loss, possibly even triumph, but what she felt was absolutely nothing.

SIXTY

Susanna allowed the letter to glide into her lap as she stared at the achingly beautiful sunset just visible over the walls of the fort. The evening sky seemed to be ablaze with fiery color, almost blinding in its intensity as it tinted the dull stones of the fort a dazzling pink, transforming it into something unexpectedly lovely for a few short moments before darkness began to settle over Staten Island, returning the fort to its normal state of serviceable ugliness.

Rising to her feet, she went to stand by the window, wrapping her arms around herself for comfort and warmth. Her sister's joyous news should have made her happy, but instead she felt as hollow as an old tree, the husk still standing tall while the inside was empty and barren. Laura was pregnant with her first child, her letter bursting with joy and excitement, the words urging Susanna to be happy for her, but bitter tears stained her cheeks as she imagined her sister's infant. It's not that she didn't wish Laura all the happiness in the world; it was just that she was beginning to feel that happiness had passed her by, choosing instead a more worthy candidate. She'd never felt as lonely as she had since Laura married Bradley and left her alone, forcing her to follow their father to America for lack of a female relative to stay with. Susanna found satisfaction in helping her father tend to the patients and seeing them recover, but the ones that didn't, left her heartbroken and bereft. One had to hold on to joy with both hands before it was too late.

The irony was that she was surrounded by men, but none of them found their way into her heart. There had been several officers who tried to court her, but she either wasn't interested or they were eventually turned off by her lack of guile and tendency to speak her mind. Sometimes she wished she could be more like Laura, who regarded flirting as a sport and frequently downplayed her own intelligence to make her husband feel superior. Susanna had to admit that although it made her cringe, it had served Laura well, landing her with a husband who adored her in a way a woman could only dream of being loved. Susanna doubted that any man would ever feel that way about her, so the best she could hope for was someone who at least respected her and cared for her wellbeing.

Susanna sighed and turned away from the window, suddenly feeling trapped in her little room. It was her sanctuary in this all-male domain, but at the moment it was close and stifling, making her feel unusually agitated. Susanna felt angry with herself for giving in to despair. She grabbed her cloak off a peg behind the door and left the room, making her way upstairs to the wall walk. She would just stroll for a few minutes in the hope that the fresh air and the violet sky reflected in the calm waters of the Narrows would clear her mind and chase this terrible melancholy away.

Susanna nodded to a sentry and made her way along the wall, inhaling air fragrant with the smell of hay, tang of the water, and just a touch of gunpowder. She leaned on the wall, enjoying the beauty of Manhattan clearly visible across the East River, great ships bobbing gently at the wharves. She watched as darkness began to settle over the city, candlelight in windows and shops glowing like stars in a night sky.

But the beauty around her only made her feel lonelier, wishing she could share it with someone who cared for her. She thought of Corporal Johnson and was suddenly jealous of a woman she'd never met, envying her the love Patrick obviously felt for her. There was something about him that touched her soul. He didn't seem like the other officers who thought war was all battles and glory, but more like a poet who found himself thrust into the wrong surroundings, his eyes seeing the suffering and fragility of life rather than mere victory and defeat. She had no right to feel anything for him, but there was something in his beautiful gray eyes that left her feeling helpless and vulnerable, wishing despite all reason that was her he was desperate to find.

Susanna had always prided herself on her good sense and pragmatic nature, but at this moment she felt like a young girl who'd read too many romantic novels, wishing the hero would finally realize his love for her and sweep her off her feet, promising a life of romance and adventure.

"You silly, silly goose," Susanna chided herself, smiling at her ridiculous thoughts. She only felt drawn to Corporal Johnson because he was injured and needed her, not because he was the hero of her dreams, but her heart told her otherwise as she descended the stairs and returned to her cold, empty room and undressed for bed. Tomorrow was another day and she would wake up in better spirits, rested and happy. But today, she would allow herself to dream.

SIXTY-ONE

ENGLAND SEPTEMBER 1624

Genevieve sat on the bed, but jumped up almost immediately, resuming her pacing. She'd prayed all night but was no closer to an answer than she had been last night when she heard from Lord Sheridan of the mysterious death of Thomas Gaines. He'd been found yesterday morning, the smell of the corpse alerting the people next door that something was terribly wrong. According to Lord Sheridan, Thomas Gaines must have been dead for several days, cause of death unknown. He'd been in good health, according to both his employer and his betrothed, who was distraught over the sudden death of her intended just weeks before their wedding. Genevieve glanced at Louisa when Lord Sheridan broke the news, but Louisa seemed unaffected, her mind probably on her upcoming wedding to Lord Carew. She was the picture of the blushing bride, happy and excited to begin her new life with an adoring husband. If only Theo knew the truth.

Genevieve sat down again, twisting her hands in her lap. She was faced with a horrible decision, one that she shouldn't have to make. If she remained silent, she might be helping to cover up a murder, but if she spoke out, she might be destroying the future she'd been so desperate to secure. Would anyone even believe her? Lord and Lady Sheridan had been warm and welcoming, but how would they react to her accusation? After all, Louisa was their beloved niece, and even though she'd sinned, she was still someone they would be honor-bound to protect and shield from the consequences of her actions. And then there was Uncle Alec. What would his reaction be if his niece accused his daughter of murder? Genevieve got up again, unable to remain immobile. She knew what her conscience was telling her to do, but every fiber in her being screamed for her to remain silent and pretend she knew nothing.

Genevieve sank to her knees, praying for guidance yet again. What did the Lord want her to do? She wasn't sure where the thought came from, but it was as if someone whispered into her ear. She supposed it was the voice of the devil, but she couldn't help but listen.

"What good would it do to expose Louisa?" the voice said. "It wouldn't bring Thomas back and he had certainly used her cruelly. If convicted, Louisa could be sentenced to death, destroying not only her life and that of her unborn child, but of everyone around her. Uncle Alec would despise you, and you would be alone again, only this time without any hope of changing your situation. You'd spend the rest of your life taking care of other people's children with no home or family of your own. You are not even sure that Louisa had gone to church with the sole purpose of walking through the cemetery and gathering yew seeds. Maybe she genuinely wanted to look at the gravestones in her state of repentance and sorrow."

Genevieve slowly rose to her feet, her decision made. After all, what she had really seen was a young girl walking through a cemetery and stopping next to an old tree.

SIXTY-TWO

PARIS OCTOBER 1624

Gentle rays of the late-afternoon sun glinted off the Seine, making the river sparkle like a ribbon of diamonds as it snaked through the bustling metropolis that was Paris, the waterway dotted by small boats. The bridges that would span the river in the centuries to come had yet to be built. The cobblestone streets were wider, flanked by stone buildings that were as beautiful as they were serviceable. Countless spires pierced the autumn sky, but none as striking as the towers of Notre Dame de Paris that rose majestically on the Ile de la Cite, which was clearly visible as the carriage passed along the river. Valerie craned her head to get a better look at the fearsome gargoyles that adorned the structure, their ugly faces meant to ward off evil spirits.

It must have just struck the top of the hour for the bells began to peel, joined by several others from nearby churches. The air vibrated with the sound, reverberating through Valerie's soul and filling it with something akin to rapture. She stole a peek at Alec. He'd been baptized a Catholic, but he'd never actually been inside a Catholic church until his arrival in France. His family had practiced in secret, housing a priest during the days of Alec's parents and then holding their own mass and seeking out a priest for major family events like weddings, christenings, and funerals. What must it feel like to be in a city full of Catholic churches, ringing their bells in fearless harmony, proclaiming their faith to the world?

"Andre, stop in front of the cathedral please," Valerie called out, unable to resist showing Alec one of the most beautiful Catholic cathedrals of all time. She'd never been to Paris, but she'd seen countless pictures of Notre Dame, its bell towers and flower window synonymous with Paris.

"What do you think, Alec?" she asked, beaming at the thought of being able to share this moment with him. "This is the next best thing to St. Peter's in Rome. Isn't it incredible?"

Alec gazed up at the Gothic structure, clearly in awe of its beauty. The rays of the sun lit up the Rose Window, illuminating the colorful shards of glass and making them glow like precious jewels in the light, the vivid colors breathtaking in their intensity.

"I've never seen anything so beautiful," he breathed, "not even Whitehall Palace. What are those things on the side for?"

"They are called Flying Buttresses. I learned about them in one of my art classes. Notre Dame was one of the first buildings in the world to use them as outer supports and they are typical of Gothic architecture. Can you believe it took almost two centuries to build the cathedral?" Valerie gushed.

"It was worth it. I'd like to go inside, but not now."

Valerie could understand his feelings. He'd been in turmoil ever since leaving Loudun. Knowing that a Catholic priest might have been responsible for the seduction and death of Rose weighed heavily on Alec, making him question everything he'd believed his whole life. He wouldn't be at peace until the last piece of the puzzle was in place, and that piece rested with Father Marc, or Cardinal Neuville, as he was now known. Alec didn't think it would be too difficult to find him and hoped he could finally attain some much-needed closure, even if it proved to be painful.

"Let's find an inn and get some supper. I'm suddenly famished," Alec suggested. "We could get you some of that duck you're so fond of."

"You seem in better spirits," Valerie remarked cautiously.

"I suppose I am."

"What if the cardinal refuses to answer your questions or denies everything outright? Will you be able to live with that?"

Valerie couldn't imagine that a Catholic cardinal would confess his sins after all this time. Alec was being naive in thinking that he could just ask politely and get an honest answer.

"Don't worry, sweetheart. I'm not leaving here until I get what I came for," Alec answered cryptically. "Now, let's go eat and maybe we'll have time to walk around the city before it gets dark. We're here on grim business, but we might as well make the best of it."

Despite everything, Alec was excited to be in Paris and eager to see the sights. Valerie frequently thought that if Alec lived in the future, he would travel the world and explore every exotic place he'd ever read about. As the head of the family, he was tethered to the land, but had he been free to pursue his own interests, he might have chosen a vastly different path, unlike Charles, who longed to be in charge. He was a true businessman at heart, exhilarated by the process of turning a profit and implementing new ideas. Valerie was grateful that Alec had been able to get away from the plantation, even for a short time, and enjoy something of France, even if the circumstances that brought him there were unexpectedly painful.

SIXTY-THREE

STATEN ISLAND OCTOBER 1777

"Mutton and boiled potatoes today," Susanna announced as she set the tray down carefully atop the small table by Sam's bed. "I'll cut up the mutton for you, shall I?"

She began to cut the meat into bite-sized pieces, not bothering to wait for Sam's reply. He couldn't cut the food for himself as the tray would rest squarely on his wound, causing him pain.

Sam sat up, watching her. He wasn't particularly hungry these days, but Susanna had taken to sitting with him while he ate, so he stretched the meal out for as long as he could just for the benefit of her company. She was the only person he'd really spoken to since being brought to the fort and he looked forward to their conversations. The other patient had been discharged, and Doctor Freeman usually blew in like a summer storm and blew out just as quickly after checking Sam's progress. Susanna explained that her father was working on creating a pain-numbing compound in his makeshift lab and was closeted in there most days, trying out different formulas and waiting for an opportunity to test them out on wounded soldiers.

Susanna never complained, but she seemed terribly lonely

at times, her beautiful eyes shadowed with sadness as she floated about the empty ward, tidying up things that were more than tidy already. Sam wasn't sure if her father meant to ignore her or if he was simply preoccupied with his work, but Susanna appeared to spend most of her time alone in her room down the hall. She'd been particularly melancholy the last few days, her eyes full of something Sam didn't understand.

"How are you feeling today?" she asked, searching his face for signs of discomfort.

"Much better," Sam lied, not wanting to complain. Lying about in a nightshirt, having his meat cut for him, and being watched as he used the chamber pot was about as much humiliation as he could handle without having her fuss over him like an infant. He tried to hold on to some dignity, but it was probably too late for that.

"And you?" Sam asked in an effort to change the subject.

"I got a letter from my sister. She's pregnant with her first child and I am very happy for her."

Susanna looked anything but happy, her eyes filling with tears and the tip of her nose turning a telltale shade of pink as she turned away from Sam. Sam put his hand over hers in a gesture of comfort, trying to understand what brought on this bout of misery in the normally composed Susanna. Why would her sister's pregnancy affect her so? He supposed it had to do with her own lack of prospects and advancing years and blurted out the first words of comfort that sprang to mind.

"You'll make a wonderful mother someday," he said, watching her face to see if he got it right. Susanna's head whipped around as she stared at him open-mouthed.

"Why did you just say that?" she demanded, her cheeks turning crimson with embarrassment.

"Isn't that why you are so sad? Your sister is pregnant and although you're happy for her, you're deathly afraid that you'll never have a child of your own."

Sam nearly bit his tongue at the look on her face. Susanna went pale, her eyes opening wide in shock. Why couldn't he have kept quiet? He'd only distressed her further. Maybe she hadn't even thought of that but now he put the idea in her head and brought attention to her age. *You blathering idiot!* Sam thought, mentally kicking himself. *What on earth possessed you to spew that bit of homespun wisdom?*

But Susanna suddenly gave him a sheepish smile, squeezing his hand in a gesture of appreciation. "Your Abbie is a very lucky woman, Corporal. Not many men would have been so perceptive. You're right; I am happy for Laura, but deep down I fear I may never experience the joy of motherhood. Love seems to have passed me by."

Sam gazed up at her, wishing she could see how lovely and special she was instead of believing herself to be plain and past the age of marriage. "Susanna, I can't proclaim myself to be a great expert on love, but I believe that sooner or later everyone has their chance. The problem is that most people don't wait for it; they grab the first person they find for fear of being passed over. It takes a world of courage to hold out for the right one and not give in to society's pressure. I wager you've had an offer or two, but you couldn't go against your heart. Am I right?"

Susanna nodded, still smiling. "So, did you hold out for the right one or grab the first one that came along?" she asked as she handed him a cup of ale, watching him with her head cocked to the side. She'd brightened up, her sorrow forgotten. "What is she like, your Abbie?"

"She's beautiful, spirited, and oh-so opinionated," Sam replied, smiling back at her. This conversation had steered him into dangerous waters, and he needed a way to gracefully change the subject.

"Do you not mind?" Susanna asked, watching him intently.

"Mind what?"

"Mind that she's opinionated. Most men find that rather an

unattractive quality in a woman, at least the ones I've come across."

"My father always said that a woman without spirit is like a night sky without the stars and the moon," Sam replied.

"Very poetic. Is your mother a spirited woman then?"

"Yes, she is, and so are my sisters—all of them. A man who is intimidated by an intelligent woman is just a coward who wants a handmaiden rather than a life partner."

Susanna looked at Sam, an expression of amusement on her face. "You're a surprising person, Corporal Johnson, and I thank you for making me feel better. You have a way of putting things in perspective. I don't usually wallow in self-pity, but I suppose everyone has their moments of doubt."

"I'm glad I could help." Sam handed the plate back to Susanna, unable to stomach another bite. All that talk of love left him feeling surprisingly sad. He was preaching about something he knew nothing about. It's not as if he had ever been in love with the right or the wrong person.

"I have some news that might cheer you up as well. The Americans have been defeated at Brandywine Creek. Washington's army fled northeast, and General Howe is poised to take Philadelphia. This might be a turning point, don't you think?"

Sam felt as if he'd been kicked in the stomach as he looked at Susanna's joyful face. She thought the news would make him happy, but he felt a cold hand of desolation squeeze his heart. Could Abbie's information have made any difference? He doubted it, feeling the crushing weight of defeat as he considered the consequences of this British victory. He'd always believed that the Americans would win, but what if Susanna was right and this was the turning point in the war? What if they lost? Sam slid down the bed, pretending to be tired. He wanted Susanna to leave so that he could grieve in peace, but she wasn't done with him yet.

"Corporal Johnson, are you all right? You look pale all of a sudden. Shall I summon my father?" Susanna put a hand to his forehead to check for fever, shaking her head in confusion.

"Thank you, Mistress Freeman; I'm quite all right. Just a little tired, I think. I'm just so overcome by the news of Washington's defeat," he added for good measure.

"Yes, it's something, isn't it? I would have told you sooner, but I didn't think you were well enough to talk about the war. Well, I'll let you rest then."

Susanna leaned over him and kissed him on the forehead, a totally unexpected gesture that left him feeling even more lonely and vulnerable. He closed his eyes to hide his misery from Susanna and kept them closed until she finally left.

SIXTY-FOUR

PARIS OCTOBER 1624

Being a Catholic cardinal must be a lucrative business, Valerie thought as the coach pulled up to Neuville's residence in the Saint-Germain quarter the following morning. The street was lined with handsome townhouses belonging to French nobility, their stone facades a testament to the world-famous architecture of Paris. Neuville's house was set back from the street, surrounded by old horse chestnut trees that provided not only privacy but shade during the warmer days of summer. Alec pushed open the iron gate and they walked beneath the green canopy of leaves toward the front door. It was too quiet, as if a spell had been cast on the house and all the inhabitants were in deep slumber, waiting for someone to come and wake them. Alec banged the brass knocker several times, but there was no answer. The house remained silent and guarded as if holding on to a secret it had been entrusted with by its owner.

"There must be someone here. I can't imagine that a house like this would be left completely unattended," Alec said, pulling Valerie around the corner and toward the outbuilding in the back, which, judging by the rutted track leading to the gate, must serve as a carriage house for the cardinal. Alec pushed open the door, peering into the dim interior. Several carriages were stored inside, cleaned and polished to a shine should the cardinal have need of them. A young boy sat in the corner, whistling a tune and carving something from a small block of wood, deftly wielding the knife as it chipped away pieces of bark.

"Hello there," Alec called out. "You are just the person I was looking for." The boy looked up in surprise, lowering the knife and the block of wood.

"How can I be of help, sir?" he asked, confused. Not many gentlemen invaded his sanctuary in this way, and the boy was clearly thrown off-guard.

"I was to have a meeting with Cardinal Neuville regarding a matter of great importance, but he seems to have forgotten all about it," Alec shared in a friendly tone. "Might you know where I could find him? It's terribly important."

The boy looked at Alec with uncertainly, torn between following orders and fear of insulting a gentleman who clearly had urgent business with his employer. Fear seemed to have won, for the boy got to his feet, coming closer to Alec and Valerie. "The cardinal left early this morning, sir. He had an urgent message from his father last night, you see. He'd been summoned home, but he couldn't leave for Loudun right away. He had an important meeting with the archbishop this morning. That's likely why he forgot his appointment with you, sir."

"Does the cardinal plan to be away long enough to warrant closing down the house?" Alec asked, gazing at the boy.

The boy shrugged his thin shoulders in a typically Gallic gesture of uncertainty, lifting his hands up and gazing heavenward as if only God knew how long the cardinal would be away. "He didn't tell us, sir, but the cardinal keeps only a small staff and sometimes gives them time off while he travels. I suspect they might have left already since most of them have family outside the city that they like to visit."

"And what about you? Don't you have family?"

"No, sir. I'm an orphan. Besides, I like being here by myself. I have the run of the house." The boy suddenly looked scared, as if realizing that the gentleman might tell on him. "That is to say, I..." he faltered, unsure how to extricate himself from the situation.

"Don't worry, son. I won't say a word to the cardinal. Your secret is safe with me. As a matter of fact, no one needs to know I was even here. Agreed?"

The boy nodded enthusiastically, happy to be off the hook. Alec pulled a coin out of his pocket, making sure the boy saw it before asking where the archbishop could be found.

"His name is Jean-Francois de Gondi, and he lives on rue Barbet de Jouy."

"Thank you, you were very helpful. The cardinal must have told me of the meeting with the archbishop and I forgot. How very thoughtless of me." Alec tossed the coin to the boy, who caught it effortlessly and bit down on it before putting it in his pocket.

"I completely understand, sir. I'm glad to have been able to help you." The boy grinned sheepishly, obviously getting Alec's meaning. For a coin, he was more than happy to forget Alec had ever been there.

"Au revoir," he called as Alec and Valerie left the carriage house and headed back to the street.

"I think we can probably intercept him before he leaves for Loudun. I would prefer not to go back there," Alec said, helping Valerie into the carriage. "I can't help wondering if someone warned him about my inquiries or if this is just a coincidence."

"I don't know, Alec, but Madame Jarnot took a great risk in telling you the truth when no one else would. I hope she didn't come to any harm. You heard what she said about the mayor." Valerie was suddenly scared for the woman. If Rose had been murdered, what was there to stop someone from murdering Berenice Jarnot?

"We came across Monsieur Barras just as we were leaving town and went to see Madame Jarnot directly from there. As far as everyone knew we left after visiting Rose's grave. I hope this is just a coincidence. No one in town told us anything, so the mayor would have had no reason to urgently send for his son," Alec reasoned out loud. "Let's see if he's still with the archbishop."

They had no difficulty finding the address the boy had given them as there were only a few houses on that street, each one grander than the next. A sleek coach stood in front of the archbishop's residence, the coachman gazing with longing after a pretty young woman who passed by with her maid. The woman stared straight ahead, but the maid turned around, giving the coachman a saucy smile, which he returned tenfold, forgetting all about her mistress.

"Pardon me," Alec said politely, "but is this the residence of the archbishop? I'm afraid we had a meeting, but I got terribly lost."

"Yes, sir," the coachman answered naively, "but he's meeting with Cardinal Neuville at the moment. I expect they'll be finished soon. We are due to leave the city within the hour."

"How foolish of me to have missed my appointment," Alec said, his face full of regret. "Thank you, young man. You were most helpful. I'll just wait until the cardinal leaves."

"Alec, what are you planning to do?" asked Valerie suspiciously as Alec climbed back inside. "You have that look on your face."

"Oh, what look is that, my dear?" Alec asked with a wicked grin.

"The look that means you have a plan and I'm not a part of it."

"Oh, you are most certainly a part of it," Alec replied. "Now, here's what I want you to do."

SIXTY-FIVE

Alec had a good view of the archbishop's house from where he stood, ready to give Andre the signal. The plan was simplicity itself. Just as the cardinal's coach pulled away from the archbishop's residence, Andre would drive into its path, distracting the coachman while Valerie would be clearly visible in the window, terrified by the near-accident and ready to swoon. The few moments of confusion would give Alec enough time to slip into the cardinal's carriage unnoticed. He would improvise from there. All he needed were a few private moments with the man, and if he couldn't see him in his home, he'd confront him in his carriage, which would give him privacy. After all, it wouldn't do to accost a cardinal of the Church on the streets of Paris.

Alec tensed when he saw a man exit through the door held open by a servant. His red robes billowed in the morning breeze, sun glinting off the gold cross just below his breastbone, a red skullcap covering his dark head. The cardinal walked toward the carriage briskly, his mind clearly on whatever he'd discussed with his superior, but even the stern look on his face couldn't hide the beauty of his features. His lean face looked as if it were carved from stone, the high cheekbones and full lips too sensual for a cleric. The cardinal's dark hair was peppered with gray, giving him an aura of mature authority that went well with the robes of office. The cardinal walked with assurance and grace, very much aware of his height and good looks. He finally got into the carriage and the coachman took up the reins, ready to navigate the magnificent coach through the congested streets of Paris.

Alec waved to Andre, holding his breath as the coach lurched around the corner, nearly colliding with the oncoming vehicle. He heard Valerie's scream as he left his hiding place and approached the cardinal's coach from the rear, so as not to be seen by the coachman who had jumped off the box and was now berating Andre in rapid French, calling him every name he could think of without offending the delicate ears of his frightened passenger. Alec yanked open the door and jumped in, taking a seat opposite the stunned cardinal.

"Good morning, Cardinal Neuville," Alec greeted the cardinal cordially, a dagger clearly visible in his hand. "I thought we might have a chat before you leave Paris. I hope I'm not inconveniencing you too greatly, but this will only take a few minutes of your time. My name is Alexander Whitfield, by the way. I'm Genevieve's maternal uncle." Alec was pleased to see a look of fear in the deep blue eyes that were regarding him with such wariness.

"Whitfield, you say? I don't believe I'm familiar with the name," the cardinal replied carefully, clearly buying himself time to think. He remained calm, his back erect and his gaze direct as he observed Alec, waiting for his next move.

"Allow me to remind you, Your Grace. You knew my sister, Rose Whitfield at the Convent of Loudun, and had fathered her daughter, Genevieve." The cardinal looked at Alec as if he were excrement on his expensive shoes, his face tightening with anger and his hands balling into fists at his sides.

"Monsieur Whitfield, I seem to remember a young woman who gave birth to a bastard and drowned herself in shame. The girl is not my child, and I resent the accusation."

The cardinal might have been proclaiming his innocence, but he grew visibly tense, his shoulders hunched beneath his robes and his generous mouth stretched into a thin line as he stared Alec down. Alec didn't think his reaction was that of an innocent man.

"So, you deny having seduced my sister, Your Grace?" Alec asked politely.

"I absolutely do. Now get out of my coach, you ruffian." He squared his shoulders, his face contorted with indignation.

"I'm so terribly sorry, Your Grace. I must have been mistaken," Alec replied, getting up to leave the coach. He could see the look of satisfaction on the cardinal's face. He clearly thought he was off the hook and would go on as before. Alec suddenly whirled around, taking a seat next to the cardinal and forcing him into a corner, the point of the dagger pressing into his neck and almost piercing the skin.

"Let's try this again, Your Grace," Alec suggested, giving the cardinal a savage smile.

"Tell me about my sister. And I'd like to hear the truth this time." The cardinal tried to move out of the way, but Alec grabbed his head, pressing the dagger hard enough to break the skin. A thin trickle of blood ran onto the robe, making an ugly dark stain on the smooth crimson cloth. The cardinal paled, his hands shaking in his lap.

"All right, you barbarian," he spat out. "I'll tell you the truth if you leave me alone."

"Whether I leave you alone largely depends on the nature of the truth," Alec replied. "Start talking, *Your Grace*," he hissed, using the title with unveiled sarcasm.

"Yes, I knew Rose," the cardinal admitted warily. "I met her in Calais on my way back to Loudon. She was very beautiful and maddeningly devout. You see, I'd never met anyone like her before. She had the type of faith one doesn't see often, not even as a priest. She was special."

"So, you seduced her?" Alec asked, his voice full of incredulity. But the cardinal shook his head, careful not to get too close to the dagger at his throat. He had the look of a defeated man.

"I never chose this vocation. I was destined for the Church while my oldest brother would inherit the estate and my other brother would go into the army. It was my father's wish and I wasn't given a say in the matter. I never wanted a life of celibacy and self-denial, but once I took my vows, I accepted my fate and remained chaste. You might not believe me, but I take my office very seriously and did so while I was a parish priest as well."

The cardinal turned his head to face Alec, a look of resignation on his face. Alec grew still, realizing he was about to hear the truth at last.

"Monsieur Whitfield, Genevieve is not my daughter—she's my niece, and I have done everything in my power to make sure that she was well taken care of and received a good education that would enable her to make a life for herself outside the convent, since she had no wish to take the veil."

"Are you saying that your brother seduced my sister?"

"Seduced is not a word I would use when speaking of my brother," the cardinal replied. "My younger brother, Henri, was the one destined for the Church, as the youngest son, but my father knew from the time he was a small boy that Henri would be much better suited to the army. He was always a cruel and violent child, who enjoyed inflicting suffering and pain. My father tried to discipline him, but he couldn't do much to change his nature, especially when my mother was always pleading his case. No amount of beatings and punishments could make him into a kinder person. When Henri was little, he limited his cruelty to animals, but as he got older, he became more interested in people and the power he could wield over them through force and manipulation. No maid was safe from him, and after he worked his way through the chateau staff, he turned his attention to the village."

"You mean, Martine?" Alec had to restrain himself from driving the dagger further into the cardinal's neck, infuriated by his calm acceptance of his brother's crimes. The cardinal lifted his hands as if to indicate that it had been the will of God and not the callous actions of his brother that had resulted in her untimely death.

"Martine was a lovely girl, and I was sorry she died. She was only fifteen at the time, but many women die in childbirth, no? My father should have sent Henri away then, but he felt that Henri was still too young for the army and kept him at home for another two years. You see, I blame myself for what happened to Rose because I unwittingly piqued Henri's interest in her. I often spoke of her to the family, marveling at her unwavering faith and devotion to God. I think Henri saw her as the ultimate challenge."

"He raped her?" Alec asked through clenched teeth. He was seething with rage, his heart burning with the need for vengeance against Henri, the cardinal, and their father, who'd abused his position as mayor and used his power to protect his son.

The cardinal nodded, having the decency to finally look contrite. "I had no knowledge of what happened until the day Rose died. Mother Superior came to see my father on the night Genevieve was born. She suspected that Henri was the father and demanded that he take responsibility for Rose and the child, since she could not allow her to stay at the convent with the baby and remain a nun. It was out of the question. My father promised to see to it that Henri married Rose and acknowledged the child as his own. He'd turned a blind eye to many sins, but even he couldn't ignore the fact that his son had defiled a nun. My father has a great fear of God, probably because he has good reason to." Cardinal Neuville sighed.

"Unfortunately, my father underestimated Henri yet again, trusting him to do his bidding. Henri strangled Rose and tossed her into the river to make it look like a suicide." The cardinal snuggled deeper into the corner of the carriage, fearing Alec's reaction to his confession.

"And you knew about this all along?" asked Alec, shocked that a priest would allow such a crime to go unpunished. "You kept your silence to protect your brother?"

"I had no choice. Henri told me everything under the seal of confession. I couldn't come forward without being defrocked by the Church. My father sent Henri off as soon as he learned the truth, refusing to do anything to punish him. We argued bitterly, but in the end, I had no choice but to go along with him, especially since my mother was mad with grief and begged me not to come forward. She wanted to take the baby, but my father refused, not wanting to give the villagers any more reason to speculate than they already had. I've lived with the guilt all these years." The cardinal wiped his cheek, although it appeared perfectly dry.

"Yes, your suffering must have been great," Alec remarked sarcastically. "You were elevated to the position of cardinal while my sister was buried at a crossroads with her soul condemned to Hell, and your niece was raised in a convent, where she was reminded every day of her mother's shame and her bastard status. It must have been hell for you," he added, his eyes glinting with anger. "And where is your brother now, if I might ask?"

"My brother died a few months after joining the army. You'll be pleased to know that he didn't die in battle but was killed by one of the other officers for cheating at cards. It was a form of justice, don't you think?"

"Not really, but I suppose I must accept it and proceed accordingly, which is where you come in, Your Grace."

"What would you have me do, Monsieur?" asked Neuville, looking nervous. He couldn't break the seal of confession even after all these years for he would lose everything, not to mention bring terrible shame on his family.

"I would have you travel to Loudun, as planned. Once you get there, you will have my sister's body exhumed and buried in the church cemetery with a proper burial service conducted by you. You will make a public statement saying that she was murdered. I don't expect you to name your brother as the murderer, but you will clear her name. You will also convince your father to make provisions for Genevieve, making sure that she's well-provided for the rest of her life. I will act as her guardian until she marries and will give her my name. Is that clear, Your Grace?"

"And if I refuse?" All the fight had gone out of the cardinal, but he wasn't ready to capitulate, still hoping to avoid having to deal with the consequences of his family's actions.

"If you refuse, you will be the next body they pull out of the river, followed by that of your father." Alec replied conversationally.

"Are you threatening me?" the cardinal asked, shocked. "You, a Catholic, would threaten a cardinal of the Church?"

"Yes, I am, Your Grace, and my threats are rarely idle. I will kill you, make no mistake. You might not have raped my sister, but you stood by and allowed her to be treated as a suicide while your brother went free."

"You know that I could have you excommunicated?" the cardinal asked loftily.

"I live in Virginia, and as far as I know, there isn't a single Catholic church anywhere within a hundred miles. You may excommunicate me, Your Grace, but it will make absolutely no difference to my faith or my life. Now, I will get out of your carriage and let you consider my proposal, but I won't be far behind. I will accompany you to Loudun and attend either my sister's funeral or yours. The choice is yours." Alec bowed to the cardinal, exiting the carriage and jogging toward his own, which had been following the cardinal's coach as instructed.

"Well?" asked Valerie, noting the blood drying on the dagger. "What did the Devil of Loudun have to say for himself?"

"The cardinal will honor my request with pleasure," said Alec with a smile, giving Valerie a warm kiss.

"Somehow I doubt that pleasure will enter into it, but I'm glad you got what you came for."

"I will be at peace knowing that Rose rests in consecrated ground. I never believed she went to Hell, but I know it would have been important to her."

"May she rest in peace," Valerie said, squeezing Alec's hand.

"Amen."

SIXTY-SIX

The day dawned sunny and bright, the cloudless sky the color of bluebells. It had grown colder over the past few days, a hint of the coming winter noticeable early in the morning and at night when darkness settled over London, chasing the last bit of warmth away and replacing it with the crisp air of fall. Louisa loved this time of year. Another week or two and a fire would be needed during the night, the lovely smell of burning wood and dancing shadows filling the bedroom. Louisa placed her hand on her belly as she did every morning, checking if it had grown any bigger. Her stomach was still flat, but it felt different, tender. Her breasts had grown larger, the nipples more sensitive and the veins bluish against the milky whiteness of her skin. Her figure was changing, and it wouldn't be long before the child inside her proclaimed dominion over her body. She had to admit that she was looking forward to this new experience. It made her a real woman. If only she could be sure that the child was Theo's. It would make things so much easier. Would she ever know who the father really was unless the child bore a striking resemblance to Theo or Tom?

"Rise and shine," her aunt sang as she entered the room, carrying Louisa's gown. "You'd better get up now if you want to have time to have some breakfast before we leave for church. Your uncle has already gone to collect Theo. They will meet us there at ten. Nervous?"

Louisa sat up, watching her aunt hang up the gown and take matching shoes out of the trunk. She seemed in good spirits, which was an improvement on the last few weeks. Louisa couldn't bear it if Aunt Lou and Uncle Kit were angry with her.

"No, Aunt Lou, I'm not nervous, but I am excited. Theo is everything I ever wanted in a husband."

Her aunt gave her a puzzled look as if to ask what in the bloody hell she had been doing with Tom when Theo was such a prize, but remained silent, not wanting to ruin the special day. Louisa hoped everything would go as planned. Theo's brothers were coming to the wedding and Walter was already at Aunt Caroline's London house having come up from the country the day before. Louisa looked forward to meeting them and hoped they would approve of their brother's choice. She knew that Robin had his reservations about Theo marrying a Catholic and a commoner. If only he knew that the Catholic commoner was also pregnant with a child that might or might not be his brother's. Louisa washed her face and sat down in front of the mirror, allowing the maid to brush out her hair before arranging it in an elaborate hairstyle. She intended to be a beautiful bride, radiant and confident despite the circumstances. Tom was gone for good, so no one had the power to betray her any longer.

If only Genevieve was happier for her. The girl had been sour and pensive since the day at the graveyard, but she wouldn't say a word. Her fear of being cast out was too great, making her easy to manipulate. Genevieve would come to the church and appear to be happy for her, but it would be a relief not to live in the same house with her any longer. The newlyweds would take up residence at their new house in Cheapside, which Robin had generously bought for them as a wedding present. The house had come fully furnished, sold by a family who'd fallen on hard times and needed to raise capital in a hurry. Louisa wasn't pleased with having to live with someone else's choice of furniture and decorations, but she would change everything in time, putting her own stamp on the house and making it a place of beauty and comfort.

Theo had a country estate as well, but Louisa was in no hurry to go to the country. They would go there next summer to escape the heat and infection of the city, but for now, she wanted to enjoy everything London had to offer. Louisa closed her eyes for a brief moment, picturing herself sitting on a blanket in a sunny meadow with a beautiful infant in her lap, his dark hair curling just like Theo's. She smiled at the image, resolving to put Thomas Gaines out of her mind forever.

The ancient church was bathed in sunlight as Louisa stepped from the carriage, holding up the hem of her skirt. Aunt Lou's seamstress had outdone herself, creating a gorgeous gown of pale-pink silk with a rounded neckline and winged collar worked with tiny seed pearls. The bodice and hem were decorated with the same pattern, leaving the voluminous skirt unadorned in between. It was beautiful, yet understated, bringing the eye to the lovely girl wearing the dress and not the over-the-top decoration that had been so popular in earlier years. A dainty hat made of matching fabric completed the outfit, perched atop Louisa's dark curls at a jaunty angle and giving her a flirtatious air. Louisa had never felt as beautiful as she did at that moment and she smiled at Uncle Kit, who came out of the church to escort her inside and give her away in marriage.

Louisa barely noticed the two handsome men who stood when she walked in or the disapproving gaze of Aunt Maud, her eyes on Theo, whose face split into a smile of joy as he saw her walk down the nave. Her life began at this moment and everything that came before was just chaff. Louisa wished her parents could be there to see her take her rightful place in London society as Lady Carew.

SIXTY-SEVEN

A light rain fell from the pewter skies, covering everything in sight with a glistening sheen of moisture. The street was quickly turning into a muddy, slippery mess, making walking at a good pace a dangerous sport. A thick mist blew off the river, the boats nearly invisible, their lanterns giving off fuzzy orbs of light that appeared to be floating out of the mist of their own accord. Boatmen could be heard calling to each other, their voices sounding strangely detached from their bodies.

Kit stared straight ahead as he walked along, concentrating on not slipping and falling into a pile of refuse. He was miserable enough without being covered in shit. He supposed he could have taken the carriage, but he didn't want anyone to know where he was going. He'd been taken aback when Buckingham invited him to come to York House on the Strand. Would he really make love to him with his wife right there in the same house? Kit wondered if the poor woman knew of her husband's proclivities, but then again, maybe she didn't care. Few marriages were based on love and desire, most being contracts between two families designed to further the political and financial interests of both parties. Lady Katherine Manners had been sold to Buckingham in marriage like many others of her station. All the same, Kit hoped he wouldn't have to face her.

The house loomed ahead, solid and imposing, a palace onto itself. It wasn't nearly as vast as Whitehall, but it had a grandeur that marked it as a residence of someone to be reckoned with. Kit could hear the splashing of water against the dock as a boat pulled up to the arched water gate on the riverbank. Was someone coming or going? Kit had a flash of hope that Buckingham had changed his mind and left the premises, but knew it wasn't likely. Whoever was getting out of the boat was alone, and Buckingham was never alone.

A liveried manservant led Kit down several hallways, their vaulted ceilings and high windows reminiscent of a church. The only sound was the echo of their footsteps on the marble floor and the oppressive sound of a house with not enough occupants and too many rooms. Kit supposed Buckingham had his private apartments separate from his wife, whom he probably visited only occasionally for the purpose of procreation.

The servant led Kit through a set of heavy wooden doors that led to yet another hallway and another set of doors. A maid scurried past them, carrying a basket of linens, but otherwise the hallway was deserted. The final set of doors led to Buckingham's private apartments—*the entrance to Hell,* Kit thought as he pushed open the door and walked inside. Buckingham didn't come to greet him this time. He sat with his feet up on a low stool, a fire blazing in the grate. It wasn't cold, but dampness penetrated everything this close to the river, the mist swirling right outside, engulfing everything in a gray shroud.

Buckingham gestured to a chair opposite his own, his eyes never leaving the merry fire. He certainly didn't seem amorous today, his hooded eyes blank and staring, a goblet of wine in his hand.

"Are you all right, Your Grace?" Kit asked, hoping he wasn't. Buckingham took a sip of wine, his eyes never straying from the dancing flames. He shook his head as he shrugged noncommittally.

"The Duke of Buckingham is always all right; it's George Villiers that has his moments of melancholy. Get some wine, Christopher," he added absentmindedly.

"What's troubling you, George?" Kit asked, pouring himself a glass of wine and sitting down. He suddenly realized that Villiers wanted more from him than just physical gratification. He wanted him to play the lover, listening and comforting him in his hour of need. That was absurd, but he supposed listening to Buckingham for a little while was a lot less agonizing than being fucked.

"Come, George, tell me about it," he invited, taking a sip of wine and watching his "lover" debate the wisdom of sharing his concerns.

Buckingham ran his hand through his unruly curls, finally turning to face Kit. "I suppose I'm just being overly sensitive, but I'm not very popular these days." He gave Kit a dramatic look, his face scrunched up like a child that was about to cry.

"Surely His Majesty still loves you," Kit replied. He'd recently heard a rumor that the king referred to Buckingham as "my sweet child and wife" in one of his letters. It hadn't been the first expression of love from their monarch, his love for Villiers an open secret at court. Was it really possible that the king himself was a sodomite, maintaining a relationship with Buckingham right under the nose of the queen?

"Sweet James will always love me, but it's the people I'm referring to. They've gotten wind of Charles's betrothal to Henrietta Maria of France, which I helped to broker. His Majesty approves the match for his son, especially since the alliance with the Spanish princess didn't come to fruition, but the people are not happy, Christopher. She's a Catholic princess; that's all they care about. What does it matter if she flagellates herself or yearns to burn someone at the stake? Her only job is to guarantee our alliance with France and spread her legs often enough to produce several heirs. It's not as if she will have a voice in anything that matters." Buckingham took another sip of wine, pouting like a girl. Kit was sure he wasn't finished with his list of grievances.

"And speaking of heirs, did you know I only have one daughter? I must have a son to inherit the title once I'm gone. A son!" He turned to Kit as if he were the one who failed to provide him with an heir. "You have a son," he added accusingly. "How happy you must be."

Maybe you're sticking it in the wrong place, thought Kit with uncharacteristic venom, forcing himself to rearrange his face into an expression of understanding and sympathy.

"You are still young, George, you'll have more children."

"I'm thirty-two, Christopher, hardly young. I should have had half a dozen heirs by now, but my wife has managed one girl. Do you enjoy lying with your wife?" he asked suddenly.

"I love my wife, George." Kit wasn't about to discuss his marital relations with Buckingham. He would not taint his feelings for Louisa by sharing them with a man who was blackmailing him and causing him such torment.

"How blessed you are to be married to a woman you love. I could never be in a legal union with the object of my affection, but it doesn't mean my love is any less real." Buckingham rose to his feet, putting his glass on a table, his hand unsteady. "I think I need to lie down, Christopher. My head aches something awful and my bowels are in a knot. Thank you for listening to me. You've made me feel better." Buckingham planted a wine-infused kiss on Kit's lips, holding out his hand. "Come and lie down with me awhile."

Buckingham carefully reclined on the bed, putting his head

on Kit's shoulder and snuggling closer in an effort to get more comfortable. Kit had no choice but to put his arms around him and hold him as he finally fell asleep, murmuring words of love and gratitude that left Kit feeling even worse than he already did.

SIXTY-EIGHT

STATEN ISLAND OCTOBER 1777

Abbie kneaded the dough for bread as if it had grossly offended her in some way. She punched it and slammed it against the table, using it to release some of her fear and frustration. Sam had been gone for over three weeks and despite all their efforts, they hadn't found a trace of his whereabouts. Finn had gone out with Jim Jenkins the day after Sam vanished, but word got around quickly that the authorities were looking for them, forcing them to stay hidden at the farm. Mr. Jenkins did his best but found nothing.

For the first few days, Abbie kept hoping that Sam would just show up, having survived somehow and found his way to them, but as time went by, she had to face the truth. Sam was gone. If he had survived, he would have managed to get word to them, but there'd been nothing but deafening silence. Abbie slammed the dough one last time before molding it into several loaf-shaped ovals and putting them into the oven to bake. She sat down, suddenly tired. She was grateful not to feel nauseated like Martha did when she was first pregnant, but she did feel awfully tired and desperate for a nap after the midday meal.

Finn encouraged her to rest, knowing that the only time she was truly at peace was when she slept.

Abbie looked up as Finn came in, carrying two buckets of milk. He set them down and looked her over. "Are you all right? You look flushed." Abbie nodded, picking up a cup and handing it to Finn to fill with milk. She was terribly thirsty. Finn gave her a cup of milk and took one for himself, drinking it in one long swallow.

"Abbie, it's time to leave." He said it quietly, but his tone brooked no argument. "It's been nearly two weeks now. The British have defeated General Washington at Brandywine Creek and are poised to take Philadelphia. We must leave while we can."

Abbie went still, the empty cup falling from her hand as she absorbed the news. How could this have happened? First Washington lost New York, and now he would lose Philadelphia. This was so much worse than any of them expected.

"When did this happen?" she asked, her eyes glistening with unshed tears.

"The battle took place on September eleventh. General Howe managed to position his forces behind Washington's right flank, breaking through and driving the Continental Army to the northeast. Jim only told me this morning."

"So, my information was useless?" Abbie asked. It rankled her to think that she would have died for nothing.

"I don't know." Finn sat down on the bench, suddenly looking defeated. "Abbie, we need to leave."

"Finn, I can't leave until I know what happened to Sam. Please, don't ask me to." Abbie looked away from him, hoping he would let the matter drop for the time being, but Finn wasn't giving up.

"We can't afford to wait any longer. Sam's gone, Abbie."

"No, he's not!" she cried, tears spilling down her cheeks. They were never too far away these days.

"Abbie, if Sam survived, he will find his way back. He is a soldier; he can take care of himself. In the meantime, you must think of our child. We have to go back to Virginia." Finn stood up, placing his palms on the table and glaring at her. He had no intention of backing down, and she knew it.

"Finn, the baby doesn't seem real to me yet, but I've known Sam all my life. He's my big brother and I love him with all my heart. How can I just leave him here?" She wiped the tears away angrily, upset with Finn for not seeing her point of view.

"I love him too, Abbie. He's like the brother I never had, but you are my priority. I swore to your father that I would bring you home." His voice was low, but she could hear him just fine. "I have never imposed my will on you. Never. But you are my wife and you will obey me in this. We will leave by the end of this week. Is that understood?"

"I'll never forgive you for this." Abbie stood up and ran to the bedroom, slamming the door behind her. She knew Finn was right, but she needed someone to blame, and right now he was all she had. Abbie threw herself down on the bed, crying her heart out and hoping that Finn would follow her and comfort her, but he didn't. The door remained firmly closed.

SIXTY-NINE

Sam was woken up by the sound of voices coming from the next room. He'd been in and out of consciousness so much, he'd lost track of how long he'd been at the fort. It had to be close to two weeks, but he wasn't sure. His days were reduced to eating and sleeping, mostly sleeping. The fever had subsided and the hot poker in his stomach had cooled some, but he was still weak and in pain. Sam reached for a cup of water, but his hand stilled as the conversation from the other room began to sink in.

"Doctor, I have orders from the colonel to question Corporal Johnson," an unfamiliar voice said.

"I understand that, Captain, but Corporal Johnson is my patient and I'm telling you that he's in no condition to answer any questions. He's just beginning to recover from the infection in his wound. What is so urgent that can't keep for a few days?"

Sam could hear the captain's exasperated sigh. "Doctor, I have my orders."

"And I have a responsibility to my patient." Doctor Freeman sounded unusually firm, ready to do battle with the captain.

"Ah, Captain Manning, if I might intervene," Susanna

piped in, trying to diffuse the situation between the two men. "I just checked on Corporal Johnson and he's unconscious. He's been slipping in and out of consciousness due to the high fever. I'm afraid you won't be able to question him even if you try, so I suggest you come back later. What is this all about anyway?" Susanna asked, sounding annoyed with the captain and curious at the same time.

"On the day the patrol found Corporal Johnson, a young woman named Abigail Whitfield was to be hanged at City Hall Park. On the way to the gallows two British soldiers ambushed the cart, killing the escort and freeing the prisoner. We believe one of them was wounded during the rescue. We think Corporal Johnson may have been involved in the incident."

"Did you say Abigail?" Susanna asked, sounding shocked.

"Yes. She was charged with spying, as was her husband, but he got away before our soldiers had a chance to take him into custody."

"Why would British soldiers ambush British soldiers?" asked Doctor Freeman. "Seems rather odd."

"They weren't really British soldiers, Doctor. Two soldiers were discovered in an alley behind Madame Mabel's bro...—eh, establishment. They'd been knocked out and relieved of their uniforms and weapons. We believe that Mistress Whitfield's husband and an accomplice posed as British officers and mounted a rescue. Corporal Johnson might not be who he pretends to be." Captain Manning was quickly losing his patience, but the Freemans weren't done with him yet.

"What will happen to him if he were involved?" Susanna asked quietly.

"He will hang, ma'am. Now, if you would be so kind as to inform me as soon as Corporal Johnson comes to. I really must speak with him. Good day to you both."

"Insufferable man!" Susanna exclaimed as soon as the

sound of the captain's footsteps died away on the stone staircase.

"I'm not interested in what he might have done. I'm a surgeon and my duty is to the patient. They can question him to their heart's content once he recovers. Now, my dear, I am feeling a bit peckish, since I haven't had my breakfast yet. I trust you will be all right here on your own?"

"Of course, Father."

Sam watched Susanna silently as she walked into the room, her eyes never leaving his face. She didn't look angry or accusing, just sad. Her eyes were full of hurt as she pulled up a chair and sat down, her hands folded demurely in her lap.

"I am guessing you heard that," she stated. "I would have never thought it true had he not mentioned Abigail. She's your wife, isn't she?"

"She's my sister," Sam said quietly. "Will you turn me in to the captain?"

"I don't know. On the one hand, you are guilty of murder and circumvention of justice. On the other, you did what any brother would do. Who was the other man, her husband?"

"Yes, my brother-in-law. They're just eighteen and were married only a few months ago. Was he supposed to let her hang?"

"Was she really spying, Patrick? Is that even your real name?" Susanna's eyes never left his, making Sam feel vulnerable and confused. It was probably a mistake to tell her anything, but he felt the need to confess, whatever the cost. If he had any chance of getting out alive, Susanna was it, and he couldn't afford to lie to her any longer.

"My name is Sam Mallory, and yes, she was spying. We serve the Revolution, not the king. Does that shock you, Susanna?"

"No. I'm not unsympathetic to your cause, believe it or not, but people very rarely ask for my opinion in these matters.

Now, get up." Susanna pushed back the chair, suddenly full of purpose.

"Why?" *She must have made up her mind to turn me in,* Sam thought as he slowly got off the cot. *She'll march me to Captain Manning, and I won't be able to do anything to stop her because I'd rather die than hurt her.*

"Because we are leaving." Susanna disappeared for a moment, returning with Sam's uniform, which had been cleaned. "Get dressed and wait for me here. I'll be back in a moment."

"How do I know you won't call for help?" Sam asked.

"You'll just have to trust me, Sam Mallory," she replied, giving him a brilliant smile. "Now hurry."

Sam tried to hurry but getting dressed was a difficult process given his weakened state and the pain in his stomach. He nearly passed out as he bent down to pull on his boots, putting pressure on the wound. It took him a few moments to catch his breath before he could tie back his hair and put on the tricorn she left on his bed. By the time Susanna returned, he was dressed and ready to go, although he had no idea where they were heading.

"Here, take this," she held out a musket, grinning at Sam's astonished face. "It's my father's, although he's never used it. I've asked the stable boy to prepare a trap. It should be ready by now. Follow me and just play along." Sam slung the musket over his shoulder and followed Susanna out of the room and into the lovely October morning. Susanna looked businesslike, with her straw bonnet and a basket slung over her arm. The trap was already waiting. "You drive," she said as she climbed onto the bench, adjusting her skirts and placing the basket in her lap. Sam mounted the bench with some difficulty, then drove toward the gates of the fort, praying this ruse would work.

The yard was surprisingly quiet, since a lot of the soldiers garrisoned at the fort were at breakfast at that time of the morning. With the British occupying the area, there was no sense of urgency or danger as people went about their business. Several officers passed by, but they did little more than greet Susanna respectfully and move on.

Two young sentries manned the gate, desperately trying to hide their boredom. They were no older than sixteen, their faces fresh and hairless. The sentries snapped to attention as the trap drew up to the gate.

"I'm on my way to collect some surgical supplies for Doctor Freeman from Richmond Town," stated Susanna.

"Yes, ma'am. Do be careful." The young sentry gave Susanna a smile, which she eagerly returned.

"I will, Bobby. Now open the gate." The boys pushed open the heavy wooden gates, allowing them to pass unchallenged. Sam stared ahead as he drove through the gate, the sound of the gates closing music to his ears. He drove in the direction of Richmond, picking up speed as they got further from the fort. Sam gazed around, trying to get his bearings and determine which way the Jenkins farm was. Finn and Abbie were likely long gone, but Jim would help him. He'd need to leave fast before the authorities came looking for him.

Sam suddenly realized that he would never see Susanna again and the thought made him unbearably sad. He'd gotten used to seeing her every day and looked forward to their conversations. The hospital had been deserted save for a few cases of upset stomach or cuts that needed to be dressed, so Susanna had been free to look after him and keep him company. Sam snuck a peek at Susanna, needing to remember her face as it looked at that moment, illuminated by the morning sun and so serious that it made him smile.

Susanna felt his gaze upon her and turned to face him, confused by his smile. "Sam, my father will be back from breakfast shortly and might raise the alarm, so you need to make your escape soon. I will return to the fort and tell them that you forced me to help you. Do you have a place to go? Will you be all right?"

"I will now. I don't know how to thank you. You've saved my life twice. I would do anything to repay you, just name it." Sam reached out and took her hand in his, bringing it to his lips. He wasn't sure what made him do it, but he wanted to touch her, to feel her skin against his lips.

"You can repay me by staying safe and getting your sister far away from here. They won't stop looking for you." Susanna shyly took her hand back, casting her eyes down as if all the answers were to be found in her basket.

Sam continued to drive, turning back periodically to make sure no one was in pursuit. He couldn't help noticing the look on Susanna's face. She sat staring straight ahead, her back rigid as a pole, her lips quivering slightly in an effort not to cry.

"Susanna, I'm so sorry I have put you in this position. I know this must be distasteful for you. No one will blame you if they believe you were in danger." Sam reached for her hand again, but drew back, not wanting to upset her further. Susanna turned to face him, her eyes full of tears as she reached up and touched his cheek tenderly, her thumb brushing across his lips.

"Sam, I helped you because I couldn't bear to see you hang, and I'm proud of what I've done. This is probably the first act of free will that I've undertaken in my whole life. And now I'm about to undertake a second one. Take me with you. Please, Sam. I don't expect you to marry me. I only want to be with you in any capacity you'll have me." She stared into his eyes, her cheeks turning crimson as she realized what she had just done.

The words came unbidden and unplanned, tumbling from her mouth as if of their own accord. She'd never been so forward in her life, but her heart knew this was her only chance, even if her mind hadn't realized it yet. The thought of never seeing Sam again left her paralyzed with pain, the rest of her life stretching before her, long and barren. She loved him, and she didn't care if he never married her. She'd gladly be his mistress if only she could have his love and affection, if only for a short time. She would take what he gave her and be grateful, happy to know what it was like to be alive at last. It was never too late to go back to her old life, taking care of her father and finding small pleasures in a good book or in the improved health of her patients. At least she would have something to look back on, a time of madness when she took love and was woman enough to give it back.

"What do you mean, take me with you?" Sam stared at her uncomprehending. "I'm an American Revolutionary and you are the daughter of a British military surgeon. Do you realize what you're asking?" He was aghast at her suggestion, but suddenly his heart filled with hope. Was it possible that she really cared for him?

"I realize what I'm asking, but the thought of never seeing you again makes me feel as if my heart has been ripped out of my chest and stomped on a few hundred times. I'm sorry to put you in this position. I should have remained quiet. Of course, you don't feel the same. It was foolish of me to assume you did; it's just that..." She grew quiet, silenced by humiliation. "Forget I said anything." She looked away, taking his surprise for rejection.

"You would never see your father again. He'll think I forced you to leave and possibly even hurt you."

Sam hated to think that the man who'd done so much to help him would believe him a murderer and abductor of women, but the unreasonable hope in his heart kept growing, filling his chest with something like happiness.

"I left him a note, telling him that I helped you and went with you willingly. I will destroy it once I get back to the fort," she mumbled, turning away from him in embarrassment.

"But won't you be sorry to leave him?"

"Sam, my mother died when I was twelve. I had to take on

the role of the lady of the house and take care of my father and little sister, who was only four at the time. They were so helpless, so lost. I told myself year after year that it was my duty to put them first and that my happiness didn't matter. I'd never allowed myself to entertain the idea of getting married or having a family of my own as long as they needed me.

I raised Laura as if she were my own child, but children grow up, and Laura left me. She got married shortly before father and I left England. Maybe it's selfish, but I'm twenty-five, and I need to think of my own happiness before it's too late. Father will just have to learn to accept that. He's a wonderful, caring man, but at times he forgets that I'm his daughter and not his wife."

Sam reached for her hand, squeezing it gently as he willed her to look at him. "Susanna, can you really see yourself with me? I'm not good enough for you."

"I'll be the judge of who's good enough and who isn't," she said, finally smiling. "I just want to be with you, Sam, and I think somewhere deep inside you feel the same."

Sam didn't say anything; he just pulled her close and kissed her with all the tenderness and joy he felt.

"Let's go then," Sam turned the cart toward the Jenkins farm, praying that Abbie and Finn were safely away by now.

* * *

Abbie set the basket of laundry on the bank, hitching up her skirt so it wouldn't get wet. She could have done the laundry in the yard, but she wanted a little time away from the house, and Finn. They'd barely spoken the past two days, and although she could understand Finn's feelings, she was still angry. He never told her what to do, but this time he was adamant. As her husband, he had the right to command her, but as her love, he should know better. How could she leave without finding out what happened to Sam? Even if they got word that Sam had died, it would be preferable to this terrible not knowing. She prayed day and night that someone took pity on him and tended to him, but most likely he was buried somewhere in a grave they'd never find. What in the world would she tell her parents? She knew her father would side with Finn and tell her that he'd done the right thing, but in her heart, it felt wrong to leave.

Finn was right, of course. Staying at the farm was no longer safe and they had to leave before it was too late. They were deep behind enemy lines, their situation precarious. Abbie wiped away a tear as she concentrated on Finn's shirt. She tried to keep busy, but her mind wasn't so easy to fool. All her thoughts were of Sam. After her twin, Luke, Sam had always been her favorite sibling. He was so much fun, unlike Martha, always playing pranks and taking her fishing instead of doing his chores. *Oh, Sam, may God keep you safe if you are out there somewhere*, she thought.

"Abbie! Come here." Finn was waving to her as he ran down the hill toward the stream. "Abbie!"

She turned away from him as if she hadn't heard, intent on her task. She wasn't ready to forgive him just yet. What could possibly be so important anyway?

"Abbie, come here," he cried. "Sam's here."

Abbie dropped the clean laundry onto the muddy bank, racing up the hill toward Finn. Had she heard him correctly? Could it really be true? Finn grabbed her hand and they ran back together, suddenly united again, all anger forgotten.

"Oh, Sam," Abbie cried as she flew into his arms. He was still wearing the red tunic, but his head was uncovered, his hair falling into his eyes as he held her close. "Are you all right? We thought you were dead."

She finally looked up at him, taking stock. He was thinner and his face was pale beneath the bronze tan he'd acquired over the summer. His forehead was covered with a sheen of perspiration and there were dark circles beneath his eyes, but otherwise he looked well enough.

"What are you still doing here?" Sam asked, looking at Finn over Abbie's head. "You should have left weeks ago. Haven't you heard about Washington's defeat? It's not safe for you here."

"Never mind that for now," replied Finn, grinning at Sam. "Tell us where you've been all this time."

"I was picked up by a British patrol and taken to the fort. I would have died otherwise, but I'll be all right, Abbie. I'll be all right." He held her close, letting her absorb the fact that he was really there. "Abbie, there's someone I want you to meet," he said once she calmed down.

Abbie hardly noticed the young woman who stood off to the side, not wanting to interfere with their reunion. She came forward as Sam smiled at her, holding out his hand. In a strange way, she reminded Abbie of herself. Her wide brown eyes were flecked with gold and her dark blonde hair escaped from her bonnet, curling around a heart-shaped face. The woman smiled shyly as she came closer, her eyes never leaving Abbie's face.

"Abbie, Finn, this is Susanna Freeman—my future wife," Sam announced, taking Susanna's hand in his own.

"It's a pleasure to meet you both," she said, searching their faces for a reaction.

Abbie turned in surprise when Finn snorted with laughter behind her. He looked from Sam to Susanna, his shoulders quaking with mirth. Susanna looked mortified, but Sam just glared at him, willing him to stop.

"What's funny?" Abbie elbowed him in the ribs, but Finn only laughed harder, waving her away.

"What's funny?" Finn asked, laughing even harder. "Only Sam could manage to find a wife while languishing in a British fort with a near-fatal wound. Well done, brother." Abbie gaped at Finn in shock, but then saw the humor in the situation and joined in the laughter, smiling at Susanna who blushed to the roots of her hair.

Finn finally stopped laughing and looked at Sam. "Sam, now that you're here, we need to leave as quickly as possible. The British are heading toward Philadelphia, so we will need to keep to the back roads and stay out of their way."

"Let's go home then," Sam said, taking Susanna by the hand.

Finn and Abbie nodded in agreement. "Let's, but I think you need to lose the uniform first."

SEVENTY

LONDON OCTOBER 1624

Heavy raindrops plopped on the roof, the pitter-patter beating a soothing rhythm that made Valerie drowsy as the coach swayed from side to side. Despite the dreary weather, she was glad to be back in London and eager to see everyone, especially their daughter. Alec had fallen asleep, his head against the side of the coach, a look of serenity on his handsome face. It was nice to see him at peace for a change.

Being a shrewd man, Cardinal Neuville had decided to comply with Alec's demands, naturally turning the whole situation around to benefit himself. Valerie couldn't help but smile as she remembered his speech to the congregation at Sunday Mass nearly two weeks ago. No one had been more stunned than Alec, but he was willing to accept the cardinal's explanation as long as he fulfilled his promise of having Rose reburied in consecrated ground. The cardinal had taken the pulpit, a look of profound grief on his face as he surveyed the parishioners whom he'd know his whole life. His own father, the Mayor, sat in the front pew, his blue eyes cold and calculating as he stared down his son, unsure of what he was about to do. Cardinal

Neuville threw his father a reassuring look before raising his hands in a plea for silence.

"Madames and Monseiurs, Father Rene has kindly allowed me to address you this morning, as I have some information that will help right a terrible wrong done many years ago to a young woman we all knew. New evidence has come to light concerning the unfortunate death of Sister Rose, who we all believe to have taken her own life. Please forgive my decision to keep the source of the information secret as it was shared with me under the seal of confession. A young boy had seen Sister Rose fall into the river and get carried away by the current. He saw her flailing her arms and heard her screams for help but was powerless to save her despite his best efforts. He's carried this terrible guilt with him for over twenty years, unable to come forward and tell the truth. Now as a grown man he can see that God, in his wisdom, would not hold him responsible, either for not having been able to save our sister in Christ or for being afraid to come forward.

In view of this, I will personally oversee the exhumation of Sister Rose's body and rebury her at the Convent cemetery. We are very fortunate indeed that Sister Rose's brother is here with us to see her laid to rest. I know I'm not alone in my sincere joy in knowing that Sister Rose's eternal soul will be with our Lord at long last."

The congregation remained utterly silent as Cardinal Neuville left the pulpit, wiping his eyes dramatically as he took a seat next to his father, who looked as if Sister Rose herself had just risen from the grave and winked at him. Valerie nudged Alec in the ribs unable to contain her indignation at the performance at the pulpit, but Alec just took her hand and smiled, shaking his head.

"What matters is the end result. As cardinal, he knows something of politics and the benefit of a good show. Let it be, Val."

"Will you really let him get away with it?" Valerie hissed, livid at the blatant distortion of facts.

"As long as he keeps his promise—yes."

He had. Rose's body had been exhumed the following day and buried in the Convent cemetery with all the pomp and circumstance of a Catholic funeral. Cardinal Neuville performed the service himself, doubtlessly sending tongues wagging for the next twenty years as he openly shed a tear, begging for Rose's forgiveness. Alec stood quietly by the grave, lost in his own thoughts and memories of his sister. He got his way, and since the cardinal made the entire thing such a public spectacle, there'd be no way for him to go back and change his mind once Alec left Loudun. Now they could finally put the whole episode behind them and return to London.

The parlor was lost in shadow despite the early hour, rivulets of rainwater streaming down the leaded windows and gushing loudly from the gutters. The maid was on her knees in front of the fireplace, blowing onto the kindling under the logs to help the fire take root and chase away the chill of early October. The house seemed unusually quiet, making Valerie uneasy. The children would be taking their afternoon nap, but where were Louisa and Kit, as well as their daughter and Genevieve? Normally at this time of day everyone would be downstairs, reading, sewing or playing a game of cribbage since the weather wasn't suitable for much else. Alec sank into a chair in front of the fireplace, happy to be home at last.

"I'll just go see where everyone is," Valerie announced, turning to leave the room just as Louisa walked in, closing the door behind her. The expression on her face was enough to make Valerie sink into a chair across from Alec, her stomach twisting into a knot. Judging from the look on Louisa's face, this was not going to be a joyful homecoming.

"Lou, what is it? Is it Kit?" she asked, noting the surprise on Louisa's face.

"Ah, no," she answered, confused. "It's Louisa, actually, but she's all right," she added hastily.

"What's happened?" Alec asked, his face tense as he leaned forward to hear the news. Louisa sat down, twisting her hands in her lap as she avoided looking at either Alec or her sister.

"I don't know how to tell you this, so I might as well just come out and say it. Louisa was married to Theo two weeks ago. We would have waited for you, but under the circumstances, there was no time to lose."

"What circumstances?" Alec looked ashen as he tried to catch Louisa's eye.

"Louisa is pregnant, and we weren't sure how soon you'd be back. She'll be starting to show soon." Louisa finally looked at Alec, needing his understanding. "Kit did what he had to do to avoid scandal. He knew you'd want him to do the right thing."

"Ah, of course," Alec said, still processing what Louisa had said. "Are you certain she's with child?"

"We are certain she's with child, Alec, but we are not certain who the father is." Louisa threw an apologetic look at a stunned Valerie.

"What do you mean? I thought you said she married Theo." Alec looked at Valerie, clearly confused. She'd grasped what Louisa said, but he was still grappling with the fact that his little girl had slept with more than one man.

"Alec, Louisa had been seeing Thomas Gaines on the sly. The child might be his."

"Does Theo know that?" Alec ran his hands through his hair, making it stand on end. "How could this have happened under our noses?"

"Theo doesn't know, and we'd like to keep it that way. He believes the baby is his and he's smitten with Louisa. This might just all blow over." Louisa smiled sadly at Alec, obviously sorry for his shock.

"What about Tom? What if he is not discreet?" Alec still

looked abashed, trying to come to terms with the fact that his daughter not only surrendered her virtue before marriage, but had done so with two men, either of whom could be the father of her child.

"Tom died several days after Louisa found out she was pregnant. No one knows what happened to him. He was found by a neighbor who noticed the smell coming from next door. He was to be married in a few weeks." Louisa stood up and began to pace the room, suddenly anxious.

"Tom died a few days after Louisa found out? How? Was he ill? Has anyone written to Annabel?" Valerie jumped to her feet, unable to believe so much had happened while they were gone. "She'll be devastated. He's the only family she had left."

"Yes, I've written to Annabel, but she won't get the letter for some time though. As far as Tom, I have no idea. He didn't appear to be ill and there were no signs of violence. He was found dead on the floor of the rooms he was renting in Blackfriars. He'd been dead for several days by the time he was discovered." Louisa stopped pacing and faced Alec and Valerie, waiting for them to react.

"Does Louisa know?" asked Alec carefully.

"Yes, Kit told her. She nodded in understanding and left the room. She hasn't mentioned it since."

Alec poured himself a glass of brandy and sank back into the chair, closing his eyes. He clearly didn't want to hear anymore.

"Was I wrong to tell you?" Louisa asked, her face full of regret. "I thought you should know the truth."

"You did the right thing, Louisa," Alec replied, "It's just a little hard to swallow."

"How are the children, and Genevieve?" Valerie asked in an effort to change the subject.

"The children are fine, but Genevieve seems a bit off. Maybe she misses Louisa now that she's gone, or perhaps she wishes it had been her. She seems so lonely. I don't suppose she's had many opportunities to meet young men and she's getting up there in age. You know how people are. Aunt Maud has already referred to her as a spinster several times."

"Do you think she's worried about her age? She's a beautiful girl and will have no lack of suitors in Virginia, although I'm not sure how many of them will be Catholic. That might be important to her, considering the fact that she grew up in a Catholic convent," Valerie mused.

"To be honest, I don't think Genevieve is very concerned with marriage right now. She's longed for a real family for so long that she's just basking in the knowledge that she's no longer alone in the world. She's still uncertain of her place here, and I think that worries her a great deal. She practically blends into the walls in her effort not to draw attention to herself," Louisa replied.

"Poor girl," Valerie said. "None of this can be easy for her, but at least she might be happier to know that her mother hadn't killed herself." Valerie poured herself a drink and gave one to Louisa.

"What did you find out?" Louisa took a sip, her face alight with curiosity.

"I'll fill you in later. I think I'd like to go see my daughter now. Alec, will you come?"

"Valerie, let's go see her tomorrow. I don't think I'm ready to face her just now. I need some time to come to terms with these revelations and speak to Kit. Where is Kit?"

"He had a meeting with Buckingham. That man always wants to meet about something," Louisa replied, annoyed. Alec stared into the fireplace to hide his reaction to Louisa's words. So, it wasn't over.

SEVENTY-ONE

Valerie had just a moment to notice how radiant Louisa looked before her daughter flew into her arms, burying her face in her mother's shoulder. "Oh, Mama, I'm so glad you are back. So much has happened. Did Aunt Louisa tell you about the wedding? It was simply beautiful. You should have seen my gown. It was magnificent. Theo's brothers are so dashing, and they thoroughly approve of his choice. Theo told me so."

Louisa tended to babble when she was nervous, and this was no exception. She was addressing her comments to Valerie, but her eyes were on her father, full of apprehension and shame. Alec stood quietly in front of the fireplace, his hands behind his back. He gave Louisa a quick peck on the cheek, but not the usual warm embrace she'd come to expect from him.

"Do sit down. Should I call for some refreshments? Theo is out at the moment, but I would be happy to show you the house. Mama would you like to see it?" Louisa sat down, her eyes darting nervously between her mother's face and her father's back.

"Dad, was your trip productive?" she asked quietly, finally realizing the depth of Alec's anger. "Dad?"

Alec finally turned around, but remained where he was, studying his daughter with an expression that made her blood run cold. He didn't answer her question about the trip, but came closer, standing in front of her so that she had no choice but to look up at him, their eyes meeting.

"I am only going to ask this once and I hope you will tell me the truth, because I will know if you aren't being honest with me. Did either Theo or Tom coerce you into lying with them or did you do it willingly?"

Alec held Louisa captive with his gaze, her face turning an alarming shade of red as she tried to look away from her father. She opened her mouth to lie, but she simply couldn't. He'd know, and then it would be worse.

"They didn't coerce me," she whispered.

"Did they hurt you or threaten you in any way?" Alec asked, his voice flat and cold.

"No."

"So, you made a conscious choice to lie with two men, neither of whom you were married to?"

Louisa just nodded, an ominous cold spreading through her body until it reached her heart, chilling her to the bone.

"And did you have anything to do with Tom's death? Tom had the power to destroy your life and he died rather conveniently. I can't imagine that my child would ever be guilty of such a heinous crime, but I have to ask."

Valerie gasped at the suggestion, but Alec held up his hand, signaling her to be quiet. "Thomas Gaines died days after you found out you were with child. Was that a coincidence?"

Louisa started to cry quietly, her face full of fear and regret. "I put yew seeds in his wine. He was cruel to me and as good as called me a whore," she whimpered, averting her gaze from Alec's.

"You are a whore," he said, turning away from her.

"I could hang for murder," Louisa whispered, her hands

shaking violently in her lap. "Would you really turn me over to the authorities? Would you watch your grandchild die?" She was sobbing now, her face blotchy and swollen, but Alec didn't seem moved.

"I will not be responsible for your death or the death of your child. It won't bring Tom back and it will ruin not only your reputation, but that of your husband and Kit's entire family. However, as of this moment, I no longer consider you my daughter. You are dead to me, Louisa." Alec walked toward the door followed by Louisa's howls of grief.

"Dad, please, I'll do anything to make things all right between us. Anything." Louisa ran after Alec, throwing herself at his feet, but he pushed her away, looking at her with an expression Valerie had never seen before.

"I might have been able to live with the fact that you have no morals or self-respect, but I can't live with the fact that you murdered a man in cold blood and tricked another man into marrying you under false pretenses. I'm grateful to Kit for what he's done for you, but I will not be a part of it. Your actions are between your conscience and God." Alec walked out of the room, leaving Louisa in a heap on the floor, crying and shaking.

"Mama," she wailed pitifully. "Mama, don't leave me."

Valerie felt physical pain in her heart as she looked at her daughter, but she couldn't go against Alec on this. Their daughter had committed murder. It hadn't even been an act of passion, but a premeditated killing that she'd planned from the moment she collected the seeds of the yew tree. She'd had time to turn back and change her mind, but she went through with it and watched Tom die for he had to have died in front of her considering the fast-acting effects of yew. Valerie rose to her feet, afraid she might collapse on the floor next to Louisa. She forced herself to walk to the door, but she couldn't leave without saying goodbye. She'd always known that Louisa was capable of far more than either she or Alec suspected, but she was still their baby, their little girl, and nothing she'd done would make Valerie stop loving her.

"Louisa, take care of yourself and may God keep you and your baby." A sob burst from her chest as she followed Alec outside, her heart breaking into a thousand little pieces. She sank onto the top step, her legs unwilling to carry her away from the place where she'd lost another child. Now all her children were gone—baby Alex dead in his grave, Finn one-hundred and fifty years away, and Louisa lost to her forever. Valerie didn't even notice when Alec scooped her up and carried her to the waiting coach, her head on his shoulder. Nothing mattered anymore, nothing. Her last baby was gone.

SEVENTY-TWO

Valerie couldn't remember coming back to the house or getting into bed, but she couldn't forget the terrible nightmares that kept her up all night. Every time she dozed off, she saw her daughter being led to the gallows, the thick rope tightening around her neck as Louisa cradled her swollen belly, begging for mercy. Valerie woke up screaming, clutching her own stomach as it twisted with the agony of her loss. She pretended to be asleep when Alec finally came to bed, smelling of liquor, his face ashen in the moonlight streaming through the window. Valerie knew he wasn't asleep as she turned toward him, wiping the tears from his cheeks and laying her head on his chest. Neither one of them said a word; just lay in each other's arms, lost in their terrible grief.

Alec rose before dawn, getting dressed quietly and tiptoeing out of the room in the hope that Valerie might get some rest. The rain that fell during the night had finally stopped, leaving the city sopping wet and strangely empty. Normally, the streets were already coming to life this early in the morning, but now no one was outside unless they really had to be, even beggars and vendors hiding in narrow doorways to avoid the rain dripping from the trees and the eaves of houses, shivering from the unseasonal cold of the October morning.

Alec walked along, unsure of where he was going until he got there. The Tower of London loomed in front of him, its gray bulk as uncompromising and solid as ever, rising out of the mist coming off the river, black crows dotting the towers like smudges of ink. Guards stood at attention at the gate, but Alec didn't go near them. He simply stood, looking at the place where his brother had died so many years ago, memories choking him with their unexpected clarity. He wasn't sure what had brought him to the Tower, but it was where he needed to be, to face this next crisis. He stood there for a long time, lost in thought until Valerie's voice startled him out of his reverie.

"You still miss him, don't you?"

"I miss all of them: Finlay, my parents, Rose, and Finn. And I will miss Louisa as well." Alec didn't bother to ask how Valerie had known he was there, she always knew his heart.

"You won't reconsider?" she whispered, already knowing the answer.

"Val, I can't. I simply can't. I could learn to live with the fact that my daughter disappointed me and that she'd manipulated Kit into lying to Theo, but I can't live with murder. I never liked the man, but he didn't force her or hurt her. She went to him willingly, fully knowing what the consequences might be. No matter what he said to her, she had no right to take his life."

Alec turned to Valerie, begging for her understanding. "God knows I've done things I'm not proud of, but I had no choice. I helped Finlay die to spare more torture, and I killed those two men in Williamsburg to save you. Louisa killed Tom out of vengeance and fear. She wanted to be sure her life with Theo would be secure. With Tom out of the way, no one would be able to hold anything over her except us, and she knows that we'd never do that. She thought it through, Val. She planned it. I simply can't live with that." Alec took Valerie's hand, turning to face her. "I will not impose my will on you. If you decide to maintain a relationship with Louisa, I won't blame you, but I can no longer be her father."

"We'll never know our grandchild, Alec. It's not the baby's fault." Alec nodded, his eyes full of pain.

"I know, but that's how it must be. I have a feeling that Louisa will get over this a lot sooner than we will. She's a survivor and she will do whatever she must to secure her own happiness."

"We'll never get over it. This will stay with us for the rest of our days, haunting us and tormenting us. Knowing that our daughter and grandchild are out there in the world and having no contact with them is worse than death." Valerie leaned against Alec, his arms going around her as the mist swirled around them, chilling them to the bone.

"Louisa and Kit will keep an eye on her," Alec said, hoping to give Valerie something to hold on to. At least she would have news of their daughter, if not physical contact.

"Maybe it's time we went home," Alec suggested.

"Yes, you might be right, although there's something I'd like to do first." Valerie took Alec by the hand, leading him away from the Tower and the horrible memories that resurfaced so frequently, especially in that place.

SEVENTY-THREE

MARYLAND OCTOBER 1777

Abbie used a stick to push the potatoes deeper between the burning logs in the hope that they would bake faster. She was terribly hungry, and the appetizing smell of the baking potatoes made her mouth water. These were the last of the potatoes, their food supplies dwindling almost down to nothing after a week of traveling. They still had a chunk of sausage left to eat with the potatoes and a few apples, but as of tomorrow, they would either have to buy food, which would deplete their meager savings since neither Abbie nor Finn collected their earnings before Abbie was arrested, or hunt for it, which would slow down their progress toward Virginia. Neither solution was desirable, but they had to eat, and with four people to feed, the supplies went quickly. Abbie tossed some ground chicory into the boiling water, making coffee to have with their meal. She didn't much like chicory coffee, but it was better than nothing, and at least it was a hot drink in her belly, warming her through against the chill of the gathering night.

Abbie inhaled deeply, enjoying the aroma of burning wood, potatoes, and simmering coffee. Sounds of birdsong filled the air as a gentle breeze moved through the trees, bringing with it a distinct smell of autumn. It would be a few weeks before the leaves began to change, but already the nights were getting colder, a warm fire a necessity for camping in the woods. Finn and Sam had gone to the river to bathe and shave, but Abbie and Susanna just washed in parts, finding the water too cold to wade in. They'd washed their undergarments a few days ago, taking advantage of a warm day and drying them on a bush while they slept. All they had were the clothes on their backs, making it difficult to maintain good hygiene, but they had been lucky to escape with their lives, making complaining just plain churlish, especially when the area was swarming with British troops after the Battle of Brandywine. Abbie never knew if her information had reached the rebels in time, but it likely wouldn't have mattered, considering the outcome.

Susanna emerged from the trees, carrying a pile of wood that she dumped close to the fire and sat down next to Abbie. She looked pale and drawn, her eyes drooping with fatigue as she stared into the flames, the tongues of firelight dancing in her pupils.

"Susanna, are you all right?" Abbie asked, taking Susanna's hand in a gesture of comfort. Susanna didn't take back the hand, but she never turned to face Abbie, speaking to the flames instead.

"I've made a terrible mistake, Abbie, and now I have to do something to rectify it." Her voice was low, trembling with deep unhappiness.

"Is it Sam? Were you wrong about your feelings for him?" Abbie asked carefully, not wanting to pry. She'd noticed that the relationship between Susanna and Sam seemed to become more strained after they left Staten Island, the two of them looking awkward and shy as they traveled south. They seemed happy when they arrived at the farm after fleeing the fort, but something had changed over the past few days, making Abbie wonder if Susanna had rushed into the relationship and was now regretting her decision to leave.

Susanna sighed, drawing up her knees and wrapping her arms around them as if to comfort herself. "He doesn't love me, Abbie. I put him in an awkward situation, and he was too much of a gentleman to reject me outright. Maybe he was hoping I'd come to my senses and leave on my own, but I stubbornly refused to face the facts, thinking he'd come around. I think I should just go back before it's too late." Susanna finally turned to face Abbie, her cheeks glistening with tears now that she finally put her feelings into words.

"Why do you think Sam doesn't love you?" Abbie had been surprised by that comment since she thought that Sam's feelings for Susanna were obvious. But then again, Susanna had only known Sam for a few weeks, so she wouldn't be able to read him as Abbie could, needing proof of his affection for her.

"He hasn't touched me," Susanna whispered, averting her eyes in embarrassment. Sam had made sure to spread his bedroll close enough to protect Susanna, but not close enough for the two of them to touch, a respectable distance between them at all times, unlike Abbie and Finn, who slept intertwined and tangled in their blankets.

"Susanna, I know my brother and he's not the type of person who would allow himself to be saddled with a wife just because he's too much of a gentleman to refuse her. And as far as the other, eh, problem goes, I think he doesn't want to offend you. You're not married yet and this is not the way to consummate a relationship. Have you spoken to him of your feelings?"

Susanna shook her head, tears running down her face. "I'm too ashamed to say anything. And afraid as well. I couldn't bear to hear him say that he wants me to go." She hastily wiped her cheeks as they heard the men returning from the river, laughing as they shared a joke.

"Please don't say anything to him, Abbie. I'd be mortified to think he felt pressured to continue with the relationship. I'll just say goodbye and leave in the morning. I think it would be better that way. No prolonged goodbyes. I hope my father can forgive me for the way I behaved."

Susanna busied herself with rolling the hot potatoes out of the fire, avoiding looking at Sam as he stepped into the light of the flames, looking years younger after his shave. He seemed to be feeling better the last few days, his wound healing well and not paining him as much after a day in the saddle. Sam tried to catch Susanna's eye, but she avoided looking at him as she divided the potatoes and placed them next to the chunks of sausage.

"I'm starving," Sam said, accepting his share and carefully peeling the potato so as not to burn his fingers. "Susanna, come sit next to me," he suggested as he watched her peeling her own potato without much enthusiasm. Susanna just shook her head, staring into the fire as if she saw her future in the flames. Sam shrugged and took a bite of sausage, his eyes never leaving Susanna's face. He seemed confused by her response but didn't persist, holding out his cup for some coffee. She poured it wordlessly, returning to her meal.

Finn's gaze met Abbie's over the leaping flames, his confusion obvious. He didn't say anything, but got up and sat next to Abbie, putting his arm around her in a proprietary manner and giving Sam a meaningful look. Sam didn't budge, continuing to eat his dinner in silence, and no longer watching Susanna.

Abbie took a sip of her coffee, watching the scene. She couldn't understand Sam's attitude. He was always so charming and confident around women, certainly not needing to be prompted to show affection, but this was different. He almost seemed scared. Perhaps Susanna was right and Sam felt trapped by his debt of gratitude to her. Maybe he didn't have the heart to tell her the truth and hoped that she would figure things out for herself and be the one to end the relationship, therefore saving what was left of her pride.

Abbie had seen Sam kiss her a few times, but he was holding back, the kisses chaste and sweet rather than passionate. Maybe he simply felt no desire for her. She wasn't the type of woman he was normally attracted to, and gratitude only went so far. Abbie felt Finn's hand on her leg and put her hand over his, thinking how heartbroken she would be if Finn didn't want her. Susanna was right to want to leave. Why prolong the awkwardness if the attraction wasn't there? Sam might feel genuine affection for her, but if he didn't desire her the way Susanna desired him the marriage would ultimately fail.

With their meal finished, Abbie rose to her feet to collect the dirty crockery and go wash it in the river before bedding down for the night. "Sam, why don't you help me?" she suggested, handing the dishes to Sam. He followed obediently, carrying the dirty dishes and humming a tune as Finn began to spread their bedrolls close to the fire, chatting to Susanna in a low voice.

Abbie turned to Sam as soon as they were out of earshot, watching his face intently. "What's going on?" she asked, taking his face in her hands as he tried to look away. "Susanna is planning to leave in the morning and return to the fort. Is that what you want?" she asked gently, trying to understand her brother's feelings. "Do you want her to go?"

Sam shook his head, looking like a sad puppy that had been left out in the rain. "Then what *do* you want?" Abbie asked, growing frustrated with him. "You seem to be avoiding her."

Sam sat down on the grass, staring out over the water slowly flowing past them, the first stars shyly appearing in the darkening sky. He sat there for a moment, looking much as Susanna had done before, miserable and forlorn.

"I love her, Abbie, and it's scaring the life out of me. I never expected to feel this way." He looked at Abbie, begging for her understanding, but she was overcome with confusion, unable to understand the logic of Sam's argument.

"Please explain this to me because I'm confused. You love her, she loves you, but the two of you look like the very picture of misery."

Sam sighed again, patting the space next to him in an invitation for Abbie to sit down. He was still staring out over the water, his eyes full of anguish. "I'm all wrong for her, Abbie. I can do nothing but ruin her life and she'll resent me and wish she'd never clapped eyes on me. She thinks she loves me, but how will she feel once she realizes that there's no going back and she's trapped in Virginia with no ties to her family or chance of returning to England? She's a proper lady, not suited to be a farmer's wife."

"Why don't you let her be the judge of that?" Abbie asked, leaning against him in a show of affection. Sam wrapped his arm around her, kissing the top of her head. "I'd rather she left me now than later. I couldn't bear it, Abbie. I just couldn't bear losing her after I allow myself to believe that she's actually mine."

Abbie pulled away from Sam, glaring at him from under her lashes. He probably couldn't see her expression in the dusk, but he could feel the force of her stare. "Have I ever told you that you are a damn fool, Samuel Mallory? I've never heard such nonsense in my whole life. You go back there, and you tell her you love her and allow her to love you. That girl has just given up everything and everyone she loves to follow you to the ends of the earth, and you are sitting here telling me you can't bear to lose her? I'd beat some sense into you if you weren't injured. I swear, only a man could be so daft."

Abbie got to her feet, gathering the dirty dishes and stepping closer to the water to wash them before turning around and glaring at Sam again. "Are you still here? Do you need a swift kick in the seat of your pants? Because I'm more than ready to administer it." Abbie put her hands on her hips, daring Sam to argue with her. He got to his feet and planted a quick kiss on her cheek before trotting back to the campsite.

"Tell Finn I need him," she called after him, hoping he'd have enough sense to talk to Susanna in private. Abbie shook her head in wonder, amazed by the foolishness of men. "Can't bear to lose her," she mumbled under her breath as she began washing the cups. "Idiot!" She couldn't help smiling as she thought of Sam. He'd really and truly fallen in love this time, finally realizing how fragile his heart was. She hoped Susanna would take good care of it for she had no doubt in her mind that she would love him with all her might if only he'd let her.

SEVENTY-FOUR

Susanna was still sitting by the fire, her eyes fixed on the flames and her arms wrapped around her knees. Sam watched her from the shadows for a few moments before finally finding the courage to join her, putting his arm around her stiff form. She didn't pull away, but she didn't lean into him either, remaining tense and unyielding, her shoulders hunched.

"I'm leaving tomorrow morning, Sam." Her voice was so low that Sam had to lean in to hear what she was saying, but her meaning was clear; her decision was made. "I should never have asked you to take me along."

Sam wiped Susanna's tear with the back of his hand, kissing her wet cheek. "Susanna, please don't go. I know I'm being totally selfish by asking you to stay, but I don't want to lose you."

"How are you being selfish?" Susanna asked, finally looking at him, her eyes huge in the firelight. "Isn't that what you want? You will be free of me."

"What I want is to drag you off to the nearest church and marry you in the sight of God and man, but I don't want to ruin your life. This might seem like an adventure now, but how will you feel once you're settled on the farm and your life consists of milking cows, mending socks, and raising children? You will miss your father and sister and wish you were back in London, living the life of a sophisticated lady. Being the British wife of an American rebel will not be easy."

"You want to drag me off to the nearest church?" Susanna asked breathlessly, her eyes full of hope.

"You did hear the rest of what I said, right?" Sam asked, amused by her eagerness. She nodded happily, smiling for the first time in days.

"I did hear what you said, but I completely ignored it. Sam, I don't want to live the life of a lady. I want to be your wife. Living on a farm with a brood of children sounds like heaven to me right now. I never realized how lonely I was until I met you and I don't wish to go back to that life. The war won't last forever, so I will see my father and sister again. I'm sure of it. I thought you didn't want me," she added shyly, averting her eyes.

"Oh, I want you," he whispered, kissing her tenderly. "I want you more than you can possibly imagine, but I want things to be right and proper. You shall have a real wedding followed by a proper wedding night once we get back home. Can you wait that long?"

Susanna nodded happily as she lifted her face up to Sam, returning his kiss. It wasn't like the other kisses they'd shared. This kiss was full of passion and longing, and so full of promise. Susanna melted into Sam, secretly wishing he'd go back on his word and make love to her then and there, but he was right. They would do things right and she would wait a little longer, knowing that every day brought her closer to a life with Sam.

SEVENTY-FIVE

ENGLAND OCTOBER 1624

Kit opened his eyes, momentarily confused by his surroundings. Where was he? It wasn't until he saw the statue of the Roman warrior that he clearly remembered exactly whose bed he was in. He couldn't believe he fell asleep with Buckingham. The man was sound asleep next to him, his arm over Kit's stomach and his thigh pressed against his. George's face looked youthful and relaxed in sleep, the mask of a master courtier removed for a short while to reveal the man beneath. Buckingham's long lashes fanned out against his lean cheeks, his mouth stretched in an enigmatic smile as he dreamed of something pleasant. Kit inched away, removing the arm and debating whether to wake George or just quietly escape.

This encounter had been different. George wished to switch roles, allowing Kit to be the dominant partner. He supposed it was preferable to feeling like a lamb being led to the slaughter. Kit was afraid that he wouldn't be able to perform what George asked of him, but Villiers teased him and stroked him until, despite all his reservations, Kit was burning with desire. George lay on the bed, submitting to Kit with pleasure, his moans still echoing in Kit's ears. Kit felt his guts twist with shame as he remembered his own pleasure as he spilled his seed inside Villiers. What was the man doing to him? He didn't want this, had fought it with every fiber of his being, but he couldn't deny that the man had the power to arouse him as much as any woman. George predicted that Kit would grow to like it, and he had to admit that with every time the act seemed less abhorrent, his body responding despite his desperate need to remain detached.

Kit nearly jumped out of his skin when George's hand reached for him, stroking him and making him hard once again, a look of hunger on his face.

"I have to go," Kit stammered, but George was already between his legs, his hot lips around Kit. Kit closed his eyes and gave himself up to the sensation. If he had to endure it, he may as well enjoy it.

SEVENTY-SIX

The rays of the setting sun glowed blood-red, igniting every window and metal surface with their fiery touch, the lavender sky beginning to twinkle with the first stars of the evening. The skyline of the city stretched for miles and miles, lights coming on and shining in windows and along the streets as the cabin rose higher above the city, giving a panoramic view of London that took their breath away. Alec held Valerie's hand as he drank in the sight, afraid to tear his eyes away from the magnificence of the city he got to see again for the first time. Valerie gazed at his enraptured face, unable to express the joy she felt at being able to share this with him.

"It's so beautiful," Alec breathed, squeezing her hand tighter as the cabin jerked slightly. "I keep looking at it, but I can't believe it's all real. Everything is so bright."

Headlights from numerous buses and cars formed a constant stream of light along the streets, zooming past with incredible speed. Alec had turned green when Valerie first took him for a ride on a double-decker bus, unused to anything going at such speed. The bus ambled along at no more than twenty miles per hour, but it was still many times faster than traveling by coach or on horseback. It took him some time to finally get over the nausea and enjoy the ride, taking in the places he'd seen only that morning in the seventeenth century.

Alec leaned out of the bus, staring at the Tower of London as countless tourists walked up the cobblestone path to the gates, ready to tour the museum and ooh and aah over the torture devices of the past, proudly displayed in the bowels of the tower where Finlay was once held. The Beefeaters looked ferocious in their finery, standing to attention until some pretty girl begged to take a picture with them and their faces broke into smiles, hamming it up for the camera.

Once he finally got tired of riding the bus, he asked Valerie to take him to an electronics store. Valerie smiled, knowing he'd be like a kid in a candy shop. She was happy to take him anywhere he wanted to go as long as it dulled the terrible pain in his heart left by the rift with Louisa. It had taken a while to convince him to come, but he finally agreed, desperate to escape his grief, if only for a few hours.

Valerie had taken a few period coins to sell, coming out of an antique shop that morning with close to £1000 that they could spend on anything they wanted. Their first stop had been the Gap where Valerie bought a pair of jeans and a long-sleeved V-neck sweater for herself and jeans and a sweater for Alec. He turned in front of the mirror, pulling on the pant legs, unable to accept that men actually walked around in such tight pants.

"These breeches are so narrow," he complained as Valerie smiled indulgently, admiring his long legs and fine behind.

"You look sexy," she growled, blowing him a kiss in the mirror.

"So do you, I think," he added as he took in her tight jeans and form-fitting sweater. "It's hard to believe how little clothing people wear these days."

"Too bad we didn't come in the summer. You'd be really shocked then." Valerie smiled, leading him to the cash register where he looked on in amazement as someone paid by credit card while talking on the phone at the same time.

The electronics store had been a hit, with Alec standing frozen in front of a TV that showed some kind of sci-fi movie. The salesperson tried to help, but finally gave up, leaving the odd couple to peruse the merchandise. Alec wouldn't leave until he looked at cameras, phones, iPods, and anything else that had buttons and was powered by electricity. He was enthralled and simultaneously devastated by all the things he was missing.

"It must have been so strange for you to find yourself without all these things," he said to Valerie as they sat in a small Italian restaurant, enjoying fried calamari, pasta, and Caesar salad. Alec had been a little suspicious of the food as it arrived, but he overcame his reservations and tucked in, enjoying the rubbery texture of the calamari and the flavor of the pasta, which he'd never tasted.

"You can't even begin to imagine what I felt like when I found myself trapped in the seventeenth century. It wasn't just the lack of electronics or modern conveniences; it was the mindset and ignorance of the people and the danger that seemed to lurk around every corner. Life can be dangerous here too, but in a completely different way. No one expects to die from the plague or be executed because they happen to practice a difference religion or misguidedly give their allegiance to the wrong person. That can still happen in other parts of the world, but not in England, not in the twenty-first century. If it hadn't been for you and Finlay, I probably wouldn't have survived. I had no idea what to do or who to turn to for help." Valerie took a sip of wine, suddenly overcome by the memory of those first days. It all seemed so long ago but having come back to the future reminded her of what she had given up in order to live in the past.

Alec nodded, silently acknowledging what Valerie must have felt. His eyes looked dreamy as he probably tried to imagine finding himself in the future with no Valerie to guide him. It would be very daunting, indeed. He speared a piece of calamari and popped it into his mouth. "This tastes chewy and strange, but I like it. What can we try for dinner?"

"What would you like to try? I thought this was relatively safe." Valerie smiled at his eagerness, completely willing to let him choose what they should do. He was so happy.

"I want to try something Oriental."

"All right. We can have Chinese, Thai, or Japanese. What would you like?" She laughed at Alec's astonished face.

"And after our Oriental dinner, I'll take you to a movie. How about that?" Alec grinned, his face alight with wonder.

"Can we see something about space?"

"Absolutely. Actually, I just spoke to the maître d' and he mentioned that there's a nice bed and breakfast only two blocks from here. We might be able to get a room without any kind of identification and stay for a few days. What do you think?"

"I think I'd love that, but I don't understand why you need identification to stay at an inn. As long as you pay your bill what does it matter who you are?" Alec was still grappling with the idea of needing a form of I.D. everywhere you went, from getting a hotel room to traveling from one place to another.

"Alec, it's different in the here and now. Everyone has a unique number attached to them for the duration of their lifetime. In the U.S. it's called a social security number, and a National Insurance number in the U.K. You can't get a job without it or any other form of documentation."

"But why are they needed?" Alec asked, still confused. "You have your name, isn't that enough?"

"It helps the government keep track of everyone in the country and make sure they pay taxes. They can track you by your credit card purchases, your cell phone and computer use, and even your bank transactions. Nothing you do is anonymous." Valerie watched Alec's face as he struggled to understand.

"So, the government knows your every move? Isn't that like spying on you? How can that be legal in this age of enlightenment, and why do people accept it as the norm?" He took a sip of wine, settling back in his chair, eager to continue the discussion.

"It's kind of a double-edged sword, really. The government keeps track of everything you do, but it also monitors everyone entering and exiting the country, which helps them stop certain terrorist activities and smuggling, and the police use the information to apprehend criminals and help find people who've gone missing or been abducted. When I disappeared, the police would have checked all my credit card activity and bank records to see if I had made any purchases or withdrawn money. They would have checked airlines and trains to see if I bought a ticket and left the place where I'd gone missing. They might have found me, had I not been hurled back four hundred years."

"I see," said Alec, although Valerie doubted he understood. "I'm not sure that I like this system, but I suppose I can see the benefits of it with so many people to govern."

Alec had been fascinated with the rush-hour crowds, overwhelmed by the number of people going about their business, all taking being surrounded by thousands of others for granted. All in all, Valerie thought he was handling it all very well, considering how overwhelming London could be even for a modern person who lived in the suburbs.

The bed and breakfast asked for I.D., but when Valerie failed to produce it, the kindly woman at the desk looked the other way, handing them a key to a lovely room on the second floor, complete with a private bathroom, flat-screen TV, and Wi-Fi. Alec was in absolute heaven. They didn't have a computer, but he spent an hour flipping channels before allowing Valerie to show him how to use a shower. Putting aside the wonder of electricity, running water that could be made hot with a turn of the faucet left him in ecstasy. Valerie barely dragged him back out in time to catch a movie and have some dinner.

The movie was a big hit, but the Japanese food proved to be a challenge. Alec was a good sport about trying sushi, but he couldn't get past the fact that he was eating raw fish, so Valerie finally ordered him some chicken teriyaki which he liked much better. He was deeply suspicious of broccoli but made a valiant effort to like it despite saying it was undercooked and looked like a little tree, which made Valerie laugh.

Alec was distracted from his vegetables by the arrival of a group of girls who were seated at the next table. They were about Louisa's age, dressed in flimsy tops and skirts that barely covered their butts and wearing lots of make-up and flashy jewelry. The girls were loud and trashy, cursing frequently and nearly starting a fight with two young men who happened to look at them a second too long.

"Val," Alec asked, "if Louisa grew up during this time, would it have been as shameful if she had relations with two men at the same time?"

"Not really. Many people see more than one person at a time, sleeping with all of them. Some people have dozens of partners by the time they finally marry, and many have children out of wedlock. People proudly share their sexual history with anyone who asks, completely undisturbed by what others might think."

"Do you think Louisa would be like these girls if she lived now?" He snuck a peek at the girls, looking away in disgust before they tried to pick a fight with him.

"I hope not. There are plenty of nice girls, even in these crazy times. Lou and I had been good girls and never gave our parents any trouble."

Valerie felt a pang as she thought of her parents. She

wished she could have at least visited their graves, but they were thousands of miles away, in a cemetery in New Jersey. She turned back to Alec, eager to talk of something else.

"So, what would you like to do tomorrow?"

Alec looked thoughtful, weighing his options. "I saw a brochure for a Science Museum at the hotel. Can we go there? I'd also love to see how a computer works. You said they have them at the library. Maybe you can show me how to, what was that word Louisa used, Google things. It sounds fascinating."

"Did you know that Louisa Googled Finlay when she found my portrait? She found references to him online." Valerie watched Alec's mouth open in a silent O.

"There are articles about my brother online in the twenty-first century? Is that really true? I want to see for myself."

"All right. There's actually an internet room at the B&B, so I can show you tomorrow morning. Are you sure you won't be upset?"

"I've learned to live with Finlay's death, but it's nice to know that he hasn't been completely forgotten, even if they refer to him as a traitor. He would have gotten a good laugh had he known that he was "online". What if we Google our Finn? Do you think something might come up?" Valerie felt a tremor of apprehension.

"Alec, I don't want to. If something happened to Finn, I would rather not know. I simply couldn't bear to live with the knowledge."

Alec nodded, instantly grasping Valerie's point. "You're right, of course. We won't look them up. I would like to look up Buckingham though. Do you think there's anything about his alleged relationship with King James?" Alec was warming up to the idea, thinking of all the things he could research. "I'd like to see that story about the convent that Louisa mentioned."

"All right, slow down. You can research everything and anything you like tomorrow. Now, I think I need to take you back to the hotel and put you to bed before your brain short-circuits and your head explodes." Valerie giggled at Alec's confused expression.

"Can that really happen?" he asked with a smile, playing along.

"No, but I think you'll have trouble sleeping tonight. You're on overload and your mind will need to process everything you've seen and heard." Valerie knew she'd have trouble sleeping tonight as well. She was on overload herself, no longer used to the pace of life in the twenty-first century.

"We don't have to go to sleep," Alec suggested sheepishly.

"Oh no, you are not surfing channels all night," Valerie replied, seeing his disappointed face. "But it would be nice to make love in the twenty-first century."

Alec smiled, the idea appealing to his sense of adventure.

SEVENTY-SEVEN

VIRGINIA NOVEMBER 1777

A fire crackled in the hearth, filling the room with a warm glow and the pleasant smell of burning wood. The warmth was welcome, the November night crisp and chilly beyond the windows, the moon already riding high in the pitch-black sky strewn with stars. The people around the table were squeezed together with barely enough room to move their arms, but the happiness on their faces was obvious to anyone who cared to look. A hush fell over the table as John Mallory rose to his feet, a cup of beer in his raised hand. He slowly looked around the table, his eyes moving slowly from person to person, filling with unshed tears.

"Two months ago, when Hannah and I heard of General Washington's defeat at Brandywine, we nearly went mad with worry, fearing that people we loved most in the world were lost to us forever. With Sam, Abbie, and Finn behind enemy lines, and Jonah on the battlefield, we stood to lose more than half our family, but God has been kind to us and blessed us in ways we never expected. Today, as we celebrate the marriage of Susanna and Sam, await the birth of our first grandchild, and rejoice at seeing Jonah alive and whole, our cup overflows, and we are so grateful." Mr. Mallory looked around the table once again, smiling at Susanna and Sam who were seated in the middle, their faces glowing in the light of the fire.

"Sam and Susanna, Hannah and I, as well as the children, wish you a lifetime of love and joy, and we are so glad that Sam, with his penchant for getting wounded, found a woman who has some medical skill." Everyone burst out laughing, but Mr. Mallory wasn't finished.

"Susanna, there's a reason why we asked you to stay with Martha for the past few weeks, and it wasn't just for the sake of propriety. We were working on your wedding surprise, and it's finished and waiting for you. Sam, take your bride home."

"Home?" Susanna asked, her mouth open with shock. "But this was to be our home."

"My dear, as much as we'd like you both to stay with us, this house is bursting at the seams, so we've built you a home of your own. It's not much, but it will be enough for two—or three. We can always build an addition later. Now, if it were my wedding night, I'd have been out the door an hour ago." Mr. Mallory chuckled as Sam pulled Susanna to her feet, already putting a shawl around her shoulders and grinning at his father.

"I don't need to be told twice," he said, winking at his father. "Goodnight to you all."

"Goodnight, and thank you," Susanna called over her shoulder as Sam pushed her out the door and into the darkness of the night.

Susanna pulled her shawl tighter around her shoulders, leaning into Sam as they walked toward their new home. He was giddy with happiness, but Susanna suddenly felt a lump in her throat, tears sliding down her cheeks and drying in the cool night air.

"Sue, what is it?" Sam asked, stopping short and taking her by the shoulders. "Aren't you happy? I thought you'd be so pleased." He looked hurt and confused, his eyes almost black in the darkness as he studied her face.

"I am happy," Susanna sobbed. "I've never been so happy in my life."

"So these are tears of joy, are they?" he asked gently, wiping her cheeks and pulling her closer. She nodded into his shoulder, wrapping her arms around him and holding on for dear life.

"Two months ago, I was sleepwalking through my days, thinking that the best life had to offer wasn't meant for me. I had no inkling that you were about to walk into my life and change everything. I never imagined that a heart can feel so much love and joy."

"Well, strictly speaking, I didn't walk into your life, I was carried, but I've never been a stickler for detail," Sam chuckled as he gazed down at her upturned face. "I thought I was fairly happy until the day I watched you walk into that ward. I had no idea what happiness was until you so brazenly asked to come with me and be my mistress."

"I never actually used that word," Susanna replied, blushing in the darkness.

"No, but you were willing to lie with me without the benefit of marriage because you were so madly in love. You wouldn't be the first, my dear," Sam teased.

"Oh, you insufferable man," Susanna giggled, smacking Sam with her palm. "I suppose I should be grateful that you made an honest woman out of me."

Sam leaned down, kissing her tenderly, his heart pounding against her chest. "Not like anyone else would have you."

Sam burst out laughing at Susanna's expression of outrage, grabbing her wrists before she hit him again. "Now, stop glaring at me and take me home, Mrs. Mallory. I believe we have some unfinished business, you and I."

* * *

Susanna gazed out the window, watching as the inky blackness of night gave way to the pearly light of dawn, the stars that had been so bright the night before fading until they disappeared from view altogether. Soon, the first rays of the sun would paint the horizon in all the glorious colors of a fall sunrise and a new day would begin, the first day of her married life. Susanna snuggled closer to Sam, enjoying the feel of his body against hers, the coarse hair on his legs a new sensation for a woman who'd only known silk against her skin. She thought she had the general idea of what happened between men and women in bed, but last night had been an eye-opener. Susanna smiled like a cat that swallowed a canary, torn between shame and another surge of desire. When she'd envisioned their wedding night, it was all very proper and quick, but what happened last night was anything but. She had no idea that her body was capable of such sensations or that she would ever allow a man to do the things Sam had done. She blushed furiously, quietly laughing at herself. What a naive fool she'd been.

Susanna's analysis was interrupted by Sam, who slid beneath the covers and pushed her legs apart, his tongue banishing all coherent thought from Susanna's mind.

SEVENTY-EIGHT

ENGLAND NOVEMBER 1624

Kit stretched luxuriously, enjoying the blissful quiet of Buckingham's rooms. He never slept during the day unless he was ill, but George liked to lie down in the middle of the afternoon, especially after a tryst. He called it a siesta, a word he'd learned in Madrid while trying to negotiate a marriage between the son of the king and Maria Anna of Spain. He was lying at Kit's side, his eyes fixed on the Roman warrior, his hand idly playing with a curl. His hair had gotten longer over the past few months, the riot of dark curls fanned on the pillow and intertwined with Kit's own. George's generous lips were pursed, a look of worry on his face.

"You seem preoccupied, George," Kit said, rolling onto his side and watching Buckingham.

"I was just thinking about the siege of Breda. It's been going on for months now and I think the outcome is a foregone conclusion. Breda will fall to the Spanish. Now that they have dispossessed Frederick V and Elizabeth Stuart, the war with Spain will finally become a reality. My dear James is not pleased with me for supporting his son in Parliament, but he can't ignore the fact that his own daughter has suffered at the hands of the Spanish. We must form an alliance with the Dutch and mount an expedition. I think Cadiz might be a likely target." Buckingham suddenly smiled, putting his hands behind his head. "But I promised that we wouldn't talk politics when away from the Privy Council, and I just broke that promise." He rolled onto his side to face Kit, a strange expression on his face.

"Christopher, there's something I want to say to you." Buckingham reached out a hand and cupped Kit's cheek, his eyes growing moist. "I owe you an apology and it's long overdue. You see, I'm a man who falls in lust often, but love doesn't come easily to me. I suppose I'm too jaded for my own good. It came as a shock when I found myself wanting you so desperately, and I blackmailed and manipulated you to get you into my bed. I thought I could make you love me."

"George," Kit began, but Buckingham put a finger over his lips.

"Let me finish, Christopher. I've watched you fight your revulsion for months, submitting to me just to protect your family, and I hated myself for hurting you. You see, I love you. I love you in a way that a man loves a woman and wants to make her his for life. I want to spend my life with you, but I know that's impossible, especially since I'm beloved by our king and not free to give my affection elsewhere, and you love your wife. I release you, Christopher. I swear that I will never summon you again or make you fear for your family's safety. Go now, before I change my mind."

Kit opened his mouth to reply but wasn't sure what he wanted to say. "Thank you, George," was all he managed as he pulled on his clothes and left the room, closing the door softly behind him and nearly running down the corridor before George had a chance to summon him back. He supposed he should go home, but he needed a little time, so he borrowed a horse from the stables and headed out of the city, needing a good gallop to clear his head.

The November afternoon was lovely, the air crisp and fresh, the trees a riot of color all around him as he trotted toward Hyde Park. Some trees had already begun to shed, the colorful leaves twirling gently on the breeze as they floated toward the cold earth and blanketed it with their glory, before beginning to dry up and rot into the soil. Hyde Park was a royal hunting ground, but certain members of the court had leave to use it with the king's blessing. Kit hoped he wouldn't encounter anyone for he just needed time alone, something he rarely got these days. The park was shady and cool, and nearly deserted. Kit saw a rider in the distance, but he was headed in the opposite direction, toward the city of London. Glorious birdsong filled the air and the breeze stirred the leaves above Kit's head, shafts of sunlight striping the narrow path into the woods.

Kit cantered along, trying to understand what he was feeling. He should have been thrilled at finally being free of Buckingham, if he were indeed free and this wasn't some ploy of George's to win his love, but his freedom felt strangely bittersweet. He'd despised the man a few months ago, but what he felt for him now was a kind of pity. Beneath the charming and confident exterior, there lay a tortured soul that just wanted to be loved and live life in a way that was forbidden to him by God and man. Kit couldn't tell if Buckingham truly loved him, but he was sure of the man's desperate need for intimacy and acceptance. Kit had grown used to the physical aspect of their relationship, but it was Buckingham's emotional need of him that kept him on edge, bringing forth feelings he never expected. He had to admit that although he would have never chosen to be Buckingham's lover, he actually liked the man and they might have been great friends had they been on equal footing and not master and slave. But the slave had become the master, and now he was free.

Kit dug his heels into the horse's flanks, forcing it into a gallop and tearing through the deserted park. He turned his face into the wind, enjoying the feeling of freedom that he hadn't felt since Buckingham first singled him out, overwhelming joy filling his soul. If he were honest with himself, he'd admit that Buckingham had wormed his way not only into his bed, but his heart, but Kit had no intention of being honest, not today. He was free at last, his family was safe, and that was all that mattered.

SEVENTY-NINE

VIRGINIA APRIL 1778

Abbie waddled out of the house to meet Finn and his parents in the yard. She'd seen them walking toward the house from the window as she dressed for the day. They had a strange way of just showing up, and never writing letters, but she didn't mind. She liked them immensely and Finn always seemed more whole somehow when they were visiting. They'd come just after Christmas and were now back for the birth of the baby. Abbie asked Finn several times where his parents lived or why they never wrote, but Finn seemed evasive and she eventually gave up, not wanting to upset him. It didn't matter.

Abbie took a deep breath of the crisp April air, relieved that spring had come at last. It had been a long, hard winter, and the budding trees and shoots of grass under her feet made her happy. Everything around them was bursting with new life as was her body. The baby kicked around the clock, refusing to allow its poor mother any rest. Abbie spent the whole night either getting up to use the pot or trying to find a comfortable position. She was exhausted and cranky, not to mention scared of the upcoming birth, but the thought of finally meeting the occupant of her stomach filled her with longing. She was eager to see the little face at last and hold the baby in her arms. She thanked God every day for being alive and well, knowing full well that things could have been very different.

Abbie walked into Alec's embrace, her belly making it awkward to give him a hug. He held her at arm's length, smiling at the size of her. "Maybe you're carrying twins. Wouldn't that be something?" He patted Finn on the shoulder, seeing the shocked look on his son's face. "Haven't considered that, have you?"

"Alec, stop scaring them. One healthy baby will be more than enough. Abbie, how's Sam?" Valerie asked, putting her arm around her daughter-in-law and walking her back to the house. Abbie seemed tired and probably needed to sit down.

"Sam's well. He's still working for the cause, but he's at home more now since Susanna is due in a few months. I don't know which one of them is more anxious. She's written to her father and had a letter back. He's having some difficulty accepting a rebel as a son-in-law, but he's starting to come around. Maybe someday he can come and visit her. I know that would make her extremely happy."

Susanna missed her father terribly, wishing she'd had a chance to say goodbye in person. She'd written several letters before finally receiving a terse reply, but it was a start. The war would end eventually and maybe father and daughter could be reunited.

"And how's everyone else?" Valerie asked.

"Everyone is well. Gil was wounded a few months ago, but Martha is taking care of him and driving him to distraction, so I think he'll be on his feet again soon," confided Abbie with a grin. "Jonah had furlough last month. He's changed so much since joining the Continental Army. His voice is so deep now, I keep thinking it's Pa talking. He's been promoted to captain, so he's over the moon. We pray for his safety every day. And the little ones are excited to meet their new niece or nephew. I'm very excited myself," Abbie added shyly, her hand on her belly.

"I can't wait," Valerie said, her heart squeezing at the thought of Louisa's baby. It would be born soon as well, maybe as early as next month. She hoped Lou would send them a letter, letting them know that all was well and tell them something of the grandchild they'd never see.

EIGHTY

Finn nearly jumped out of his skin as another scream tore through the house, his face pale and taut. Both Alec and John Mallory put a hand on his shoulder, forcing him back down, but Finn wouldn't stay put.

"I can't take it," he moaned. "She's in such pain. I'm scared for her." He looked at the older men for support, helpless and frightened, but they seemed calm.

"Mistress Baker knows what she's doing, son. She's delivered more than half the children in this parish. It's normal to be in pain, but it will be over soon. Now sit down and have another drink."

Mr. Mallory poured Finn another cup of ale, but he pushed it away, his hands shaking with anxiety. Abbie had been in labor since early morning and it was nearly dusk now, the sun hanging just above the tree line for a few minutes before sinking below the horizon.

"Why don't we go for a walk?" Alec suggested, pushing back his chair and getting to his feet. "Maybe you'll be a father by the time we return." Finn didn't protest. He joined his father outside, walking away from the house and toward the stile where he could no longer hear Abbie's screams.

"Did Mama suffer when I was born?" he asked suddenly.

"Yes, she did, and even worse with Louisa. It's a woman's lot, son. There's nothing you can do, no matter how much you want to take the pain onto yourself. Just pray that everything will be well, and you'll have a healthy baby. Abbie is young and strong; she'll be all right."

Alec felt bad lying to Finn, but he needed to reassure the poor boy. Many young, healthy women died in childbirth, but he prayed that Abbie wouldn't be one of them and that she would be delivered soon. Valerie was in the room with Mistress Baker and Hannah Mallory as per Abbie's request, but Finn hadn't been allowed to stay. The formidable Mrs. Baker pushed him out the door, bidding him to stay out of her way until the babe was born.

"Dad, how is Louisa? Have you had any word?" Finn was aware of what happened in London, but he still hoped for a reconciliation between his parents and sister. He knew that deep down his parents loved her and thought of her every day, praying that she was all right.

"According to your aunt, Louisa is well. The Sheridans saw her and Theo at Whitehall, but Louisa has probably started her confinement by now. Theo dotes on her and Louisa enjoys being the grand lady," his father replied sadly. "I miss her more than you can imagine."

Finn looked at Alec, his eyes full of hope. "Do you think you might be reconciled one day? I think Mama would like that."

"I'm sure she would. I don't know, Finn. Time will tell, but right now it's too soon. I only hope that she's well and happy." Alec looked heartbroken, but he was still firm in his resolve. He'd forgiven her the disgrace, but he couldn't forgive the murder. That would take time.

Finn suddenly stilled as a baby's wail pierced the quiet of the early evening. He sprinted toward the house, his sister forgotten. Alec followed at a slower pace, praying all was well.

Abbie was sitting up in bed, her hair cascading around her shoulders, her face flushed. She looked exhausted, but a smile of pure joy split her face when she showed Finn the little bundle she was holding. The baby's face was pink and wrinkled, its eyes closed, its crown of golden fuzz plastered to its tiny head. It looked content as it lay on Abbie's breast wrapped in a wooly blanket. His mother and Mrs. Mallory left the room, giving them a few minutes of privacy as they escorted the midwife downstairs to offer her some refreshment and payment for her services.

"Can I hold it?" Finn asked, looking at the little person that was now his responsibility.

"It's not an it; it's a her," Abbie giggled. "It's a perfect little girl. What should we call her do you think?" They'd discussed names, but nothing came to mind, so they decided to meet their baby and see what name fit.

"Whatever you like. You are the one who labored to bring her into this world. I'll be happy with any name you choose." Finn held out his arms as Abbie put the bundle into them, making sure that Finn's palm supported the head. His daughter opened her eyes, looking straight at him, her green gaze so like his own.

"What about Diana?" Abbie asked, watching Finn's face.

"After the Goddess?"

"No, after the whore. If it hadn't been for Diana's help, you and Sam would have never rescued me and neither one of us would be here right now. What do you think?"

"Diana Whitfield," Finn said experimentally. "I like it. Diana it is." He kissed the baby's tiny hand as it came out of the blanket, the fingers touching his face. Abbie smiled when Finn wiped away a tear of joy.

"Diana it is," she repeated, reaching for her daughter.

EIGHTY-ONE

LONDON JUNE 1625

Louisa Sheridan opened her eyes, instantly aware of the chill in the room. It was unusually cold for June, driving sheets of rain lashing against the window and filling the room with impenetrable gloom. Louisa snuggled closer to Kit, needing his warmth and comfort. He was fast asleep, but he wrapped his arm around her as she wiggled her butt against his thigh. He looked relaxed and at peace, making Louisa smile. He'd been much happier since Buckingham went off to Ireland two months ago, sent there by the king to assess the current situation with Irish Catholics. Louisa wasn't much for politics, but she knew there were some instances of unrest as Catholics protested having to pay the penalty for not attending Protestant services. It must have been Buckingham that caused Kit such anxiety, summoning him at all hours of the day and keeping him away from his family. Louisa hoped that vain and arrogant libertine would stay in Ireland for a good long time.

Kit seemed more like his normal self since Buckingham left, the haunted look in his eyes replaced by something like contentment. Louisa was thrilled to have her husband back, and relieved to know that there had been no mistress. Buckingham must have been putting terrible pressure on Kit, demanding his counsel and loyalty in meetings of the Privy Council. Kit had to walk a fine line between doing what he thought was right and showing unwavering support for Villiers, despite his reservations about the coming war with Spain. Buckingham was a dangerous man to cross and the consequences of his displeasure could be dire.

Louisa suddenly felt a chill that had nothing to do with the temperature in the room. *Buckingham's name is George,* she thought suddenly. *Could it be possible that 'G' stood for George?* Louisa shook her head, annoyed with herself for that crazy thought. Buckingham was a known sodomite, but he was the rumored lover of the king, and even if he weren't, Kit did not share his proclivities. How silly she was being for even going down that path. Kit would be furious if he found out she thought him capable of carrying on a flirtation with Buckingham. Louisa was about to close her eyes again when she heard Robbie's wail coming from the nursery.

"Coming," she mumbled as she got out of bed, reaching for her brocade dressing gown. Robbie was standing in his cot, his feet cold as ice as he reached out for her.

"Want milk," he announced, wrapping his arms around Louisa.

"Go back to bed," she said to the nurse who came running into the nursery, her round face creased with sleep. "I'll just take him down to the kitchen for some warm milk. Neither one of us is going back to sleep."

Louisa wrapped Robbie in a blanket and carried him downstairs, his cheek warm against her neck, and his little arms wrapped around her in a gesture of trust and love. She hoped Cook had already lit the fire so she could warm the milk as well as her frozen feet. Louisa was just about to go down into the kitchen when a knock on the door startled her. Who would come so early in the morning unless it was bad news? Louisa passed Robbie to Cook as a manservant entered the kitchen, his face apologetic and red with cold.

"I have a note for you, my lady," he said, handing Louisa a folded piece of paper. "It's from Lord Carew."

"Have something warm to drink," she told the man as she unfolded the note with shaking hands. Theo wouldn't write unless something was wrong. The note was brief, written in Theo's firm hand and asking her to come right away. Her niece had been in labor for three days and was asking for her. Louisa ran upstairs to get dressed, her guts twisting with worry. She knew Louisa was in the care of Doctor Wells, but in this day and age, anything could happen.

The coach was outside, waiting for her as she stepped into the cold rain, her shoes instantly soaking through. What bliss it would be to have a pair of rain boots, Louisa thought, annoyed for thinking of something so trivial when her niece was in agony. Funny how the mind sometimes turned to mundane things in time of worry, Louisa thought, looking out the window as the coach made its laborious progress down the street, maneuvering between wagons making their morning deliveries.

Theo looked like hell, his face ashen and his eyes full of fear as he met Louisa in the hall. His crumpled clothes and unshaven face indicated that he hadn't slept in days, his soul torn to shreds by his wife's screams. Robin put a hand on his shoulder in a gesture of comfort, but Theo never even noticed, his eyes on Louisa.

"She's been laboring for three days, but she's no closer to delivering the babe," Theo moaned. "I'm so scared for her, Aunt Louisa. She's growing weaker by the moment. She's been asking for you since last night, but I didn't want to disturb you unnecessarily. I hoped she might have had the baby by now, but nothing yet. The doctor won't let me in. I'm scared," he said again, looking like the twenty-one-year-old boy he was.

"I'll go up and see her," Louisa promised, giving his hand a reassuring squeeze. Her heart raced as she walked up the stairs and toward the sound of the heart-wrenching screams echoing through the stone corridor. The house around her was unusually quiet, as if holding its breath, the rain lashing against the windows the only sound aside from the terrible screams coming from Louisa's bedroom.

The room was lost in shadow, only the feeble light of a rainy dawn infiltrating the gloom and barely reaching the small, frightened figure in the large bed. It hadn't been aired out in some time, the overpowering smell of sweat, fear, and blood filling the air and nearly making Louisa gag. Her niece lay in a tangle of blood and sweat-stained sheets, her face nearly indistinguishable from the color of the linen, her hair plastered to her forehead and her eyes closed in exhaustion. She might have been dead, if not for the barely noticeable rise and fall of her chest as she braced for another contraction, which came as soon as Louisa approached the bed.

An older woman, presumably the doctor's assistant, sat on the side of the bed, holding Louisa's hand and whispering words of encouragement as she bore down, her face turning beet-red and her eyes bugging out of her head with the gargantuan effort of trying to squeeze something the size of a watermelon though a keyhole.

"Ah, Lady Sheridan," Dr. Wells said, turning to face Louisa. He looked exhausted, the dark circles beneath his eyes testament to the fact that he obviously hadn't had any sleep in days either. He ran his hand absentmindedly through his disheveled hair, his eyes on his patient as he shook his head in dismay.

"Aunt Lou," Louisa whispered, her voice hoarse from screaming, "Thank God you've come. I'm so scared." Another scream tore from her as a contraction rolled through her body, leaving her limp and exhausted.

"What's happening, Doctor?" Louisa asked, afraid to hear the answer.

"I'm afraid her pelvis is too narrow, and the baby is stuck. I've offered to perform a cesarean section, but she refuses, and I can't go against her wishes. It's a risky procedure with a low rate of success. The only other option is to use the hook."

"No!" Louisa roared from the bed. "I forbid you to use the hook." She looked terrified, her eyes wild with pain and fear, but still lucid enough to know what using the hook meant. The baby would be extracted in pieces in an effort to save the mother's life. "I forbid it," she whispered, tears choking her as she considered the alternative. "Save my baby."

"I will do everything I can, Lady Carew. Now try to save your strength and rest between contractions. I must speak with your aunt."

Doctor Wells walked off toward the window, motioning for Louisa to follow him. In the murky light from the window he looked even worse, his skin sallow and his jaw covered with a day's stubble that was surprisingly gray compared to his dark hair.

"What am I to do, Lady Sheridan? Lord Carew is paralyzed with indecision and if I don't act soon it will be too late for them both. She wants to save the baby, even if it means giving up her own life in the process."

"Save the mother, doctor," Louisa whispered. If it was a choice between both of them dying and only saving the mother, then it had to be done. God willing, Louisa would be able to have another baby, one whose paternity wouldn't be in question. But she was desperate to save this baby. Was it because she hoped it was Tom's or because of the guilt she felt over taking his life? Agreeing to let the doctor butcher the baby would make her a murderess in her eyes, and she couldn't bear to have two deaths on her conscience, especially if this child was all that was left of Tom.

"Is there nothing you can do to save the child?" Louisa asked, already knowing the answer.

"There is something," the doctor said, searching Louisa's face as if unsure of whether to mention it, his lips clamping tight as he looked away from her, gazing into the dreary morning.

"Well, what is it?" she hissed, annoyed with the man for being so secretive.

"Lady Sheridan, I have a friend, a French Huguenot who fled his homeland to escape religious persecution. He's invented a device that can be used to pull the child from the womb without harming it, but he prefers to keep it a secret for fear of persecution by the Church. Some might feel that this device interferes with the will of God and blame the person who invented it. I have the object in my possession but have never used it on a patient."

Doctor Wells continued to study Louisa's face, his own showing signs of fear and doubt. As court physician, he had much to lose and very little to gain by saving one child. Medical progress was not something that was encouraged by the king or the Church, and not worth risking position and personal safety over, not to mention the safety of the doctor who invented the device. He'd suffered enough religious persecution and only wanted to live in peace in his adopted homeland.

"Doctor, please, I beg you, use the device. I won't breathe a word to anyone. Your secret and that of your friend will be safe with me. Louisa is in no condition to understand what's happening, and your assistant can be sent out of the room. You have my word that no one will hear anything from me."

Louisa grabbed his wrist in her agitation, her eyes never leaving his. She knew what device he was referring to but couldn't let on. "Please," she repeated, seeing his resolve weaken. "I beg you, save them."

The doctor gave an almost imperceptible nod as he turned

to his nurse. "Please go to the kitchens and get some hot water," he instructed her, not wishing to arouse suspicion.

"Yes, Doctor." The woman bobbed a quick curtsey and scurried from the room, eager to do something to help. Doctor Wells quickly turned the key in the lock before reaching for his medical bag. Louisa had never seen forceps firsthand, but she'd seen pictures and heard of forceps deliveries. The object was crude, but surprisingly similar to the ones she'd seen in the twenty-first century. It was made of some type of metal which caught the meager light of the room. Louisa desperately wanted to ask Doctor Wells to clean the instrument, but she had to remain silent, knowing that the notion of germs and infection from unsterilized tools was foreign to him. She breathed a sigh of relief as he used a wet rag to wipe the forceps before turning toward the bed.

"Hold her," was all he said as he positioned himself between Louisa's legs. His muttered prayer was drowned out by Louisa's desperate scream as the forceps entered her body, tearing it apart further. The doctor's brow was furrowed in concentration as he maneuvered the tool until he was sure he had it around the baby's head securely, ready to attempt extraction. Louisa took her niece's hand in both of hers, holding on tight, and talking to her as the doctor began to carefully pull the infant from her body. Louisa went rigid as a board, her body refusing to cooperate as another contraction ripped through her, forcing the doctor to wait.

"Louisa, look at me. Doctor Wells will save your baby, but you must let him. Try not to fight him, allow your body to relax." Louisa smoothed a strand of hair from her niece's face, trying to soothe her.

"I'm trying, Aunt Lou. It hurts so much," Louisa wailed. "I can't take it anymore."

"Just a little bit longer, my love, just a little bit longer."

"Aunt Lou, please tell my parents that I'm sorry. I'm sorry

for everything I've done. Please ask Dad to pray for my soul and to put a marker for me in the cemetery," she whispered. "Please."

"You can tell him yourself once you are feeling better, and no more talk of markers. Now, concentrate on your breathing. It will make the pain more bearable."

"I want my mother," Louisa sobbed as Doctor Wells pulled the baby's head from between her thighs, her face crumpling as tears ran down her cheeks. "I just want my mother."

"She's not here, love, but I will be right here with you. I won't leave you. Just do as the doctor says. Trust him."

Louisa nodded, too exhausted to reply. The pain must have been unbearable, but she clenched her teeth, squeezing her aunt's hand to the point of cutting off circulation. Doctor Wells grunted with effort as he pulled the shoulders out, easing the baby gently out of Louisa's body. He cleared its mouth and nose of mucus and wrapped it in a blanket before turning his attention back to Louisa.

"She's hemorrhaging badly," the doctor said as he wadded up two towels and stuffed them between Louisa's legs in an effort to reduce the bleeding. "Please clean the instrument and hide it in my bag before you unlock the door."

Louisa did as she was told, opening the door just in time for the nurse to barrel in with a basin of steaming water and more rags.

"God be praised," she exclaimed when she saw the baby lying quietly on the bed next to its mother, but no one was paying attention to the infant. Louisa was no longer screaming, just lying silently, her face white against the linen of the sheets. The towels between her legs were the only splash of color in a colorless world as the fabric absorbed the blood, pouring out of her body at an alarming rate.

"Here, look at your baby," Louisa urged as she placed the mewling bundle into her niece's arms. "Look at him, Louisa."

She knew there was nothing to be done but hoped the sight of the baby might give her strength to hold on. "He's beautiful."

Louisa gazed at her son, her face full of rapture. The little boy was still covered in smudges of blood, but the golden fuzz and blue eyes were unmistakable. Louisa smiled beatifically, planting a kiss on the baby's downy head.

"He's perfect," she said. "Just perfect."

Louisa never turned around as Doctor Wells stepped away from the bed, his hands covered with her niece's blood. She didn't need to look to know that there was nothing more he could do. She was still bleeding profusely, the blood pooling between her legs and soaking through the sheets, its metallic tang filling the room.

"What would you like to call him?" Louisa asked, tears running down her face. She could see the life slipping out of her niece as her lips turned bluish, her face going from pale to gray.

"Tom," she whispered. "I want to call him Tom." She smiled at the baby one last time before closing her eyes forever.

"I'm so sorry. I did everything I could," Doctor Wells said, taking the baby out of Louisa's arms. The child looked at him with round blue eyes, completely unaware that a great tragedy had just befallen him. "Will you tell the father?"

Louisa nodded, unable to find her voice. Tears blurred her vision as she stumbled to the door to break Theo's heart. He stood outside, his face full of hope until he saw Louisa's face.

"I'm so sorry, Theo," Louisa managed to say before doubling over, silent sobs tearing her apart from the inside. She couldn't bring herself to say the words, but he knew. Theo's face was frozen in an expression of such grief that Louisa had to turn away from him, unable to see his pain. He walked into the room, sitting down next to his wife and smoothing away the hair from her face. Doctor Wells placed the baby in his arms, giving him a chance to study his son. Theo pulled back the blanket, caressing the cheek with his finger, tears rolling down his face.

"I'll take good care of him. I promise you," he whispered, kissing Louisa on the forehead. "Do you know what she wished to call him?" he suddenly asked, turning to Louisa, his eyes slightly out of focus.

"Tom," Louisa said and ran from the room, unable to bear the grief any longer.

EPILOGUE

VIRGINIA NOVEMBER 1625

Valerie stepped outside, eager to get away from the din in the house. She could hear Louisa scolding Evie for something she had broken, Robbie chasing Harry through the house followed by an irate Genevieve, and Kit arguing politics with Charles as Annabel begged them all to be quiet for fear of waking the baby. Mrs. Dolly and Minnie were in the kitchen preparing the midday meal, while Fred Taylor set off on his daily walk in the woods, probably just as eager to escape the loony bin. The sound of hammers punctuated the noise as the workers went about building the addition to the house, which would add a large parlor downstairs and two smaller bedrooms upstairs to accommodate the extra people now residing at Rosewood Manor.

The day outside was picture-perfect, the sky a cobalt-blue with fluffy white clouds floating lazily across the brilliant sun that cast a golden glow on the changing trees, their foliage ablaze with the vivid colors of fall. Birdsong filled the air, rivaled only by the incessant croaking of frogs coming from the reeds surrounding the pond. The sun was deceptively warm for

November, almost letting one believe that winter wasn't around the corner and that Thanksgiving wasn't next week.

Valerie strolled toward the pond, taking a seat on the bench and enjoying a short-lived moment of peace and quiet before someone found her. She didn't really mind the noise or overcrowding; they were a blessing she was thankful for every single day since the Sheridans turned up in Virginia a few weeks ago, fleeing the worst outbreak of plague in years. The disease marched across England, wiping out thousands with no sign of abating as long as the weather remained warm. Valerie cringed every time Evie sang *Ring Around the Rosie*, which she taught to Robbie and Harry, not realizing that the song, which hadn't even been written yet, but had been misguidedly taught to her by her mother, was actually about the plague. Her young voice rang through the house, singing, "Ashes, ashes, we all fall down," making Valerie run from the room in a fit of grief.

Poor Theo had been one of the first to die and was buried next to his young bride only a month after her death. Thankfully, he'd had the foresight to send baby Tom and his wet nurse to the Sheridans as the first symptoms appeared, knowing that they would care for the child and try to keep him safe from the plague. Aunt Maud followed, dying all alone in her home without anyone to care for her in her final moments, having been deserted by the frightened staff and left without food or water, lying in her own waste for days before finally succumbing to the illness.

Kit wasted no time in getting the family away, having lost his first wife and mother to the plague all those years before. The Sheridans sailed from Plymouth before the plague reached that part of the country, with Kit personally inspecting the crew to make sure no one was ill, and the family wasn't in danger of being infected. Normally, he would have needed permission from the king to leave court, but under the circumstances, the formalities had been dispensed with. People were running like rats from a sinking ship in a desperate effort to save themselves and their loved ones.

News of Louisa's death had come only six weeks before, devastating the family. Valerie still couldn't think of Louisa without an unbearable pain seizing her heart and a sense of hopelessness rolling over her with such force that it left her frozen with misery, unable to cope, but she had to go on. She was needed more than ever, especially by Alec, who was torn apart by grief. He'd shut down after receiving the news of his daughter's death, unable to accept that Louisa died thinking he hated her and hadn't forgiven her. Deep lines were etched into his face, more gray sprinkling his dark hair. They clung to each other like two drowning people, joined in their misery, and torn apart by their guilt. Valerie feared to think of what might have happened had the Sheridans not arrived so unexpectedly, bringing them back to life.

Alec honored his daughter's wish by putting a marker for her in the cemetery next to the one for Finn. They couldn't explain why they would choose to honor their daughter in death, but not their son, so a marker had been erected for both children, tearing their souls just a little bit more. Seeing those forlorn crosses side by side was more than either one could bear. Valerie had waited until everyone but Alec had gone back to the house before reciting a poem by Mary Elizabeth Fry that her grandmother had taught her when she was a girl. It had been read at her grandfather's funeral and Valerie had been deeply touched by the words, finding comfort and a sense of peace in the message. She took Alec's hand, speaking the words of the poem "Do Not Stand at My Grave and Weep", her heart filling with the balm of hope.

They walked away, their hands still linked, their hearts united by loss and sorrow. It was time to heal and move forward; there were too many people who needed them to remain strong, especially when there was so much to be done.

The charges against Louisa and Kit had never been dropped, so that was something that needed to be addressed as soon as they set foot in Virginia. Fortunately, a new governor of Virginia Colony had been appointed on September 18th, replacing Sir Francis Wyatt with Sir George Yeardley, who was a good friend of Alec's. He agreed to close the case, providing that Lord Sheridan made a healthy donation to the church fund and kept his wife in check from that moment on, promising to beat her if necessary. Kit was also asked to compensate the guard he'd assaulted during Louisa's rescue with a few coins of silver. Kit had never been so happy to part with money or to make a pledge to beat his wife, a promise which he took great pleasure in, reminding Louisa of it every time she disagreed with him.

Valerie waved to Alec as he came out of the house, heading in her direction. He looked tired but content, thrilled to have the family together again and safely away from danger. Alec sat down next to his wife, smiling at the sleeping baby in her arms.

"He looks more like Louisa every day despite his coloring," Alec said, his voice thick with emotion.

"I know. He looks like his father too, and Annabel is beginning to notice that. She remarked on it just the other day. I think she's starting to guess at the truth." Valerie kissed the rosy cheek, enjoying the lovely smell of the infant who slept peacefully, oblivious to all the goings-on at Rosewood Manor.

"I don't think I even remember how to do this anymore," Alec remarked, watching the infant with a look of pure love. He'd barely let baby Tom out of his sight since the Sheridans arrived, needing to be close to him for fear of losing another part of his daughter, a part of her that so easily could have died during the birth or of the plague.

"Don't worry. It's like riding a bike," Valerie chuckled, smoothing back a blond ringlet.

"Whatever do you mean by that?" Alec gaped at her. "Actually, I would very much like to learn to ride a bike, and I'm sure Tom would as well." He grinned sheepishly, reaching for the baby and cradling him against his chest protectively.

"I hope you're not suggesting we take him to the future?" Valerie asked, surprised. "If we did, we'd have to stay there. No child would be able to keep such a secret, much less be happy in either place having known the other. Someday, Tom will go back to England and claim his inheritance, but for now, we've been given another chance, and for that, I'm truly grateful."

"You're right," replied Alec, studying the sleeping infant. "I'll always grieve for Louisa and miss Finn, but at this moment, I'm almost happy."

"Me too. It's a new beginning for us all," replied Valerie, putting her head on Alec's shoulder as Tom wrapped his tiny hand around her finger. "Let's see what it brings."

A LETTER FROM THE AUTHOR

Huge thanks for reading *A Game of Shadows*, I hope you were hooked on Valerie and Alec's epic journey. It continues in book five, *Shattered Moments*. If you want to join other readers in hearing all about my new releases and bonus content, you can sign up for my newsletter.

www.stormpublishing.co/irina-shapiro

If you enjoyed this book and could spare a few moments to leave a review that would be hugely appreciated. Even a short review can make all the difference in encouraging a reader to discover my books for the first time. Thank you so much.

Although I write several different genres, time travel was my first love. As a student of history, I often wonder if I have what it takes to survive in the past in the dangerous, life-altering situations my characters have to deal with.

Thanks again for being part of this amazing journey with me and I hope you'll stay in touch – I have so many more stories and ideas to entertain you with!

Irina

KEEP IN TOUCH WITH THE AUTHOR

facebook.com/IrinaShapiro2

x.com/IrinaShapiro2

instagram.com/irina_shapiro_author

Printed in Great Britain
by Amazon

61905121R00234